Raccoon John Smith

*"Behold, I have set before thee, John, an open door,
and no man can shut it."*

FROM THE REVELATION OF ST. JOHN

Books by LOUIS COCHRAN

RACCOON JOHN SMITH

THE FOOL OF GOD

HALLELUJAH, MISSISSIPPI

ROW'S END

BOSS MAN

SON OF HAMAN

BLACK EARTH

FLOOD TIDES

THE LOWLY GNOME

RACCOON JOHN SMITH

A Novel Based on the Life of the Famous Pioneer Kentucky Preacher

by

LOUIS COCHRAN

College Press Publishing Company, Inc.
Joplin, Mo. 64802

Second Printing 1989

Printed and Bound in the
United States of America

Cover Art by Paula Nash Giltner

International Standard Book Number: 0-89900-277-3

To

Bess, the author's wife,
who is as much a part of this book as he is

Author's Note

ALTHOUGH told here as fiction, this is essentially a true story—the people lived; the events, indelible threads in the fabric of history.

In a sense, Raccoon John Smith was not a great man, but he had greatness in him, symbolic of that greatness in the host of pioneer John Smiths who with Bible and ax and rifle cleared the wilderness and widened the pathway to the Eternal City so all Christians could travel it together.

The hero, however, is not so much the man as the revelation that the love of God is more powerful than the fear of Him; the unity of His people the most important fact in time.

CONTENTS

Book 1

"I have heard of thee by the hearing of the ear . . ."

CHAPTER I

JOHN could hear the murmur of voices even before Zebulon topped the rise of the southern Kentucky hill. He drew back sharply on the reins, and sat for a moment, horse and rider in sentinel outline against the darkening sky, a quickening in him at the sight below. Never had he seen human beings in such numbers.

Here was the Muddy River meeting of the great McGready religious revival. The ridge upon which he stood was like the rim of a saucer, its rounded bottom hemmed by trumpet vines and wild ginger clamoring among great leaf cucumber magnolias, and chestnut and sycamore trees, their solid, matted front broken by wagon trails cut by impetuous hands long used to carving through the wilderness. Directly across from him Muddy River belied its name, meandering in a flowing, glistening course in and out of the ring of trees, and half encircling the saucerlike prairie where two parallel circles of wagons surrounded the great open field. In the center of the field a square platform, formed by wagon beds lashed together, with puncheon steps on two sides, supported a high speaker's box behind which, John knew, a good shouting preacher could be seen and heard by folks all over the encircling prairie. People were teeming about in little swarms and eddies, thousands of them, tending to their horses and mules tethered to the wagons or to trees, or their low-bellowing oxen herded in the narrow corral along the river bank, gathering their children, preparing their evening meal, some about campfires, others cooking over the hickory flames leaping in an open trench alongside the river, getting earthy tasks done before the night service would begin.

John had heard strange and marvelous stories of this meeting, of how even the Presbyterians would shout and leap and fall in agony in a final triumphal ecstasy of their souls. Pa Smith was a strict Calvinist and Regular Baptist, but he was curious about the talk of it, and so was Brother Isaac Denton, the preacher at the Clear Fork Baptist Church back in Stockton's Valley.

"You might have the revealing experience there, John," Brother Isaac had told him as the three of them had stood together at the hitching post just before John had ridden away. "The Lord God could reach you through the preaching of his word, even by those who have only part of the truth, much better than he ever could on some fiddling frolic in the barrens."

"Son John is not a fiddling man," Pa had observed truthfully. "And his feet are too heavy for him to dance. He's but a lad of seventeen yet; filled with a ready tongue, and the will to laugh and joke his way through life, I fear, to his soul's damnation."

"John hath an unco sway and say among his fellows. 'Twould be the mercy of God if he were saved." Brother Isaac spoke in that stern yet kindly way of his, the twinkle in the dark depth of his eyes like a distant gleam in a deep cavern. He had great power with the Lord, and there were some who said he could gather the saved from the damned at a glance.

"He won't be saved there," Pa said ruefully. "From the accounts of all the ruckus, the meetings are in the hands of the shouting Methodists and their crew; they would make a mourner's bench of the Lord's plan of salvation, and kick and scream their way through the pearly gates."

"Aye!" agreed Brother Isaac. "Even a Methodist may be saved if the Lord wills. I hear good reports of some. And there are Presbyterians there, too. James McGready himself is one, and he started it all when he moved to Russellville now five years past from the Carolinas, and waited not even two years before he lit the fires of revival at the Red River sacramental meeting. And the preacher brothers, William and John McGee, one a Presbyterian and the other lost to Methodism. They can make men sway like the mountain wind." He nodded at John standing before them, erect as a young sapling, unconscious of the wonder which had crept into the lean outlines of his face. "But there are no Baptists there mocking the Lord with their ravings. I canna see harm for him to listen for an hour and report to us in due time. The Lord has marked him or he has not. No man can turn the hand of destiny."

"I see no good in going out of my way through Logan County

just to listen to such goings-on." John spoke deep-throated like a man. "But it would be pleasuring, and George can wait for me to get to Christian County and help him move back here. He took his time waiting after the Harpes nearly killed him, writing us about it. But I won't be looking for any revealing experience, Brother Isaac. I'm a sinner and I know it, and so does the Lord."

"Well said; the Lord sees no good in you, John," Brother Isaac agreed gently. "Before the sun and the stars were made, or the moon hung out, it was God's own pleasure to either choose you or not choose you as one of his Elect—and that without any reference to your character or your good works. That is our *Philadelphia Confession of Faith* as taught in the Scriptures, and nothing can change the truth of God."

John turned away. Such talk got them nowhere. "I'll rest my fate with God; I'm not given to worrying overmuch about it."

"You will do more than worry about it." The preacher spoke sternly, an anxiety in his voice. "You will pray and agonize in dust and ashes that the scales may fall from your eyes in order that you may find yourself in the presence of God."

John flushed, his high cheekbones reddening under their sunburned bronze, for a moment a flash of temper in him which did not escape the older man. "I'll go by the meeting place," he said. "Maybe the Lord will strike me down, and the scales will fall there. Or maybe I'll dance and sing. As he wills!"

The two older men, strong in the faith and secure in their salvation, stared at him and at one another as John vaulted into his saddle. With a broad grin and a wave, he wheeled his horse about and was gone.

"He is my son," said George Smith softly. He blinked away a mistiness in his mild gray eyes. "He is the ninth of the thirteen children the Lord has given wife Rebecca and me. And sometimes I think the most promising, and impudent, of the lot."

"And my Timothy," answered Brother Isaac Denton gruffly, "... if the Lord wills. I love him, too."

It was three days later, May 1, 1801. John had traveled the Cumberland Trace westward across southern Kentucky by way of Blue Springs and Graham Springs. He had passed several wagon trains heading west on their long, tedious trek, and twice buffalo had crossed the trace, but for the most part he had the company only of flocks of pigeons and darting rabbits and chattering squirrels. At a fork in Logan County he left the trace to follow a barely discernible Indian path through fields of cockleburs to this valley.

He pushed his horse forward, his long, sinewy hands grasping the reins loosely; a lean, stringy youth in leather breeches and moccasins, his brown linsey shirt faded to a dingy hue, a cotton kerchief knotted loosely about his long neck. He rode well, his lean body at one with the sure-footed Zebulon; his tanned cheeks, barely roughened with the sandy-sprouting whiskers of young manhood, framing a long, almost belligerent nose under a pair of sky-blue, craggy eyes. A round, close-fitting raccoon cap was snugged back on his high forehead, against ears which stood boldly out under tufts of brown, reddish hair as though poised for instant flight.

He patted the rifle strapped against the saddle, and felt again of the three United States dollars in the small leather sack beside the hunting knife inside his belt; and with a final tug at the leather whangs binding his saddlebags, hastened his long descent into the valley, singing softly, as he often did when riding alone, a ditty he had learned as a child from his Cherokee Indian friends:

"*Tsa gi, tsa gi, hwi laki,*
Gei, gei, hwi, laki.
Upstream, upstream, you must go!
Downstream, downstream, you must go!"

The song reminded him of Nalgi, tall and lithe, and brown as a nut, whose grandfather had been a white man. The Cherokees believed in one God and in immortality, but for them there was no original sin, nor fear of eternal damnation, nor hope of celestial reward in that final life. What men did on earth, good or bad, was practiced for its own sake and not through any craven fear of a vengeful God. But that was not the religion of Brother Isaac Denton and Pa and Ma Smith, nor the crowds of men and women now milling about in the valley below like swarms of gathering ants. He thought of the hymn given out by Brother Isaac at the Clear Fork Church last Sunday. It was Brother Isaac's favorite, he had told them, although it was written by a British Seceder, Isaac Watts, but it summed up the will of God as well as any hymn of praise outside the Bible itself. In lowered key but singing lustily, he rode into the valley:

"Not all the outward forms
Nor rites that God has given
Nor will of man, nor blood, nor birth
Can raise a soul to heaven.
The sovereign will of God alone
Creates us heirs of grace;
Born in the image of his son
A new peculiar race."

He paused at the end of the narrow trail which had led him from the Cumberland Trace, and then rode on rapidly into the valley. Around a bend he came in sight of a square log meetinghouse. That must be the place where, Brother Isaac had said, fire had spread from the Red River Presbyterian Church after it had first been struck there among the sinners and the damned by the Presbyterian preacher, James McGready, now over a year ago. The revival had blazed in this church, too, until the small building could not hold the crowds and the meetings had spilled over to the adjacent prairie, with people coming for forty miles or more to be a part of it all, and it was threatening now, folks said, to spread out from Logan County in all directions, even to Stockton's Valley.

The church was on a slight knoll, sloping to the riverbank on the far side of the wagoned circle. The splintered, whitened trunk of a dead oak, called to its destruction, John guessed, by a single stroke of lightning, stood beside it like a finger of the Lord summoning the faithful from a similar doom. People were milling about the church, men and women entering by separate doors. John dismounted and made his way, reins in hand, toward the open-trench fire site to heat the remnants of the deer meat and corn pone in his saddlebags.

"You just in?" A slack-jawed man greeted him with a toothless grin as he reached the trench. "Folks swarming in, and it be only Friday!" He waved his hands expansively. "The prairie won't hold 'em all by Sunday. McGready stirred 'em up last night, ripping into 'em with his Dry Bones sermon, and he'll go at 'em again tonight. And John Page from Ebenezer, and Bill and John McGee will preach, too, and the Lord knows who else. Preachers pouring in from everywhere, sending the sinners to hell!"

"You're drunk, Silas!" The thin, stooped woman behind him pushed her bonnet to the back of her head, stirring the steaming kettle on the open fire. "And the boy is hungry!" She motioned John toward the pot. "There's a-plenty here," she said. "Hep yourself, boy. And there's corn in the wagon for your horse."

"I got meat in my poke here," John said. "And corn, too. But I thank you, ma'am." He shifted his feet uncomfortably, ashamed of his revulsion at the pair.

"He had the jerks last night." The woman spoke as though the man were not there. "He'll get 'em again tonight and tear a wagon wheel off sommers if he ain't downed first. Whiskey won't help him, the swine!"

"Thou she-devil!" the man roared. "The Lord will smite thee tenfold for thy viper's tongue!"

"Ah, hold your jaw!"

John moved on, a tightness in him.

Most of the assembly, he saw, consisted of families—men with their wives and children, who had come prepared with food and pewter plates and pots and wooden spoons and forage as though for a long stay, bedding down on pine-needle pallets on their wagon beds, or on the bare ground beside the wheels. He led Zebulon to the river, and while the horse drank, he loosened the girth and slipped the deerskin feed bag with its nubbins of corn about the animal's neck and tied him loosely to a sycamore tree. Then he drew the last of his venison and corn bread from his saddlebags and, with his tin cup and plate, walked back to the trench behind the church to find some smoldering hickory embers.

A deep voice, gruff, but with a lightness about it, suddenly hailed him from beside the corral behind the dead oak tree.

"Hey, son! I been watchin' you. It's a long ride you've had for a fat sermon or I'm no judge. Where's your home?"

John stared at the cool, gray eyes with the glint of humor in them, the lips tugging at the beginnings of a smile. He was uncertain whether the man was laughing at him. "Cumberland County, sir," he said. "Stockton's Valley. I'm on my way to Christian County to see my brother George and his family."

"From the land of the saltpeter caves and the possums and the raccoons. The Legislature is cutting up your county of Cumberland, come fall."

"That's what Pa heard. But Stockton's Valley will still be in Cumberland, and proud of it."

The man glanced at his fur cap and leather breeches. "You're riding well for the trail, but you'll sweat in that outfit before the summer's full here." He motioned to the food in John's hand. "Put that hardtack away. Fine stuff during the Revolution, and good enough for the trail, but we got better eatin' here." He slapped his arm about John's shoulder, and John warmed to him. The man was old, maybe forty or even fifty, but sturdy like a plow horse and with a look about him as though he held a secret joke.

"I'm Peter Cartwright from over Ebenezer way," the man went on. "I got a boy about your age; you come eat with us. What are you called?"

"I'm John Smith. Heading west to help my brother George and his family move back from Christian County; he was most killed by the Harpe outlaws there a while back."

"Big Micajah Harpe and Little Wiley Harpe!" the man said, his voice almost jovial, as they made their way across the churchyard. "The big one's dead, and his head's stuck on a hickory sapling. The little runt got away, but their murdering women are in jail in Russellville, thank God. A devil's horde if there ever was one. How come your brother mixed with them?"

"I don't know rightly; that's what I'm aiming to find out."

They stopped beside a woman kneeling over a simmering kettle of squirrel stew, near her a stocky youth about John's age, square-built, round-faced, his curly black hair falling almost to his shoulders, standing straddle-legged, eating from a tin plate.

"Peter was hungry," the woman said almost defensively, glancing up. "We waited a long spell."

"My woman and my son, Peter," the man said, waving toward them. "The lad's named for his Pa, and he's a chip off the old block because he likes card gambling and horse racing and dancing just like I do. But he's like his ma some, too, trying to get religion." He reached up and tousled his son's hair affectionately, and jerked his thumb toward John. "This is John Smith from Stockton's Valley, over in the raccoon country." He turned to John. "Son, you ought to be called Raccoon, to tell you from all the other John Smiths hereabouts. Raccoons are maybe my favorite animal; smart and fearless; sweet, good meat, too. And the critters even die with a grin on their faces." He laughed heartily, and pushed a plate toward John. "He's on his way to bring his brother back from the Harpe country," he said to his family.

"He could take some Methodist preaching with him," the woman said sharply. "That's a bad section."

"No worse than the Rogues Harbor here in Logan County," the man countered. "Even the Regulators find it tough, keeping the law in these hills."

"That's the reason for these meetings," the woman said to John. "It's the Lord's hand, cleaning out his stables."

"And a foul stench it is." The man's voice was harsh as though to end the matter. "I hope I never see a son of mine rolling on the ground, and slobbering, and barking like a dog."

The woman filled a long-handled gourd with squirrel stew and ladled John's plate full of the steaming food. "Our son's name is Peter," she said, looking him full in the face, "like the disciple who denied the Lord three times, and then lived to become the greatest of the apostles. It's a proud name."

The man turned half-apologetically to John. "I'm not much of a church-going man," he explained. "But I believe. It's just that ever since I began to read Tom Paine during the Revolution, I see things different. I can't abide all these camp-meeting monkeyshines. They unman a fellow. I don't want nobody upsetting my reason. Like Tom Paine said, we gotta use our common sense."

The two boys squatted on their heels, facing one another, eating hastily, a stilted, self-conscious silence upon them both. And then the black-haired Peter stood up.

"I'll show you around," he said, his voice guttural. "You want to see things?"

John finished his food before he spoke. "I'm much obliged, ma'am," he said, getting to his feet, addressing himself directly to the woman. "I've tasted none better." He turned to the man. "Pa was in the Revolution, too," he said. "In Virginia. But I never heard him talk none of any Tom Paine. Was he a general, or maybe a Baptist?"

The man laughed, good-natured. "He wasn't no general, and he sure wasn't no Baptist. He was a fighter, though, with his pen, and his pen was worth a legion with guns." He waved the boys away. "You be back, Peter, before services. Your ma wants you when the preaching starts."

"Pa don't take much stock in preachers," Peter said when they were out of earshot. "But his bark is worse than his bite. He's trying to live sober, but he still says that card games and fast horses, with a little whiskey now and then, when the need is on him, never hurt any man. Ma says different; she's dead set against them all, and it hurt her something awful when I gambled with cards and run race horses. But that's all over now. I'm under conviction, and I'm trying to get saved."

They explored the field, an understanding growing between them, a rising exuberance in them which their own unfathomed yearnings could not entirely squelch. People were settling themselves on the split-log, backless benches, in family groups, or with friends, or with total strangers. Others were milling about, young men and women pairing off, some of them wandering to the thick grove of trees opposite the riverbank, a few flaunting whiskey bottles, raucous laughter occasionally wafting back to echo against the hills. Pine torches began throwing their yellow, flowing light from the four corners of the wagoned rostrum, while within the double line of wagons which sealed the meeting place campfires cast weird shadows over the gathering, restless figures.

"I was a card-playing hellion myself!" John spoke suddenly, his voice defensive, as though eager to assure himself an equality with his companion. "I was a card-playing fool until Pa caught me with my brothers Joe and James gambling in the woods last spring."

"And he beat hell out of you?" asked Peter.

"Naw. He never said a word. But we knew he was worried, thinking that hell is lined with spot cards, like our preacher says. So we just quit, and I'm staying quit. But I'm still a sinner. All men are sinners, only some by God's mercy are among the Elect, and they'll be saved; the rest are headed for hell, and there's nothing they can do about it. I'm going to hell."

"You can pray," Peter said as they pushed slowly ahead, walking aimlessly. "You've got to have conviction of your sin and get on the mourner's bench and pray and beg and repent. If you mean it, and aim to live the good life, God will have mercy and give you the sign, and your sins will be washed away in the blood of Jesus. That's what I'm waiting for now, a sign that the Lord has forgiven me."

They stopped before the door of the meetinghouse, and John stared inside. The little building was crowded with humanity, the air stale and enervating, even with the two wooden shutters on either side flung wide for the freshening breeze; the long candles in the wall notches were lighting the place dimly, burdening the fetid atmosphere with an acrid tinge.

"The preaching is done outdoors," Peter said, "but there's a prayer meeting going on all the time here inside the church. Except at night. People sleep here nights, them that don't have a wagon, and can crowd inside." They stood silent for a moment, staring into the room. And then Peter gave John a little push. "You'd better go in and pray if you're a Baptist, because you're bound for hell."

"No quicker than if I was a Methodist," John spoke sharply. "Or a Presbyterian either. But I'm nothing—nothing at all."

He stepped aside as a fat, gallused man was pushed out the church door, his breath thick with the fumes of whiskey, his face bloated. Two men held him by either arm, hastening him on.

"The big man with the red beard helping that drunk is Brother McGready," Peter whispered to John. "He's the man who started all this revival business at Red River over a year ago. He's a Presbyterian and preaches regular at Red River and Gasper River, and for this church at Muddy River, too. Ma says he's almost a Methodist, only he won't admit it. Anyway, he's got a voice like a trumpet; when he gets going good you can hear him all over creation."

"Who's the other man?" John asked curiously, watching the slender figure help the reeling drunk to a pallet and cover him with a blanket.

Peter shook his head. "Never saw him before; likely as not he's another preacher." He turned to leave. "I've gotta go. I promised Ma I'd set with her tonight."

John looked after him for a moment. The fellow said he was under conviction; maybe tonight he would get the jerks and bark like a dog. He frowned, and stepped inside the church.

All seemed orderly confusion. Elderly men, clean-shaven and with an air of authority about them like church elders, moved about quietly. Women with infants openly at their breasts, and others with small children were arranging pallets on the log benches on one side of the room as though preparing for the night. Separated from them by a rough bark railing, men and boys were jammed together, some sleeping, some sitting upright, staring at the pulpit stand, others eying the young women covertly, a few brazenly.

"No services here again until prayers for the lost at ten o'clock in the morning, son," an elder said, touching him on the arm. "And nobody allowed inside after preaching begins except women and children and the sick and ailing."

"I was just poking around," John explained. "Looks like some of these folks are palleting down for the night."

"Folks who got no place else to sleep can bed here after preaching as long as there's room. You got a place?" the man asked. "Your folks here?"

"I got a place," John said, "right by old Zeb, my horse."

The elder pushed him not ungently toward the door. "That's where you'll belong after preaching," he said. "Us elders got enough to do at these meetings besides being watch wardens. There's no bundling here, not even for married folks. This is the Lord's house." He peered at John sharply. "Are you saved, son?"

"I'm a Baptist connection," John said.

The elder placed his hand on John's arm, a quick warmth in his eyes. "I'm a Separate Baptist," he said. "But we're not Baptists or Methodists or Presbyterians here. We're just sinners."

CHAPTER II

THE moon was late, and by the time preaching was to start the gloom of the night had become a murky darkness merging into the brooding, unbroken thicket of trees ringing the little prairie in blurred outline, their blackness intensified by the yellow blaze of pine torches. John tried to make his way closer to the preaching rostrum, stepping gingerly among the people massed on the ground, most of them sitting silently or speaking in hasty, low-voiced tones as though conscious of the Awful Presence.

There had been no rain for weeks, and the ground was dry and dusty, scuffed bare by trampling feet of the sweet clover that covered the countryside. He edged into a space between a broad-hatted bearded man, squatting with grim intentness on his heels, and an equally silent woman sitting cross-legged on the ground, lean-shanked, a stubby hickory snuff stick in her mouth, her linsey skirt pulled tight about her knees, and stood for a moment looking about. The people for the most part were in compact groups, huddling together as if for comfort; clusters of men stood on the outskirts against the fringe of wagons, their cheeks bulging with tobacco quid, as curious and as anxious as their womenfolks, but with an independence in their stance as befitted men who had conquered the wilderness and asked no odds of man or the devil, or even of God.

A stirring on the platform, and John saw Brother McGready's red beard glisten in the torchlight as the big man raised his hand for prayer. A silence as profound as the most distant star fell over the crowd. A thousand people, maybe two thousand, maybe more waited—hushed, expectant. John had never seen so many people together, enough to make a city as large as New York or Philadelphia, which Pa Smith had seen during the Revolution. He recognized the slender, erect man, who had helped the drunk, sitting not far from him, leaning forward, his gaze intent on Brother McGready.

"Almighty God, Creator and eternal ruler of heaven and earth and hell, we come before thee in all our guilt and shame." The deep voice reverberated over the throng, against the thick dark of the trees, not loudly but intimately, pleading. And then it rose in volume and became a trumpet call, a roaring fullness about it which swept through the air like a blast of wind. John closed his eyes and listened as the words, clear and distinct, were hurled at the Lord as from a warring prophet. And then his eyes opened, and he looked directly into the face of the preacher.

The preacher's eyes were open, roving the assembly like tiny searching torchlights, by long habit seeking out those who could be numbered among the penitent, marking the scoffers, the defiant, the indifferent. For a moment the probing stare came to rest on John standing in ramrod erectness, and he stared back, his breathing suddenly hushed, the veins on his neck standing out like cords. Then the eyes passed on, and John relaxed, his hands moist with perspiration. Brother McGready did not know him, and yet John felt he had singled him out from that massed, hushed throng as if with the eyes of the all-knowing and all-seeing God. Because he was not of the Elect. He was doomed to hell from the day he was born.

The prayer ended, and half-stifled cries for mercy arose here and there about the crowd, then frantic pleadings bespeaking terror, and then the low rumble of guttural approval from the saved and the sanctified. The preacher waved for silence and began limning out the One Hundredth Psalm, the comforting words rising and falling in a rhythmic chant from the throng.

"But his everlasting mercy is not to the unrighteous nor to the sinful," Brother McGready trumpeted as the Psalm ended, and began quoting, "For the ungodly are like the chaff which the wind driveth away. Therefore the ungodly shall *not* stand in the judgment, nor sinners in the congregation of the righteous, for the Lord knoweth the way of the righteous, but"—he paused and waved his arms in threatening wrath—"the way of the ungodly shall perish!"

John shivered, and moved slightly forward, and found himself directly behind the young man he had noticed that afternoon helping the drunk. He eased himself to the ground and hugged his knees to his chest. Brother McGready stood silent for a moment as a stir went over the crowd, and people shoved and jostled about in little whorls of motion, settling themselves better to hear this thunderous, red-bearded man of God, to taste to the full the maledictions and promises he would hurl at them.

"Woe to the rebellious children, saith the Lord, that they take counsel," he read from Isaiah. "The breath of the Lord is like a stream of brimstone." The voice paused as though filled suddenly with deep pity and understanding for the people huddled in the half-darkness before him, for the finite, groping minds, so less certain than he of their fate in the future world. "We are to understand," he went on not unkindly, "that all the ranks and classes of ungodly, unrepentant sinners collected into one horrible company, will be bound up in bundles and piled together, to be consumed by the eternal fire."

Low moans and whimpers began again to be heard. John leaned back and looked into the heavens. The stars seemed to dart out and then disappear, and to come again like peepholes into a paradise which would be forever closed to him. Brother McGready was quoting the parable of Dives. As his voice rose and fell, John could see the rich man clothed in purple and fine linen, and the beggar at his gate, full of sores, yearning for crumbs which fell from the rich man's table. He squeezed his eyes shut and clenched his hands as the picture unfolded, tasting the rich man's death, his torments in hell; hearing his piteous pleading that Abraham send the beggar, Lazarus, now in heaven, with a single drop of water to cool his parched tongue. "But Abraham said," the voice rolled on, "In thy lifetime thou receiveth good things and Lazarus evil things, but now he is comforted and thou art tormented. And between you there is a great gulf fixed."

A woman near John began suddenly to scream, a long, low wailing sound, a desperation and despair in it. John braced himself and stared straight ahead. The slender back of the young man who had been Brother McGready's companion was rigid. Other cries arose, shrill and piercing, or hoarsely guttural. The preacher stood silent and commanding until the cries died away, and then he began again to speak, his voice less harsh now, his tone almost benign.

"Hear ye the final warning as given in the book of Revelation by the Apostle John as he was given the vision of the last day before the end of the world," he said, and began to read, the words rolling in the hushed air:

> "And I saw a great white throne, and him that sat on it from whose face the earth and the heavens fled away; and there was found no place for them.
>
> "And I saw the dead, small and great, stand before God; and the books were opened, and another book was opened which is the Book of Life; and the dead were judged out of those things which were written in the books, according to their works.
>
> "And the sea gave up the dead which were in it; and death and hell delivered up the dead which were in them; and they were judged every man according to his works.
>
> "And death and hell were cast into the lake of fire. This is the second death.
>
> "And whosoever was not found written in the Book of Life was cast into the lake of fire."

As the reading ended, whimpers began filling the air, and low, hissing moans as from between clenched teeth. Somewhere a child, aroused to uncomprehending primitive fear, gave a spasmodic cry. But the preacher ignored the cries now, his voice taking on new urgency.

"You false, professing Christians," he shouted, "you self-anointed Elect of the Lord! You choose to go to hell with your devil's idols of money, property, and fine clothing rather than to take up the cross of Calvary in self-denial. You drive your neighbor to poverty and want with your hard bargains, your cheating in horse trading, your curses and blasphemy, your brawls and parties, your horse racing and gambling, your treacheries and infidelities. You are filled with anger and malice, and a hot thirst for revenge; you covet the flesh of slaves, and the blood of our Indian brothers, rather than teach them the ways of the Lord; your bitter, unforgiving temper against your fellow man fills all the heavens with woe. You choose to go to hell for the sake of the bottle, the drunkard's Christ, which will rob you of your senses and of everything clean and decent and godly about you, and send you to hell quicker than anything under heaven.

"And what is hell, you ask? I will tell you: It is a lake of fire, burning with brimstone, a bottomless pit, a place of growing torments for the unmilled wrath of a sin-avenging almighty God!"

The words ended like the hiss of escaping steam from a hot kettle, and John noticed for the first time that the man on his right had slumped against him, a dead weight, his eyes screwed shut, his face twitching in violent, irregular, uncontrollable contortions. And then he noticed others stretched on the dampening ground, jerking and twitching spasmodically as though some inner demon were seeking to escape its prison of human flesh; others were sitting motionless and rigid, as still as that false death into which they had entered; a few were kneeling in stark immobility like stone-carved figures. Those still possessed of their senses paid them no attention, enthralled beyond all caring.

"What is that hell?" Brother McGready's voice seemed to come from a long way off, and John pushed against the man slumped against him. The man toppled the other way, and John jumped to his feet. As he did, the press of the crowd forced him forward and his knees dug into the back of the slender man who had helped with the drunk.

The man turned and glanced up at him, and John stared back. In the dim light John could not make out his features but he sensed a calmness strangely at odds with the tension about them. He started to speak but the voice of the preacher boomed through the air.

"What is that hell? If all the pains and torments that were ever endured by all the human beings that ever existed upon earth were inflicted upon one person, and add to this ten thousand times the horrors endured by Spira, yet all this would not bear the same comparison to the torments of the damned in hell that the scratch of a pin will to a sword run through a man's bowels. That is hell!

"And what is still more dreadful, that which constitutes the essence of hell, the very emphasis of damnation, is its eternal duration. They go away into everlasting punishment, where the worm dieth not, where the fire is not quenched, and the smoke of their torment ascendeth forever and ever, and where they have no rest, day or night. When they have spent ten thousand ages sinking in this bottomless hell, their torments will be but begun."

Gasping moans and muted cries mingled with shrieks. All about him John could see people doubling as if in pain, straightening only to thrash their arms, falling back stiffened, and then sitting up to jerk and shake, some uttering hoarse, barking cries, some rising to dance in jerky motions. But Brother McGready ignored it all. His voice went on and on, as if intent on reaching still others who sat in shocked silence or in gaping wonder, or in defiance.

"This hell, this bottomless pit of torment which stretches between the heavens and the earth, can be escaped," he cried in a final tone of triumph. "There is still hope for the repentant and regenerate sinner to escape the awful judgment of the Almighty. But he must experience a spiritual rebirth; he must be born again. He must be recast as a child in the image of the everlasting God. In that awful day when the Universe Assembled must appear before the quick and the dead, the question, brethren, will not be whether you were a Presbyterian, a Seceder, a Covenanter, a Baptist, a Methodist, but: Did you experience the new birth? Did you accept Christ and his salvation as set forth in the gospel?"

John felt a sudden tightening in his stomach. He could stand no more. He turned, his hands clenched, the cords in his neck taut. He stumbled over a jerking form and, as he steadied himself, he felt a hand grip his arm.

"Wait a minute." It was the young man he had been standing behind. "I'll go with you."

They picked their way carefully over the bodies of those slain of the Lord, the words of the preacher indistinct but the tone that of hoarse, vehement command. John looked back. The sermon had ended but the big man was still talking, mopping his brow, striding in dignity from the platform to walk among the fallen.

"Brother McGready is a friend of mine," the man with John said as they came to a cleared space and stood in a pool of silence at the edge of the crowd. "But he doesn't have all the truth. I heard him preach like this back in North Carolina"—he glanced at John sharply—"when I was about your age. It upset me, just as I see it has upset you. But then I heard a young preacher, William Hodge, about the same age I am now, explain that God is also a God of love and that Christ died for all men, not just a few. That changed the whole picture for me; it perhaps saved me from infidelity or worse. Because it's true; God may punish, but he loves us, too."

"You talk like a preacher," John said, shifting his feet uneasily.

"I am," the man smiled. "My name is Barton W. Stone. I started out to be a lawyer, but the Lord called me to preach."

John eyed him closely. "You a Baptist preacher?"

Stone shook his head. "Presbyterian," he said and hesitated before he went on. "At least I guess I still am. I don't agree with all the Presbyterians teach. I have a church at Cane Ridge up in Bourbon County, and I came down here to see for myself what was going on in this revival. I don't approve of all of it, but I can see it is doing great good. Out here on the frontier, with the old restraints gone, people need something like this."

"Well, I don't hanker to it," John said. "These people are scared to death. Is that religion?"

"No." Stone faced him squarely. "Much of this is hysteria, even terror. The devil has always tried to ape the works of God. But it can't be wholly Satan's work if it brings people to forsake their sins, to solemn prayers, to sincere repentance and a godly life. How old are you?" he asked suddenly. "You're almost grown, aren't you?"

"I am grown. I'm John Smith of Stockton's Valley, and I'm seventeen years old. I'm on my way to Christian County to bring my brother George and his family back home from the Harpe country." He spoke defiantly, standing firmly rooted to the ground, straddle-legged. "How old are you?"

"I'm twenty-nine," Stone said.

"Where's your wife?"

Stone smiled. "I'm to be married this summer, probably in July," he said. "That's one reason I'm down in these parts. I've been visiting my promised bride in Greenville in Muhlenberg County just a few miles from here."

"Well, I wouldn't mix preaching like this with sparkin' a girl,"

John said. "Back home, Brother Isaac Denton, our preacher, lets go about hell and damnation sometimes, but not this bad. And my own pa and ma agree with him, but it's hard for me. I'm just not of the Elect, I reckon. I was born damned."

"No man is born Elect, and no man is born damned," Stone said. "Those who are damned will damn themselves because they refuse to receive the testimony—that Jesus is the Christ, the Son of God, and that believing on him brings us eternal life." He stopped abruptly. "I don't mean to preach. Let's go back. John Page, the Methodist, is going to speak pretty soon, and tomorrow there'll be preaching by the two McGee brothers—John, a Methodist, and William, a Presbyterian. You're a Baptist, you say?"

"I don't know," said John doubtfully. "I'm nothing yet but a sinner. Pa's a Baptist, and so is Brother Isaac Denton, and better people never lived."

"It doesn't matter what label we wear here—we're all just Christians," Stone said. "I've been thinking lately there's no reason we shouldn't call ourselves that all the time, that and nothing more." He turned to go back to the meeting. "You better come back with me. It's too early for bed. Where are you sleeping?"

"On the ground, right by my horse."

"You'll get cold before morning; you're no Indian."

"I'm almost part Indian," John said. "I was partly raised with them, the Cherokees, the Creeks, and the Shawnees, back in Sullivan County, Tennessee, where I was born. The free state of Franklin they called it then. I've been hunting with them lots of times. I like Indians. They wouldn't be doing like some of the folks here, running around on all fours and barking like dogs." A sudden desire to stand well in the eyes of this young preacher came over him. "I can even talk Cherokee a little," he said proudly.

"You can?" Stone exclaimed. "So can I. *Yandaska ga hunyaka ska,*" he said, and when John shook his head, not understanding, he went on, laughing. "It's my pronunciation. I never could get it right. Anyway, it means, 'The fault-finder will die,' There's one word I can get right, though. *Canaly!*"

John laughed. "*Canaly!*" he repeated. "Friend! Of course I know that." He extended his hand, a lasting friendship in the gesture. "Good-by, *Canaly* Stone. I'm leaving early in the morning, but if I ever get up that way, I'll come hear you preach at Cane Ridge."

Barton Stone held the extended hand for a moment. "If you do, you'll hear a sermon on God's mercy, not on his wrath. Remember, God is love!"

For a moment they stood, the tall, gangling youth with the deep-set brooding eyes, and the young preacher in the full flush of maturity, and then Stone turned and walked back toward the wagoned circle, stopping now and then to help a fallen figure; a slow, irregular march across the battlefield of the Lord, ministering to his slain.

John found Zebulon drowsing comfortably beside the sycamore tree where he had tethered him, and as the horse snugged at him he rubbed the flesh between his tender, twitching nostrils. He pulled a thick wool blanket from under his saddle and folded it for a pallet on the ground beside the horse, tramping down a growth of wild onions.

Shouting, preaching sounds came to him faintly against the breeze. That would be John Page, as Barton Stone had said; it could go on all night, and all week, and longer, until only the hopelessly damned would be left, defiant and helpless, sneering at their Lord on the brink of hell. He pressed his head against the horse's flank. He'd sooner be lost in hell than come under conviction in that crowd and go through such jerks and twitchings and goings-on. He would never do it; he would prove he could resist it to the last. On impulse he pushed the blanket back under the saddle and retraced his steps.

Circuit Rider John Page was a younger man than Brother McGready, John noticed as he stopped on the edge of the crowd. He was less sure of the wrath of God, and John warmed to him as he listened. Here was unexpected, reassuring hope.

"Ye have the choice," the preacher cried. "Ye may go to eternal paradise and sit with Jesus and the angels on the right hand of God, the Father, or ye may go to the bottomless pit of everlasting torment. It is as ye choose. Repent ye! Tomorrow is too late! Tomorrow is always too late! Repent now! Repent! Repent! Come, my brother, come!"

He motioned the people forward, and there was a movement among them, a surging and then an ebbing like the tides of the sea. John had never seen the sea, but Pa Smith had seen it during the Revolution, and John had been fascinated by tales of the irresistible, inexorable ebb and flow of that relentless tide which a man could not start, nor halt. John was pushed forward, but he braced himself, and the crowd surged by him—men with tears streaming down their cheeks, women wild-eyed and disheveled. He turned to go, and found himself staring into the flushed, round face of young Peter Cartwright.

Peter had been kneeling, his mother beside him, but now he was getting stiffly to his feet, muttering incoherent words of petition and gratitude, pressing toward the platform and the mourner's bench. If he saw John he had no sign, and John said nothing, a curious reverence, almost an awe, displacing his revulsion. Peter's face was shining with the same quiet light John had glimpsed on the face of Barton Stone, a look of complete transcendence, of utter dedication to the will of God. There was no physical movement, no twitching, no jerking, only a complete assurance. Peter Cartwright, John was sure, had found the forgiveness he was seeking; maybe he had even found God.

John walked away quickly, stiff-legged, rubbing his knuckles across his eyes. He would get Zebulon and ride on tonight, not waiting for morning; he would sleep better in the woods, away from all this, away from the preachers and the saints and the sinners, and the saved.

He was saddling his horse when he heard the preacher limning out the words of a familiar hymn. Hesitantly at first, and then with a lustiness and fervor, the crowd took up the words, the rising chorus of voices heard clearly through the night air:

"Thy mercy, my God, is the theme of my song,
The joy of my heart and the boast of my tongue;
Thy free grace alone, from the first to the last,
Hath won my affection and bound my soul fast."

Even after he had ridden past the little church, crowded now with weary sleepers, with the elders sternly parading the aisles, and past the double row of wagons, and had entered the narrow trail that would lead him back to the Cumberland Trace, the words came to him in fading crescendo, a huge, hoarse-voiced, untutored, magnificent choir:

"Thy mercy is more than a match for my heart,
Which wonders to feel its own hardness depart;
Dissolved by thy goodness, I fall to the ground,
And weep to the praise of the mercy I've found."

CHAPTER III

TWO days later Zebulon carried him from the narrowing Cumberland Trace into the shadow of Pilot Rock, which dominated the Green River section of Christian County, where George had thought to settle, building a two-room cabin for his bride there four years before. In sheer exuberance of spirit, and to announce his arrival as he neared the cabin, John began to sing at the top of his voice:

> "When I was a bachelor bold and young,
> I courted me a girl with a clattering tongue;
> She promised she'd marry me; she didn't say when;
> The kisses I gave her were a hundred and ten,
> The kisses I gave her were a hundred and ten,
> The kisses I gave her were a hundred and ten!"

He turned into a short lane leading up to the cabin and paused as a lusty hail came from behind the cow shed nestled in a grove of beechwood trees. His lanky, sandy-haired brother came into view. At the same time a woman with two identical little girls clinging to her voluminous calico skirt appeared in the doorway of the cabin, and, at the sight of him, came running, holding a child by either hand.

"Dismount, stranger!" George's voice was high-pitched with excitement. "There's vittles on the table and fodder in the barn. We been looking for you for more'n two days now."

Beulah scooped the little girls before her, her thin face wreathed in smiles, her eyes dancing with excitement. "It's Uncle John!" she cried. "He's come to help us milk the nanny goats!" The children buried their faces in the folds of her apron, peering out at John like startled kittens. "He's a lot nicer uncle than he sounds when he sings like that. Don't let him scare you!"

John rode up to the door of the cabin and reined Zebulon to a standstill, and leaning over, spoke directly to the children. "For a couple of three-year-olds, you twins don't look scared to me. The way they look to me," he said to Beulah, "they want Uncle John to sing them the rest of the song." He looked at George. "Ain't that the truth, George?"

"No," said George. "It'd scare the nanny goats. You don't want them to hold their milk, do you?"

At a twisted prod of the heels, Zebulon lifted his right forepaw, a trick John had taught him as a colt, and John turned in mock solemnity to his brother's wife, noting, for all his teasing banter, how stooped and thin she looked. "Old Zeb says to sing it all," he said, "all seven verses. What do you say, Beulah? It's a love song all the boys are sparkin' the girls with back home."

"I don't rightly trust you, John." She laughed up at him. "You'll scandalize us. There's no telling what you'll sing. Maybe it's something little Rose and Sharon oughtn't to hear."

"Maybe it is," John said. "Maybe you're right. I'll just sing the last verse." He tightened the reins in his hand, and while Zebulon turned his head as though to listen, he rose in his stirrups the better to send his voice echoing against the surface of great Pilot Rock in the distance. "There's a verse for every day in the week, but it's the Saturday one the boys like best, after the fellow had married his girl and lost her." Lustily he began to sing:

"Saturday morning, breakfast time,
I had no wife to bother my mind;
So my week's work is now at an end,
And my brandy bottle is my best friend,
And my brandy bottle is my best friend!"

He tossed the reins to his brother and jumped to the ground, grabbing his twin nieces under either arm and jogging them playfully on his hips while they screamed with delight. "Maybe they'd rather play Chickama Craney Crow," he said, and jogged them more vigorously, chanting the words of the game he had known since childhood:

"Chickama, chickama, craney crow,
I went to the well to wash my toe,
When I got back my black-eyed chicken was gone.
What time is it now, little witch?"

They clamored for more, their timidity gone, but he placed them on the ground and turned to face his brother and his wife.

"It's plain to see you've been on some kind of rampage," George said, shaking his head vigorously. "Pa must have hastened you up here to save your soul. We've got no brandy, though I reckon I could spare a dram of bitters to a sick man. But we got plenty of fresh goat's milk, all waiting to be tuck."

"I'd a fixed some squirrel stew if I had known when you was getting here," Beulah said. She turned to her husband. "Maybe we could have some tomorrow if you boys will catch me some squirrels."

"I had me some squirrel stew a couple of days ago over in Logan County," John said, his face sobering. "I stopped over one night at the big camp meeting on Muddy River, and I had me a time!" He shook his head. "I'm all messed up worse than ever, George, about God and such."

"For a young colt, you ponder too much. It ain't natural." George's soberness suddenly matched John's own. "Like Brother Isaac always said, we don't have any say-so about such things. We're either Elect or we're not."

"That's what bothers me," John replied, tossing his saddlebags across his shoulder and starting to unloosen his horse's bellyband. "Maybe we do have a choice. Some preachers say we do."

"That's Methodist talk. Better not let Brother Isaac hear you say that," George warned. "Nor Pa either."

It was not yet full dark when they finished supper and the three-year-old twins were put to bed in the trundle cot beside their parents' pole bed cleated to a corner in the big all-purpose room of the cabin. Across the dogtrot a pallet had been spread in the smaller second room where John would sleep. The only lighting in the house was from fire logs of pine knots in the hearth, except for the glow furnished by a string hung from a hollowed piece of iron holding bear grease that George had made for Beulah to keep by their bed for use if the children got sick in the night. The evening was too warm for fire logs, so George carried three cane-bottomed chairs he had latticed the year before to the front yard, and far into the night the three of them sat under the stars and talked. Instead of brandy, they drank fresh goat's milk, as George had promised, warm and filling, and as pungent as old cheese. And although John told them about the revival in Logan County, he did not go into details. He mentioned the Peter Cartwrights, father and son, but he said nothing at all about his conversation with the young Presbyterian preacher, Barton Stone. George had inherited his father's name and also his unquestioning faith. He would not understand, and the strange views would only fret him.

"I've got a concern about God same as you," George said as John finished his brief recital of the meeting. "But I'm Elect, and I know it; God gave me the sign when he saved me from the Harpes last year. That's the way it will happen to you, too, John. A miracle will happen like that to you one of these days, and you'll know you're saved. There's nothing you can do about it until then but wait."

John gave a short laugh. "I somehow don't feel right about such signs," he said. "I heard one old fellow tell once how he tumbled over into Big Little Fork while he was drunk, and when the water sobered him, and he crawled out, he knew he was of the Elect. He even made the preacher baptize him in the same spot where he fell in. It was some kind of holy water, he claimed." He picked up a twig and broke it into small pieces, and then glanced over at his brother. "It's plumb peculiar to me that God would make you get all shot up by mistake as a member of the Harpe crowd, just as a sign of salvation. Was it God that made the mistake, or the devil?"

"You talk downright sacrilegious, John!" Beulah spoke sharply in reproof. "It ain't like you. You know God never makes a mistake, even though we don't always understand." She sighed. "You take us. I been telling George all along we ought to move back to Stockton's Valley where the young'uns maybe can get a little schooling. This country's still too much a wilderness. And I was right. This trouble with the Harpes was a sign we ought to move back, just as much as it betokened George is of the Elect."

"That's right," George said. "I promised the Lord last year when the Harpes had me that if he got me out alive, we'd quit our hankering for new land and move back where we come from. It was a sure sign of salvation, and a covenant. Beulah is right. That's how come I wrote Pa about the trouble and asked would he send you to help me move back."

Despite himself, John could not resist a skeptical shake of the head. To conceal his feelings, he grinned and tilted back in his chair.

"Maybe God just moved in on Beulah's side," he said, a teasing ring in his voice, "because he likes her. Just like I'd do in a family argument." He turned to George. "I'm busting to know what happened with the Harpes. Your letter just said they tried to kill you; it had Pa worried sick, and Ma, too, until we heard the Big Harpe had been shot dead. That's why Pa didn't hasten me on more'n he did; we figured you was in no quick danger any longer, not from the Big Harpe anyway."

"Daytimes, it seems like it never happened; nights, I get so shivered it could of happened yesterday," Beulah said, breaking the silence that blanketed them for a moment. "I was alone with the babies that day. George was out rounding the stock into the sheepfold because we'd heard there was thieves about. Seems like the Harpe gang was prowling along the road the day before leading down to the mouth of Green River, and night come on and they was close to the Stegall place. Clem Stegall was over at Woods Settlement, and Mrs. Stegall was there alone with her three children. They had a nice three-room house of planed lumber, and when Big Micajah Harpe come to the door, with his brother, Little Wiley Harpe, looking over his shoulder, and claimed they was Methodist preachers riding the circuit, she took them in and fixed them supper and bedded them down for the night. And some folks say Big Harpe even said prayers that night, blaspheming God."

She paused, a catch in her voice, and stared unseeing through the dim light at the flat blackness of Pilot Rock. The moon had risen, half-full, but clouds scurried across the sky almost obscuring it.

George waited a moment, and then took up the story, holding his voice with difficulty under control. "The Harpes killed them that night while they slept," he said. "They done it with axes. Chopped them to pieces, the young'uns and all. Then they plundered the house and set it afire. All for the hell of it." He was silent, and John could sense the terror of the moment as they relived it. "They camped somewhere in the woods," he went on, "and the next day was when I sighted them three miles from here, north of Green River. They'd made camp, and their three women were cooking when I come on them. I was walking, looking for my stock, and mistook them for new settlers. Anyway, I had my rifle and felt safe enough. So I just walked right in amongst them, holding my rifle butt-end foremost.

"The two men, Big Harpe and Little Wiley Harpe, was just standing around like they was waiting to be fed. They didn't say nothing, and directly one of the women asked me was I hungry. The women was real cheery-like, and I said I was always hungry, and we started talking. I was fixing to prop my gun against a tree while I ate some grub, when the two men grabbed me, one fore and one aft. They wrestled the gun out of my hand, and then Big Harpe twisted my arms behind my back and got a Indian hold on my scalp. He faced me about so Little Harpe could shoot me with my own gun. With my own gun! I thought I was a goner!" His voice hoarsened at the recollection, and John shivered involuntarily.

"That's where the Lord took over," Beulah said. "If Little Harpe had pulled that trigger, you wouldn't be here now. It was the Lord's hand that reached down and took charge."

"It was a miracle you got away," John muttered. "What happened?"

"That's what I been telling you," said George. "It was a miracle. What happened was the women started hollering; they didn't care if I was killed, but they yelled to take me back in the woods and do it. So Big Harpe shoved me down the trail a piece, close to where their horses were, and tried to turn me around so Little Wiley could get a bead on me. But Little Wiley couldn't work my rifle and threw it down, and Big Harpe loosened his hold a bit on my scalp to throw him his own gun. When he did that, I jerked free a hand and grabbed his arm, and there we were, prancing around, holding on to each other like a couple of drunk Indians—him trying to get me in the sights of Little Wiley's gun, and me trying to use Big Harpe as a shield. Big Harpe must of weighed all of fifteen stone, and he had a hold like a bear. I was just about ready to give up when the women started hollering again. Then we heard horses and men yelling, and it sounded like a whole army. Big Harpe dropped me and jumped quick on his horse, but Little Harpe couldn't get to his horse, and he lit out on foot in the thicket."

Beulah got up and stood beside her husband, her hand on his shoulder. She looked apprehensively at the darkening sky. "Old Pilot Rock is calling up his thunderbirds," she said. "It's fixing to weather."

George placed a reassuring arm about her waist. A mist drifted and curled from the creek behind the shed, and John felt its moistness on his hot face.

"Who was it coming?" he asked.

"It was Clem Stegall and Captain John Leeper, and about a dozen neighbors who'd joined in right after Mr. Stegall got home that morning and found his house burned and his family murdered. I knew most of them but they didn't recognize me, squirming there on the ground, my clothes tore half off and my face bloody from where Big Harpe had dug into my scalp. They knew I wasn't one of the Harpe brothers, but they thought I was one of the gang, so they shot me in the leg and pushed on after Big Harpe on his horse. They'd seen him take flight. The women run into the thicket after Little Wiley, and they caught them, but Little Wiley got away. They said he went south, down in Mississippi Territory. They got the women still in the jailhouse over at Russellville in Logan County."

"And then you made it home?" John went back to the story, prodding him, anxious for all details.

"I was thinking I would bleed to death, lying there in that mud and dirt I don't know how long. I hollered and hollered. If nobody was about to hear me, I figured God would. And then some folks on their way to Woods Settlement for trading drove by in a wagon, and brung me straight home."

"He was a sight," said Beulah. "All covered with blood like a stuck pig. I thought my man was gone." She covered her face with her hands at the recollection.

"But they got Big Harpe?" John asked. "Mr. Stegall shot him?"

"Captain Leeper caught him," said George. "It was a good ten miles before he could get close enough for a good shot. He's fought the Indians, and he knew how to bring him down, him and his horse both, without killing him. He shot him in the groin, and then he held him down until Stegall come up, and Stegall shot him right between the eyes."

John shuffled his feet on the dry ground. "I heard that gang of cutthroats killed Marcus and Tobey Brown in Logan County before they got up here in the Green River country," he said. "And there's other murders they did, too. It's a mercy they were caught."

"Wiley is still loose. That's why me and Beulah carry guns in the fields, and never let the twins out of sight. But Big Harpe is gone; he's sure gone." George got stiffly to his feet. "After Stegall shot him, they cut off his head and stuck it on the end of a hickory sapling with all the branches trimmed off, and it's there now at the bend in the trace just about five miles from here as the crow flies. Folks are beginning to call that section Harpe's Head. We'll pass it when we ride down to Stockton's Valley. We'll see it then."

Beulah shivered, and reached up and smoothed the loose brown hair which hung in ragged lengths over the neckband of her husband's hunting shirt. "I'd be pleasured enough if I never heard that tale again," she said. "It's time we was going in. The peeper frogs are hollering, and that's a sign it's ready to rain."

As though to refute her words, the dark, low-hanging clouds began to drift away in a sharp breeze, and the long, rolling spaces of the valley emerged before them in the shadowy moonlight.

The next day John found now that the time had come, both George and Beulah seemed sorrowful to leave the Green River country where they had homesteaded four years before. The twins had been born in the big front room with the fieldstone chimney George had built with his own hands; the clearing was quiet except for the birds, and darting rabbits and woodchucks and occasional foxes; and the limestone valley soil was every bit as good for tobacco and corn as could be found in Cumberland County. But the closest market was Woods Settlement, too far away for George to take the corn and tobacco and hogs and sheep he tried to raise and leave Beulah alone, now that she was in the family way. After the encounter with the Harpes he had offered the place for sale, and a buying settler with hard money had been secured almost at once. It showed that Beulah had been right all along; it was the leading of the Lord.

George still had doubts about leaving, John could see, as they rode about the valley for the last time two days later, rounding up the last of the little drove of hogs and sheep and goats George had managed to nurse through the bitter cold of the winter.

"You can be a comfort to Pa," John tried to reassure him. "Pa ain't pert any more. He's past seventy, and he hankers for his family to be around him. He got Philip to put in a claim for a eighty-acre parcel for you on Otter Creek, and he's been over there with Philip, making a clearing for you to raise a house. Joe and Willy are talking to the Ryder sisters; you recollect them, Susie and Margaret. Ma was saying she wouldn't be surprised if there wasn't a wedding before snow flies."

George laughed, the soberness which had settled on him gone. "If we hustle real sharp, maybe we can pull out of here tomorrow," he said.

But it was two days more before the little procession finally pulled away from the valley of Green River and the shadow of Pilot Rock. George and Beulah, with the twins between them, sat in the wagon with all their possessions, driving the two black mules George had bought the year before and had never been able to fatten. John followed the wagon on Zebulon, herding the stock.

They made camp early the first night near a blue hole, and George entertained them with stories he had heard of unwary travelers lost in such bottomless pits. The next morning they passed Harpe's Head, the skull of Big Harpe now a mottled, pinkish, gaping mask, whistling in the wind atop the swaying hickory sapling. Although only Beulah pretended not to look at it, the somberness it cast upon them all was not relieved by their forced gaiety, or their silence.

Four more days of slow plodding over the rutted Cumberland Trace, luxuriant now with climbing vines and wild grapes and berries, the air sweet with honeysuckle growing in riotous profusion among the dogwood, and then the climb again into the shadow of Poplar Mountain. And at last, in midafternoon of the fifth day, they topped the rim of the valley named for its first settler, Thomas Stockton.

"Pa said I was to bring you right to the house," John told them as they drove into the valley and headed for the two-hundred-acre farm on Smith Creek. Pa had secured the place as a military grant when he moved from Holston Valley, Tennessee, six years before, and it was home to all his children.

"There'll be a family reunion after preaching on Sunday," John said, riding abreast of the wagon. "Even if it is Sunday, Ma'll let us play games and have fun."

In soaring spirits, now that the long journey was almost over, John drove the stock ahead of the wagon, his voice lifted in the strains of the ancient rhyme they had known since their earliest days:

> "King William was King George's son,
> Upon a royal race he run!"

Not to be outdone, George speeded up the lumbering wagon as best he could, and in high good humor the little party drove past the spicewood thicket and splashed through the shallow creek which cut the George Smith farm in two, and stopped with much clattering and noise and jubilant shouts beside the single giant locust that shaded their father's house.

CHAPTER IV

THE following Sunday morning John squirmed uncomfortably in his seat beside his younger brother, Jonathan, in the men's section of the Clear Fork Baptist Church. The day was warm, but Ma had insisted he wear his oldest brother Philip's store-bought wedding suit and white cravat because Brother Isaac Denton was going to call on him to tell about the Muddy River revival. Philip had married three years before, leaving the suit at home to be worn on important occasions by the younger boys as they grew into it, but it was woolsey and itched in the heat. As Brother Isaac's sermon droned on for an hour and a half, John grew hopeful he had forgotten the request. He had no wish to relate again, as he had for the family, the experience of that nightmarish time, its sharp edges dimming now in the light of normal things. He would like to forget it all.

But Brother Isaac had not forgotten, and John mopped his brow with his cotton kerchief as he strode to the front of the room and stood before the tightly packed meetinghouse with more confidence than he felt, relating the story. He told of the throngs of people and the flaring torches, of the shouting sermons and the distraught, hysterical people, of their contortions and their cries as they came under conviction and sought to be born again. He mentioned the young Methodist, Peter Cartwright, as one of those converted, and of the nickname the boy's father had given him—Raccoon John—which brought a titter of laughter. He spoke of his encounter with the Presbyterian preacher, Barton Stone, and with a touch of eloquence that surprised himself, he related his ride back into the Cumberland Trace with the singing of the multitude in his ears. But he did not tell of that radiance he had seen in young Peter's face, nor of Barton Stone's gentle words, "No man is born Elect, and no man is born damned. God is love!"

As he finished and was preparing to take his seat, Thomas Stockton leaned forward in his place among the elders, his devouring eyes fixed on John.

"Did you come under conviction, boy? Did you get saved?"

John drew in his breath sharply. Thomas Stockton was the biggest man in the community. He had been the first settler, and the valley was named for him. He had given the land on which the meetinghouse stood, and his word was law in church affairs. John had always stood a mite in awe of him; his stern face and erect figure, his massive chin and flowing white hair put him sometimes in mind of God. He had no mind to displeasure him.

He shifted his feet and cleared his throat, tugging at the unaccustomed cravat. "Can't say I did, Mr. Stockton," he said, his voice hoarse. "I didn't feel the notion to jump and shout and roll on the ground, and all that. It may be the workings of the Lord on some folks, but I'm just not made that way. It somehow ain't right to me." He tugged again at his cravat and mopped his forehead with his sleeve. "It scares me some."

"And so you ran away," Mr. Stockton said. "You left, like you said, with those good people singing a great hymn at the gates of heaven. You were privileged to attend this revival where a mighty fire is being struck for the Lord, and you turned your back on it." He waved John aside as he got to his feet and turned to face the group. "My friends, the boy is young and knew no better. In time he will realize the folly of his ways." He looked over at John, his tone not unkindly. "A man who turns his back on God will live to regret it," he said, and then he turned back to the narrow platform where Brother Isaac was sitting with bowed head, his face deep in thought. "Tell us the story of Jonah, Brother Denton; burn it into our hearts before we leave this place of worship."

Brother Isaac Denton got to his feet and stood with one hand on the puncheon stand, sympathy and understanding for John in his face, yet stern in the knowledge Thomas Stockton was right. Simply he related the story of the young man who had rebelled against God and had fled from his duty; and of how the Lord had caused a storm to come up while the young man, Jonah, was at sea, and of how the sailors had cast Jonah into the sea, where he was swallowed by a whale and spewed up after three days on dry land—a lesson, mighty and enduring for all time to all men.

John listened, his eyes on the floor, at first accepting the rebuke as part of the discipline members felt called upon to give each other, and then in mounting irritation. He was not like Jonah; he had not rebelled against the will of God. He felt somehow betrayed and incensed. He was tired of being preached at, and made the butt of sermons; no man should be penned up and held like a stray calf for the butcher's knife. If the Lord had not chosen him, all the preaching and prayers of Brother Isaac and Thomas Stockton and Pa could not change the divine decree one jot or tittle.

He hurried from the meetinghouse when Brother Isaac concluded the benediction, and ran across the churchyard, Jonathan at his heels.

"Don't take on so, John," Jonathan called to him, panting, as he caught up with him at the end of the fence thick with dogwood and forsythia. "Everybody knows you can't help it if you ain't had the revealing experience. Mr. Stockton didn't mean nothing, except he felt sorry for you."

"I'm walking home," John said. He had no mind to discuss the rebuke. "You tell Pa I'm cutting across the creek and will be there quicker'n he can get the folks there in the wagon." The air in the meetinghouse had been close, and the breeze felt good. "I can be there and help Ma lay out the dinner."

Four hours later John's irritation had been dispelled. He looked at Pa Smith leaning back in his hickory rocker in the yard under the giant locust, sucking gently on his pipe. The safe return of George and Beulah had been the occasion, as John had foretold, for a family dinner after the preaching, and the big yard, clean as if it had been broomed, was still filled. No mention was made of the happenings at the church as they gathered about the long trestle table and heaped their tin plates with Ma's succulent turkey stew and ham slices and corn bread and pickled walnuts and quince tarts, topped off with the season's first watermelons. Not every man so close to his allotted time, John thought, looking at his father, could sit with his wife on a sunny May afternoon and watch every one of the thirteen children the Lord had given him, and their wives or husbands and children, frolic and sing and play together on the Lord's Day.

It was because Pa and Ma believed the Lord made people to be happy and enjoy his blessings, and his day. John grinned as he saw his father lean over and pat the ridged, worn hand of the woman sitting in unaccustomed ease in a rocker beside him.

"Brother Isaac spoke well at the dinner table before the blessing," he said to her. "Like the Good Book says, 'Eye hath not seen nor ear heard, neither hath it entered into the heart of man what God hath prepared for those who love him.' "

"Faith, 'tis true," Ma answered, nodding. "And did I believe in the idolatry of my people in old Dublin, I would give a couple of my boys to the priesthood in thanksgiving. I do believe God has touched at least one of them." She glanced fleetingly at John, and although her voice was gay, there was a conviction in her tone which caused him to stiffen. Ma saw more with her heart than with her two eyes, sharp as they were, Pa always said.

"That's reckless talk for even an old Irish colleen." Pa smiled gently, his furrowed face flushed with the excitement of the day, his deep-set gray eyes twinkling under his shaggy brows and shock of snow-white hair. "If I didn't know you as well as the sole of my shoe I'd think you would make one of them the Pope."

"My people were Druid worshippers before they became Catholic Christians," Ma continued dreamily. "And before that they worshipped stones, and the tides. They were friends of unseen spirits, the little people; the leprechauns fairly bedeviled and bewitched them. That is, before my blessed grandmother, Molly Mageehan, God rest her soul, found the true Christian faith with the Baptists in Pennsylvania and spared not the rod that I might walk in the true light."

"Sister Rebecca, I misdoubt but that you are still something of a pagan." The deep, warm voice spoke suddenly from the rope swing, where Brother Isaac Denton had been pushing two of the children. Now he came slowly toward the old couple, easing his stocky frame down near them on a backless workbench the boys had brought in from the shed for the occasion. "I sometimes suspect you still believe in fairies!"

"Indade I do!" She pushed herself up from the rocker and pretended to make a little skip, swishing her white apron and gray hodden skirt around her plump figure, her reddish hair now tinged with white drawn back tight into a low bun on her neck under a crisp white cap, her round face with its network of laughter lines sparkling with high humor. "Whatever one doubts, one never doubts the fairies, my grandmother Mageehan always told me. They stand to reason. Even Saint Patrick, rest his soul, with all his faith could not have driven the snakes out of the auld sod without the help of the pookas."

"For shame, Sister Rebecca," said Brother Isaac in mock severity. "Sometimes I would doubt your own sainthood did I not know you so well."

"I'll wrap her in a wether's skin yet," said Pa. "A demon has her!"

"I've seen pookas," said John solemnly. "You remember a bird dog I had once. Ma named him Pooka, and he was the best setter I ever had. He froze the birds with his eyes."

"Nor must I forget the banshees," Ma continued, ignoring the interruptions, lost in her fancies. "They live in the damp bogs and travel in coaches drawn by headless horses. Nor the merry pixies, or the brownies and the gnomes and little dwarfs. I would be false to the ancient kings of my native land," she continued, "their Royal Majesties Conchobar and Cochulainn, not to mention King Mongan, did I deny them!"

"You're a pixie yourself, Ma." A tall young woman, cradling a sleeping infant in her arms, called to her lightly from across the yard where she was sitting in a rope hammock swung between two beech trees. "It's hard enough for me to raise my children as Christians without hearing such talk from their own grandma."

"Fiddle-fan, Rebecca," her mother called back, shaking her finger at her eldest daughter, who bore her own name. "We've had serious talk enough for today; let your children know there are happier things to speak of on the Lord's Day lest we disgrace his holy name."

"Sister Smith is right," Brother Isaac said, wagging his head, his white hair, long about his neck, lifting in the breeze. He was a stocky man, square-built; his wide mouth was set in a broad arc under a short, upturned nose, and his blue eyes looked out in a penetrating, perplexed gaze from under thick brows, his skin weathered and brown. "Such things are spoken of in Holy Writ; it speaks of good spirits, joyous spirits who spake with tongues and cymbals, and of demons and such perverse creatures as the witch of Endor, who tortured the soul of Saul."

The family was scattered about the yard, the children in swings, or playing teeter-totter on planks placed over fallen logs; the girls making daisy chains; the young people lolling in the cool stand of hickory adjacent to the yard, laughing, chattering; the older ones joining them from the kitchen after clearing up the last disorder of the dinner.

Philip came over and laid his hand on the shoulder of his father. Ma glanced at him, and suddenly sobered. "We must call the family roll," she said, and seated herself again in the rocker beside her husband, "before they scatter. Philip's fixing to leave, I can see it in his eyes."

"And good reason," Philip said, an air of importance about him. "But I'm proud-turned to answer to the roll. I'll answer for wife Millie, too, and our little Polly, and especially for the lazy rascal who dropped into our house just the day George and Beulah came back. That's why Millie can't be here today."

"No speeches!" Nat Stockton, Rebecca's husband, called from where he had sat down beside his wife in the hammock. "Just answer to the muster!"

"He's got the same first name as the daddy of King David himself." He looked about the group. "Who was that?"

"Jesse," John answered quickly. "You're not thinking you're the only one knows the Bible, are you, Philip?"

Philip ignored him. "And our Ma's maiden name—Jesse Bowen Smith he's named, the first and only son of me and Millie, called into service in this life on May 24, A.D. 1801!"

Pa rose from his rocker and put his arm about Philip's shoulder, his kindly face in contrast to his eldest son's stern countenance. "I'll answer for the rookie," he said. "It's a proud day for the Lord."

"You mean it's a proud day for George Smith," Ma corrected him. "It's a sinful pride you be having in your first grandson to carry the name forever of Smith. As though you be forgetting all the other little ones because they're females." Her eyes roved the group, separating them. "I'll call the roll of them myself," she said, and began counting them off on her gnarled fingers. "Besides Philip and Millie with their Polly and now baby Jesse, there's George and Beulah with their Rose and Sharon; and Rebecca and Nat Stockton with their three; and Polly and Ben Livingstone with their two; and Betsy and Ezra Matlock with their yearling." She stopped, her eyes suddenly clouded. "That's all of the married girls; they're doing their part. It's my boys I'm getting fret about."

"From the looks of things, Ma, you won't have to fret much longer about Willy and Joe," John called out.

They all turned to where the two boys were sitting on the fence rail beside Maggie and Susie Ryder, a self-conscious constraint upon them, flushing at the sudden, teasing attention. Ma smiled, nodding. Margaret and Susannah were both smart girls from over on Pea Ridge, blooming now in their early womanhood, old enough to settle down to a lifetime of hard work and having babies. They would make good wives for Willy and Joe; the two brothers had been sparking and talking to the sisters now for over a month.

"It's James you better be lighting a fire under," John went on. "He's all of twenty-three, and he ain't never been sparkin' a girl yet."

James, a lanky, thin-faced youth with close-set eyes, hugged his knees tighter to his chest, sitting on the stile. He had helped Pa make the fence of gnarled honey locust, riving out the planing boards, making them fast with taut leather thongs, and he had been mending a broken cleat. He frowned at the sally and made no reply, and John went on. "And there's me and Jonathan and Henry. What about us?"

His mother dismissed him with a wave of her hand. "You three youngest of the brood, you have time to grow on. And same's true of Fancy Mae and Jane. I'm pleasured to have some of you still underfoot."

"We ought to have a kissin' game before we break up," Nat Stockton called from the well, where he was lowering the wooden bucket on the windlass. He was a gay blade, as the whole countryside knew, little resembling his uncle, Thomas Stockton, but he was a good farmer and shrewd trader, and a devoted husband and father. "Especially as some are here with marrying notions. They won't feel too much like frolicking once they hop the broom."

"For shame, Nat," his wife, Rebecca, said. "Talk like that is enough to scare the notion right out of any girl's head."

"Not mine," Maggie Ryder said frankly. "I'm not that scary. Willy makes a lot of talk, but I haven't heard him say nothing to the point yet."

"You ain't been listening," said William stoutly. "I been talking my head off all month. Let's do a little hopping," he said as if to change the subject. "James has a fiddle, and John could call the tunes."

"I ain't fiddled for a coon's age," James spoke up. He gave a warning, sidelong glance at the faces of his father and Brother Denton, their obvious disapproval only partially offset by the still sparkling eyes of Ma. "Being it's the Lord's Day, maybe we shouldn't be hopping, but it would be right and proper for John to call the numbers. Raccoon John," he paused as though to emphasize his pride in his younger brother, "the man that named him who must have seen how smart he is. He knows more lively tunes, and he's got the best calling voice of any boy caller this side of the Gap!"

"I'm a pore foot-shuffler, but I do know some good callin' tune songs," John admitted. He turned to his father. "You recollect the time you sent me to Horine's mill up on the Dix River with a couple of pack horses for seed corn that first winter we was here?" he asked, and shivered as though feeling again the cold. "Br-r-r-r! It took me a week, and when I got there I found a dance going on at the miller's cabin, and it was a spell before anybody noticed me. I got the corn all right the next day and got back, the Lord looking after me. But that fiddler, Jeremiah Vardeman, I've never forgot him. He wore a striped red coat and velvet breeches, and he was a fiddlin' fool. And I ain't never forgot the song they was steppin' to." He turned to the two sparking couples and, rising on tiptoe, swung into the merry chant, the rest of them keeping time with a clapping of their hands:

"High up in the cherry tree,
The riper grows the berry;
The sooner a young man courts a gal,
The sooner they will marry!"

In the laughter that followed, George and Beulah rose to go, each holding a twin by the hand. They were bedding down at Philip's place over near Sinking Creek, a good twelve miles away, and Philip was anxious to be on the way.

"Sunup comes early," George said, "and those that are helping with my house-raising in the morning better be there." He looked about the group. "Hank Grigsby and Willy Wood said today after preaching they was coming, and Beulah's two brothers, Flea and Quillen Thompson, will be there. We ought to raise it in a day."

"Rome wasn't built in a day," Fancy Mae spoke up. "Was it, Pa?"

"But this house will be, or my name won't be Smith," Pa answered. "We'll be there, George, you can count on us all," he said as George made a dash for Sharon, who had broken from his hold. He picked her up and placed her in the wagon bed and put Rose beside her, and helped Beulah hoist herself on to the plank seat between them and climbed in himself beside the waiting Philip, staring in disapproval at the frolicsome children.

For a few minutes there was silence as the wagon disappeared around a bend in the lane, and then Ma sighed deeply. "I'm that grateful to the Lord for the care he took of them," she said. "I don't know as I could of stood it, losing George."

"Tell us about the banshees and the pookas again, Ma," nine-year-old Jane called. "We can hear sorrowful talk any time."

"You're an impudent little colleen," Pa said firmly, but there was no harshness in his voice. "Like your ma when she was young, you need the rod more often than you get it."

"Tell us about the Indians!" Not to be outdone by his sister, Jonathan, fifteen, spoke from a crotch of the great locust tree, now casting long shadows across the yard. "Tell us about Uncle Reece and how he killed a b'ar!"

"It was Dan'l Boone who killed the b'ar," John said, and chanted, "Old Dan'l Boone he killed a ba'r; he killed a b'ar that wasn't thar."

"I had two brothers traveling with Dan'l Boone at one time or another," Ma said pridefully. "Reece and William. But it was your Uncle Reece who killed the b'ar. He crushed it to death against his chest, which was solid bone and muscle; they do say he broke every bone in that b'ar's body."

"That be a likely tale," Pa interposed. "Reece Bowen was a stout man, but he wasn't all that stout. The way I heard it, he grabbed the b'ar by the throat and choked it to death."

"Anyway," Ma shrugged and went on, "they were brave men, and we mightn't be here today if they hadn't killed b'ars and Indians. But they was friends of the Indians mostly. There were good and bad Indians, but mostly good, I always said; not all of them were warpath-minded. White men wasn't all good either."

"Some of them became Christians," Brother Isaac said, rousing himself and pushing back his hair from where it had fallen partially over his face as he nodded, leaning back on the workbench against the trunk of the locust. "We take pride in the fact that the first missionary to the Indians was our own Roger Williams of the true Baptist faith in the state of Rhode Island."

"John is practically an Indian himself," Jonathan said, eying his older brother pridefully. "He talks Cherokee when he doesn't want me to know what he's saying."

"*Tsi tsa lagi;* that means, 'I'm a Cherokee,' " John replied promptly. "You was too little to be one when we lived back in Holston Valley, Jonathan. That's when I picked up what I know."

"John was always one to pick up a thing quick-like," Pa said, observing him thoughtfully. "He's reading the Scriptures for us now at morning prayers," he said to Brother Isaac, "and he's helping the younger ones to read, too. He's a good reader."

"But I still can't cipher much," John said, a note of wistfulness in his voice. "I wish we could have us another school here."

"That we should," Brother Isaac said firmly. "Some day the state will have it, public and free for all, so all can read the Scriptures and do more than sign their mark."

Dusk had come, and the air was sweet-smelling with wood smoke; the wind had stilled. Ma motioned to John.

"Get from the house the three holy books," she said. "Brother Denton might read from them all before we go inside."

"I've been preaching all day, more than I intended," Brother Isaac demurred. But he accepted the books when John brought them from the house and turned the pages rapidly. As if not finding what he wanted, he put the *Philadelphia Confession of Faith* and the Hymnal down, and got to his feet, holding the thick, worn black Bible open in his sensitive hands.

"The Lord called Samuel, and he answered, 'Here am I!' " He ringed the silent circle with his eyes, a deep gravity in his face. He finished reading the account of young Samuel, and then began speaking of their blessings and their responsibilities, and of that gift which each among them possessed in unique measure above the others, and of the need to use it wisely in the service of the Lord. And although he singled out no one of them, John felt the message was directed at him above and apart from all the others, and he felt again the familiar rebellion rising in him, mingled with an uncertainty and a restlessness he could not analyze.

It was after the younger ones had gone to bed and Pa and Ma were in their rockers before the sandstone hearth, a low burning of hickory logs transmuting the chill of the night mountain air into a rhythm of comforting warmth, that John voiced the feelings he had kept submerged all day.

He uncrossed his legs and crossed them again, sitting beside Jonathan on the floor before the fire, and cleared his throat. It was a big, comfortable, cheerful room, he thought as he looked about, filled with peace and family pride, a refuge where not even Governor Isaac Shelby or Dan'l Boone would dare enter unless Pa said so. Back in the corner adjacent to the kitchen was the six-legged, four-posted bed of his parents, its feather mattress so high a stool was required to plunge into its depths. A round oak table, hand-hewn, was near the center, holding four thick, foot-high tallow candles, about which the family gathered for Scripture reading. The Bible was on it now, beside the Hymnal and the *Philadelphia Confession of Faith* where Ma had placed them when she came in, her holy books, she called them; and alongside was an Almanac distributed that spring to all the farmers by Matt Lyon, campaigning for Congress. Ma's spinning jenny and sounding wheel were pushed against the far wall, quiet now that it was Sunday but humming every other day; soon they would be transferred for the summer to the shade of the big locust before the house, where Ma and the girls could get the breeze as they worked with their piles of wool and flying cards.

Occasionally the family even ate their meals in the room, especially when visitors were present or all the married ones and their spouses and children were at home, but for the most part the meals were in the long, narrow kitchen with its rows of pots and kettles and pans hanging by the wide-mouthed hearth over the ever-smoldering embers. Open cupboards lined the caulked kitchen walls, holding the tin and woodenware, as well as earthen jars of jellies and preserves and pickles sealed with coatings of bear grease and tallowed paper. The family sat on backless benches at a long table before the hearth, but when not in use the benches were pushed against the wall of the kitchen on either side of the door leading to the deep, cooling cellar where meats and milk and root vegetables were stored.

A bedroom at the back of the big room was reserved for the girls, the boys climbing the puncheon steps near the kitchen door to the two big loft rooms overhead, while a square fifteen-foot company room on the other side of the family room was kept ready at all times for visiting preachers, or the married children, with its feather bed fluffed high under Ma's best white quilted coverlet, and the pewter bowl and pitcher kept shining on the walnut stand under the framed mirror, once the property of Grandma Mageehan. This mirror had been brought by Ma as her only dowry when she married the orphaned lad, George Schmidt, later changed to Smith, thirty-five years before in Botetourt County, Virginia, and, by the grace of God, it had escaped breakage during its long travels across the wilderness trail.

"I didn't hanker to what Brother Isaac said at preaching this morning," John said almost explosively, his deepening voice seeming high-pitched. "I'm not like Jonah, running away. I'm not trying to hide from anybody."

Jonathan rolled over on his back, his hands behind his head, and looked at him curiously. Ma glanced sharply at her husband, compressing her lips, and Pa removed his pipe, holding it at arm's length, studying it.

"Are you sure?" Pa asked gently. "A man has to make himself receptive to God's will, that's all Brother Isaac meant. That's where Jonah failed; he was proud-turned and hardened his neck against God."

"But I'm not Jonah!" John protested, hugging his knees to his chest. "And the Lord hasn't made his will known. I've exposed myself, waiting for the experience. I just can't say truthful one has come. What else can I do?"

" 'Seek and ye shall find,' " Jonathan quoted. " 'Ye shall see the heavens open and an angel of God descending upon the Son of Man.' "

"You're too quick given to Bible-quoting, Jonathan," John said, poking at him impatiently. He turned to his parents. "Maybe I ought to leave home; I'm most eighteen now. If I could get some more schooling, I might be a lawyer like Micah Taul up at Monticello and go into politics. Or I could start homesteading a place of my own. I want to amount to something before I die and go to hell."

"Hush, son!" His mother spoke sternly, her face drawn in troubled lines. "No Irish son talks like that!"

"There'll most likely be plenty of Irish sons in hell," John said. "I won't be lonesome there." He squirmed about to face his parents better. "I've been doing more sober-minded thinking than folks give me credit for. No matter how low-down the Lord has ordained me, I want to amount to something, and I'm thinking it's time I begun."

"You've begun," Jonathan pushed himself to a sitting position, his back to the hearth, facing John and his parents. "Maybe John ought to be a preacher, bothering all the time like this about things." He rubbed his chin, feeling the first faint fuzz of down on his skin. "Once you tuck to preaching, John, it'd ease off your mind and you could go on about your business and maybe amount to something."

John ignored him. "I want more schooling," he said firmly. "I like farming well enough, but I got a feeling there's more I can do than plowing and hoeing and digging in the mountains for ginseng. Maybe I could be an arithmetician."

Ma looked up, her eyes startled. "A what?"

"Like ciphering," John explained. "It makes me feel good to figure things out, like with numbers. I like to reason things."

Ma laughed quietly. "You still want the answer to that question you asked of that drunken schoolmaster three years ago. 'How many grains of corn does it take to make a square foot of mush?' was what you asked of him." She laughed and wagged her head. "Your Pa should've switched you for being so pert. Maybe then you wouldn't of dropped those hot coals into the schoolmaster's coat pockets when he was drunk that time, and made him run away. It's partly your own fault, John, that we don't have a schoolmaster now in Stockton's Valley. You run the last one off, and he gave out the word. They're afraid of your pranks."

"That drunken sot deserved to be chased off," Pa said. "Though not to have his coat set afire. The Lord would have seen to such burning soon enough." He laughed quietly.

"If you want more learning, you can keep on with your Dilworth's grammar and speller and your Pike's arithmetic, like you're a-doing, and in reading the Scriptures. There's no finer study book than the Word of God," Ma said thoughtfully.

"What's wrong about digging ginseng root?" Jonathan inquired. "It makes good medicine."

"There's nothing wrong about digging ginseng in the woods after crops are laid by, and before planting time," Ma said. "It serves as medicine, and if it never cured anybody it's never done no harm as I know of either. And it's something to swap at the trading posts in Burkesville and at Joe Beard's store in Monticello."

"I didn't say there was wrongdoing in digging ginseng," John said defensively. "I like to dig it because it takes me to the woods. God's there, in the trees and everything, and he might give me the revealing experience, but I ain't expecting to have it in places where people roll over and over and bark and jerk and yell and cavort like they did at that revival. I can't see God in such goings-on." He shrugged in resignation. "Maybe that's why I've never had the experience."

"That's why, all right," Jonathan said solemnly. "Like Pa said, you've hardened your neck."

"You keep still!" John made a half-threatening gesture at his brother, frustration filling him.

"Hush, boys," Pa spoke firmly. "You're both young; in some ways you are both like children. It's time you were putting away childish things. You both judge too harsh. You got to grow up; now you see through a glass darkly, like the Bible says." He looked directly at John. "You've got to have patience, son, with God and with yourself. Who are you, my boy, to say that the signs you saw at Muddy River were not the works of God?"

John dug his knuckles into his eyes and then got slowly to his feet. "I'm only a sinner," he said, "and I reckon like you say, I got no right to judge."

"The admission of sin is the beginning of salvation," Pa said quietly.

Ma got up from her rocker, easing herself erect. "My joints are plumb creaky," she said. "Tomorrow's the house-raising of George and Beulah. It'll be a busy time, even with all the logs cut and notched and ready for the raising crew. Pa and the boys worked hard last week while you was gone, John, getting things ready. But the womenfolks still got all that cooking to do. It's time to bed down. James is still out, Lord knows where, and Willy and Joe won't be in till late, taking the Ryder girls home clear over to Pea Ridge. No use waiting up for them."

Pa nodded, and rising stiffly, knocked out his pipe on the stone chimney and wiped his lips with the back of his hand. And then, slowly and deliberately, he raised his hand and led the little group solemnly and reverently into the presence of their Lord in prayer.

CHAPTER V

IT was a full hour after sunup the next morning when John brought the wagon carrying the family to a halt in the cleared space alongside Otter Creek, the reins taut in his hands, seesawing the bit in Beelzebub's mouth with a double-handed steady pressure which even a mule understood. A final heave forward, and then a quick, jolting halt, and John braced himself against the footboard to avoid plunging forward, the reins now slack in his grip.

"This he-devil remembers when you had him snaking logs in here last week from the woods; he's still mad about it." John spoke to his father standing beside him, holding to the wagon side. "Old Beelie's as smart as Balaam's ass. He hates work. I'll bet he's cussing now under his breath if we just knew mule talk."

"Mules and men are kin," Ma said from her seat on a plank behind them. She watched Fancy Mae and Jane scramble out as the wagon came to a halt, and then gingerly eased herself over the edge of the high sideboard, grabbing Pa's extended hand for support. Jonathan and Henry were already on the ground, and she motioned for them to fetch the pans of chicken and the iron skillet of corn bread and the big reed hamper under the seat with the other food. She had been up since before dawn, preparing for the noonday dinner.

"Get the fire going under the kettle," she said to John, who had unhitched the mule and was tethering him to a sapling. "The others'll be coming any time now. I hear the boys already whacking out there in the woods."

James, with Willy and Joe, had left before the wagon, riding horseback to the clearing with the tools, and the sound of their felling ax and their double-handed saws reverberated through the clear morning air.

John started the fire and stood for a moment, studying the clearing. George and Beulah would like it. Pa had entered a claim for it in George's name, and the eighty-acre parcel was a good selection. It ran along a gentle ridge of scrub pine and locust, sloping on one side to Otter Creek and falling off on the other side to a hazelnut thicket which grew to the edge of a meadow surrounding a gushing spring a hundred yards from the space Pa and Philip had cleared for the house. There had once been an orchard here, John could tell, planted probably by the Indians; plum and peach and apple trees were scattered here and there, bent and gnarled and showing the lack of care but still thrusting sprigs of early green toward the sun, contrasting with the coarser, hardier pine.

A call from the roadway, and George and Beulah drove up with Philip and Millie and the children, Millie bundled in blankets and pillows in a chair in the wagon, holding her new baby. It was her first time out since the baby's birth, and the wagon was immediately surrounded as the men lifted her out, chair and all, and placed her in a shaded spot near the fire already sputtering down near the spring.

John had always enjoyed house-raisings. Something about them measured a man and gave him a feeling of building the country. He had been at plenty of them, and even as a boy did his share of the work: felling and hewing and scalping the logs, notching and helping with the clinch work, and even with the snaking-in of the felled trees with mule and brake and chain. He liked it all. But most of all he liked the frolic of it, the singing, the banter among the men while the womenfolks, talking endlessly, prepared the big dinner, their full skirts billowing about them as they stooped to push the corn pones in the ashes of the kettle fires, their faces excited and flushed as they took turns lugging wooden buckets to the working men filled with whatever thirst-quenchers were to be had. Sometimes it was just pure spring water, sometimes sweet-slaked metheglin brewed from the pods of the honey locust; a few times the fiery homemade usquebaugh familiar to the Scotch and Irish settlers. And once or twice it had been plain charcoaled, brown-flecked or water-clear unmellowed mountain whiskey, which plenty of good church people brewed with a steady fire, an iron kettle, and a long iron pipe from the juice of the bruised and fermented corn. But Pa frowned on such. He enjoyed a warm toddy sweetened with honey, or a little wine for his stomach's sake, and sometimes drink a little stronger, especially at a wedding or a shivaree or an infare. But when there was steady work to be done, he said, the drink should be of another color.

More people were arriving. The Grigsby brothers, Hank and Bill, and Alexander Hayes and William Wood; Beulah's two brothers, Flea and Quillen Thompson, from beyond Wolf River, were hobbling their horses, swinging their axes over their powerful shoulders, their womenfolks sliding to the ground from their perches behind the saddles where they had hung to their men for the ride over, balancing their hampers of food as best they could. Nat Stockton had already taken his place as the lead corner man to supervise the exacting clinch work of the notched logs when they would be lifted and fitted snugly into place. An uneven notch, or one too shallow, or too deeply cut, could lift one end of the log higher than the other and throw the whole thing out of kilter. But when fitted true and firm, they would hold the house together, and make the roof ride straight and keep the corners from sagging.

Pa motioned the group together. "The raising for George and Beulah will begin as soon as I finish my speech here, and keep on till the work is done or dark comes," he announced. "At midday I'll take a bearing on the sun and give time off for a bait of food. There ain't no reason the house won't be raised by full dark with all the stout menfolks we got here, but if it ain't, we'll leastwise raise the main room and the rafters, and George and the boys can finish up later. It'll give George and his family four walls and a roof." He paused for breath and pointed to the pile of felled logs. "Them's cedar, and they're heavy. Forty or more of them in all, and every one a foot thick and not one under twenty foot long. We want eight logs for the front and eight for the back wall. Side walls will take sixteen logs, each about eighteen foot long, and some shorter logs that'll take some trimming and notching to fit the gables."

He stopped and the men began crowding about. "Here, you, George," Pa called. "You place these four big stones where you want the four corners of your house. You, Willy, and Joe, you help Nat Stockton and Willy Wood as corner men, to clinch the logs snug. You, Henry," he called to his eight-year-old son, chasing a rabbit that had darted across the edge of the hazelnut thicket, "you keep the wood coming for the women and their kettle fires, and keep the drippin' piggin filled with water from the spring."

Hastily now, instructions were called to the others, and John found himself hoisting logs with Quillen Thompson and Hank Grigsby. Steadily the logs were lifted and clinched into place by the corner men with the powering force of their broadaxes. By midmorning the four walls had been raised, a rough opening hewed in either end for windows, and a narrow doorway hewed out in the front. Smaller poplar logs were lifted overhead for the loft, a bare ten feet above the earthen floor which would be covered later with puncheon logs, and stout cedars hoisted into place from gable to gable to serve as joists for the roof. The ridge pole was in position by noon.

The Ryder sisters and their aging father, Tom, who had lost an eye under General Braddock in Pennsylvania before the Revolution, drove up in their buggy, and Pa whistled for the noon meal. Tom Ryder couldn't help with the raising, but he lugged from in back of the buggy seat a half-barrel of metheglin and a two-gallon keg of usquebaugh for the workers while the girls carried over to Beulah a side of jerked deer meat and a keg of pea seed as a housewarming gift. And then, as if not to be outdone, Brother Isaac Denton's horn was heard, and he came into view, bouncing on his horse, his flat-crown, broad-brimmed hat low over his eyes.

"I dinna come just to pray with you," he said, dismounting. "I want to help a bit. I brought my hand adz to help smooth the inside walls, and here's my round saw if you need it."

He laid the tools beside a pile of logs and joined the others, milling now about the kettle fires with their pewter plates where the women were ladling out the food. Brother Isaac had been widowed for as long as John could remember, living alone, tending his own place as best he could in the time he took from his preaching. But it was common knowledge he was only a tolerable farmer, and no cook at all. He ate with the brethren on all special occasions as well as other times, always a welcome guest, and John noticed now he took a hearty helping of food.

"I think Brother Isaac was plumb hungry," John said, his voice low, edging over to his father. "You figure he's got any vittles at all on his place?"

Pa shook his head doubtfully. "Only what folks send in, and that ain't regular. He raises hemp mostly and sells it for hard money, but he gives away freely, and I've never known him to have a quid on him."

The thirty minutes' break Pa had allotted for the noon meal was over almost before it had begun. The women cleared the plates, and the men found themselves back at work, setting on the joists the long white oak clapboards which had been salvaged from an abandoned sugar mill on Wolf River, to make the roof firm against the weather. Then slender barked hickory butting poles were pegged over the clapboards to keep them in place. While this was going on, a mud and stick chimney was erected above the sandstone hearth by Nat Stockton, who boasted with reason that he was the best hearth and chimney man in the Cumberland region. Others edged and smoothed and laid the floor puncheons of ash and beech; Brother Isaac, true to his word, smoothed the inside walls, and John helped cleat a pole bedstead into the side wall, opposite the hearth. George would later hew a doorway in the back wall that could lead to any rooms he wanted to add.

"A fair reward for hasty effort." Brother Isaac pronounced his judgment as they began to gather their tools and clear away the rubbish before darkness fell. He came over and stood beside John, who was talking with Willy and Maggie Ryder. "Another year or so, John, and maybe we'll be raising a house for you."

"John is a slowpoke," William said. "He's a man grown, and if he's bundled with any girl in the county yet, nobody ever heard tell of it. It'll be a long time before we'll be putting up a house like this for him. I got an idea he's hankering for a rich wife."

John dug his heel in the soft earth. "Whether she's rich or pore, when I get ready I won't waste a lot of time hedging around about it like some folks I know. It won't take me forever to make up my mind."

"You ain't talking about me, John," William said. "My mind's been set for a long spell; I just been waiting for a chance to talk to the preacher here."

Maggie giggled. "It ain't fitten to do it with me a-listening," she said. "That's man-to-man talk." She gathered her skirts in her hand and ran to her father's buggy. The half-barrel of metheglin had been placed in the shade of the buggy and, excitedly, she began ladling gourd dippers of the honeyed brew to Nat Stockton and Quillen Thompson and others who gathered about her.

William reddened, a tightening in his jaw, and kicked at a clod of earth. "Maybe it ain't fitten to speak to you here, Brother Isaac;

anyway, matters ain't full set yet." He turned and followed Maggie, and John and Brother Isaac looked after him, smiling.

"I been waiting for a chance to talk to you, Brother Isaac," John said, "even if Willy ain't. I been talking already some to the folks." He lowered his voice and drew the preacher partly aside. "I don't feel too good about what you said, comparing me to Jonah. I know you didn't mean me no harm but it irked me some."

The preacher's eyes softened in quick understanding. "It was because I love you like a son, John; I want you should be all that the Lord intended you to be."

"That's just it," John said. "I don't rightly know what the Lord's got in mind for me. I been thinking some I should leave home and go out on my own. Maybe the Lord would reveal himself to me quicker." He paused and looked searchingly at the old man. "What do you think of that?"

Brother Isaac pursed his lips. "All young men feel that way," he said. "You'd best pray about it."

John frowned. "I'm most prayed out," he said sharply.

Brother Isaac smiled, and laid his hand on John's arm. "You're thinking only of yourself," he said. "Your father is an old man, John; perhaps the Lord is revealing his work for you, and you're not of a mind to see it. But it's plain to me you're needed here."

The shadows had grown long and folks were beginning to leave. There was still work to be done at the new cabin; a corn and fodder loft to be clapboarded, pens to be made for the stock, milking stalls to be roofed, and a lean-to built against the side of the house for farm tools. There was timber and brush to be cleared, and stumps to be pulled and burned to prepare the ground for turning. George would do most of it, but he would still have assistance from his brothers and the neighbors, who would expect and receive a return of the work as they in turn needed it.

Summer descended on the land with its enervating heat. Once a month John attended the Sunday preaching at the Clear Fork Baptist Church with the family; on the other Sundays, when Brother Isaac was preaching and exhorting at other settlements, the family worshiped at home, with John usually reading the Scriptures as the best reader in the family and each member commenting or questioning as the mood seized him, the intimate service closing always with prayer by Ma or Pa. The harvest would be good, Pa said, but he cautioned again, as he always did in a prosperous year, against the accumulation of riches. "A display of wealth is an abomination to the Lord," he said when Ma suggested getting a store-bought coverlet for the girls' bed when she sold her egg surplus to Joe Beard in Monticello. "Riches corrupt," he said, and quoted from the Epistle of James: 'Your gold and silver is cankered, and the rust of them shall be a witness against you and shall eat your flesh as it were fire.' "

It was while they were harvesting corn in late August that John reminded Pa of his concern over provisions for Brother Isaac. "The church here at Clear Fork ought to give him something regular," he said. "Not paying a preacher in hard money is all right, but letting him go hungry is bad."

Pa agreed, and within the next week he had circulated a subscription form among the brethren, similar to one Brother Isaac had shown him at one time that some Baptist churches in the Elkhorn Association up north had drawn up for their preacher, John Shackleford:

	Salt	Corn	Wheat	Pork	Flower	Beaf	Tallow	Whiskey
George Smith		3		1				
Thomas Stockton	12½				100			5
Tom Ryder			2					
William Wood		1				50		
Henry Grigsby							2	
Alexander Hayes			1			10		4
Flea Thompson		4						

Brother Isaac's gratitude was pathetic when he was told of it, Pa said later. "He didn't admit it, but I do believe he's been going hungry when he couldn't set down with some of us. Us Baptists set store by the fancy saying, 'A free gospel for a free country,' but the Bible says a preacher is worthy of his hire, and a man's got to eat."

In September the hogs were rounded up and driven to the market at Burkesville, twenty miles to the northwest. Later in the month John and Jonathan drove a wagon of corn and hemp to the straggling settlement of Monticello, fourteen miles north and eastward, the seat of the new county of Wayne. Here traders were beginning to come every month to pick up what they could for shipment down the Cumberland to the fabled Mississippi River, where other traders would ship it to distant cities like St. Louis and New Orleans; or sometimes it went overland to Lexington, or to Frankfort, the state capital, or even to Cincinnati and Pittsburgh.

Driving away with their load, John felt with his moccasined feet under the wagon seat to be sure Jonathan had not forgotten their sang hoe. He drove slowly down the lane around the bend and pulled the horse to a stop in a thicket which lined both sides of the narrow trail, and whistled to the hounds yipping in the hills as though they had holed a fox. Jonathan grinned on the seat beside him, and they both jumped to the ground. Ma was resigned to not having the store-bought coverlet; maybe it was a sinful display. But she wanted some calico cloth bad, and even Pa would say the shifts she wanted to make out of it for the girls were not pure vanity. They raced through the thicket to the slope of Poplar Mountain and hastily dug in the rich mold for the five-leafed, red-berried ginseng root. They could barter it at Mr. Beard's store for the calico.

It was nearing noon when they got to Monticello. They completed their barter with Mr. Beard's clerk, Ben Gholson, and tucked the calico under the seat. Then they disposed of their hemp and corn, receiving hard United States coin, tying it in the deerskin bag Pa had made for the purpose, reserving for each of them a pointed silver four-bit piece to jangle in their pockets as Pa had told them to do. It would make them appreciate money, Pa said, to have a piece of their own. He encouraged them to raise garden stuff to sell, and gave them each in turn a yearling calf to raise and sell. It was not that he was against money; it was the love of money and the sinful pride of vanity that church people should be shed of.

They were almost to the hitching rail to climb back into their wagon, their two hounds, Obediah and Jezebel, at their heels, when Thomas Stockton rode up in a whirl of dust. It was a brassy hot day, and Stockton's horse was lathered, his stern face red and perspiring. But John sensed a friendliness about him he had not noticed before as the older man wheeled about to face them, pushing his wide-brimmed hat to the back of his head. The dogs barked furiously, darting about the feet of the strange horse.

"Those are sweet-singing bitches you boys have there," he said. "Nat tells me they're good coon dogs, and even helped tree a bear once. Want to sell them?"

John grinned. "Only Jezebel is a bitch, Mr. Stockton. Obediah, well, I think he wishes he was sometimes. But they're good hounds. And they're not for sale."

Thomas Stockton slipped from his saddle while the hounds subsided their noise to murmuring yips and began gently nuzzling each other. "I'm just back from a cattle-buying trip up north around Lexington," he said. He tethered his horse and then seated himself against the hitching rail and stretched his long legs in front of him. "And I saw something of the Lord's wonders." He looked at John. "It was something like what you must have seen at Muddy River, young man."

John's eyes puzzled. "You mean a revival meeting?"

Mr. Stockton nodded. "And I met a friend of yours."

"I don't know nobody up there," John said. "The biggest place I've ever been is Burkesville."

"Maybe it was the little Harpe," Jonathan said. "Maybe he's after you this time, John."

"You do know somebody up there," Mr. Stockton insisted. "He said to tell his young *Canaly*, John Smith of Stockton's Valley, that he expected to see him up that way some time."

"*Canaly?*" John echoed.

"He was a Presbyterian preacher, Barton Stone," Mr. Stockton said. "He met you at Muddy River; he had stopped there on the way to visit his intended wife, Eliza Campbell, at Greenville. They were married in July. I knew his father-in-law, Colonel William Campbell, when he was in the state senate at Frankfort. He died last year at Lexington. They are fine folks, the Campbells."

John's eyes kindled in recollection. "Of course I remember Barton Stone," he said. "I liked him, too; he's a good man."

"A very good man," replied Mr. Stockton, his face sobering. "He's being used of the Lord. He carried back to Bourbon County the fire that was kindled in the Logan County revivals, and it's changing the complexion of the whole northern part of the state." He fanned himself with his hat, his shoulder-length shock of white hair lifting slightly in the current of air.

"Did you hear Mr. Stone preach?" John asked. "I'd like to hear him some time; he seemed, well, kind of different from most preachers."

"Yes, I heard him," Mr. Stockton said. "I went over to Cane Ridge meetinghouse, where the revival was; it was the last night of the meeting, but I'd heard about it in Lexington, and I cut my business short and went." He gave a low whistle. "Greatest sight I ever saw; must have been over twenty thousand people there. Wagons everywhere, hundreds of them, people living in tents, sleeping on the ground, preaching going on all the time." He turned and looked at John. "Mr. Stone preached on God's redemptive love; I'll never forget it." Slowly he quoted: " 'For God sent not his Son into the world to condemn the world, but that the world through him might be saved.' "

"That sounds like he talked," John said.

"You say different preachers were shouting at the same time?" Jonathan queried. "How could that be?"

"There were dozens of preachers all over the place," Mr. Stockton said, his eyes burning with the intensity of his recollection. "The meeting started in Barton Stone's meetinghouse at Cane Ridge on a Friday night, but such was the power and presence of God, it kept on all that first night; the next day, Saturday, so many people had come they had to build a pulpit stand outdoors. Then the crowds kept increasing, and other preachers came, and they began preaching at just about every cleared space they could find. And from that time on, all through the next Wednesday night, preaching went on all the time with a dozen sermons going on at once in different places."

"Was there any Baptists?" Jonathan asked.

"A few," Stockton said. "We Baptists have got to wake up. There was one Baptist preacher I recall, name of Moses Bitt, and he shouted and stomped just like a regular Methodist. But people didn't pay no mind to what sect they were. There was Richard M'Nemar and Matthew Houston and David Purviance, and a Methodist named William Burke."

"Was they jerking and falling down and such?" John asked, his voice cautious.

"It was like Judgment Day," Stockton said slowly. "And we'd best be prepared for it. Yes, the people were crying and moaning and falling to the ground; there was even a little boy preaching on the shoulders of some old man, and a little girl, she looked like an angel, exhorting the people. It was a sight all right, with the lanterns strung on trees bobbing up and down, and pine torches flaring on posts everywhere."

"When I saw Mr. Stone at the Muddy River revival," John said thoughtfully, "he didn't seem to like all that carrying-on too well."

"I'm not sure he does yet," Stockton said. "Although he told me that religion had sunk so low among the people that nothing common could stir them up again. He's feeling that God is sending such uncommon agitations to pull the people away from the snares of the devil. His sermon was good, but I felt he was a little too easy on the sinners, although plenty of people fell before him, thick and fast. It was after his sermon that I spoke to him. When I told him I was from Stockton's Valley, he gave me the word for you. You must have made an impression on him." He eyed John with new respect.

John said nothing for a moment, his eyes on the ground. He raised them with an effort. "It's because I could say a few words of Cherokee. I wish I could have heard him preach." He hesitated, and then his voice rang out stubbornly. "But I still don't see how he could think such carrying-on was God's work. It's belittlin' of God just to think he'd do it."

"You're wrong, lad, you're wrong!" Thomas Stockton shook his head and eased himself from the hitching rail, tugging at the belt of his leather breeches, clapping his hat back on his head. "There's plenty of Bible authority for hell and damnation sermons. Hellfire and damnation are awaiting the sinner. That's real preaching, the kind of preaching we need here at Clear Fork. And I'm going to see we get some of it in this valley. We need a revival camp meeting, with people living on the grounds and preaching going on for days." He paused, and started to loosen his horse, and then stopped and flipped his long forefinger at John. "Who are we to question the works of the Almighty? If sin strikes men down in jerks and faints, who are we to stop them?"

"Brother Denton won't like a revival here," John said stubbornly. "He's a good Baptist, and he believes we're born either saved or damned, and no amount of revival preaching is going to change a goat into a sheep. That's what Pa thinks, too."

Thomas Stockton slapped his riding crop as though for emphasis against his leather breeches. "Well, we'll stir up the saints, and if we can't save the sinners, at least we'll make them sorry as hell they're going there. Tell your Pa that. No matter what Isaac Denton says, we're going to have a revival at Clear Fork. We're going to stir up the Elect and set fire to the sinners, or my name's not Thomas Stockton." He vaulted into his saddle with an ease which belied his sixty years, and cantered away.

"It takes more'n believing to be saved," John spoke low-voiced to Jonathan as they watched Stockton disappear around a bend of the town creek. "It takes more than repentance and baptism and good works. It takes more than prayer. God decided it all at the beginning of the world. That's what Brother Isaac and Pa and even Ma believe, and there ain't no truer Christians. That's what I believe, too." He paused, reflecting. "I reckon I do," he added almost to himself.

"I believe it," Jonathan said stoutly, "and there ain't nothing going to change me. I know I'm saved, but if you're not, John, I'll stick with you, even if you go to hell."

They were pulling the harness off the horse in the barn lot, telling Pa, honing a knife on the whetstone, about the trip when Joe and William rode up, riding double on Willy's horse, a bustling, important air about them. Ma waved her apron at them from the barn loft, where she was gathering eggs, when she heard the clatter, and eased herself down the barn ladder, the eggs in a hempen bag on her arm. The boys slid off the horse and Joe stood, a sudden hesitancy about him, as if waiting for William to speak.

"Tomorrow I'm riding over to Beaver Creek," William said, loosening the horse's cinch belt and pulling off the saddle. "Mr. Ryder told me about a man there who wants to sell forty acres of good farm land to get money for a trip back to Virginia, and I'm aiming to buy it. I've saved most of my part of the hog and cattle money," he said, looking at his father, "and I can pay the full cash price."

"What're you trying to tell us, son?" Pa had stopped the whetstone and stood, a puzzled, amused look on his face.

"There's a run-down, two-room poplar log house on the place by a spring," William went on, ignoring the question, "and a fodder-loft barn house. It's a good buy."

"What he's trying to say," Joe spoke up, "is that Brother Isaac is marrying Willy and me in a double wedding ceremony, me to Susie and Willy to Maggie. We've fixed up the marriage bonds today at the courthouse in Burkesville. Susie and me will live with Mr. Ryder for a while, until we find our own place, and Willy and Maggie will live in this new place he's getting. It'll be a big wedding, Mr. Ryder says, and all the county will be there for the shivaree!"

And it was a big wedding. On October 15, 1801, at the Ryder homestead on Pea Ridge, Brother Isaac Denton performed the long-drawn-out, high-sounding double ceremony in the presence of all the relatives of both families and more than a hundred friends and neighbors from as far away as Burkesville. Pa Smith mildly boasted, at the infare which followed the next day at the Smith cabin, that it was not only big but promising, creating two more good Smith families in the growing valley.

As though not to be outdone, or maybe, as Nat Stockton told Rebecca later, while under the influence of the stout usquebaugh ladled out at the shivaree by old man Ryder, James shipped as a poleman two days later on the river packet *Natchez Belle*, bound with a cargo of hemp and tobacco for the faraway river town of New Orleans.

"James is like my brother Reece," Ma said, her eyes moist, when John brought home the news as related to him by William Wood and Nat. "Reece was a good boy, the oldest and the steadiest of my brothers, and then all of a sudden, when he was about twenty-five, he up and flew the coop, and went out west to fight Indians with Dan'l Boone. And he never came back."

"James will be back," Pa said, comforting her. "He's just got the itching foot. He's got a good home to come back to, and your brother Reece didn't. With all the to-do about Willy and Joe getting hitched, I figure he felt out of it and just took off. He got caught up in a roaming spell. I've felt like that myself when I was a young'un."

"And you went to the war with General Washington, but you had reason. You was all alone, with your folks dead, and you living there on Colonel Buchanan's place in Virginia." She folded the mending in her lap and leaned back. "I reckon that's why I married you, you was so alone, and I could see you was fixing to take off again. And you did take off—to Tennessee, and then on here to Kentucky." She wagged her head at recollection of the long trek over the wilderness trail. "But you never got away from me."

Pa laughed and spat reflectively into the fire that burned in the coolness of the October evening, and wiped his mouth with the back of his hand. He winked solemnly at John, looking up from Pike's arithmetic at the big table where he had been ciphering. "A wife is what James needs; that'll keep him home. Every man needs a wife and a passel of young'uns and a piece of land to settle him down."

John flipped the pages of the book. Like Brother Isaac had said, Pa was getting old. He was thinner, and he tired quickly. He ate less and sat longer and longer before the hearth of a night, peering through his steel-rimmed spectacles at the big-lettered Bible he had brought as a young man from Virginia, until he would begin to nod and Ma would gently take the book from his hand.

But Pa was not joking about wanting his boys to marry and settle down. He was glad to have William and Joe settled, and he was hinting now, John knew, at him. He drew some whorls on the paper, and then crumbled it in a small ball. He liked girls, and he took pleasuring in games with them at cornhuskings and such and even barn frolics if there was a quick-snapping fiddler to string the tunes, although his feet were too big and his rawboned body too jerky and clumsy when he tried to whirl the girls around. Pa and Ma frowned on such didos as worldly and sinful for church folks, and maybe they were. Anyway, there was plenty of time to wallop a woman on the behind after the preacher said the binding words. But he wasn't hankering for that; he wanted more book learning.

Winter came on, and in December word reached the valley that the common-law wives of Big Micajah Harpe and Little Wiley Harpe were released by order of the Logan County Court without trial from the jailhouse at Russellville. The victims of the Harpe men did not want to relive their horrors by witnessing against them, and no contest was made to their claims of innocence by reason of coercion in the bloody swath cut by their men through the Kentucky Barrens. Besides, the judge said, there was no sense boarding such women at the expense of the people forever, especially since Little Wiley Harpe had met his just end and had been hanged in Mississippi and was as dead as his brother's leering skull still atop the swaying hickory sapling in Christian County. Except for a general sense of relief as at the fading of an evil dream, there was little mention of it, even by George and Beulah, now settled in their new house, and winter plowed on, and spring came again to the valley.

CHAPTER VI

IT was Moses Bitt, an itinerant Baptist preacher afflicted with a constant burning in his bowels to warn the people of the eternal fires awaiting stiff-necked sinners, who eventually brought the revival to the Clear Fork Baptist Church in Stockton's Valley. It was on the last Sunday in May, 1802, that he first preached.

Brother Bitt had been roaming the countryside, visiting among the brethren, bedding down mostly at Thomas Stockton's house. And although Brother Isaac Denton was due to preach on the last Sunday, Thomas Stockton let it be known that he had asked Brother Bitt to speak, and it was a blessing of the Lord that he did, he explained, as he introduced the new preacher at services to the waiting congregation, because Brother Isaac had been detained at the meeting of the Cumberland Baptist Association at Burkesville. "Brother Bitt is a harbinger of God in accordance with the true Baptist Confession of Faith," Stockton said by way of further introduction. "The harvest is plentiful, but the laborers are few."

John sat beside Pa in the men's section, and as he listened to the visiting preacher his rising suspicion became a certainty that Thomas Stockton, his countenance beaming and the rhythmic crunch of his jaws indicating approval, had planned it, as he had said he would do. He had brought the revival to the valley. The sermon was on Paul's warning to the Romans that the wages of sin are death, and within minutes Brother Bitt was parading before the pulpit stand, consigning the lost to an eternity of torment, his stinging words emphasized by his stomping feet, his damning accusations flowing in a torrent the little log-ribbed meetinghouse had never heard before. And when the Widow Simmons, whose boy had been drowned in Wolf River the week before without ever having had the revealing experience, began to moan aloud, others began to cry out, and the meeting ended with such shouts and groans that even the benediction could scarcely be heard above the din.

The people scattered about the churchyard in little knots and groups, bewildered, frightened; but Ma pleaded an aching in her bones and announced she was going home with her brood and wouldn't stay for the dinner-on-the-grounds and the afternoon preaching service. The hampers of food she had prepared were put back in the wagon to be spread instead in their own big yard, and there the family sat about the long trestle table under the great locust tree, eating in silence for the most part, each seeming to wait for the other to speak on the experience of the morning. Finally Pa pushed back his chair and pulled out his corncob pipe.

"Brother Isaac wouldn't of preached such a sermon," he said, as if they had been talking about it all the time. "But that don't mean we don't need that kind of preaching, even though I was considerable shook up by it myself." He got an ember from the smoldering yard pit where the hominy cakes had been baked, and put it to his pipe, sucking on the stem, blowing out a cloud of smoke before he spoke again. "Ever since the fall of Adam, we have all been born in sin, and it helps people to be reminded of it. We're all headed for hell unless we get under conviction."

"Did that preacher mean I'll go to hell if I don't say my prayers every night, Ma?" Jane asked, her round childish face clouded with worry.

"No!" Ma bit off the word sharply.

"Brother Bitt will be preaching every night this week, Tom Stockton tells me," Pa went on. "Your Ma and the girls don't have to go," he paused and looked askance at his wife, "being as how she says without saying so she'd druther not. But you boys should; you might have the revealing experience under preaching like that."

John sighed and ran his hands through his hair. "All right, Pa," he said. "I'll go. I'll do my best to get the revealing experience. Maybe I'll do like poor Widow Simmons and groan and carry on. How'd you like that?"

"The people were put in mind of their sins," Pa said. "It's enough to give them fits when they think of all the bad they've done. And it should—the convicted sinners acted like that in Bible days. Jesus rebuked and cast out devils from the people more than once. When Peter preached at Pentecost, three thousand sinners spoke in tongues, and no telling what else they did that might sound crazy to us. But they were saved; it was the revealing experience for them." He shook his head almost sadly. "We can't question the ways of the Lord; whatever works for good is from the Lord."

"There's no call for you to fault yourself, Ma," John said in quick defense of his mother, noticing her worried expression. "You've got a right to your druthers."

She sighed deeply. "I don't misdoubt anything the preacher said," she said. "Like your Pa says, whatever works for good is from the Lord. And if he can start people living better with such talk, I don't know as it would be becoming of me to be offish."

"He'll start a revival, all right," John said. "I can smell it coming. He'll gather in some Methodists and Presbyterians, too, and we'll all forget who's what and be just Christians."

Pa frowned. "That's bad talk, son," he said. "True, the disciples were called Christians at Antioch, but before that time the followers of Christ were called Baptists after John the Baptizer who baptized our Lord. If there are any true Christians other than our Regular Baptist people, it is not according to the word of God as revealed in the Scriptures."

Ma nodded in vigorous agreement. "The Baptist faith is the one true faith, no man can deny," she said emphatically, and then her eyes grew reflective, and she spoke more gently. "But let none of us doubt the power of the Lord." She stood up and motioned for the girls to clear the table. "And that's not just my Irish tongue a-talking. If Almighty God should choose to save them who worship him under other names, neither Pa nor me nor anybody else can question his will."

Brother Isaac Denton returned from the meeting of the Cumberland Baptist Association at Burkesville in time to attend only the last preaching service of the revival. John had worked late, rounding up the sheep, and the preaching had already started when he reached the church. The room was packed with sweltering humanity, people sitting on the window ledges and on campstools in the side aisles. He stood outside the door, peering in. Brother Isaac was in the front row, his hand cupped behind his ear, his round blue eyes wider than usual, intent on the speaker's face. The sermon rang with threats of hell, and John started to turn away when Brother Bitt suddenly began swinging his legs in what looked like a dance. He skipped and kicked and spun about on the narrow platform, and then leaped over its low railing and ran up and down among the people, jumping over benches and stools, at times singing, pushing a hesitating sinner to his knees, jerking erect a saved one, slain before the Lord. John watched, wide-eyed at first, and then turned away in disgust, sensing the old rebellion rise in him, a sickening in his stomach. He was glad Ma had not come.

To his surprise, he discovered the next day when he rode over to help Brother Isaac hoe his corn, that the old preacher seemed to mildly approve of the manifestations.

"I canna say na to it," Brother Isaac said, drawing a last long drink of buttermilk from the earthen jug John had brought as they finished a noon lunch under a clump of pines on the edge of the corn field. "I dinna say it would have been my way, but the Lord touched Brother Bitt to dance and sing while he was preaching. Many fell who otherwise might not have been put under conviction."

"Brother Bitt had a fit," John said bluntly. "A spasm. If I hadn't of knowed the reason, I would have tied him up. I'd a roped him like a bucking steer to keep him from hurting himself."

Brother Isaac shrugged, and handed the buttermilk jug to John. "I would have preferred one of the other exercises, like Tom Stockton said they did at Cane Ridge. Maybe the singing exercise." His frame shook with silent laughter. "If he'd a got me to singing, I would more than ever be convinced the Lord's hand was in it, for I canna carry a tune. Or maybe the laughing exercise, provided it was a holy laugh and not too loud; or the running exercise." He wagged his head of white hair. "I would have known for certain then, for I'm not as fleet of limb and sound of wind as I once was. The last choice to me would be the jerks and the barking exercise. But to Brother Bitt came the dancing exercise." His face broke into another broad grin. "Truly, it was only by the Lord's grace a man so heavy could be so nimble."

John took a long drink of the buttermilk, and smashed the corncob stopper tight in the jug with his fist. "He had a spasm!" he insisted grimly. He looked at the old preacher curiously. "You mean, Brother Isaac, you would have one of those exercises if the notion came on you?"

"I would do anything to make a sinner feel the presence of God," the preacher said quietly. He picked up his hoe and after a moment's pause, John swung his own hoe over his shoulder and fell into step and, wordless, they walked together across the stubby field.

As the summer advanced, the religious fervor in the valley seemed to mount. Camp meetings were held in every village and in many remote settlements, along riverbanks and on the ridges, in open clearings and in groves, and not even two traveling shows of performing bears detracted interest from them. Preachers swarmed the countryside, Presbyterians and Methodists and even a sprinkling of staid Episcopalians as well as Baptists, and people fell and writhed and came under conviction, and multiplied in numbers and in righteousness.

Several times a week, Pa loaded the members of the family in the wagon and drove to some meeting, and John went along, although he resisted being caught up in the frenzy and excitement they engendered. But Henry, together with little Jane and Fancy Mae, became so wrought up under the preaching of a Methodist brother from Russellville late in July they would have been sprinkled into the clutching Methodist body had it not been for prompt action by Ma, who saw to it they were lectured the next morning by their father on the faith and practices of the true communion of the Regular Baptists according to the doctrines of the Philadelphia Confession of Faith. Thereafter, they were never outside her sight or reach. Conviction of sin and the revealing experience were direct manifestations of the Lord, Ma said, but to join any church other than the Regular Baptist was a distortion of the teachings of the Scriptures and a mockery of the Lord's plan of salvation. After that scare they all seemed relieved when the cooling months of autumn brought molasses-making weather and hog-killing time, and fox hunting drew the men to the hills at night, and the meetings came to an end.

But despite his distrust of the revival, John began to sense a lessening of tension in the atmosphere of the community. People seemed to deal with one another in more kindly fashion; there was less faultfinding. It was as if they had discovered life was more than a grubbing existence. He even imagined that men stood straighter and walked taller, and a mood of contrition enveloped him. He had been too harsh in his condemnation, like Pa had said. As if to make up for it, he began reading the Bible intently. Night after night he pored over it, pondering its meaning, rereading it until he found he unconsciously had memorized whole chapters.

At the end of the year William increased his land holding on Beaver Creek by securing a grant of three hundred and eighty acres adjacent to his place. A good house was already on the place, built by early settlers and abandoned when they moved on; substantial enough with a little fixing and adequate as a permanent abode. The house was further east in Wayne County, all of ten miles from Stockton's Valley as the crow flies, and following the road it was twice that. Ma demurred at their moving so far away, but Maggie was pregnant with her first baby, and William wanted to get settled. There would be no need for another house-raising, he told Pa.

And 'twas just as well, Pa said; he wasn't up to another raising. His strength had ebbed as the cold of winter penetrated the valley. Ma thought he was pining for word of James. But no word came from him, and then a rumor was brought by Nat Stockton, who had talked with two river men in Burkesville, that James had shipped away to sea at New Orleans. Pa accepted the news without a word, and James was mentioned less and less until it seemed to John his parents numbered him among the dead, their only hope of again seeing him in the glorious resurrection.

It was late the following summer that, just at daybreak, the sickness came on Pa with a sudden retching of his stomach. It lasted all one night and the following day, and Ma gave him melted mutton tallow and tea from spikenard roots and made him chew sweet-gum bark. The retching passed, but a slow fever came, barely discernible in the mornings but increasing by evening, burning away his vigor with its slow, steady intensity. Ma added sulphur and molasses to his food, and the bitter ginseng tea prescribed by the Burkesville doctor who finally stopped by the house two weeks after John had ridden over to tell him of his father's condition. The man was also a blacksmith and a Methodist preacher, and his business would not allow him to come sooner, he explained. Pa got better, and was up and about the house for a month before he was taken again. This time there were pains in his stomach and a hacking cough, and he was glad to stay in bed, his form thin, his face haggard. Ma grew fearful it was the fatal milk sickness.

Winter would bring relief, the doctor had promised. But with the first cold snap he seemed to shrivel, and all the comforters and quilts Ma would pile on him brought no warmth to his body. The weeks stretched into months, and he lay as in a stupor, groaning occasionally, talking irrationally at times, lying quiet as death most of the long hours.

It was late in the afternoon in the middle of March that Ma stopped John as he was entering the house after watering and bedding down the stock.

"I think he's a-dying," she said simply. "He's quiet now, but he's had the trembles all day. He wants to see you."

John slipped into the back bedroom, which had been given over to Pa when he was first taken, and stared at the thin, white-whiskered, gaunt figure, the deep, billowing waves of the feather bed making him appear skeleton-small, almost shrunken, beneath the wool blanket. Pa opened his eyes and moved his hand in a feeble gesture, and John covered his father's hand with his own.

"Yes, Pa?"

"You're my oldest boy at home now," he said, his voice wheezy with effort, the words coming in little spurts and gusts of strength. "You be the head of the family; you're . . ." His voice trailed away, and his eyes closed. To John he seemed to shrink inwardly in a slow relaxation, as if the tired body lay unhinged.

"I'll look after things, Pa," he said. "Don't fret, Pa, you hear?" He leaned over and listened for a moment to the quiet breathing, and then tucked the thin hand under the covers and tiptoed from the room.

A week later, on March 20, 1804, George Smith of Virginia and the Free State of Franklin in Tennessee and of Stockton's Valley in Cumberland County, Kentucky, died so quietly with his wife and eight of his thirteen children about him that it was a good five minutes before they knew he was gone. And it was John Smith, his sixth son and the ninth of his children, who crossed his hands and closed the vacant eyes by placing silver dollars on the shrunken lids.

The death was the first break in the family, and although it was expected, John knew the high-backed hickory rocker before the hearth would never be filled. When Brother Isaac Denton preached the funeral sermon at the Clear Fork Church three days later, he said as much, and when a group of neighboring menfolks lowered the pine box into the grave in the burying plot beside the church, they voiced the same opinion. His like would not soon be seen.

Spring rushed on with its avalanche of farm duties, smothering the family's grief, and John found time only at fleeting intervals to reflect on the irony of serving as head of the family in Pa's place when he was not even a convicted sinner. Maybe he was being stubborn, resisting conviction. The thought troubled him increasingly.

"Stubbornness is wrong when it means sticking to something you know is bad," Ma told him, when he mentioned the problem to her one morning as she was sitting in the yard shelling a turn of corn into her apron for a late mess of hominy. "Stubbornness is proper when it means standing up for right against wrong. Your pa was stubborn like that. When he knew he was right, nothing could change him." She looked over at Jonathan mending a bridle under the locust tree, pulling tight the whang, looping and knotting it, and then at Henry, coming in from the orchard with a bucket of cherries, watching him as he set the bucket on the ground and sat down on the bench beside John, who was honing a knife.

"Do you boys recollect when your pa refused to buy a couple of slaves back when we lived in Holston Valley? John maybe remembers, but Jonathan and Henry was too little, I reckon." She smiled as if flooded with the warmth of the recollection, and then went on. "Your pa had a chance to buy a stout black and his woman dirt cheap from a man moving into free territory, and us needing help real bad. Philip and George was both off on some Indian hunt under Governor John Sevier, and you young'uns too little to do more than get in the way. Pa was working hisself to death, but he said no. He held it wrongdoing. That's one reason we pushed on her to Stockton's Valley; he'd heard there was no slaves here."

"Mr. Stockton's talking some of getting one," Jonathan said. "He's taking up more land and putting in hemp, and he told me at the revival meeting one night he'd be needing more farm help. He says blacks make good Baptists."

Ma snorted. "Tom Stockton will wind himself a bonny pirn," she said. "Slaves bring trouble; they make a man proud-turned, besides the wrong of it."

"Maybe I got the wrong kind of stubbornness," John said. "I argued with Pa once that there couldn't be enough iron nails made to build those fancy houses over in Burkesville. I'd seen him hammer and chisel out a few nails, and I figured it'd ruin all the chisels in the world to make enough to build a whole house. Wooden nails seemed better, anyway."

"That's your trouble, John," Ma said, shaking a finger at him. "You have to all the time see a thing before you'll believe it. The Bible says that you got to have faith."

"Faith is the substance of things hoped for, the evidence of things not seen," Jonathan sang out, airing his knowledge.

"Some day, please God, you'll know that, John," Ma said, "or you'll stick your horn in a bog."

John laughed. "That means I'll get myself in a fix, don't it?" he said. "Ma, you ought to quit mixing up your Scotch and your Irish and take to talking plain American."

"Them that will to Cupar maun to Cupar," she said, teasing. "That means a willful man must have his way, so I guess I'm stubborn, too. But I'm not mule-headed. Neither was your pa. He just wouldn't do what he figured was wrong. He didn't hold with church folks making worldly display or hankering after riches, and many's the time I've seen him lay a silver dollar on a block and cut it up into four-bit pieces rather than let the devil tempt him to spend it all. And when grain was scarce back in Holston Valley, and the rest of the neighbors was getting a dollar a bushel and more for their corn, Pa refused to take more than the old price of two and sixpence a bushel. He didn't hold it was Christian to take advantage because folks was hungry."

Long after sleep had descended on the house that night, John tossed on his mattress of shuck ticks, troubled in spirit, uncertain in mind. What if he never had the revealing experience? He thought of the Harpe brothers; they could claim ignorance of right-doing but he had been instructed in every duty and in every Baptist doctrine. He would be reckoned, then, more dead in sin even than such notorious bad men. He threw back the quilt and put his feet on the floor.

The house was quiet and only a floorboard by his door squeaked as he made his way down the puncheon ladder steps. It was warm, and the night air felt good as he pushed open the kitchen door and peered out. He took a few deep breaths and considered walking around the yard, but the hounds would probably start yipping, so instead he turned back into the room and took an ember and lighted the candle on the table by the rocker Ma kept there. He sank down in the chair and picked up the copy of the *Philadelphia Confession of Faith* and stared at it. Ma must have been reading it; she and Pa had ruled their lives by that book, and the Bible. Without plan he began to turn the pages.

> Man, having brought himself under the curse of the law by his fall, it pleased the Lord to make a covenant of grace, wherein he freely offered the sinners life and salvation by Jesus Christ, requiring of them faith in him, that they might be saved; and promising to give unto all those that are ordained unto eternal life, his Holy Spirit, to make them willing and able to believe.

He read the words again. They were in Chapter Seven, headed, "Of God's Covenant." Their meaning was unmistakable; unless a man was ordained by God himself, he could not receive the Holy Spirit, and unless he received the Holy Spirit, he could be neither willing nor able to believe. John was then as hopelessly damned as the Harpe men. But what if the Harpe men had been predestined as Elect from the beginning of time? Would they be saved in spite of their wrongdoing? It didn't make sense, even if the smartest men since the Apostles had written it. He turned the pages almost in anger.

> Although God created man upright and perfect and gave him a righteous law, which had been unto life had he kept it, and threatened death upon the breach thereof; yet he did not long abide in this honour. Satan, using the subtlety of the serpent to seduce Eve, then by her seducing Adam who, without any compulsion, did willfully transgress the law of their creation and the command given to them in eating the forbidden fruit which God was pleased, according to his wise and holy counsel, to permit, having purposed to order it to his own glory.

A slow-rising gorge of revolt, almost of incredulity, arose in him. There was no understanding the ways of the Lord, and only fools would try. Brother Isaac had always said as much; God's ways were past understanding, and a sinful man could only worship and hope and pray and do the best he could. He read on:

Our first parents by this sin, fell from their original righteousness and we in them; all becoming dead in sin and wholly defiled....

They being the root and, by God's appointment, standing in the room and stead of all mankind, the guilt of the sin was imputed, and corrupted nature was conveyed, to all their posterity, and all other miseries, spiritual, temporal and eternal, unless the Lord Jesus set them free.

He read the last line again. "Unless the Lord Jesus set them free." Here was hope! He stared at the words as though he had seen them for the first time, and then held the book closer to the candle and read on:

Although the price of redemption was not actually paid by Christ until after his incarnation, yet the virtue, efficacy and benefit thereof was communicated to the Elect in all ages successively from the beginning of the world ... and all of free and absolute grace, without any condition in them to procure it....

These angels and men thus predestinated and foreordained, are particularly and unchangeably designed; and their number so certain, and definite, that it cannot be either increased or diminished.

He closed the book and blew out the candle and leaned back his head against the high back of the chair. That was it; he could only wait for the divine communication; there was nothing he could do.

He must have slept, for when he jerked himself erect, Ma was standing beside him, her long white nightgown and her tasseled nightcap making her seem a ghost, her worn hand shielding the lighted candle she held aloft. She was peering at him anxiously.

"You sick or something, John?" she said. "I thought I heard moans."

She reached out to feel his forehead, but he pushed her hand away. His body was cramped and cold, and he rubbed his face with his hands, kneading himself into reality.

"I'm the chief of sinners, Ma," he said.

"You're bilious. Get to bed; it'll soon be milking time."

He got to his feet and impulsively, for a rare moment feeling like a child, he gave her a quick hug, and groped his way to the loft room.

Two days later John drove over to Brother Isaac's place to deliver some of the corn Pa had subscribed for the preacher. Brother Isaac had just come into his one-room cabin from milking and, after the corn was unloaded, John sat with him, enjoying a noggin of the warm milk.

"I fell to reading the *Philadelphia Confession* the other night," John said finally, "and I'm ready to give up. Off and on for three years now it's been death in the pot for me. I'm going to quit trying to find God."

"You'll never quit," the old preacher said, his eyes smiling. "You'll be seeking God all your life. But you'll never find him; you have to let him find you."

"He don't seem of a mind to seek me out," John said. "I'm the chief of sinners, Brother Isaac, worse even than the Harpes. I'm . . ."

"You say that but you don't really believe it," Brother Isaac interrupted. "Even while you tell God himself in so many words you're a great sinner, you don't believe it. You're not rightly convinced that you're a sinner, even though you know the church teaches that you were born in sin, totally depraved, and are hopelessly lost unless the Lord has elected you to be saved. Your mind is committed, but your heart isn't. That's your trouble, John."

John stared at him thoughtfully, considering his words. "I guess that's the truth," he said after a moment. "I don't rightly believe it. I got a feeling deep down inside me that there's something to be said for me; there's always something to be said for the other side."

"You're lukewarm, John," Brother Isaac said. "The Lord had a word for lukewarm folks. He sent through John a message to the church at Laodicea. 'I know thy works, saith the Lord, that thou art neither hot nor cold. I would thou wert hot or cold. Because thou art lukewarm, and neither hot nor cold, I will spue thee out of my mouth.' " He paused and looked at John. "I figure the Lord maybe loves a cheerful sinner better than he does a lukewarm Christian."

John frowned and got up and placed his noggin on the hearth. "Looking at both sides doesn't mean a man's lukewarm; maybe he's just fair-minded. I still think there's two sides to everything," he said, his voice stubborn. "Maybe there's truth even on the wrong side; maybe there's no final truth at all!"

"That's heresy!" Brother Isaac spoke sharply. "You sound like you're tainted with the Separate Baptist doctrine. Don't talk so!"

John grinned. The term, Separate Baptist, had floated outside the rim of his consciousness since he was a child. The words were almost bad words; they represented something not quite respectable, but he had never bothered to wonder why. He started to ask the old preacher about them, but it was late and he should be on his way.

"Reckon that makes me worse even than the chief of sinners," he grinned, an unexpected mischief in his face. "I'm getting on home before the devil gets me."

But he spoke with more cheerfulness than he felt.

For days a depression took hold of him he could not shake off. He went about his work as under the threat of doom. High on the ridges the blue huckleberries ripened, and he slipped off to pick them, stooping and bending until his body ached, but the solitude did little to help. He became short-tempered, and Jonathan told him bluntly he seemed afraid to smile. Even Jane and Fancy Mae began avoiding him, or spoke in whispers when he was about. And although in self-reproach he tried to assume the appearance of gaiety, he knew he deceived no one.

Ma alone seemed unperturbed. Sometimes he caught her looking at him with unmasked eyes, puzzled, but she said nothing. And when he reported for County Muster Roll a month later at Burkesville, and Nat Stockton and Quillen Thompson asked him to sing at the jamboree which would follow the parade, his reply made them stare at him as though they were looking at a specter they had never before seen and had no wish to see again, and then walk away without a word.

"No, boys," he said. "I have played the fool long enough. Unless I find my soul, I'll never sing again!"

CHAPTER VII

LATE in October Brother Isaac Denton rode up to the Smith cabin and slid from his horse. It was a warm day, and he wiped his forehead with the sleeve of his worn black alpaca coat, his face worried and drawn.

"I've been over to Stubbins Creek," he said, sinking heavily onto the bench under the locust, "and all hell has broke loose."

John looked up from the pail by the back door where he was washing his face. It was noon, and Ma had called dinner and was heaping golden ears of sweet corn and ham slices on the big pewter plates, watching with half an eye as Fancy Mae and Jane came out from the kitchen, swinging between them the iron pot of cowpeas, tilting it to run off the fat-back liquor before setting it in the center of the trestle table.

"Set a while and eat, Brother Isaac," Ma said, motioning them all to seats about the table. Jonathan and Henry had come in from stacking creek-bottom corn and were wrestling down near the fence. "Dinner's on, boys," she called, and as they grouped about, she glanced at the preacher. "You'll give us the blessing," she said, her voice carrying a tone that bent all heads.

At the conclusion of the familiar grace, all eyes fastened in frank curiosity on Brother Isaac.

"What happened?" John said.

"It all started when a young whippersnapper of a Methodist preacher came over to preach a funeral sermon for a back-sliding Methodist. The Methodists got no meetinghouse there, so they used ours." He ate vigorously of his food for a moment, and John felt a hardening in his jaws.

"Wasn't that all right?" he asked, his voice querulous. "What've we got a meetinghouse for? When Baptists ain't needing it, why can't the Methodists use it for their needs?"

"That would have been right and proper," Brother Isaac went on, "but it was like a mule getting his nose in the feed bag. The young fellow stayed on, and used the meetinghouse for preaching services day and night for a week. He most converted all our Baptists to the Methodist way of thinking."

Ma laid down her fork and spoon, indignation flooding her face. "That's sinful!"

Brother Isaac leaned forward. "He not only did that, but last week, after I got Brother Tom Mason and another elder from Burkesville to come over and help me gather the people back into the true fold, the young fellow came to our meeting and near broke it up."

Ma shook her head, incredulous; the children looked their consternation, and even John felt a rising resentment. An attack on the Baptist church was like an attack on Brother Isaac, or Ma herself.

"The fellow got up in meeting and reported he'd had a revealing experience," Brother Isaac went on, talking between bites, "and pretended he wanted to join the church. I wasn't minded to doubt him until he got contrary when we fixed to baptize him; that's when we knew for certain he was out to raise a ruckus and take advantage of the crowd to air his views. So we didn't pass him the Holy Communion after our baptizing service, and he went out and got on a log and started a preaching service of his own, lambasting us for excluding him from the Lord's Table."

"How come he was a preacher if he hadn't been baptized?" Jonathan asked.

"He was a Methodist," Brother Isaac explained patiently. "He claimed he'd a-been baptized by that sprinkling they do. That's no baptism; read your Bible, Jonathan, you should know that. Paul made it clear: 'We are buried with Christ by baptism into death that, like as Christ was raised up from the dead by the glory of the Father, so we also should walk with Christ in newness of life.' " He pushed his plate aside and stood up, leaning on the table, speaking earnestly. "Baptism is to picture the death and burial of the Savior by going down into the water, and the resurrection by coming up out of it. Even the Methodists know that, but they're just lazy and take to sprinkling because it's more convenient. But unless a man's put under the water, he's not been rightly baptized, and if he's not baptized he's got no call to take a seat at the Lord's Table."

"That man blasphemed God," Ma said solemnly. "We should name him in our prayers for God's mercy. Who was he?"

"Name is Peter Cartwright," Brother Isaac mumbled indistinctly, wiping his mouth with his sleeve. "From over by Ebenezer. The Lord save him!"

John's eyes widened. He was on the point of helping himself to another slice of ham, and he held the long iron spearing fork in midair for a moment. "Peter Cartwright?" he repeated.

Brother Isaac nodded. "Could be the same fast-talking young fellow you run across at the Muddy River revival; some day he might be a power in the land though I misdoubt it would be to any good. He's a bold one, coming over here to our valley, setting up Methodist churches right and left. He's that perky it wouldn't startle me would he turn up at our experience meeting at the Clear Fork Church this Saturday night."

"We're having an experience meeting?" John asked.

"We're having one," Brother Isaac said firmly. "It's needful in times like these with the Methodists making raids on us as well as the devil." He looked at John. "You ready to give one, John?"

John hesitated, feeling his mother's eyes on him. "I'm not sure," he said. "The *Confession of Faith* says all sinners got to go before the congregation for a quizzing about their experience. It scares me."

Brother Isaac smiled, his eyes warm with understanding. "I'd be easy on you, boy. But your conduct's good, and your hold on the doctrine is sound. The Lord's called you."

"I haven't heard any call," John protested.

"Maybe you been listening with a tin ear," Jonathan chided.

"Except in your heart," Brother Isaac said, "you may never hear. The *Confession of Faith* tells us that man is wholly passive and God's call is not from any power in his creature but only by God's grace." He turned to Ma. "Do you recollect when old Jim Shanahan related his hope of salvation before the church couple of years ago?"

Ma laughed. "That I do. One eye wept while the other stood dry as tinder. He stopped right in the middle of his telling and said that was a sign he was a hypocrite. Folks thought he was plumb fevered."

"And he was," Brother Isaac said. "He's still outside the fold." His face sobered. "A man can expect too much of God, John, in the way of a sign. No two revealing experiences are alike. Just you come to the meeting and let the Lord lead you."

The weather turned cold, and by Saturday a light frost was predicted. John reached the meetinghouse late to find the seats filled and the double plank doors closed against the chill air, the mud and stone chimney emptying itself in spirals of black smoke from the dampened wood in the wide hearth beside the pulpit stand. Ma had decided to stay home, and he had not urged the others to come. He would rather be alone, deciding in the solitude of his own soul what he should do, as the Lord moved him.

He tethered Zebulon at the hitching rail and joined a few latecomers outside the door, peering in through a crevice in the log wall. The fire in the damp wood was struggling into flame; soon it would burn with a rich, belching heat, and the people would squirm and flush in the warmth, and the door would be opened for the cooling air. He had been to experience meetings before, listening sometimes in awe and wonder at the miraculous tales, more recently in derision and downright disbelief. But tonight was different. The news about Peter Cartwright goaded him. If that round-faced bumpkin of a boy he had seen converted at Muddy River could become a Methodist preacher, cavorting in Baptist strongholds and upsetting true believers, maybe the Lord needed what help John Smith could give him. At least, John felt, he could quit his stubbornness and offer himself, and see what the elders said as the Lord gave them utterance when he placed his case for salvation before them.

He peered more closely through the crack. Someone had opened the door slightly, and he could hear old man Jenk Hawkins, his white chin whiskers bobbing up and down as he stuttered through the telling of an experience he hoped the saints of the church would find linked him to the Elect.

"I saw the devil," the old man said. "I saw the devil as plain as I see Brother Denton there. I wasn't drunk neither, though I do take my dram every night like a man oughter. I had been asleep in my bed when something woke me. It wasn't daybreak, and I stepped out my cabin on private business, just a week ago. And there I saw the devil!"

"How did the devil look, brother?" The question came from Thomas Stockton, sitting at the side out of John's range of vision. "Did he have horns and a tail?"

The old man swallowed as though bracing himself, and then spoke huskily. "He was about the size of a yearling, a white yearling calf. He was a yearling. He was standing on a little slope just back of my barn, looking at me with big round yellow eyes like fireballs. And he didn't open his mouth or move a hair. He just looked."

A woman near the hearth began to cough, and a scattered, spasmodic scraping of heavy boots on the puncheon floor punctuated hoarse masculine throat clearings, as though the elders were readying themselves for more questions. But old Mr. Hawkins went on, a sudden desperate aloneness in his voice, a clinging to hope.

"Brethren, I declare 'fore God I was that set back, I couldn't even pray. I was struck dumb. I went back into the house, quivering and shaking. And when I came out again about sunup, I went to the place where I seen the yearling. But there was no yearling there. There never had been a yearling there. I knew then the Lord had sent me a vision; I knew it was the devil I'd been beholding, and that the Lord had saved me out of his evil hands. God help me!"

The old man turned to take his seat, and John drew back, suddenly conscious he was cramped and chilled, a revulsion and a pity in him. He brushed against a man standing beside him, and in the half-darkness looked into a round face, the mouth set in a wide grin, the eyes friendly and amused. For a moment they stared at each other in growing recognition.

"I know you," the man said, a pleased surprise in his deep voice. His black eyes pierced John's tentative smile, and he pushed at his tousled black hair straggling from under a woolen cap flattened against his ears. "We've met before somewhere."

John straightened, sterning himself against the contagious friendliness of the man. He did not offer to shake hands. "Yes," he said shortly. "At Muddy River, three years ago. You got converted there. But I would hardly a-knowed you if I hadn't been halfway expecting you to pop up here. You're Peter Cartwright."

"That's right," Peter said, "I remember now. You ate with us that night. You're John Smith, Raccoon John, my pa called you; and you're a Baptist, and you thought you were bound for hell."

"It was because I couldn't see visions like you did; I thought then I had to. I saw you that night acting like you was seeing visions."

"I didn't see the devil as a white yearling calf," Peter said pointedly. "But I did get converted. I joined the Methodist Church at Ebenezer that June, and I started preaching some a year later on the Red River Circuit in Logan County. But I got my own circuit now. I go all around; I even been preaching some here in this valley."

"So I been hearing," John said. He pushed his raccoon cap further down on his head and thrust his hands inside his deerskin jacket.

"You come to this valley to save souls from hell or from the Baptists?"

Peter shrugged. "I don't mind converting Baptists whenever I run across some needing converting," he said frankly. "I've been on the Waynesville Circuit, and that covers this part of Kentucky as well as dipping down into Tennessee and up into Ohio and Indiana some. I go anywhere in my circuit where I feel the need."

"Well, you ain't needed here," John said, and instantly regretted the sharpness of his words. "I mean I don't like what I heard you did," he went on, his voice more kindly, "pretending you wanted to join the Baptists at Stubbins Creek without being rightly baptized, and by trying to take the Lord's Supper when you knowed you didn't have a right to it."

He turned and started toward the edge of the churchyard where the wagons were drawn up and the horses could be heard stomping in the frosty air, tethered to the rail. Peter fell into step beside him.

"You were in a Baptist meetinghouse," John turned to him angrily. "If you wanted to spout your Methodist doctrine, you ought to have called your own meeting somewhere else."

"That's just what I did," Peter said. "I preached on an old mossy log so slippery I most slid off and broke my neck. I knew the Baptist preachers were upset, but I was upset myself, coming back there after my week of preaching and finding my converts about to slip into error again. I had to act quick to save them."

"You didn't get them all back the way I heard it," John said.

"I saved some; they're Methodists again, including them I sprinkled into the church the first time."

"You call that saving them?" John said. "Sprinkling ain't baptizing, and you know it. And only a truly baptized person has got a right to sit at the Lord's Table. That's what the Bible teaches, and that's what us Baptists believe. We got a right to worship God in our own way without folks like you trying to break up our meetings. You was just lucky I wasn't at Stubbins Creek!"

"It's the duty of us preachers to point out error, and that's what I was doing." Peter's voice was quiet but firm. "And I'd do it again. I don't believe in your Baptist doctrine that God limited salvation to a few Elect. All men can be saved if they'll just follow Jesus Christ. When those Baptist preachers denied me the right to take Holy Communion like I was a heathen sinner, they went too far."

"It was because you weren't rightly baptized," John said.

"That's what you think, but I think different. The Scriptures say that baptism is not just the putting away of the filth of the flesh, but the answer of a good conscience. And a little sprinkling from a water noggin is just as good as dunking a man in the River Jordan. Water never saved anybody!"

John snorted. "Well, water may not do the saving, but one of these days some thirsty galoot is going to drink your Jordan dry before you can get him sprinkled." He kicked at a clod of earth. "And nobody claims water can save a man. Baptism," he went on thoughtfully, "has nothing to do with salvation except to proclaim it as a fact after the chosen one has his revealing experience from God that he is saved. It's a symbol, sort of, that a man is born again, just like Jesus died and was buried and was resurrected, and no amount of sprinkling, or pouring, from a cup or a gourd or a noggin or a barrel or anything else can do it. It's like trying to bury a man by throwing a few clods of dirt on his coffin. It don't reason out."

"Lots of things don't reason out," Peter said. "So I quit trying. Pa says I'm wrong. You recall Pa?"

John grinned. "That I do; I liked him."

"He's still reading books by Tom Paine and trying to reason everything out like that heretic says should be done. The folks live in Lewiston County now, down towards the mouth of the Cumberland River. They'd be proud to see you, even if you are a Baptist. Ma's a strict Methodist, but Pa thinks Baptists are good people, too."

"I got nothing much against Methodists," John admitted, "except some of them are uppity. Fact is, I sometimes get a wonder on me that all the churches, Methodists and Baptists and Presbyterians and all the others, ought to get together and quit their fighting each other. They sermonized together at the revivals; what's to hinder them from doing it all the time?"

"You're a heretic, saying that"—Peter laughed—"most as bad as Tom Paine." The sound of singing came from the meetinghouse, and Peter waved toward it. "But at least you're not seeing the devil in a white yearling calf. The meeting must be about over. I'm riding on. Tell Brother Denton if he felt bad about me doing what I did, I apologize."

"You coming back this way soon?" John asked, almost sorry now to see him go.

Peter shook his head. "Elder William Burke from Green County is coming here. The annual conference at Mount Gerisim is assigning me to the Salt River and Shelbyville Circuits come next year. I'm an exhorter, not a deacon or elder yet. I'll be traveling south from the fork of Green River and north to the Ohio River, and even cross into the Illinois Grant before I cover my rounds."

John saw him to his horse and watched him ride away, a mixture of pride and chagrin in him. Peter Cartwright was still the boy he had known at Muddy River, and yet he had changed. They had stumbled together across the camp meeting grounds, groping for what neither of them could comprehend, and Peter had found it. John turned back toward the meetinghouse. The singing had stopped, but as he drew closer he could hear a low-pitched cracking voice droning on and on. He had no stomach to listen to another tale about a white yearling calf. He stood, undecided for a moment, and then turned back to the hitching rail and got on Zebulon and rode slowly home.

Ma had left the bear-oil lamp lighted on the kitchen table; the family was all asleep. He blew out the lamp and started for the loft steps. But he was not sleepy. The window shutter creaked on its leather hinges, and he stared in sudden alarm at his mother's door. She called out faintly in her sleep, and then he heard her deep, regular breathing. He went to the window to fasten it more securely and looked out, and then on impulse threw his legs over the ledge and jumped to the ground.

Even the drowsing night noises seemed suddenly hushed; the late moon wrapped the world with a warming beauty. He could smell the tantalizing, musky odor of the spicewood thicket a hundred yards away. It was a heavy thicket, the spicewood deep like a latticed, tangled veil, matted with vines of honeysuckle and wild grape. He was drawn to its fragrance as if by a magnet. Once, when he was just beginning to be a man, he had stood for an hour in the rain in the thicket, experiencing a curious oneness and an aloneness with the earth and the dark night.

He pushed into a cleared space Pa had made in the center of the growth and sat down on a puncheon bench. The girls had got George to build the bench years before and put it here where they could do some sparking, but Pa had disapproved and for a while it had been moved into the clearing by the house. But Willy and Joe had probably moved it back, and now John ran his hand over the rough bark of the hickory limbs that served as arms, the warmth of the family's closeness filling him.

For a long time he sat, a dreaminess upon him, oblivious of the quick, tight stillness that his presence had caused, until he heard the slow twittering, slithering sounds which told him the night creatures had accepted him. The moon edged from behind a slow, careening cloud, and he watched it disappear behind another. He could see his breath in the frosty air. Slowly, the faintly pulsating stirrings of the covert crept into him, and in his mind began a rhythmic chanting of a passage Saint John had written in Revelations:

> I know thy works; behold, I have set before thee an open door, and no man can shut it; for thou hath a little strength and hast kept my word, and hast not denied my name.

He leaned forward, his elbows on his knees, and buried his face in his hands. Ma said he had been named for John, the beloved Apostle, and the thought flashed through his mind that the Lord could have been speaking to them both: "Behold, I have set before thee, John, an open door."

A light breeze stirred the thick matted growth about him, sounding almost like Ma's rustling skirts. Ma was not bothered much by doubts; she knew she was saved. "I'm one of the Elect," she had told him only the other day, "and so was Pa. And I'm not fretting about you, John. Them that really want to be saved, and prove it like you are a-doing by your Christian living, will find their names on the glory roll." And then she had quoted her favorite passage, written by the Apostle John:

> For God so loved the world that he gave his only begotten son, that whosoever believeth in him should not perish but have everlasting life.

"You see," she had paused at this point to explain, "Jesus didn't die on the cross to send the good people to hell. He died to save the people who believed on him. 'For God sent not his son into the world to condemn the world, but that the world through him might be saved.' And that's a God's truth!"

John had paid little attention to her at the time, but now his mind held like a vise to the words. God had sent his Son to save all who believed on him. All sinners. That included John. He raised his head; feeling a queer lightness, a sudden lifting of his spirits. The words of the familiar hymn sung often at the Clear Fork Church came to him:

So great, so vast a sacrifice,
May well, my hope revive;
If God's own son thus bleeds and dies
The sinner sure may live.

He stood up, shaking his feet to rid them of the chill and dampness of the night, wondering at his blindness. God was not only an omnipotent being of awful justice; he was a being of infinite wisdom and love and mercy.

The next day Ma nodded her head when he told her of the hour in the spicewood thicket. "The pookas have been bedeviling you overmuch, John. Let the good fairies come into your life again. Tell your experience before the saints, and be done with it. You've suffered enough with dark thoughts."

"You are converted," George told him as Beulah nodded gravely in assent. "You had the revealing experience right there at Muddy River, only you wouldn't admit it. We knew that when you came after us at Pilot Rock. You was always a contrary-minded fellow, John. You need a good dunking in the creek, or a paddling."

George moved as though to wrestle his brother when Beulah spoke, her voice solemn in protest. "And to think you compared yourself to the Harpes! That was the sin, John. You've been too solemn; go before the church and tell them all you've been through. And then start your singing and your joking again."

"You're young enough to wait a while," Philip said, shaking his head. Philip was sixteen years older, and acted it, John thought, listening politely. "You should wait a while. I waited until I knew for a certain I'd had the experience."

"What was it?" John asked.

Philip pulled at the stubble of a beard on his chin he had been growing since serving as an elder in the Concord Baptist Church up on Sinking Creek. "I heard a voice calling me in the dead of night. I was wide-awake, because I'd been eating green apples and had the stomach-ache. I thought Pa was calling at first, but it wasn't Pa at all. It wasn't anybody. And then I knew it was really the Lord calling. It was like the call to Samuel."

Jonathan was inclined to side with Philip, John learned, when he finally asked his younger brother his opinion. "No," he said solemnly, "you ain't had it yet. When you do, you won't go about asking folks; you'll know. I've had it twice, and it's always the same. I dream I'm about to be dropped into hell, and I can near feel the flames, they're that close; then I hear a voice, and I wake up. There's always a whiteness before my eyes, like an angel. Some day I'll tell that experience before the church and get myself baptized. But there's no hurry for me like maybe there is for you, John, because I'm Elect and I know it."

But it was William who gave John the most hope. Willy had been baptized for half his life now, since he was fifteen, and John knew Pa had considered him the most practical Christian of all of them. He just took the Lord for granted and didn't fret.

"You're converted, John," William said when John rode over to Wayne County early in December to talk to him. "There's no doubt about it. Go before the church right away and tell about it." He was pouring water on the grindstone by the shed, turning it slowly, holding his ax against it. "Quit argying with the Lord. That's what you been doing for months. You're as stubborn as all hell, John. You're hard-headed. Maybe you think the Lord ought to send you an angel on a big white horse blowing a trumpet, and all? But you ain't that important. You got to be humble and have faith. Faith that has to have things proven ain't faith at all."

John grinned, and reached down and patted the deerskin cap on the baby, Jacob, trying already at ten months to stand alone in the heavy moccasins and leather shift Maggie had made for him to wear outdoors while Willy worked.

"You ought to get married, John," Willy said, observing him. "You need to get settled. You been studying too much and getting yourself addle-brained. That old Indian hunting ground over here in Horse Hollow along the Little South Fork is being opened up for settlers. I can help you get a headright on some good land there. I'll help you open it up and get you settled." He paused at John's doubtful shake of the head, and then went on. "Jonathan is old enough now to look after things at the home place, especially with the rest of us close by to help out. I figure Ma'd be proud if you'd get yourself a little farm of your own and settle down with some nice girl for a wife. She's bound to be fretting about you, what with four young'uns still at home, and all."

John pursed his lips, considering. He had been thinking much the same things. Willy was level-headed, and Pa had always listened to his advice. But he shook his head. "No," he said, "when Pa died, he said—"

"Shucks," William interrupted. "I thought you'd be saying that. Pa didn't mean for you to stay there forever like a knot on a log. You know that. Pa wouldn't want to tie you down like that." He laid down the ax and came over and slapped John on the back. "Think about it, John. That land's open for settlers, and it'll be took up soon. I'd like to see you get a parcel of it."

Three weeks later, on Saturday afternoon, December 26, 1804, John presented himself before the regular monthly business session of the Clear Fork Baptist Church and, without sparing himself, told of his struggles and his doubts and his hopes and his fears and his prayers. And with Brother Isaac Denton as moderator, the congregation voted unanimously that in the opinion of the saints he had experienced the revealing grace of the Lord and was deemed worthy of salvation.

The following day, Sunday, in the bright clear cold of early morning, ice was broken in Clear Fork Creek, and together with old Jenk Hawkins, who had seen the white yearling calf, and two weeping women, he was immersed by Brother Denton in the name of the Father and of the Son and of the Holy Ghost.

CHAPTER VIII

WINTER descended on the valley with cold fury. Snow fell for two weeks in January, and John was kept busy clearing a path to the barn, feeding and watering the stock, helping Jonathan keep wood chopped for the fires. In February there were fences to mend, broken under the weight of ice, and then the air warmed and a steady rain fell for days, swelling the creek to a roaring river, tearing out the footbridge behind the spicewood thicket.

It was March before John had a chance to ease up on his labors. The ground was too water-logged for the spring plowing, and he took advantage of the lull to ride over to Wayne County. He found William had already bespoken for two hundred acres of hillside land for him in Horse Hollow, on a ridge sloping to Little South Fork.

"I just took the bull by the horns," William explained the next morning as they sat about the table after breakfast in the kitchen in William's cabin. "Billy Barnes had put in a claim for a leasehold on the place, but he's anxious to get going, and I feared somebody else would snap it up." He puffed on his corncob pipe in contented wonder. "Ma 'lowed to me right after you was converted she wanted you to get out on your own. A man ain't been tested rightly until he wrestles with his own soil."

"That's right poor land, though," Maggie said thoughtfully from a corner in the kitchen where she had begun churning, plunging the dasher up and down, slowing the motion now and then to feel the cream thickening into butter. She was midway in her second pregnancy, and her body was swollen and awkward, but she kept one foot extended, guarding the toddling Jacob from reaching beyond the confines of his railed-in playpallet. "I went over it with Willy one day; it looked like sheep-skull rock to me, and what soil there was looked thin and full of bull nettles high up there on that ridge. I reckon that's why Mr. Barnes is willing to sell his claim."

"He's nursing the jug," William said. "That's why he's getting out of these hills." He nudged a hot coal into the bowl of his pipe and puffed deeply. "It's too lonesome, too, he says; there ain't enough folks around."

"There's plenty for me!" Maggie said firmly. "That's why I like it here in Wayne. Over near your Ma's place, and over at Pa's, too, on Pea Ridge, it's getting too crowded. You don't have to even blow your horn there to be heard; you can just holler!"

The place was six miles from William's land, and by nightfall the brothers had completed a survey of it. It was hilly and wooded, as Maggie had said, but a two-acre clearing had been made near a swift-flowing creek, and a flimsy one-room cabin erected, and even if the soil was thin, the leasehold was worth possessing. John's interest increased the more he explored the place.

"You can live with me and Maggie while you're clearing more land," William told him. "You'd be a big help to me. Maggie's expecting in about four months, and the last few weeks she won't be much account in the fields."

John stayed with William for a week, talking over plans, and on the second day of April, 1805, John Smith, bachelor, and citizen of the state of Kentucky, for the total consideration of forty assorted skins and the sum of fifty dollars hard money, paid to William Barnes at the log courthouse in the county seat village of Monticello, became the owner of the leasehold to two hundred acres of unimproved land, fourteen miles southeast of Monticello, located in the wilderness known as Horse Hollow in Wayne County, created only five years before from parts of Cumberland County and Pulaski County, and named in honor of General "Mad Anthony" Wayne, who had bedeviled the British so successfully during the Revolutionary War. He was a man of property now, John thought, as he folded the grant deed in the pocket of his leather jacket. He was a landowner and would be a working farmer as soon as he could clear another acre or two and plant a crop. He would raise hogs and cattle; he would get rich and buy more land and more land, and some day he would be as big a farmer as Thomas Stockton, and the ridge would be known as Raccoon John Smith Ridge. And the Lord would know where to find him, as Ma said, if the Lord wanted him to preach.

He frowned at the thought and tried to drive it away, but it persisted, nagging at the corner of his mind as he tossed that night on his pallet after William and Maggie were asleep. Brother Isaac had comes frequently to the house after John's baptism, pretending his errand was to bring John books to read, but actually to press upon him the possibility of doing some exhorting.

"The Lord needs quick-talking people like you, John, to awake other souls to the fullness of salvation," he had said.

"I would be of a mind to preach," John had admitted, "but not just because I'm quick-talking. The Lord would have to call me. I wouldn't hanker to be like Uzzah. He put his hand on that Ark, thinking only to steady it, and the Lord struck him dead because it was Uzzah's own notion and not the Lord's idea."

He recalled with a grin that Ma had agreed with him. She was glad Brother Isaac had brought him the books but she looked the old preacher straight in the face when she said, "There's a difference between a call from the Lord and from a preacher, even though he himself be a saint. Bear a mind to it, Brother Isaac."

"Here's my thumb," Brother Isaac had said solemnly. "I'll not beguile him, and I'll not venture to stand in the way of the Lord."

"So be it," she had said. "Every wight has his weird. It is as the Lord wills."

It would, indeed, be as the Lord willed. The words went through John's mind as if Ma had just spoken them; his tension released, and he felt himself sinking into sleep.

The next day he returned to Stockton's Valley and began his preparations to move. Ma was thinking of selling off a parcel of the old farm, and Jonathan and Henry could manage the rest; Fancy Mae and Jane were getting boy-looking, and it wouldn't be long until they would be finding themselves husbands. They could manage at home without him.

"Horse Hollow is a wild, lawless country." Brother Isaac shook his head as he stood with John beside his barn when John had ridden over to return the books. "The smell of the devil is still on the place, even if the horse thieves that hid out there are all gone, them that wasn't strung up. There's nary a church meetinghouse in the whole Hollow."

John nodded absently, concentrating on the books as he handed them to the old man. "I've read all of Toplady's *Reply to Wesley*, and most of *Pilgrim's Progress*," he said. He thumbed through the Bunyan book, flipping the pages idly. "Bunyan spent a lot of time in jail, didn't he?"

"He did that; twelve years in the Bedford jail." Brother Isaac's voice trembled, as if speaking of the troubles of a brother. "All because he insisted on preaching the true faith of the Baptists. He turned blind there; his eyes plumb gave out. But he wrote his books in spite of it; he turned a great burden into a great blessing." He turned to John. "I want you should read his book, *Grace Abounding to the Chief of Sinners;* it tells how he had struggles, just like you, John. I'll give it to you to take over to the Hollow; you'll need reading like that to keep your mind right-thinking. Memorize some of his sayings, like: 'We are called with a holy calling, not according to our works but according to his own purpose and grace, which was given us in Christ Jesus before the world began.' Bunyan was a true

Baptist, and all through the book he quotes things like the Apostle Paul saying: 'Whom he did predestinate them he also called, and whom he called, them he also justified; and whom he justified, them he also glorified.' " He smiled, his blue eyes twinkling. "You are now glorified, John, in God the Father. You are one of the saints in Christ."

John kicked at a clod of earth. "You're a saint, Brother Isaac, not me. I'd never understand the Lord making me one."

"That's your weakness, my boy," Brother Isaac said gently. "You fret yourself trying to understand when all you need is to have faith that the Lord knows what he's doing, and obey him. I'm only a little preacher in this remote corner of the world. I often stumble; I have few gifts. But I do have faith. I know my Lord."

John turned away, embarrassed by the emotions flooding him; for a moment almost overcome by the love and sympathy and tenderness he felt for the old preacher. "I'd purely like to have that book you mention," he said. "I want to keep up with my reading."

"Which reminds me," Brother Isaac said, "I've been hearing that a wheelwright from Virginia named Robert Ferrill, and said to be something of a teacher and a smart man with books, is dickering with Tom Stockton to live on a piece of his land. He might open a school here in Stockton's Valley." He looked at John, his eyes wide with sudden hope. "You'd like that, wouldn't you? Would you be coming back to the valley if we got a school?"

John shrugged. "It'd be a tempting piece of news if it happens," he said.

It was a week before John was ready to leave for his new home in Wayne County. He helped Ma and the girls plant the garden, and planned with Jonathan and Henry on the crops, and twice he attended neighborhood frolics. One evening he went with all the family to the Stockton's Valley Debating and Spelling Bee Association at Tom Stockton's house. Jonathan won the spelling bee, but John's gift of gab, as Ma called it, came in handy in the debate which followed. It was on the merits of corn versus cane as fodder, and he found himself taking both sides before the evening was over, his banter and repartee sparking the group of friends into uproarious laughter.

"It'd be a fair sight to see you and that young Methodist exhorter, Peter Cartwright, lock horns on matters of church doctrine," Brother

Isaac told him at the close of the evening. "You might set the heather on fire in his soul and make a Baptist out of the rapscallion."

John laughed, but the remark troubled him as he drove the family home in the wagon. Peter Cartwright was sure of himself, certain of his destiny. No conflicts troubled him. John felt a tinge of envy. But as he pulled off his boots and stepped out of his leather breeches and slid under the quilt on his pallet beside Jonathan, he comforted himself with the thought that at least he had made a start toward his own destiny; he had a farm. Tomorrow he would finish packing his things and leave.

"You was talking again in your sleep, John," Ma told him the next morning. "You shouted out like you was trying to preach." She eyed him, and John felt his face flush. Ma was devout and saved of the Lord, her faith firm in both her Irish fairy folk and in the angels spoken of in Holy Writ, but her feet were on solid earth. "Because you think you can charm the birds out of their nests with your silver tongue is no sure sign you ought to be a preacher. I've seen such self-anointed preachers, and I'd no more trust one than I would a British Tory. There be plenty of other ways to serve God. You could maybe be a lawyer like that young fellow at the gathering last night, Micah Taul, from up at Monticello. He's got a ready tongue just like you." She took a deep indrawing of breath. "But in my heart I know there be no better life than a farmer. Get a good girl and settle yourself down. There be no better way to serve the Lord than working his soil!"

She helped John pack his clothing and books in a hamper and filled his saddlebags with slabs of turkey breast and venison wrapped in deerskin for Maggie, while Jonathan helped by hoisting them on a crosspiece over the saddle, securing them with a surcingle of leather whangs.

John swung up on the saddle and pulled at the reins. Brother Isaac had ridden by, and they stood for a few minutes, a small, tight group, quietly talking.

"I'll let you know about that school man if he comes," Brother Isaac said. "I'll write you a letter to Monticello. The postrider told me last time he was through Burkesville he's stopping there now that it's a county-seat town."

John laughed. "It'll be my first letter from the post office. I'll be proud to get a letter from you, Brother Isaac. And I'll manage to read it, too, even if you write no better than I do."

"And if I know aright, you'll do what the letter says, if I send one," said Brother Isaac. "I'll pray you will, and there's power in prayer."

John had never doubted the power of prayer, but he was reminded of Brother Isaac's remark when, on the last Saturday in May, William returned from a trading trip to Monticello and brought him a square-folded letter. John was at the well house, washing up after a day's chopping in the brush below the creek, when William handed him the thick, rough envelope.

"Joe Beard handed it to me just when I was leaving his store place," William said. "It's from Isaac Denton; it came with the postrider last Tuesday. Why would Brother Isaac be writing you a letter when you was talking with him only last month?"

John dried his face with the rough hempen towel and ran the cloth over his hair, smoothing it down. He took the letter and glanced at it, and then pushed it in his blouse pocket. "I was sort of expecting it," he said, "but I wasn't certain. That's the reason I never mentioned it. I'll hold it through supper and savor it. It's my first post office letter, and if it's what I think it is, it sets me up a problem."

And William agreed it was a problem when the envelope was finally spread open and the sprawling, black-inked script of Brother Isaac Denton was deciphered. Robert F. Ferrill, a wheelwright and a scholar from Virginia, had been in Stockton's Valley two weeks now, the preacher wrote, and with the help of neighbors was raising him a house and a shop on some of Tom Stockton's land five miles north of the Smith cabin. Wheelwright business was slack, and as soon as spring planting was through about the first of June, he was opening a school. It was the Lord's blessing.

"I'm not agreeing it's a blessing," William said soberly when John finished reading. "Here you're just starting on your own place, or getting ready to, and you're being tempted to drop it all. It don't make sense!"

"It might be a setback to you, John," Maggie interposed mildly. "It's not like as if you was a little fellow; you're all of twenty-one; a man grown. You think you could take to schooling?"

"I'll be twenty-one come October, I'm not that now," John said a little testily, "and I ain't aiming to quit the farm. I'd be coming back. But I don't aim to miss a chance to get any education I can get, either. Brother Isaac wouldn't of written me if he hadn't thought I needed it, and he's a heap sight closer to knowing what's best for me in the sight of the Lord than anybody else."

"Sin ain't in Brother Isaac," Maggie said. "I reckon the land will be waiting for you, John. You haven't put your hand to your own plow yet, so you won't be looking back exactly. Good thing this come up before you got rightly started. Don't you reckon so, Willy?"

"I reckon," William said slowly. He looked up, a slow grin of resignation on his face. "I reckon as how maybe I was figuring on you being with us for a spell, that's the bottom truth of it." He pushed back his chair and stood up. "Go on back to the school if you've a mind to. We'll be a-hold of the land; it won't run off." He filled his pipe and puffed on it for a moment. "But don't come back too big for your breeches; you got more book learning now than you'll ever need, even if you was to tuck to preaching."

Robert Ferrill's sharp gray eyes held a look of annoyance when John presented himself for instruction with Henry and Jane and Fancy Mae at the hastily erected log schoolhouse near the creek on Tom Stockton's land six miles from the Smith cabin. Jonathan had pleaded duties on the farm as an excuse not to report, and John was the only grown person among the group of excited pupils who had arrived an hour after sunup on the last day in June, a shy eagerness about most of them which John knew would develop with the passing days either into a noisy indifference or a hunger for more learning. The schoolmaster was a short, bald-headed man in his early forties, with the air of a Bantam rooster as he walked about in his knee breeches and long stockings and buckles on his shoes. He motioned John to wait outside the door as the others filed in, and after settling the room to quiet, he came out and shook John's hand without enthusiasm.

"The preacher told me you might be attending," he said, "but I'm not sure it will work, having you recite along with the rest. He said you were a right smart man."

John flushed. "I can read and write, and do ciphering good. That's about all."

"What makes you think you want more schooling then?" Mr. Ferrill asked, his tone critical. "You plan to be a Baptist preacher, don't you? Isn't that all they need to know? Doesn't the good Lord put into their mouths all they need to say?"

John was not sure he was joking, but he grinned. "Some think it's plenty; some think a preacher's mouth is like an empty dipper, and the Lord pours into it all that needs to come out. But I figure that's putting too much burden on the Lord." He looked at Mr. Ferrill steadily. "Anyway, I didn't say I wanted to be a Baptist preacher; I ain't certain yet. But if I do, I want to be able to help the Lord a little. I don't believe he aims for any man to be more ignorant than he has to be."

Mr. Ferrill's manner warmed at John's frankness, and he smiled, tiny lines latticing about the corners of his eyes. "Here's what I'll do. I'll have you sit in the back of the room and help keep an eye on the unruly. You can read the books I'll give you, and I'll hear you recite after the others are gone."

As the weeks passed, John found himself liking the bouncing schoolmaster. Beneath his peppery manner was a genuine devotion to learning, and for an hour before the others came each morning and for two hours after they had left, John and the schoolmaster talked, discussing the books John had been given to read. The younger pupils confined their study to the Bible and their own copies of Dilworth's *English Grammar and Speller* and Pike's *Arithmetic*, which almost every family owned, but Mr. Ferrill soon found John had mastered these and introduced him to the orations of Cicero and Demosthenes, to Sir Walter Raleigh's *History of the Ancient World*, to Boswell's *Life of Samuel Johnson*, the essays of Francis Bacon, and Matthew's *Manual of Arithmetic*. His father had owned the books before him, he said, and he valued them, carting them about the land with him as he went from place to place, plying his trade as a wheelwright.

Brother Isaac Denton came each Wednesday morning to inspire the students with a talk and to lead in prayer, and supplied the school with a big-lettered Holy Bible and a copy of *Pilgrim's Progress;* and before the first month was out, Thomas Stockton appeared with an illustrated copy of *Aesop's Fables*. It was written by a Greek slave, he said, over two thousand years ago, and Mr. Ferrill had John read it aloud to the class.

"You read well," Mr. Ferrill told him, "and you're pretty good in arithmetic, but your spelling and your scripting is poor. Master these tools; then store your mind with the knowledge in books, and practice retelling it. Do some speech-making every chance you get; you can even do it to the animals in the fields. Fill your mouth with pebbles, as Demosthenes did, and learn to enunciate so clearly you can be understood even with that handicap. And improve your grammar; you know the rules, but you forget and lapse into your old way of talking too easily."

Mr. Ferrill was patient with ignorance, but his temper was short when he encountered indifference, and his discipline was strict. He taught with a hickory switch in one hand and a book in the other, and John was often called upon to remove one of the bigger boys from the room.

"Some people are just not made for book learning," Mr. Ferrill told John one such time when classes were over. "They have to learn by experience, and I'm not running that kind of school. That's the Lord's job, with the assistance of the devil. All I'm willing to do is light a spark for learning, and I figure," he paused and looked at John knowingly, "I figure that's as noble a job as bringing souls into redemptive grace."

At such times John was uncertain whether the man was mocking him or testing him. Religion was a subject they rarely touched upon, and John began wondering if it was his duty to show a concern for Mr. Ferrill's salvation. In little snatches and explosions of reminiscence, Mr. Ferrill had revealed that he had been a member of the Church of England back in Virginia, where he had a wife and an infant son. But the wife had left him, and instead of trying to bring her back, he had given free rein to his yearning to see the world and, learning the trade of a wheelwright, had wandered through North Carolina, Tennessee, and now was in Kentucky, intending to push on again as the mood seized him. He loved the roaming life, he said; it gave him opportunity to add to his knowledge and time to read and study his cherished books.

"But what do you want with all your learning?" John inquired.

"Knowledge is an end in itself," Mr. Ferrill replied with a shrug. "Just as virtue is its own reward."

Brother Isaac shook his head doubtfully when John relayed the conversation to him. "I misdoubt the man should be teaching the young," he said. "He's a learned man in books, but I dinna ken when I urged him to open the school that he had a wife and child and him parading as a man with no responsibilities. He's shed himself of his obligations, and it's a bad sign. And him a member of the Church of England and a renegade."

As August drew to a close and harvest time approached, work on the farms increased, and the pupils were needed more and more at home. Demands grew for spindles and wheels, and at the close of the month Mr. Ferrill announced the school would close. John was not surprised, but his disappointment was deep. He had only tasted of the feast of knowledge locked in Mr. Ferrill's books; like Moses, he had been shown the promised land but had not yet fully entered it.

The schoolmaster sensed his disappointment. As they closed the door of the schoolhouse for the last time and walked together to the creek where the road forked and they usually separated, Mr. Ferrill put his hand on John's arm.

"With winter coming on," he said, "you won't be able to do much at that Horse Hollow hill farm of yours. Why don't you stay until the end of the year at my cabin?"

John turned, startled at the idea. Mr. Ferrill occupied a one-room cabin that had once been a smokehouse on Thomas Stockton's land. It was within a mile of the narrow road leading north to Monticello, and adjoining it was the shed he used as a shop for whirling and molding and polishing wheels. "With you?" he echoed. "What could I do?"

Mr. Ferrill shrugged. "What you've been doing—read mostly."

John felt an excited glow, and then he sobered. "I'd have to stay with Ma if I stayed on here in Stockton's Valley," he said. "It wouldn't seem right." He looked down the road, scarcely more than a trail, that followed the twisting course of the creek.

"Your mother is more anxious for you to continue your schooling than she is for your company," Mr. Ferrill said. "She as much as told me so at the singing school last Friday."

John smiled in recollection. All the neighbors had assembled at the schoolhouse on the last Friday to celebrate the closing of the school with a singing. Jonathan had come, driving Ma and the girls and Henry, and John had led the singing with such abandon, his clear tenor heard above the rest, Ma had held her hands over her ears in mock horror.

"But I'd like your company," Mr. Ferrill went on. "You could help me some in the shop with my work, and nights we could read together, and talk."

John jumped the creek, and then turned and extended his hand. "It's a bargain, Mr. Ferrill," he said impulsively, pumping the man's hand across the moving stream. "I'd be proud to stay with you. I'll get my things and be over tomorrow." They stood for a moment on either side of the creek, its whirls and eddies, its floating twigs and dead leaves sweeping along with relentless movement.

" 'Tis a blessing of St. Patrick," Ma said when John told her of the plan. "You stay with him until Christmas time, and you'll still have time aplenty to get settled on your farm before spring planting begins. You learn something of his trade, too, John; it can come in handy should you need it. Good Baptist that I am, I don't misdoubt the good saint keeps a canny eye on sons of the auld sod who try to better themselves." She wagged her head, her white cap slightly askew, her eyes warm with affection and pride.

But Brother Isaac was not so sure it was a good plan. "You have enough learning now in secular knowledge," he said. "And you'll become beholden to this man for your keep. What if the Lord should call you to preach?" He shook his head, his face showing his distress. "You would not want your mind overlaid with worldly thoughts. The Bible is a sufficient book for you; it is itself the greatest library in all creation. I'm not sure I was wise in urging you to take more schooling; I didn't fathom your thirst for it."

"I'll not beholden myself," John said. "I'll work in the shop and in the fields as he needs me. And the Lord can find me there; I won't be hiding from him."

When John rode old Zebulon over the next day, he carried with him a pallet of corn shucks Ma had given him, and his own wash-bowl and eating fork and spoon. He placed them in one corner of the single room, and went out to the shop. It was little more than a lean-to on the south outside wall of the cabin, and Mr. Ferrill was busying himself at the bench, his fancy Tidewater clothes replaced by the rough working garb of the valley people. All day John worked with him, their speech reduced to few words, Mr. Ferrill's hand guiding John in turning the lathe and polishing the spindles. At noon they sat in the shade of a giant dead sycamore and ate corn pone and jerked venison John had brought with him, washing it down with noggins of spring water. Then Mr. Ferrill left to secure provisions in Monticello, and John went into the creek bottom garden patch and shucked corn and dug turnips. He washed the green tops at the creek and pushed them into Mr. Ferrill's single iron pot. They would make good eating.

It was with a warm, comfortable feeling they sat about the hearth that night, burning with a slow fire to ward off the first chill of autumn that invaded the valley. Mr. Ferrill sat in the single ladder-back chair and John stretched out on the floor, his feet extended to the fire. After they had scraped their pewter plates clean, and washed them in the creek, and stacked them away on the shelf by the shop door, Mr. Ferrill pulled out a box from under his pole bed opposite the corner where John had placed his pallet, and kneeling down beside John before the fire, began extracting books John had never heard him mention before: *A History of the Ancient World* by Madison Forbes; a work on physical science by Paul Silversmith; a copy of Winston's *Mathematics*.

Ferrill smiled, a twinkle in his eyes, at John's excited murmurings as he turned the pages. He lighted a tall tallow and placed it between them on the floor. "This is only a taste, John," he said. "Here's one you'll especially relish." He fondled the book, turning to its title page. "*Poems, Chiefly in the Scottish Dialect*, by Robert Burns," he read. "It's a copy I bought in Boston fifteen years ago. Whenever you find yourself getting too big for your breeches—as preachers sometimes do—read Robert Burns."

The days ran together. They worked side by side during the daylight hours in the shop and in the fields, and at night sat before the blazing pine knots, an understanding silence between them, the schoolmaster giving unobtrusive guidance to John's reading. The rudiments of mathematics were easy for him, and the smattering of science in the scattered textbooks fascinated him, but his chief delight was in the literature of Shakespeare and Milton and Robert Burns. His imagination soared with Milton's description of the rebellion of Satan and the expulsion of Adam and Eve from paradise, the story gripping him with the same power he felt in reading the lamentations of the prophets in the Old Testament. He pored over a thin, leather-bound copy of *Poor Richard's Almanac* until its small type hurt his eyes.

"That's a rare book," Mr. Ferrill told him. "It's the 1752 edition.

Ben Franklin published his Almanac every year for twenty-five years, and I suppose more people in this country read it than any other book, except the Bible. And maybe Tom Paine," he added.

"Tom Paine?" John looked up, expectant. "You got something he wrote?"

Mr. Ferrill shook his head. "I had his books, but I loaned them out and lost them. His book *Common Sense* did a lot to help win the Revolutionary War, but Paine was misunderstood. He's an old man now, living in New York State, and ignored. People misunderstood his *Age of Reason*, too, thinking it an attack on the Bible when actually it was in defense of it. Tom Paine is a deist, a believer in God, but he doesn't go along with the Christian myths."

"They're not myths," John said, frowning.

"Mr. Paine thought they were because they didn't stand to reason; they were against all evidence of our human senses. You'd better watch out, John, or you'll be thinking that way too. You seem to always want a logical explanation for everything, but it's not always forthcoming."

John studied the fire, troubled. "That wouldn't make me a deist; I'd always believe in Christ. There's bound to be explanations of what people think are miracles and myths in the Bible; we just haven't discovered them yet. There's no harm in wanting to understand."

"Maybe there are some things we aren't supposed to figure out; maybe we need what your church calls faith," Ferrill said quietly. "Take this book, *The Confessions of St. Augustine*," he said, holding up a volume. "It was written fifteen hundred years ago by a man who really was a saint. I don't understand all he says any more than I do his book *The City of God*, but I read it just the same, and it sort of seeps into me." His voice trailed off into silence, and John watched, wondering if now was the time to speak to him about his salvation. But he thought better of it and after a moment resumed his reading.

The scrub pines below the ridge showed white with frost in early November, reminding John that Christmas and his time of leaving were not far off. Time and again he tried to talk to Robert Ferrill in terms of the *Philadelphia Confession of Faith* and the true Baptist religion, but he found his tongue halting and thick in his mouth. Mr. Ferrill was a good man, even if he was a renegade Episcopalian, and he was his friend. But that made it all the more John's bounden duty to speak to him and bring him before the Lord.

It was the day before Christmas when he finally mentioned the matter. He was leaving the next day, and he waited until they had cleaned up the supper things and were settled by the fire before he spoke.

"It'd pleasure us all, Mr. Ferrill," he said, "if you'd ride over to Ma's and have Christmas dinner with us tomorrow. She'll have a big lot of food, and she'll bring out her blackberry wine. Brother Isaac will be there; he likes that wine."

"Isaac Denton is a good man," Mr. Ferrill said, searching in his pocket for a scrap of leaf tobacco. "I'm going to hear him preach some time. I never have, you know. Maybe he'd give me the sacraments."

"He won't," John said soberly. "He probably thinks a Church of England man is even worsen than a Methodist." He caught Ferrill's pained expression and corrected his grammar. "Worse, I mean. The Baptist church is the only true church, you see." He paused, doubtful how best to press his attack, a certainty upon him that he would not have the chance again. "Brother Isaac could prove that to you easy. Maybe you could be converted, Mr. Ferrill. You're a good man."

Ferrill laughed, an unexpected, metallic hardness in his voice. He got up and emptied his mouth into the hearth. "That depends on your point of view, John." He stood, his legs wide apart, his hands thrust into his pockets. "I'm not even a good Anglican. I'm a heretic."

John looked at the floor, embarrassed. "I was called a heretic once," he said. "But the man didn't know what he was talking about."

"Few men do when they go name-calling," Ferrill said. "But I have beliefs contrary to those of your established churches, so that makes me a heretic. Like your Separate Baptists."

John looked at him, his eyes puzzled. "What are the Separate Baptists?"

Mr. Ferrill gazed off into space for a moment before he spoke. "They're some of your Baptists," he said finally, "who began to think for themselves in Virginia. They held to the essential beliefs of your Christian faith, but they discarded the nonessentials. They didn't exactly break with the church, but the idea that a man didn't have to accept everything just because the church did was in the minds of some of the folks who came over the wilderness trail in that traveling church, and it's been like a burr under the saddle of the Baptists in Kentucky ever since. The folks who got hold of the idea clung to it pretty tenaciously; some of them considered it more precious than their seed corn." He slowly put a burning twig to his pipe and puffed on the stem for a moment before he went on. "I admire them, but even they are too rigid for me." He waved his pipe at John. "I guess I believe what Ben Franklin said he believed when the president of Yale College asked him. He said, 'I believe in one God, creator of the universe; that he governs by his providence; that he ought to be worshiped; that the most acceptable service we render him is doing good to his other children; that the soul of man is immortal and will be treated with justice in another life respecting its conduct in this.' "

John sat silent, his mind digesting the words. "That's not enough, Mr. Ferrill," he said boldly, getting to his feet. "You're on the right road, but you've just started. You . . ."

"Here," Mr. Ferrill interrupted him. "I'm giving you this copy of *Hamlet*." He spoke as if he wanted to change the subject, and thrust the book into John's hands. And then he picked up his cherished copy of *Poor Richard's Almanac*. "And I'm giving you this, too. It will help you start your library, and also," he smiled a little wistfully, "help you remember me."

John held the two books uncertainly, overcome for the moment by his gratitude. He already had three books of his own, Pa's copy of the *Philadelphia Confession of Faith*, which Ma had given him; a copy of the Holy Bible, which he had bought himself with part of the money from his first run of hogs when he was fourteen; and Toplady's *Reply to Wesley*, the gift of Brother Isaac. And now he had two more. He blinked his eyes, groping for words to express his appreciation.

"Don't try to say it, John," Ferrill said, understanding. "I know how you feel."

"It'll take me all day tomorrow to let you know, I'm that grateful," John said. "Ma will be that glad, too; she'll maybe bring out even her special scuppernong wine."

Mr. Ferrill smiled. "I like your mother. She's Druid Irish, and the look of the Portadown heaths is still about her. But I'll not be at the

Smith homestead for Christmas dinner tomorrow. 'Tis the glory day, as the Irish say, and all the pixies and the leprechauns will be there, even if it is a religious festival in celebration of the birthday of your Christ."

"You're wrong, Mr. Ferrill," John said, surprising himself with the tone of authority in his voice. "Christmas is no actual celebration of the birthday of the Savior by the Baptists. If Jesus Christ had wanted his birthday celebrated, he would have said so. We'll have prayers, of course, and Scripture reading, but we do that every day; Christmas is just a happy time of giving gifts and eating ourselves drowsy. Ma says it goes back to the time of the Irish kings. She'd put a black pooka curse on both of us if you don't come."

"Well, that I can stand!" Mr. Ferrill laughed and shook his head. "No, I'll be spending the day chopping down that dead sycamore. It'll keep me warm and furnish me wood, and keep memories from being stirred as by a family gathering."

CHAPTER IX

JOHN had never known a winter to fly so quickly, nor a spring to come so early. The last snow of mid-February melted in splotchy patches, and the next day the earth seemed to come alive with soft stirrings. Within a week tree buds were swelling, and William began talking of turning the garden.

"I'll help you do that," John said, "and then I'm moving on to my own place. I've dallied long enough."

"That cabin ain't fitten for you to bed in," William said. "You stay on here and help me with spring planting, and slack times we'll both do clearing on your place and fix your cabin up some."

John demurred, but he knew William was right. The cabin was a shambles, little more than a half-camp, the earthen floor uneven, the openings for windows shutterless, and the sagging door unhinged. The days had passed so swiftly since his return after Christmas, nothing had been done to the place, but now that the weather had opened, he and William could spend some time on it, clearing ground and maybe putting in a planting of corn. Meanwhile he could stay on with William. He knew he was needed. The new baby, Joel, was almost six months old, and Maggie had her hands full with him and the scampering Jake; John had taken over the milking to relieve her and the care of the stock, and he knew William could use what help he could give in the spring planting.

And it was a pleasant life. All along the Little South Fork, smoke trailed out of the squat chimneys of friendly cabins dotting the narrow bottom land and edging up into the hills which seemed to nudge the sky, massing in the distance. Visits among the neighbors were frequent. Elisha Franklin maintained a blacksmith shop behind his cabin below the river bend, and up through the Hollow were cabins belonging to Joseph Hurt and Lewis Coffey, and Sam Hinds and Amos Wright and James Townsend and John Parmley, the biggest landowner in the section. Mr. Parmley's house was big and sprawling, but not as imposing as the two-story house with its veranda across the front where Joshua Jones, the county surveyor and reputed to be the smartest man in the county, lived with his elegant wife, Hannah Todhunter. In addition to visits with the neighbors, Joseph and Sue often came over to William's place from the Ryder cabin, where they still lived with Mr. Ryder on Pea Ridge, a fifteen miles' distance, to spend a day or a week, sometimes bringing Jonathan with them. Often they all went to George and Beulah's place on Otter Creek, or up to Philip and Millie's cater-cornered cabin of solid cedar logs back of a buffalo trail near the settlement of Bethel on Sinking Creek. Philip had a constant worriment about the almost defunct Concord Baptist Church where he was serving as elder, and John felt less and less in sympathy with his staid and sober nature, and regretted that his influence on the literal-minded Jonathan was plainly growing.

Never less than twice a month, and generally once a week on Friday night, the neighbors assembled at one of the cabins, sometimes for a frolic, often for a working bee, frequently a preaching, providing for each other social warmth and spiritual comfort, as well as plenty of good food. Tables laden with turkey breasts and bear steaks and dried peas and succulent sweet potatoes and corn puddings were uncovered at the close of most of the evenings together except the preachings, and if occasionally one of the men became too well fortified with a brew of corn, he would be good-humoredly ignored. Every house had its own jug of applejack, and everybody partook according to his swallowing capacity. John had no taste for the burning, bitter flavor, or for its effect.

"It's unreasonable," he told William one night after a frolic at Amos Wright's cabin, "that a man would take into his stomach anything that would make him unsteady in his mind." He shook his head. "I'm thinking more than one good dram, except for sickness or tooth-pulling or setting a broken leg, is too much."

He enjoyed the frolics and the fence buildings and the log rollings, but it was the preaching services he liked best. No church was established in Horse Hollow, and even the small, square-hewed Concord meetinghouse on Sinking Creek, where Philip was an elder, stood vacant and beaten by the elements, bereft of regular preaching except for the quarterly congregational meetings or when some itinerating Baptist preacher chanced by for a week of soul cleansing and examination among the faithful. At other times the only spiritual guidance to be had was in the cabin gatherings of neighbors. John found that his clear singing voice, his familiarity with the Scriptures, and his facility in praying made him the leader of such gatherings more often than he wished.

"The fact that I'm sure of my salvation without more of a revealing experience than I had, Philip thinks is sinful pride," he confided to William after a Friday night service at Philip's house. "But it's not pride; it's faith. The only reason I can find to doubt my salvation is that I have no doubt about it now at all."

It was Elisha Franklin, the blacksmith, who finally persuaded John to speak at a preaching service. John had taken Zeb to him for a limp in his left front leg early in April, stopping on his way back from Young's mill. A new shoe was needed, and after the work was done, he and Elisha Franklin stood together in the opening of the smith's shed.

"You got a good horse here, John," Elisha said, "and it's good sense to keep him well shod; he won't limp any more for a while now. It's the same way with folks. We got to keep well shod before the Lord or we go limp and lame and no-count. The Lord needs some blacksmiths to help keep us going. You got the makings of a good one, John. How about you building up our foundations a little? We could use some solid preaching when the folks come to services at my house next Friday night."

John shook his head. "I haven't had a call to preach. It would be an offense to the Lord should I preach without a call."

"You could exhort," insisted the blacksmith. "There could be no harm in exhorting us a little. Maybe we can get a regular preacher come summer, but you could help now, holding the folks to right-doing. You got the gift of speech more'n any young buck I know. According to my way of thinking, when the Lord makes a gift like that, he aims for a man to use it."

"Elisha's right," William said when they talked it over that night. "I reckon the Lord put it into you, because if there's anybody can spout off easier than you, I've never heard him." He spat reflectively into the hearth. "I'm thinking of the Bible story of the men with the talents. Could be the devil's trying to argue you into hiding yours."

"But you couldn't start regular preaching," Maggie said, "marrying people and all that, before you get the call. You can exhort, though. Maybe that's why the Lord had it come about you should move here to Horse Hollow where a preacher's needed."

John rode over the next day to tell Elisha Franklin that he would exhort at the meeting next Friday night at the Franklin cabin, and the word went out through the neighborhood. He chose as his text the parable of the talents as reported in the twenty-fifth chapter of the Gospel of St. Matthew.

Friday was five days off, but every waking moment he practiced his speech, while plowing or tending the stock, or sitting with William and Maggie in the evening. Back in Stockton's Valley he had been in the debating society organized by Brother Isaac, and in spelling bees at neighbors' homes, and in discussions at the Clear Fork Church he had been quick and ready of tongue. But this was different, and he felt an uneasiness in his mind. The Lord had not called him to preach, not that he knew of.

"You won't be preaching," William reassured him with quiet patience. "There's a sight of difference between preaching and exhorting. Preaching is proclaiming the Gospel; exhorting is more like argufying, stirring up the people to do better than they been doing. A man can exhort all his life and never be a preacher. That don't mean he won't be doing a lot of good. Take that young Methodist fellow who almost broke up Brother Isaac's church at Stubbins Creek; he was only an exhorter, but he sure did pull up stumps."

"That was Peter Cartwright," John said, musing. "He may be licensed to preach by now."

"That's just it," William said. "Before some shouting Methodist like that comes along hereabouts to lead people astray, you'd better be doing what you can to make them less liable to fall. And it'd make it easier on the Lord to reach you should he ever take a mind to call you to preach."

Friday a thin rain fell, and it turned cool. Not many of the neighbors would come, John thought hopefully, glancing at the darkening sky as he finished plowing and led the horses to the watering trough before bedding them down.

But the family room in the Elisha Franklin cabin was crowded when he and William and Maggie arrived with the two babies. They had driven over in William's new wagon drawn by his two black, spanking mules who could be depended upon, should the rain become heavier and wash out the road, to get them home. Elisha's wife, Silence, a large, raw-boned woman with a kindly face, was standing at the end of the lane by the clearing, her cap and wide skirt covered by an enormous bearskin, directing the wagons to the hitching rail behind the barn. Inside, John greeted the men standing near the hearth, lean, weather-worn, sinewy men for the most part, in rough skin clothes, their hard-limbed, heavily shawled and petticoated women sitting on one side of the room, chatting cosily. A few of the men stared at him, appraising him, wondering if he was acting bumptious before the Lord, but kindly enough, withholding their judgment. The women embraced him with their eyes as though in renewal of their own youth in his lithe figure with his warm handclasp and shock of reddish hair. Most of them were Baptists, and he liked them all: Nicholas Koger and Amos Wright and John Parmley and Micajah Van Winkle and James Townsend. Mr. Townsend was said to be a freethinker, but he was tolerant and, being widowed, he mingled with the Baptists for social warmth, and his daughter Anna, a pretty, slender reed of a girl, always came with him. She seemed different from the other women, almost fragile enough for him to crush in his arms if he had a mind to, and he spoke to her tonight with pointed courtesy, but his thought was on his speech, and he had no urge to talk. He frowned as he saw Nathan Weems standing near the hearth, his hands clasped behind his back, his short legs astraddle, talking as though he were lord of all creation.

Nathan Weems had moved to the region from North Carolina and was plainly not one of the hill people, and was proud of it. He walked with an arrogance that irritated John, a young man of his own age, and boasted of the land he owned in Tennessee. He was not farming in Wayne but was developing a salt works with Tom Beatty on Bear Creek over by Big South Fork, and he kept himself groomed in finery no mountain man wore who worked in the open. Now he was making his way over to sit with Mr. Townsend and his daughter Anna. He had let it be known that he, too, was a free-thinker, although he came to the cabin preaching services and once or twice had even read the Scriptures.

William and Maggie found seats near the far wall, the children both already asleep in their arms, and John anchored his Bible more firmly under his arm and seated himself on an upturned wooden bucket near the door beside a big-bosomed, red-faced woman he did not know, her arms folded across her breasts, staring in torpid silence into nothingness. At a small table in front of the hearth Philip, as an elder in the Concord Church, was rapping for order. He would lead in prayer, John knew, and then there would be hymn singing and another prayer, and then he would be called beside the table to exhort the people.

His throat felt dry and his face prickly hot, but as he opened the door beside him a crack, the fat woman hugged herself closer as though for warmth, and he closed it quickly. The first prayer was over, and the hymn singing had begun, a doleful tune that dragged through six stanzas depicting God's vengeance on all sinners. It came over him that Philip could have selected a happier tune; maybe his brother thought he had uncommon boldness, presuming to exhort without a call. He bowed his head as the hymn ended, and Philip called on John Parmley to pray. As the prayer droned on and on, John glanced up from under his lowered brows to see Philip's eyes on him, motioning to him. The prayer ended, and he fingered his Bible, marshaling his thoughts, conscious of a taut, waiting tenseness; imagining baleful, suspicious eyes boring into him, questioning his audacity in speaking to people about their sins, about the use of their talents for the Lord. He was not a Daniel, nor a Paul, nor even a Peter Cartwright; he was plain John Smith, nicknamed "Raccoon," a chief of sinners, stumbling on to holy ground he had no right to enter.

Philip mumbled a word of introduction, and he moved to get up from his seat. The fat woman next to him turned to stare at him curiously, her yellow, near-sighted eyes stripping him of all claim to sanctification and of his right to tell other people of their sins. He walked to the table and stood rigidly erect, trying to assume a confidence he did not feel, gripping the Bible to hide the tremble in his hands, conscious only that the room was very still and that a blur of eyes peered at him, waiting to pronounce judgment.

Philip and John Parmley pushed their chairs back noisily from the table, giving him the center of the space by the hearth. In a barely audible voice he repeated from memory the parable of the talents, and then he stood, his mind blank, his voice paralyzed. Frantically he tried to recall his carefully thought-out talk, but no words came, and the room began to rock before him.

The fat woman beside the door gave a sudden wheeze, a spasmodic throaty sound which might have been of sympathy or derision, and then, as though to divert attention from herself in the muted silence of the overheated room, sweltering now with warm, moist bodies, she leaned over and opened the door slightly, as John had done, fanning herself with the hem of her apron.

In two giant strides John was across the room and out the door, swept like an automaton into the cooling darkness of the night, his legs, wobbling like long stilts, about to collapse under him. His foot struck against a half-uncovered elbow-shaped root of a walnut tree not ten feet from the door, and he sprawled forward, his arms outstretched, his breath depleted. He lay for a moment, stunned and senseless, before the dankness of the wet earth restored him to reality. Light streamed from the open door, and the stillness was unbroken, as though the people waited—startled, expectant, both a hope and a fear in them.

"Arise and stand upon thy feet!" The words of Jesus to the fallen Saul on his journey to Damascus came to John out of the darkness beyond the rim of light as though they had been spoken aloud. "Witness both of these things which thou hast seen, and of those things in which I will appear to thee."

He got to his feet, brushing his knees where he had skidded on the soft ground, running his fingers through his hair, and under a power not his own he stalked back to the house and to his place beside the table. Like Paul who had been called Saul, like all those who had known salvation, he was suddenly, completely, unshakably confident he was called to witness unto Christ of those things he had seen and of those things yet to be divined, a workman who needeth not to be ashamed, obeying only the command of Christ three times given to Peter, "Feed my sheep!"

He felt the firelight from the hearth dance on his face as he began to speak, low-voiced, utterly assured, in a tone of authority he had never used before. The faces were clear now, puzzled at first and then listening, approving. Even Philip tightened his grip upon his crossed knees in unconscious admiration, while Elisha Franklin beamed at him, wagging his head in triumphant confirmation of his predictions. Beside him his wife Silence sat with an impassive face, as though not to be rushed into a final verdict. From the far side William let out a long breath, a curious pride and beaming approval on his face. And on the other side of the room John saw the smirking grin on Nathan Weems' face fade to a grudging respect as he sat with folded arms between Mr. Townsend and his daughter Anna. For a moment John looked directly at Anna, at her slight figure in a high-necked blue calico dress, a red shawl about her shoulders, a white cap sitting primly on her dark hair parted in the middle and drawn in tight coils over her ears. She was leaning slightly forward, her blue eyes wide, drinking in his words. Then his eyes swept on over the group, cataloguing the people instinctively into family groups and individuals; into saints and sinners, into unconverted believers and disdainful scoffers. But the Townsends were none of them; they were not scoffers nor were they groping, unconverted sinners. James Townsend simply held there was no necessity for conversion; he was not even trying to get it.

John finished his talk and stood for a moment, uncertain, and then he held up his hand and pronounced the benediction. Not until the people crowded about him, sluggishly at first and then with hand-shaking approval, did he remember that he should have taken his seat and allowed Philip as an elder to offer the final prayer; he had assumed a privilege he did not possess; he had acted with rudeness and arrogance.

"Maybe I wouldn't of noticed you were acting out of order if it hadn't been the way Philip looked so disapproving when you pronounced the benediction." William flapped the reins against the mules as they jogged comfortably home an hour later. "He didn't like you doing it, that's for sure, but he liked your talk." He turned to John on the plank seat beside him, a glow in him and an appraisement of which John was only dimly aware. "You're a born preacher, John. You held them people hanging on to their seats with your words."

"They did seem right interested," John acknowledged. "But maybe it's because they wondered what I'd say, knowing I'm contrary-minded. That's the reason, I reckon, I came back after I ran out like I did; I just couldn't stand to be run out by the devil like the cast-off of the Lord."

"Maybe the devil had you," Maggie said from her seat behind them on a low plank stretched across the wagon bed, a sleeping child in each arm. "But if it was, Old Nick miscalculated. I think you done a powerful lot of good, John, when you come back. You sweetened our souls and stirred us up something powerful. You got us to see none of us is doing what we could with what the Lord has given us."

"The devil did have me," John admitted. "He had a downhill drag on me, I was that scared. But when the Lord tripped me up on that walnut-tree root, and I lay there flat on the ground, I could hear plain as day the Lord telling me I was to witness. When I heard that, I wasn't scared any more. That's how I come to go back right away. The Lord wasn't fooling."

"Maybe that's your call to preach," said William earnestly. "The fact you come back is reason enough for me. I felt mighty low-down when you run out of the room; I reckon everybody did. We just set there, waiting for somebody to say something. And before anybody could, here you come back, and your face a-shining even with the dirt on it. I knowed then you was all right. It could a been the call of the Lord to preach."

John stared into darkness. "It could a been," he said, "but I'm not trespassing on the Lord without knowing for certain. Paul says in Second Timothy that the Lord would call us with a holy calling if he's a mind to. 'Not according to our works but according to his own purpose and grace which was given us in Christ Jesus before the world began,' and Peter made it even more plain. He said, 'Give diligence to make your calling and election sure, for if ye do these things, ye shall never fail.' I trespassed on the Lord's mercy enough when I went before the church for membership without having more of a revealing experience. I never did have any miraculous sign. I just felt the Lord's salvation in my bones, and I still feel it."

"I noticed Anna Townsend looking at you with all her eyes, like she was on the point of being converted," Maggie said.

"She didn't look that way to me," John said, feeling his face flush. "She looked like she wasn't even listening."

"You must of eyed her right sharp to notice that," William said, and chuckled. "She's a pretty little thing, but she'd not make a good wife for a farmer; she's too frail-like. And old Jim's not aiming to be converted. He didn't say nothing disapproving of your talk, but he didn't say nothing approving either. He was showing around a book by Tom Paine, a big friend of General Washington; we should all read it, he said. You read it, John?"

"I've heard of it," John said. "Mr. Ferrill talked about it, but I haven't read any of his books. He's a freethinker, too, like Mr. Townsend."

Summer came on with a rush. John found time to clear an additional two acres about his cabin, and with William's help he turned it to the plow, planting an acre to corn and an acre to rye. Maggie went to the place with them twice, inspecting the cabin, doing what she could to clean it of dirt and cobwebs, scrubbing the hearth with a piece of soft deerskin. But the place remained a shambles, scarcely more than a shelter, and John knew he would have to practically rebuild it before he could live in it.

Twice he exhorted again at the fortnightly gatherings, winning Philip's grudging acknowledgment that he had the gift of the Holy Spirit in his speech, and should use it.

It was the morning after a gathering at the Joshua Jones big house that William found the mangled carcass of one of his hogs, dragged to the edge of the clearing, the tracks of a bear plainly visible. The dogs had not bayed him; the wind had been in the animal's favor.

John had seen similar sights on the Stockton's Valley farm, but Pa had never been one much for bear hunting, and he had been too young to do more than tag along with George and Philip as they roamed the hills, rifles in hand, the dogs loping in delighted frenzy about them, scenting the trail. Twice the bear had been found and killed, but John had little stomach for the hunt, and the slaughter sickened him.

But now he felt the urge to kill. The sight of the mangled, half-eaten sow stirred him to righteous wrath; it was the instinct, he knew, of self-preservation, now that he was a man with a farm and soon would have stock of his own. He was ready to meet life on its own terms. All day he and William roamed the woods with their cocked rifles, crashing through the matted undergrowth, following the trail of the dogs, hearing their bays echo against the hills. But the bear eluded them, and they returned empty-handed except for two rabbits taken as they started home, and which Maggie gratefully used for their supper.

"A bear's only doing what's natural when he comes stealing food," she said. "A man's given a brain by the Lord to protect himself and his stock. He should do it by using his head instead of always running for his gun. Pen the stock up better, I say. That sow had been foraging in the thicket and wasn't even in the pen; you plumb asked for it, Willy."

Chagrined by their failure in the hunt and stung by her words, William and John ate in silence. It was not until they had pushed back their chairs and Maggie started to clear the table that she told them that Elisha Franklin had come by in their absence and invited them all to a corn husking at his place the following Friday.

When John rode up early Friday afternoon to Elisha Franklin's cabin, the men were already gathered about the double corncrib and fodder loft, talking in little groups, the warming rays of the late Indian summer sun filtering through the autumn haze. William and Maggie were coming later in the jolt cart, and would wedge it in among the wagons ranged in circular fashion end to end around the barn lot, the animals tethered to a rail in the center, a custom adopted during the Indian Wars and which some of the people still occasionally followed.

John tied old Zeb near the other animals, his ear catching the chatter of female voices floating out of the house. The women, he knew, were grouping about the quilting frames, strung with long cowhide thongs from the rafters, and would talk all day. He smiled at the thought and joined the men.

"You're a sight for sore eyes." Elisha hailed him from his blacksmith shed on the far side of the cabin, where he had been tending one of the neighbor's lame horses, and came toward him, wiping his hands on a rough hempen cloth. "Some of the boys been saying you wouldn't be coming; that you'd druther be going to Hanging Fork to hold a prayer meeting. But I told them there's more than one way to beat the devil around a stump."

"Come on, Elisha; choose your captains!" Nathan Weems stood, a broad grin on his face, his hands on his hips, a taunt in his deep voice. "We got a lot of jug passing to do before we crib all these nubbins, and time's a-wasting."

"He's plain wanting to be one of the captains," Elisha said to John in an undertone. "He claims to be a champeen shucker. He needs taking down a peg; you be the other captain and you do it."

John laughed uncertainly. "You got me 'twixt a knot and a hard place, Elisha," he said. "Get somebody else to wrestle with him; I'm no champeen."

"It's brains more'n muscle that counts," Elisha said. "Nathan drove up with the Townsend girl, and he's aching to show off."

John pulled at his belt, tightening it. "Let him then. Just let him. He needs to do a little showing off."

Elisha swung around and called to the group. "I name Nathan Weems captain of Team One. Who'll volunteer as captain of Team Two and take him on and topple him?"

Nathan stepped forward, his flat blue eyes in his red face under its mop of jet-black hair already alight with the tussle, his stocky body in an arrogant posture. "I'm starting to choose my team," he called. "Here, you . . ."

"We'll do it regular fashion, by turns." Elisha waved him back. "There's plenty of men for both sides. Who'll volunteer?"

John shifted his feet. Nathan Weems would be a hard man to beat. And he'd be good at crowing afterwards, too. Involuntarily, he stepped forward at the thought. "I will." He spoke as if the words were blown out of him, an explosion of pent-up force.

"A lily-pure lamb for the slaughter," Weems laughed. "But good pickings, easy pickings."

"I got a heap of corn in that pile." Elisha waved an unpeeled hickory stick at the group. "It'll take a heap of husking to get it done before vittle time comes. Let the judges step forward and divide it fair and square before us all!"

The group parted, and Tom Merritt, a long, gangling tobacco-spitting man, came forward, matching his steps to Henry Tuggle's short legs as both men began pacing slowly around the mound of corn with appraising eyes.

"Tom, you make the first estimate," Elisha said to the knob-jawed man cudding his tobacco quid in solemn appraisal, "and Henry'll make the second. And if you judges don't agree, I'll divide the heap myself."

"Pass the applejack," piped a shrill voice. "We're thirsty."

"Not yet, you don't get any," Elisha grinned. "You do some husking first."

The two judges paced again back and forth, squatting now and then on their haunches to view the mound of corn better, nodding as though in unspoken discussion. Tom Merritt stood on tiptoe and, closing one eye, took careful sight across the top of the ridge and then walked around the base as if pacing the distance, and again took his bearings with one eye shut, his jaws working rhythmically. Tom had the reputation of being a knowing man; he said little and was a good horse-trader.

"I calculate as how that there's fifty wagons of corn in that heap," he said finally. "You must've been saving it for a long spell, Elisha." He looked at Elisha through half-closed lids. "I 'low as how there's a heap sight more corn in this end of the pile than in the other, but this here seems mainly to be long yellow seed and powerful easy to shuck. The other end is a lot of little, flinty hominy-seed corn with a right smart sprinkling of nubbins." He paused and rubbed his chin as though in final decision. "All things considered"—he stopped to squirt a stream of amber juice judiciously at his feet—"I 'low as how the lawful thing to do is to divide the pile right down the middle, and let the teams cuss it out."

"I reckon Tom's about right." Henry Tuggle spoke with his usual moonfaced benignity, bobbing his head up and down, measuring his words as though conscious of his uncertain reputation for offhand guessing. "I 'low as how whoever gets hold of them nubbins will get sucked in. There's a desperate sight of nubbins there. But I calculate the heap ought to be divided down the middle, and it would be fair to all."

Elisha laughed. "All right, boys. The judges have decided. Measure the corn, right down the middle. And get a caper on."

With much digging and scooping and good-natured banter, the men made a separation down the middle of the heap, dividing the mound into two piles, with the hominy and nubbins and long yellow seed corn distributed between the two. Two hickory poles were laid between the heaps, denoting the boundaries, with a two-foot clearance on either side, and the husking match was ready to begin.

"We'll start at this end and work toward the barn," Elisha announced. "And make sure you pitch the shucked corn into the crib and not over the barn. I'll clean up the shucks later, and whoever wants can have them for mattress stuffing." He motioned for John and Nathan Weems to come forward. "Now, captains, choose your men and choose your corn!" With the words he tossed his hickory stick twirling toward them. A quick leap upward, and Nathan Weems grabbed it firmly at one end with John's hand just above. Rapidly, with hand-smashing plunges, their hands gripped the stick, rotating one above the other, the broader hand of Nathan Weems crowding John's shorter fingers until his spreading grip reached the top of the stick.

"Captain Weems wins first choice of men," announced Elisha. "We toss again for choice of corn heap."

Again he twirled the stick high in the air. This time John jumped upward and grabbed it first, but again the broad, expanding grip of Nathan Weems edged him out at the end.

"This your off day, preacher?" Weems grinned at John. "Maybe you been spending too much time in prayer meeting."

The women had come out of the house to watch, and John saw Anna Townsend standing near the door, her white hand shielding her eyes as she followed the match. He mopped his forehead with his sleeve and made no reply.

"Weems wins first choice of corn," announced Elisha solemnly, avoiding John's eyes. "Make your choices, Weems."

"I'll take this side," Nathan said, waving his hand toward one side of the heap. "I'll wager there's more big yellow ears there, and I'll leave the nubbins to the other boys. And for my right-hand man, my straw boss," he let his eyes rove over the men, "I'll take Amos Wright." He pointed at a big, two-hundred-pound man with broad-spreading, calloused hands, who stood grinning beside him.

"I'll take Sam Hinds," John said as Elisha motioned for him to choose.

Spiritedly, the selection went on until the men were all chosen except the two judges and Elisha, who were to pass on the cleanness of the husked corn and see that an equitable division of the brown jug was made as it passed from hand to hand among the grunting, sweating men.

Husked ears of corn began flying from the mounded heaps into the crib, John standing in the middle of his team while Nathan Weems placed himself at one end of his group, both shouting encouragement to their men, sending good-natured insults to their opponents. At first the teams seemed evenly matched, but as the corn kept flying, John noticed his side was falling back. More of the flinty hominy corn and the nubbins seemed on his side, slowing the men, although he could see the other side had plenty of the bad stuff too. But Nathan Weems was powerful, and he pushed his men with a gusto John could not match, and soon catcalls of derision came from the other side, ending in a final triumphant cry of victory.

Doggedly, John's team completed its heap, grinning in its defeat, sending a steady stream of stripped ears flailing against the walls of the crib after the others had finished, until their share was done.

"Nathan always wins," Sam Hinds said to John as they finished and stood wiping their faces. "Fair play or foul, he always wins."

"He won fair enough," conceded John.

"That's fair spoken," Nathan Weems said, suddenly appearing beside them, brushing corn silks from his hair. "Fair spoken, that is, for a preacher." He grinned and walked away.

"He don't like you somehow, John," Sam said, tossing a last nubbin into the crib. "I seen that look before. You've got to convert him or whip him."

John shook his head and grinned as they made their way to the barn to wash up before supper and the frolic which would follow.

It was two weeks later that John made his announcement. "I'm getting me a wife," he said.

Maggie stopped clearing the table after their supper and turned and stared at him, a load of dishes in her hands. "I knowed it all along," she said, the smile on her face broadening. "I can even tell you the girl you're aiming for, it's that plain."

"I misdoubt that," John said, pushing back his chair and getting to his feet. "It's just lately I made up my mind, since the frolic at Elisha's place."

"It was the frolic at Elisha's as taught me," explained Maggie. She took the dishes to the dry sink and came back to the table and wagged her finger at John. "Right after Anna Townsend left with Nathan Weems, I could see the party was over for you. Your heart walked out the door when that girl left."

"She frolicked with you quite a bit," William commented, stuffing his pipe with leaf tobacco, "and Weems did his share of glowering at you. I could see that. But I didn't see what Maggie saw. Women got eyes in the back of their heads, I reckon."

"She hung on your arm in that promenade, too," Maggie went on. "Women notice such things. I could see her looking at you hungry-like when you promenaded with the others."

"Like as not she's already beholden to Nathan," William said. "He's been talking to her now at several of the gatherings."

"It's her, all right," John admitted. "It's Anna Townsend I'm taking to wife. And one of the reasons I'm going to wed her is she needs protection from Weems. He's a blow dandy, and a nice girl like Anna Townsend got no call to tangle with him. I'm going to have Brother Isaac come over and say the binding words."

William's laugh filled the room as he slapped his open palm against the table. "Maybe you better ask the girl whether she wants your protection before you jump off the wrong end of the log," he said. "That fellow Weems is worth a barrel of money, folks say, and he's a bad one to cross when he's riled. He's lately got himself a saltpeter cave and is figuring on making gunpowder."

"I aim to ask her," John said, "but I'm speaking to her father first."

"He'll be a tough nut to crack," William said. "Since his wife died, he sets a store by the girl. The old granny lives with them, looking after the two young'uns, a boy and a girl, both younger than Anna, and she ain't aiming on losing Anna's help with things."

"Willy's right," Maggie said. "You'd better be talking to the girl some afore you make her pa a proposition. How do you know she'll have you? You ought to start wooing her some; a woman needs wooing." She eyed him thoughtfully. "You're smart in books, John, but you're plain simple about women. It takes more'n you think to make a woman want to marry up with a man, and what with you maybe liable to turn out a preacher and away from home half the time."

William grunted. "Don't set your heart on it, John. No sensible girl has got a call to turn down a rich man like Weems to camp out in a broke-down cabin like your place on the ridge. But you can try." He shrugged. "You never know."

"I'll try," John said firmly.

Late the next afternoon John stated his proposition to James Townsend when he located him in his barn not far from the house. But somehow his carefully planned words did not sound as confident as they tumbled out of him; he felt his shell of assurance crumbling beneath the kindly, half-humorous inquiry in Townsend's eyes.

"Miss Anna may not be expecting this," John admitted. "In fact, I don't think maybe she is. But I'll go right in and start talking with her if you don't object, sir. I suppose the sooner a young lady has notice of a thing like this the better."

Townsend spun a big ear of yellow corn into the trough, and as his horse nuzzled the ear, he rubbed the animal between the eyes. "You planning on being a preacher or a farmer?" he asked, his gaze quizzical. "I got nothing against preachers; give or take a little, they're as good as most. But a preacher is generally a pretty poor provider for his family. Anna's used to good living; she's not given to working in the fields."

"Maybe I'll be a preacher," John said, "but I'll always be a farmer." He shifted his feet awkwardly. "Preaching, I'll have to wait and see if the Lord calls me."

Mr. Townsend looked his disgust. "I don't follow that line of thinking," he said. "In my notion, a man's a free-will agent; he does his own deciding." He looked at John, puzzled. "Us Townsends ain't church members. Why would you be wanting a wife who couldn't be yoked even with you in your thinking?"

John tightened his jaw. "I think I could convert her," he said. "Leastwise, I'd try. I wouldn't want to risk losing my wife in eternity."

"It'd not take a lot of doing," Townsend admitted. "Anna is not given to reasoning things out like me; she even puts store waiting for miracles to happen."

"Maybe you got somebody else picked out for her?" John asked boldly. "Is she beholden?"

A hint of a smile crossed the father's face. "You better ask her," he said. "If you got a mind to speak to her, go ahead. My two young'uns, Hiram and Pensy, are visiting their dead ma's sister over the line, and Anna's alone up there except for Gramma Jennie. Gramma's old and wore out and won't pay you no mind."

John studied him, uncertain whether this lean, saturnine man was encouraging him or leading him to humiliation. As he stared, the older man grinned, a sudden, somehow heart-warming grin, and John grinned back. The man was telling him he liked him, and Anna liked him, and that she was not beholden to Nathan Weems. He swung about and started with long strides toward the house, where smoke drifted in a thin spiral from the chimney, a sudden lightness of spirit upon him that sent him whistling as he walked.

But he was not whistling when he left the house a half-hour later. A dazed bewilderment was on him, an uncertainty, and he walked with stumbling steps to Zeb waiting in drowsing patience at the hitching post.

Anna had listened with an air of shy gravity as he had made his purpose known. He had found her in the kitchen with Gramma Jennie, her cheeks flushed with the heat of the fire, her pinafore covered with a huge apron stained with cherry juice she and the stooped, gnarled, gnomelike grandmother were canning. She had hastily untied the apron and cast it aside as she led him into the big sitting room and motioned him to a chair, seating herself erectly in a high-backed armchair like a queen, he thought, her hands clasped sedately in her lap, her dark hair coiled high under her white cap, its crispness made slightly limp from the steam in the kitchen.

He had come straight to the point as he had planned to do, and told her of his farm and of his prospects, and of his ambition to be a preacher in the Baptist faith if the Lord so willed. If she was not beholden to another, he said, he would be glad to take her to wife.

She had heard him out, her blue eyes at first veiled as she glanced demurely up at him, and then growing puzzled, staring at him openly, but she had not said a word as he had alternately stood and sat, fluent enough, he thought, and logical, although he had stumbled a little at the last.

There was silence for a moment as she twisted at the kerchief about her neck, and then, half-shy, half-bold, she said, "Is that all?"

He looked at her blankly. "All?" he echoed.

The dirt daubers buzzed in the rafters as they stared at each other. And then she stood up, her face flushed in anger.

"No," she said. Just the one word, no. She turned toward the kitchen, pressing her small, clenched fist against her mouth, but stopped before she reached the door and turned to him, a frozen, tight smile on her lips, tears welling in her eyes and, as if not trusting herself to speak, offered him her hand.

The hand felt tiny in his grasp, and suddenly he felt a desire to crush her slight figure in his arms, and even kiss her. He had never kissed a girl, not counting the play-party kisses at neighborhood frolics with everybody watching, but then he had never before wanted to.

The door to the kitchen was pushed open, and the bent figure of Gramma Jennie stood in the opening, her eyes blinking rapidly in annoyance.

"Your jelly's a-boiling over, Annie," she called in a high, cracked voice.

It was then John had left, stalking without a word through the kitchen door as the old woman pushed herself back to let him pass, and through the kitchen and out into the yard.

Jim Townsend was standing beside Zeb at the hitching post, and John frowned at him and started to tug at the horse's tether, his throat dry, an anger welling in him.

"I sort of thought you'd be coming out mad." Townsend cleared his throat. "Going in like you did, like you was going to buy a horse or a sack of meal." He eyed John. "You don't know women, son.

A woman wants loving. Anna's had a chance to wed a man with good prospects, better'n yours, I'd say offhand, and she's turned him down."

"Nathan Weems?" John said, his eyes narrowing.

"I'm not telling names," Townsend went on. "I'm just saying a woman wants more'n a farm under her feet and a roof over her head, no matter how fancy. Women are queer that way. They like a man to talk to them some."

"It's silly," John said, "this business of a man and a woman talking for weeks; it's a waste of time if a man is ready to take a wife and has a farm."

Townsend shrugged. "You'll learn," he said. He pursed his lips, eying John. "Do you love Anna, son?"

John drew in his breath. He had never asked himself the question; he had no need to. He felt a swelling urgency in him for the girl, a desire he could not put into words. It consumed him suddenly with a fire he had never before known. "I reckon I been plain stupid," he said, his voice hoarse. "I love her, all right."

Townsend whacked him on the back. "Then tell her," he said. "You got my consent. I'd be proud if she'd take you." He gave John a little shove and stood grinning as John gulped and then turned and started back to the house, his long, swinging steps breaking into almost a run as he neared the kitchen door.

CHAPTER X

"YOU'RE a fast worker." William spoke with admiration when John told his story the next morning at the breakfast table. "I could tell by that cat-swallowed-a-fish look on your face when you was feeding the stock that she must have took you. You're a real tall man, brother Raccoon John."

"If it had been me, I'd made you beg a little," said Maggie. "And you'd a done it. You'd come around."

John grinned. "That's just what she did. It shook me up considerable, too; I hadn't figured on begging. And now I got to bring

Mr. Townsend around to the notion of a quick wedding. He's wanting us to put it off until spring."

"You're smart about pushing for an early wedding," William said sagely. "Too many things can happen, what with a rich young fellow like Nathan Weems hanging around."

"He don't worry me none," John said. "Anna told me she never liked him after the corn husking and the frolic, the way he acted there, strutting so big. What worries me is getting my cabin in fit shape. Anna's used to nice things."

"But all them nice things the Townsends got have no place in a church member's house," Maggie said. "They savor of sinful pride."

"Even so," William said, "that cabin's hardly fitten for a beast, let alone for a man to take his bride. I'll help you with it."

"Anna said she'd be willing for the wedding as soon as the place is ready," John said, "and I figure on having that done in a month. It won't be no place that'll give cause for sinful pride, but it'll be tighter'n a drum before I'm through with it. I'll have me a puncheon floor and an inside cellar for root stuff, and I'm thinking I'll even build me a loft room with a stairway, not a ladder, mind you, and I got a mind to build another room right behind the chimney, and I'll start me a barn."

"That's mighty big talk," William commented.

But as word of the impending marriage filtered through the Hollow, John's big talk crystallized into deeds. Neighbors fell to, and the cabin began taking on new shape. Marshaled by William, men appeared at the cabin each day—Solomon Turpin and John Parmley and Nicholas Koger and Henry Tuggle and Sam Hinds and others—helping with the redoing under John's supervision. A new chimney of red clay and sandstone, latticed with stout hickory poles and burnished with a broad sandstone hearth was as good as any in the county, according to Elisha Franklin's critical eye, and when the loft room began to take shape, with its clapboard shutters and two window openings facing the front, even Philip and Millie, who had come over to help, had to admit it was as likely a house as the Lord would look with favor on a church member owning. To the left of the fireplace and facing it was the real stairway of puncheon logs, and in the center floor space a trap door led to a three-foot-deep rock-walled cellar for the storage of root vegetables unsuited for the smokehouse or for the loft room. The clapboard roof of seasoned white oak, laid in overlapping rows and held in place by long butting poles, was the special pride of Sam Hinds, who considered himself an expert with the maul and froe and the smoothing plane, and it was as waterproof and tight as a new-stretched drum.

John himself made the pole bed, placing it in the corner opposite the stairway. He found in the woods a young dogwood tree, forked at the proper height from the ground, and dragged it to the cabin as the corner post of the bed. He let one end into the floor with the auger, fastening the other securely to a joist in the roof. Two hickory poles served for rails, placed at right angles to each other in the fork of the post, their other ends in the crevice of logs on each wall of the corner. Across this frame he placed peeled hickory rods in close parallels for slats, covering them with strips of linden bark he had torn from trees in the creek bottom land. The goose-feather mattress Anna would bring would make the bed complete.

The house was nearing completion when Anna and Gramma Jennie visited it on the last day in November. Gramma's eyes were critical but approving, and Anna was delighted.

"Pa didn't think you could do it," she whispered to John as they went over the rooms hand in hand. She reached barely to his shoulder, her delicate features and slight frame seeming out of place in the rough, unfinished rooms, and he put his arm about her in a surge of protective urgency.

"It'll be done next week," he said. "All we need then is some furnishings. Maybe we could get married before Christmas."

"Christmas?" chortled Gramma Jennie climbing down the stairway from where she had been inspecting the loft room. "Why should a pair of healthy young'uns fret for each other once they got a fitten place to live?" She came down the steps, clinging tightly to the railing. "Anna's going to bring over her ma's old skillet and Dutch oven, and her pa is giving her a couple of stools and a block table. She don't want none of her ma's real silver pieces because they ain't fitten for a church member's house, but she can have the pewter plates I brung over the trail. What with stuff other folks will give you, you got enough to start up housekeeping."

John snugged Anna closer to him. "I've already spoken to Brother

Isaac Denton," he said. "All I have to do now is get the marriage bond. We could be ready by Christmas easy."

"Anna come into the world on the ninth day of December, 1786," Gramma said, seating herself on the steps and stuffing her hickory snuff stick between her almost toothless gums. "It would be fitten if she was born into wedlock on that same day twenty years later."

A week later John stood with James Townsend before County Clerk Micah Taul in the new log Wayne County Courthouse in Monticello and listened as the dapper little lawyer-clerk recited the formal provisions of the marriage bond as written in his fine Spencerian script according to the laws of Kentucky.

" 'Tis a solemn obligation," Micah Taul said, leaning over the counter, his deep-set gray eyes appraising them both with genial shrewdness. "If this union is not solemnized, the Commonwealth of Kentucky could claim a forfeit of fifty dollars. Read it yourself." He handed a sheaf of papers across the counter to John.

John took the papers, and after a pause, unmindful of the grinning farmers crowding into the tight little room, began to read aloud, his voice rolling in unconscious relish over the sonorous phrases:

> "Know all men by these presents that we, John Smith and James Townsend, are held and firmly bound unto his excellency, Christopher Greenup, Esq., Governor of Kentucky, and his successors, in the sum of fifty dollars current money for payment thereof, well and truly to be made, we bind ourselves and heirs, and jointly and severally firmly by these presents sealed and dated this 6th day of December, 1806."

"It sounds pretty serious." John interrupted his reading with an attempt at pleasantry. "What if a fellow ain't worth a fifty-dollar bond?"

"It is serious," said Micah Taul. "You don't fool around with the state of Kentucky. Or with getting married. Read the rest of it; you're just getting to the meat now."

"I'm consenting to this marriage." Townsend spoke directly to Micah Taul. "But I'd druther not sign any bond like I was trying to get shed of my girl. Far as I'm concerned, Anna can marry or not marry, as she chooses. She's got a mind of her own, and she's not spoiled. I'm not anxious for her to marry John here; but I'm not objecting either."

"He who seeks equity must do equity," explained Taul. "Nobody is forced to sign a bond in Kentucky, neither the happy groom or the unhappy father, or vice versa." He grinned, and the bystanders broke into loud guffaws. "Read on," he said to John. "See what it says."

John turned the page, his face flushed, fighting against a rising discomfort. His voice was strained as he read aloud:

> "The condition of this bond is such that whereas a marriage is shortly intended to be had and solemnized between the above bound John Smith and Anna Townsend if therefore there be no lawful cause to obstruct the same, then this obligation to be void, else to remain in full force."

"There's the core of the apple," Taul said smoothly. "If there be no lawful cause means if the girl backs out, or the man." He looked at John. "Well, that's lawful cause. The bond just shows the expressed honorable intention of John Smith, and your signature, Mr. Townsend, as security for John is to show that you consent to the union. Not that you have to consent, mind you. The marriage would be legal anyhow, as your daughter is of legal age. Now sign here, both of you; I got other things to do."

He indicated the line and slowly, soberly, they affixed their signatures, James Townsend writing his name laboriously under John's, his face clearing as he wrote.

"It'll be a good marriage." Townsend spoke to no one in particular. "John's a stout worker, and he can talk the bark off a tree. He'll make a tolerable son-in-law."

Taul nodded in grudging agreement, pulling the paper back toward him. "I'll sign as witness, and I'll add this line." Hastily he scribbled:

> Parents consent proved by the oath of James Townsend.
> M. Taul.

He pushed the paper to one side and reached into a drawer under the counter and produced a sheet of thick brown paper. "I'll file the bond in the Book of Marriage Bonds of Wayne County. This here is your license to wed." He began to write, reading aloud as his pen raced along on the paper:

"Monticello,
Wayne County, Kentucky

"Any minister of the Gospel, legally authorized, is hereby licensed to celebrate the rites of matrimony between John Smith and Anna Townsend of this county, and this shall be a sufficient warrant therefor; he having executed bond with security as required by law. Witness Micah Taul, Clerk of said County, this 6th day of December, 1806."

He signed his name with a flourish and sprinkled finely powdered sand from the box before him to dry the ink, and pushed the document toward John. "When you aiming to marry?" he asked.

"In three days," John said briefly.

"It's to be on my girl's birthday, December ninth," Townsend said, "at my place. We'd be proud to have you come over, Mr. Taul, you and your lady."

John's eyes brightened. "That we would," he said. Micah Taul, as clerk of both the County Court and the Court of Quarter Sessions, was already a man of note in the county, young as he was, better known even than John Parmley or Elisha Franklin with all their land holdings. He had more learning in the law even than Joshua Jones, and was respected even if it was rumored he sometimes drank too much and gambled more than he should. The last time John had exhorted at Joshua Jones's place, Micah Taul had been there, with his young wife Dorothy, listening and nodding his head even though he was not a Baptist.

"I may be jogging over," Taul said. "I've heard you talk a sermon; I might as well see you take a wife. You're a good talker, Raccoon John, like Mr. Townsend says; and a hardheaded man with the gift of gab and not afraid to work could make a fine lawyer." He looked at John, appraising him. "I was thinking some you might like to read law in my office. The state needs good lawmen, maybe more than it needs preachers. Think it over."

John shook his extended hand, laughing. "I'll think it over," he promised. "But I got a feeling the Lord wants me to preach. I'm just waiting for a sure sign."

From the courthouse John and James Townsend made their way

to Beard's Store, an easy companionship upon them. John made several purchases, and as they left the store and approached their horses tethered to the town hitching rail above the springs, Townsend put his hand on John's shoulder.

"That was a right smart deposit you had shored up with Joe Beard. A forty-pound, six-shilling credit ain't no riches, but it's pretty good for a young man who ain't been in the Hollow on his own no longer'n you have. You got a head for business better'n I thought."

John grinned, swinging into his saddle. "I wanted you to know you didn't run no risk by going my security on that marriage bond. That's the reason I let you do it. And Joe Beard treats everybody fair and square. He paid me fifteen pence a pound for the jerked meat I sold him this fall, going shares with Willy, and that's fair enough. But with the new suspenders I bought me, and my beaver hat, and a new bridle for Zeb, I'm set back a little. I was aiming to buy me some cashmere cloth for a wedding suit, but I figure that would purely be sinful pride."

"A cashmere suit wouldn't be no account in the roughs," said Townsend. "But that don't mean it would be sinful pride to own one. Not as much, leastwise, as that decorated bridle you bought your horse. That's shore a waste of money."

John patted the horse's neck affectionately. "I just didn't want Zeb to think I was forgetting him 'cause I'm taking me a wife."

On Wednesday, December 9, 1806, John and Anna Townsend were married in the big family room of the Townsend two-story house by Elder Isaac Denton of the Clear Fork Baptist Church in Stockton's Valley before more than half a hundred neighbors who had broken trail through the early December snow to crowd the room, festooned now with evergreen and holly and myrtle leaves. William and Philip, with their wives and children, were there, and Jonathan had ridden over from the valley with Brother Isaac and Robert Ferrill, but Ma was suffering from a chronic hurt in her lungs and had not ventured the twenty-mile trip. Micah Taul and his wife, Dorothy, had arrived just as the ceremony was starting in the early dusk, riding over in their two-seated carriage with Joe Beard and his wife. When the binding words of the simple ceremony were finished, as spoken by the short, square-shouldered Baptist preacher standing in solemn dignity in his store-bought black alpaca suit, the stiffness of the room suddenly lifted as John bent to kiss his bride, and it became filled with warm gaiety and friendliness.

"They been practicing that part real steady now." Gramma Jennie waved her clay pipe at the couple with a quick circular motion. "You'd a thought it was the most important part of the ceremony, and it ain't no part a-tall. The preacher just made it sanctified instead of sinful!"

They were late in leaving the Townsend house the next morning after the shivaree and frolic that had followed the wedding ceremony, with only a three-hour rest before daylight in their upper-story bedroom. Anna perched snugly atop the sledge in the middle of her big goose-filled mattress, surrounded by assorted pots and kettles and stools and her spinning wheel; she held in her lap the Dutch oven in which Gramma Jennie had packed two freshly boiled hens wrapped in soft deerskin. She wore a dark-red velvet cape and hood that had been her mother's wedding wrap, and which all but concealed her small frame, only her smiling blue eyes and pert button nose visible beneath the ruffled hood. But she managed to extract an arm to wave gaily to Gramma Jennie and her father and her brother Hiram and younger sister Pensy as John swung his long whip over the brace of oxen his father-in-law had given them. Behind the sledge old Zeb, his new bridle fastened with a leather whang to the end runner, tossed his head and snorted as they moved out of the yard and struck the trail across the lower end of Horse Hollow to John's place, a distance of twelve miles.

The snow grew heavier, falling for three days, enveloping the Hollow with a sharp stillness. The enforced seclusion gave time for Anna and John to get settled, the world shut out, the warmth of their cabin and their love filling them with a vast contentment. Then the weather cleared, and work on the place claimed John's attention, and neighbors began dropping in with housewarming gifts and greetings and well wishes, and the fortnightly prayer meetings were resumed with John now accepted as the regular exhorter.

It was after the prayer meeting at John Parmley's house the third week after their marriage that Anna told John she wanted to join the Baptist church. John was fastening the door against the night, and Anna had dropped onto the floor before the fire. They had talked often of religion, and of John's hope to be a preacher, and he had tried to explain to her the meaning of predestination, and of the Holy Spirit and the revealing experience it would bring. She had listened attentively, her eyes on his face, but he had been conscious his influence on her was growing, and the fear gnawed at him that she might tend to accept not only his faith but his tenuous revealing experience as her own.

"I believe in Jesus," she had said several times. "Isn't that enough? You understand all about the Doctrine of the Elect and the totally depraved and the revealing experience, and if it's all true to you, it is to me, too."

He came now and sat down on the floor beside her, taking her hand in his, groping for an answer. "In good time, Anna," he said softly, knowing he must be very guarded with her, and gentle. "In the Lord's own good time he will reveal himself to you. All you can do about it now is wait and pray." He felt a blankness in his own mind as he spoke, but he went doggedly on. "You must come under conviction as a chief of sinners, Anna. It is not up to you to make the decision to accept the Lord; it is up to the Lord to let you know if he has accepted you."

"I want the revealing experience." She pounded the floor, half-joking, half in earnest, with her small fist. "I want it right away."

"You can't make demands on God, Anna." He rose stiffly to his feet and pulled her close against him. "You must wait and pray and read the Bible. God will open the way. Wait until we organize a church here in Horse Hollow. Brother Isaac asked me again about getting one started when I saw him last week in Monticello."

"Then could I join?" she asked hopefully.

"If you rightly believe." He smoothed her hair, his voice troubled. "The elders would have to pass on the reality of your revealing experience after it comes to you. It's a troublesome matter, and I'll not be one to say a person wanting the Lord as you do ain't under conviction." He sighed, a deep, lingering indrawing of breath. "I dunno; the Lord help us!"

Christmas came, and they were drawn into its pleasuring. At a play-party at Sam Hinds' cabin John learned that Nathan Weems had sold out his interest in the salt works and moved on to Tennessee. As the new year lengthened into weeks and then into months, duties about the place engrossed them both. Anna made curtains for the two window openings to conceal the bear-greased paper that covered them, and wove bright-colored rugs for the floor, and as John plowed the newly cleared fields, she followed the furrows, dropping seed corn. He risked planting corn in the bottom land rather than on the thinner soil of the ridge because the growth would be quicker and the harvest heavier once it survived the hillside downpour of the spring rains. He finished building the barn and a smokehouse, and erected a two-railing fence about the barn lot, extending it to enclose a portion of the creek where the stock could water, with Anna helping to hold the posts as he leveled the rails.

He worked furiously at times, reminding himself of a man running from the devil. He was getting too fond of pleasuring and of worldly things; he had done nothing to organize a church in the Hollow. Brother Isaac had rightly seen one was needed, and had even suggested a preacher, a man named Richard Barrier from up on the Big South Fork in the northern part of the county, who would be willing to pastor it for a while.

"It's because you're newly wed," William reassured him when he rode over to his brother's place late in March, plagued by his conscience. "A man's a right to laze away a time. The Lord will remind you of your duty soon enough. Wait until the babies begin to come, with their colics and their crying and their empty stomachs needing filling, you'll sober yourself then."

But his words served only to disquiet John more. He had been married close to four months now, and there was no sign of a child on the way. Was the Lord taking this means to punish him?

Within a week he made the rounds of the neighbors with Baptist connections, outlining his plan for constituting a church which would be faithful to the Scriptures and the true Confession of Faith as adopted by the Philadelphia Association at Philadelphia, Pennsylvania, on September 25, 1742. Some of the neighbors were indifferent, content with the fortnightly gatherings in the homes; a few, like Philip, lived on the outskirts of the Hollow, too distant to be included, and they suggested another church be constituted closer by; but about twenty-five signified their interest.

When John spoke to Elisha Franklin he was surprised at the reaction of the hearty blacksmith.

"I'm not a hide-bound creedist," Elisha said, chewing soberly on his tobacco, stroking the horse he had been shodding. "The Bible is my creed and nothing else. I've a deep concern for keeping the word of God alive in the Hollow; that's why I got you to do some exhorting at our gatherings. But I've no truck with either the London or your revised *Philadelphia Confession of Faith* that the Baptists put so much stock in."

"But you're a Baptist," John protested, "just like the rest of us."

"Not exactly, now that you pin me down," Elisha said. "My folks were taken with the Separate Baptist talk back in Virginia, and I reckon some of it spilled over on me. It sorta goes with the free life here on the frontier, every man shedding himself of them binding creeds just like we got shed of our political bonds."

John frowned. "If a Christian is a Baptist, he's a Baptist," he protested. "There's no such thing as a Separate Baptist."

Elisha wagged his head. "Of course I'm still a Baptist, like John the Baptizer, the forerunner of Jesus Christ. But I'm not swallowing all they teach. I don't hanker to all the gloom and damnation of the *Philadelphia Confession of Faith*. I read some of it, and I'm not reading it no more; I just follow the Bible." He looked at John, his eyes frank. "If you let me do that and have my own opinions about creeds and such, and let every man do the same, I'll let you make me a deacon in your new church. If you don't, well, I'll probably join up anyway, but I'll not be anything but a listening, believing Baptist Christian, and a paying member."

"You wouldn't be listening to me," John said, confused, anxious to change the subject. "We'd have to get us a steady preacher."

Elisha rubbed the stubble of beard on his chin before he spoke. "You're a born preacher, John; I can see it plain as day," he said. "You're just too pigheaded to admit it."

John gave a short laugh. "I could be pigheaded, but I'd be in a worse fix than Balaam's ass if I tried to preach without first getting a sign from the Lord that he had me in mind for it."

The blacksmith shook his head firmly. "When the church decides a man ought to preach, it's an order. The church is the body of Christ, and its voice is the voice of God. You stop turning your ear away and listen to it."

CHAPTER XI

WITHIN two weeks John secured the promise of twenty-three neighbors, saved and sanctified, to constitute a regularly organized Baptist congregation after the pattern set out in the Scriptures and the *Philadelphia Confession of Faith* in the rugged southwest hill country of Wayne County, which had once been the hiding place of horse thieves. The next day he wrote to Brother Isaac Denton to get his best preaching clothes ready and prepare to come to the Hollow to formally constitute and consecrate the new group as soon as it got itself a meetinghouse.

To John's surprise and delight, Elisha Franklin offered a plot of ground on a clearing he had made three years before, where the soil was too thin for cultivation, as a site for the new church. It was on a western ridge overlooking the Hollow. "Wife Silence calls it Franklin's Folly, my clearing this spot, because it's been no good." He spoke with heavy humor as he and John stood on the ridge. "No good, that is, up to now. But it'll be a proud place for a house of God, and I'll give it, and that parcel adjoining, too, in the scrub pine, for a burying ground. Horse thieves and fighting Indians and maybe even the Harpe gang once used this land, maybe this exact spot, as a lookout against the law. Having a church here will serve folks this end of the Hollow; later, maybe we can start another up aways. That'll show the fancy people in northern Kentucky we're getting civilized down in these parts."

Like fire in a tinderbox, enthusiasm for the new church spread. Logs were cut and hauled and spliced by practically every able-bodied man in the Hollow, and in four turbulent days in late August the meetinghouse was raised complete with puncheon benches and a gum-tree pulpit stand, and even a fancy two-foot latticed steeple ready for a bell when they could find one.

The day of consecration was set for the last Sunday in August, and on Saturday afternoon Brother Isaac Denton rode up to John's house, accompanied to John's delight by Jonathan and Thomas

Stockton. It was a happy, joyous occasion. The new preacher, Elder Richard Barrier, would be on hand in the morning, Brother Isaac said, and would sermonize thereafter for the new church once a month. Other friends dropped in—the Parmleys and Sam Hinds and his wife, and Elisha and Silence Franklin, and Joshua and Hannah Jones—and James Townsend and Gramma Jennie, and William and Maggie. After a pitch-in dinner served by the women, with Anna fluttering about in a state of high excitement, they made plans for the following day's service and the future of the church.

"It was from Mount Pisgah that the Lord let Moses see the vision of the Promised Land," John reminded them as they were preparing to leave. "Nobody's said much about a name for the church. How would Mount Pisgah do?"

Brother Isaac slapped him approvingly on the shoulder. "You can see your own vision from your own Mount Pisgah!" he said. "A wonderful name!" He held up his hand to quiet the group. "All in favor say aye!"

A hearty chorus of assenting voices responded, and as John and Anna walked with Jim Townsend and Gramma Jennie to their wagon, Anna slipped her hand in John's and spoke quietly to her father.

"From Mount Pisgah people got a vision, Pa, and I've got one, too. I'm joining the church tomorrow." She waited a moment for him to reply as John's hand tightened on her fingers, tensing in surprise. She had not told him of her intention. But her father said nothing, helping Gramma Jennie into her seat in the wagon. "Do you mind?"

He picked up the reins and started to speak, but Gramma's cracked voice stopped him. "A woman's man decides things after she gets one, not her pa," she said. "Go along with you, Anna; John decides things for you now."

"John didn't decide this." John's voice was firm. "Nobody decided it but Anna and her Lord. She's asking only your blessing, sir."

Townsend looked at them soberly, and then he shook his head. "I reckon the bottom truth is I envy the lot of you," he said, "but I could never bring myself to join you. Yes, Anna has my blessing. I wish I had whatever faith prompts her."

For an hour after the others had left, John and Anna sat with Brother Isaac and Thomas Stockton and Jonathan in the yard, talking quietly of pleasant things, reminiscing, gazing into the ricocheting fields of moonlight in the cleared bottom land below them. And then John brought to the surface the problem he had been mulling over ever since his talk with Elisha Franklin.

"I thought we had twenty-three people signed up for the new church," he said. "But now I figure there'll be only seventeen. The five of the Amos Wright family aren't coming in. They think we're too rigid, constituting this a regular Baptist church according to the *Philadelphia Confession.* They were Separate Baptists back in North Carolina, Amos told me, and they say they won't compromise like Elisha Franklin is doing."

Brother Isaac's face clouded. "Mr. Franklin was a Separate Baptist?" he inquired.

"He still is," John explained. "But he's willing to go along with us because he thinks it's a sin to cause division. He said the church is like a man and wife; he doesn't agree with everything Silence does, but that doesn't mean he's willing to break up the union of marriage. He believes in the one church of the Apostles, which is the united Baptist church." He paused, reflecting, and then went on. "I don't understand it. A man can deny the truth and be a Methodist or a Presbyterian or a Tory Episcopalian, or even a Catholic. But how can a man think he's saved and not be a regular Baptist?"

For a full minute there was silence while they waited for Brother Isaac to answer, and Anna began quietly to pass around a plate of molasses cookies filled with hickory nuts and to fill the noggins with buttermilk from a stone jar. As she handed a noggin to Brother Isaac, he spoke directly to her.

"As fond as I am of your husband," he said, "I canna see he's content unless he is ever winding himself a bonny pirn over something. Even the truth for him is shifting sand. He will ever find ground for another question." He took a long drink of the buttermilk and set down the mug.

Jonathan shifted his feet noisily. He had become a deacon in the Clear Fork Church and was feeling the call to preach. "The truth is plain enough," he said. "A man is a Baptist, or he ain't a believer. There's no such Christian faith as a Separate Baptist."

"So it has been decided by the dissenters themselves," Brother Isaac said. "But there are some who still insist on styling themselves as such an absurdity, especially in our Kentucky. It is the devil's work, as are all schisms in the body of Christ. We have a few of these dissenters in Stockton's Valley but I had hoped none in Horse Hollow."

"Where'd these Separate Baptists come from all of a sudden?" John asked. "I remember Pa talking about them some, and my old teacher, Robert Ferrill, talked some of them, but I thought they'd died out."

"I heard one of them preach over near Burkesville," Jonathan said, "an old fellow named Rice Haggard. He preaches a sort of every-man-decides-for-himself religion. I got no use for that."

"It's not that bad, Jonathan," Brother Isaac rebuked him mildly. "There are many honest, conscientious people among them. They practice the true baptism by immersion, and they preach the infallibility of the Holy Bible." Slowly, as though reluctant to voice recollections he would prefer to keep in the back of his mind, he went on. "I reckon it really began with old Jonathan Edwards and George Whitefield back in the colonies along about 1740. That was the real beginning of the revival we witnessed in Logan County a few years back and which spread up north to Bourbon County and came to Stockton's Valley too. Shubal Stearns was one of those great preachers, too, and there were others while I was still back in Virginia. They were the first to preach against creeds; but they didn't oppose creeds as such but only the errors in them."

"You're too easy on them, preacher," Thomas Stockton said. "My folks back in North Carolina ran head on into them, and backed away. The rascals thought they were ordained to literally resurrect all the ancient customs of the early church, such as feet washing and the holy kiss and anointing the sick, and love feasts and the laying on of hands and weekly communion. They even appointed new apostles to replace the original twelve. As I recall, a man named Samuel Harris was named as the first apostle."

Brother Isaac laughed softly. "But that didn't last long. Not even the Arminians, who claim everybody is saved and will believe anything, could take that. Most of the people came to their senses and came back into the true church, and it was decided that even the names Regular Baptist and Separate Baptist would be buried and forgotten, and we'd be known only as United Baptists."

"You can't bury and forget an idea," John said, "once it gets inside a man."

"That's why we need to keep firm control," Thomas Stockton said. "Too much liberty is dangerous. These die-hard Separate Baptists are sowing their seed all over the state; they're tainting even the Presbyterians. You recall, John, that Presbyterian preacher, Barton Stone, you met at Muddy River? I liked the man until I heard on my last trip to Lexington that he'd become almost a freethinker. He left the Presbyterian church with four other men and started what they called the Springfield Presbytery, but they had a falling out and split up. Two of them went back to the Presbyterians, and two went with that anti-marriage bunch, the Shakers. But Stone wouldn't go with anybody. He's started a church of his own, repudiating creeds and sitting down to the Lord's Table with anybody who'll sit with him. He calls the people who join him Christians, but folks are calling them New Lights or Stoneites and other names not so good."

"Barton Stone is a good man," John said warmly. "Whatever he's done, he's a man of God. He'd make a powerful good Baptist preacher, Brother Isaac."

"Not with his views." Brother Isaac shook his head. "He's too much tainted with plain heresy if he thinks all men can be Christians."

"And Separate Baptists are getting even into politics, preaching against slavery." Thomas Stockton almost exploded. "When I was in Lexington I heard that a Baptist preacher in Mount Sterling, David Barrow, had gone so far as to organize some outfit to actually abolish slavery!"

Brother Isaac cleared his throat, a warning sound. "If Elder Barrow considered slavery a great evil, it was his duty to act against it. It was a matter of conscience."

"If he had kept it as a matter of individual conscience, it would have been all right," grumbled Stockton amicably. "But when he sets up an organization he calls Friends of Humanity, to abolish an institution sanctioned by the laws of our own government, and by the Scriptures, he went too far. I've got two slaves now, and I've made Christians out of them, good Baptists, both of them. I look after their souls as well as their bodies. The blacks are not ready to be free people; they'd be helpless and revert to the jungle in no time. Africans are the sons of Ham, who shamed their father, Noah, in his nakedness, and they must work out their salvation in subjection and toil, according to the Scriptures. It's the Lord's plan blacks should be here as slaves; it was predestined by God before the foundation of the world for the good of their souls. Slavery is not an evil to these people; it's a blessing. It..."

"No! No!" Brother Isaac interrupted him, shaking his head vehemently. "The enslavement of man by man is an evil thing."

"You're a good man, preacher." Thomas Stockton smiled in friendly tolerance. "But if you had the care and responsibility of a few blacks, you'd be a wiser man. It's a privilege to have them, but it's also a burden given to us by God himself." He looked at John and Jonathan. "Every man in these mountains ought to get away for a while and get the feel of what's going on in the world. We're isolated down here. Things are happening in Lexington and Frankfort that are making history."

"Like what?" asked John pointedly, irked at the man's tone of condescension, troubled by his flat pronouncement on the rightness of slavery. Thomas Stockton didn't know everything. "I read a copy of the *Kentucky Gazette* last month when I was in Monticello. Didn't seem to me much was going on." He spoke gruffly, half-conscious of an effort to conceal his hunger for news; unwilling to admit the unrest that filled him.

"Well, they had a big party for Aaron Burr at the Governor's Mansion in Frankfort the day after Christmas, that set people's tongues wagging," Stockton said mildly, as if trying to offset any note of condescension. "Of course he was our vice-president under Jefferson, but since then he's killed Alexander Hamilton in a duel, and he's been arrested for treason, trying to organize an expedition against Spain."

"We shouldn't of honored such a man," Brother Isaac said, a note of sadness in his voice. "Dueling is wrong; the man is a murderer. I hope Henry Clay wasn't there."

"He wasn't," Stockton said. "He has no use for the man. Henry Clay is a credit to the state. I heard him orate at a burgoo at Versailles, and he's a powerful speaker. He might even be president some day."

Anna spoke suddenly from her seat on a low stool beside John's chair. "Did you say there was some anti-marriage people up there? I didn't know anybody was against marriage."

Stockton grunted in derision. "They're called Shakers, and they're as active in spreading their queer doctrines as even the Separate

Baptists. But they won't make as much progress, I'll guarantee you that." He laughed hoarsely.

"They're well named," Brother Isaac said. "The time will come when they'll all shake and scream in torment at the enormity of their sins. God help them."

"They preach that a woman, Anna Lee, is the reincarnation of Jesus Christ," Stockton continued, speaking directly to Anna. "The term 'Shakers' is a nickname because they shake all over when doing their holy dance. They think marriage is a mortal sin, and husbands and wives are forced to live apart when they join the outfit. They even give up their children to be raised separately."

"How could a religion like that take hold?" John's disgust showed in his voice. "It's blasphemy."

"Three of their missionaries showed up at Turtle Creek only a couple of years ago, and they've been gaining recruits of a sort ever since. They've even established a colony in Jessamine County, and they're aiming to start another over here near Russellville," Stockton said. "They're lunatics!"

"And they don't believe in marriage?" Anna repeated in wonder. "They must be fevered."

A wind had come up, and she got to her feet, steadying herself with a hand on John's shoulder. "I believe in marriage," she said. "I even agree with the Apostle Paul that the husband is the head of the wife, even as Christ is the head of the church, and that wives are to submit themselves to their husbands as to the Lord." She smiled at Brother Isaac. "You see, sir, I've been reading the Bible."

"Husbands also have an obligation," Brother Isaac assured her in quick, approving humor. "Husbands are to love their wives even as Christ loved the church, and a man shall leave his father and his mother and shall be joined unto his wife, and the two shall be one flesh."

"I'm glad you said that," Anna said. "If we are to be one flesh, I've come to realize we should be one in spirit, too. My husband's religion is good enough for me. That is what you might call my revealing experience, Brother Isaac. The Lord has shown me I should join John in his church. I intend to offer myself for membership in the church when it is organized tomorrow, and I want you to baptize me just as you baptized John."

John stood up and put his arm protectingly about her small waist.

Anna was genuinely, utterly, sincere; he would not allow her to be hurt by any rejection of what she considered her revealing experience, not if he had to defy the whole Baptist church. He started to speak, but Brother Isaac stopped him with a wave of his hand.

"I have never heard a more convincing experience, Sister Anna," he said quietly, "nor a more Scriptural one. God love you!"

No one was surprised the next day, following the sonorous sermon by lanky Brother Richard Barrier and the election and ordination of two elders and four deacons by the seventeen members of the new church—not counting the twelve visitors including silent, brooding James Townsend and chattering Gramma Jennie—when the congregation voted upon John's motion that the name of the church be known as the Mount Pisgah Baptist Church of the Stockton's Valley Association in Horse Hollow. Elisha Franklin seconded the motion, and John's face burned as the man added that he felt young Deacon Raccoon John Smith inspired when he conceived the name, proof, if any was needed, that he had been touched and set apart by the Lord. Nor was there anything but shining agreement when after the morning service and the noonday dinner-on-the-grounds, and Brother Isaac had reassembled the group for the consecration sermon and the receiving of experiences, Anna had pledged her faith and asked for membership, with a sincerity and devoutness no one could doubt.

"The discernment and obedience of Anna Townsend Smith to the pronouncements of the Apostle Paul relative to the position of husband and wife in the family relationship is a credit to Christian womankind and an example her sex could well follow," Brother Isaac said in moving her acceptance. And while the women nodded in affirmation, their enthusiasm appeared somewhat less emphatic than that of their men.

Two other women and a craggy, weather-beaten farmer from below Young's mill reported miraculous experiences of sudden seizures and nocturnal calls, and were voted into membership, and the four recruits were immersed forthwith in the creek at the base of the ridge, and the little congregation had grown to twenty-one souls.

"I'm troubled in my mind for you, John," Brother Isaac said soberly as John walked with him toward the horse enclosure to join Jonathan and Thomas Stockton for the ride home. "You've done well in starting this church, but I can see you've also done well with your farm. Your stock is increasing; you must have all of fifty head ranging these hills; you got a good start in hogs; you got a fine house. It's plain you got the turn of making money." He shook his head. "You got to watch, John, or it will breed in you sinful pride; it could turn your eyes from the furrow and take your hand from the holy plow. The Lord has given you much; much will he be expecting from you."

"I've used my head." John spoke more defensively than he intended. "That's why I've done well. There's nothing wrong with working hard and being careful in business dealings. I'll use it for the glory of God."

"You have much to use," Brother Isaac went on as if John had not spoken. "I can see it more clearly every time we meet. You have a Scotch toughness of mind combined with the ready tongue of the Irish, and a touch of worldly ambition. A heady mixture, and a rich one. I've mentioned your special gifts to Brother Barrier."

John frowned in quick resentment. "Brother Barrier will learn soon enough what I can do, and what I cannot," he said.

Again Brother Isaac ignored his remark. "There need be no supernatural call to preach," he said as if they had been talking about it all the time, his eyes fixed upon Jonathan riding toward them, leading the preacher's plodding mare, while Thomas Stockton followed on his own sleek, high-spirited animal. "I tell Jonathan that, too. That boy does not have your gifts, but he has a conviction in him; a deep certainty that is like a steady anchor in these skeptical times." He spoke hurriedly now, with rising emphasis. "The ability and the desire to meet a need is God's call." Jonathan rode up to them, but Brother Isaac kept on talking. "Most women have a curious touch of intuitive wisdom. Anna has her share. Listen to her, John; she may be your conscience." He put his foot in the rope stirrup and, with a quick boost from John, hoisted himself into the saddle. Jonathan and Thomas Stockton waved and pushed ahead, and the old preacher watched them for a moment and then, before joining them, turned back to John and raised his low-crowned hat in a solemn gesture of farewell.

CHAPTER XII

WHATEVER Brother Isaac had said to Elder Barrier, the tall, solemn elder seemed in no hurry to single John out for any special attention, although he called upon him to dismiss the congregation after his second preaching service, and listened attentively enough whenever John spoke at the business and experience meetings of the church on Saturday afternoons. So John listened with surprise when he heard the preacher propose to the congregation on the fourth Saturday in November that Deacon John Smith, sometimes known as Raccoon John, be licensed by the Mount Pisgah Baptist Church of Horse Hollow to exercise to the best of his ability, and the limits of the patience of the people, such powers as the Lord had given him as the official exhorter of the church.

The matter was voted immediately and, almost in a daze, John received the congratulations and well wishes of the members as they filed out. He lingered behind, waiting for the preacher, while Anna went with William and Maggie toward the wagons.

"I don't rightly know this was wise, Brother Barrier," he said as they started together out of the church. "I don't know as I should be officially licensed. I do exhorting as needed, but to be licensed, well, that's almost the same as being ordained. That's being set apart, and I've got no sure sign yet that God's wanting me to be set apart."

They stopped in the center of the churchyard, out of earshot of the others climbing into the wagons in the horse enclosure.

"It means only that you are a beginner, a probationer before the Lord, John. In a sense, you're on trial." The preacher spoke slowly, stroking his stubby chin whiskers in emphasis. "You have no authority to perform marriages or baptisms, or administer the Lord's Supper, or to conduct funerals or any other ministerial duties except that right given to any Christian in the absence of an ordained saint. But you can exhort as you have been doing, only it's official now."

"Sounds in a way like I'll be neither fish nor fowl," John said. "That's about it, ain't it?"

"That's about it." Brother Barrier looked at John soberly, and then his eyes twinkled. "And who would want to long remain in that state?" The words were more a statement of fact than a question.

He started toward his horse, tethered at the far end of the enclosure, and John followed him, a gradual conviction filling him that he had taken another step toward an inevitable destiny. With it was a curious sense of relief. Brother Barrier loosened the bellyband on his horse and began to smooth the wrinkles from the saddle blanket.

"How does a man get himself ordained, once he feels he's had the call?" John asked.

"Ordination may be accomplished only after fasting and prayer and proper examination and the laying on of hands by the elders as prescribed by the Philadelphia Confession of Faith, and in no other manner." The preacher vaulted into the saddle and wheeled about to face John staring up at him, an unconscious eagerness in him.

"What do they ask on that examination?"

Brother Barrier pondered a moment. "Not all the questions may appear pertinent at first blush, but they're based on profound wisdom," he said. "Some may seem rather foolish at the time. But hath not God made foolish the wisdom of this world?" A smile quivered at the corners of his mouth, softening the solemnity of his long face. "I recall one of the examining elders at my ordination asked me if I had ever known a sheep to turn into a goat, or a goat to turn into a sheep. It sounded like a foolish question, and of course I answered no. To my surprise the elders were satisfied. It was not until later that I learned that in my ignorance and confusion, I had answered wiser than I knew. I had forgotten that the foreordained Elect of the Lord, even before conversion, are the sheep of Christ; that no sheep can ever change his nature and be a lost soul; that once a sheep, always a sheep." He studied John's upturned face for a moment and lowered his voice, leaning slightly forward. "Few of the Elect of the Lord are called to preach, but those of us who are cry with the Apostle Paul: 'For though I preach the gospel, I have nothing to glory of; for necessity is laid upon me; yea, woe is unto me if I preach not the gospel.' I think you feel that necessity, Raccoon John Smith. Why do you resist it? That is your call to preach. The fields are white unto the harvest." With a sharp slap of his palm on the mare's rump, he wheeled about. "Remember this, my friend," he said, reining in his horse for a moment, "the place whereon thou standeth is holy ground." A final wave of his hand and the preacher spurred his horse into a loping gallop down the rutted roadway.

John went toward William, backing his mule to his cart, snapping the trace chains fast, and William grinned up at him.

"You and the preacher were doing a spell of gabbing," he said. "Was he laying down the law and the gospel or just plain giving you hell?"

John tousled the hair of little Jake, standing restlessly between Maggie and Anna, and forced a grin. "I'm not sure. He reminded me the fields are white unto the harvest. Reckon he meant for me to get to work."

"You look scared," Maggie said.

"I am scared," John replied. "I can't figure it all out."

"You couldn't be scared, John." Anna slipped her hand through his arm. "You're made in the image of God; there's nothing that could scare you."

William snorted. "He's not made plumb in His image," he said. "The Lord nodded a little when he made John. He's got a mite of the devil in him, wrestling with the Lord about everything. He's that contrary!"

"All men have the devil in them," said Maggie, "some more'n others. I got a notion the Lord allows it on purpose to test the mettle of their womenfolks."

William slapped little Jake on the haunches as the boy climbed over the wagon wheel and seated himself on the single plank seat. "The Lord put the devil in men so they could match their women. It all started with Eve getting Adam in trouble in the garden," he said. "Even preachers have some of the devil in them; they call it sin. But we can get the best of the devil if we've a mind to; that's the truth of it."

"The Lord's got to help," John said. "We can't do it alone."

"It's the Adam in men that makes them blame their women for all their bad ways," Maggie said, climbing into the wagon with the sleeping Joey in her arms, pushing Jake over to make room on the seat. She turned to Anna. "But I sorta like the devil in men myself. It sorta humanifies them. They even make up to their women a little better when they think they're sinning a little. And what need would there be for preachers and churches and meetings like this if men stayed too pious and sanctified all the time?"

William chortled and climbed in beside her and picked up the reins, and with a sudden lurch the wagon started on its jolting way.

December was unusually mild; the intermittent snows were light and dry, and the roads remained open. John took advantage of the clear spell to take Anna on a trip to Stockton's Valley, timing the visit to coincide with their first anniversary. Anna had not yet had a chance to meet her mother-in-law, and their encounter was pleasant enough, although John could see that his young wife, accustomed to Gramma Jennie's grumpy ways, was not prepared for Ma and the merry Irish tales with which she regaled them, flouncing about the house still as chippy and feisty as ever. Jane and Fancy Mae had become young ladies, their heads and eyes full of young men who drifted in and out during the visit. Henry was a man now, almost as sober as Jonathan, and there had been no news of James, Ma told him briefly, dismissing the subject with a shake of her head, revealing a sadness that had no expression in words. George and Beulah had come over, and they had relived the Harpe adventure; and Robert Ferrill had dropped in, too busy with his shop, he said, to think of teaching school again, a reserve and a withdrawnness about him even when John turned the talk to books.

"It's because he's an agnostic," Brother Isaac told him. "A man canna live apart from God and prosper in his spirit. He dries up if he thinks he's nothing going nowhere."

Brother Isaac was as genial and friendly as ever, but somehow his manner puzzled John. There had been some talk of the church at Clear Fork, and the old preacher had listened as John told of his license to exhort. But not once did he remind him to harken to the call to preach. And when John told of his farm, and of how Joe Beard had told him his hogs were the fattest in the market that fall, and of how the hemp he had planted in the limestone soil on the slope was as fine-fibered as was to be found anywhere in the Cumberland, the old preacher turned away. And not even to George did John confide that he had been able to bank over half of his earnings in the iron safe in Lawyer Micah Taul's office in the log courthouse in Monticello.

The new year brought heavy snows, blocking them into the snugness of their cabin, and a biting, penetrating, soggy coldness followed. The wolves ran gaunt and ravenous over the hills, a constant menace to the stock huddled under the shed in the cow lot, and in March the winds seemed strong enough to tear at all creation.

Elder Richard Barrier, like the hickory-tough man of God he was, never failed his appointments at the Mount Pisgah Church, no matter what the weather, even bringing with him occasionally two other preachers, Isham Burnet to do added praying, and Isaac Storey, who always brought along his wife, Abigail, as they were thinking of settling in the Hollow. And the little congregation never faulted him, although many had the winter sickness, reducing the saints in number on one Sunday in March to a mere half-dozen. But the old preacher's sermons never seemed more God-ridden, nor his exhortations more sanctified, than on that day. Twice during the winter John exhorted at the church, following Brother Barrier's sermon, and once at a midweek socializing and prayer meeting at Elisha Franklin's house.

It had been a long winter, John reflected one afternoon late in April as he jerked at the reins of old Zeb, pulling the plow through a stubby new clearing he had made during the cold weather at the edge of the scraggly pine slope which shadowed his farm. But it had been a good winter, with plenty of time for study and meditation, and even love-making. He mopped his forehead, taking a bearing on the sun. It was all of three hours past high noon. The day had turned warm, bringing the feel of summer heat, and he was thirsty. He felt suddenly tired. A man weakened quicker, Pa used to say, after the shut-in months of winter.

He pulled the horse to a stop and propped his long-handled plow against the stump of a cedar tree at the edge of the clearing and uncorked the jug of cool water Anna had filled for him. He took a long drink and sat down on the stump, his feet braced wide apart on the damp, matted underbrush, his thoughts centered on the exhortation Brother Barrier had asked him to give next Sunday following the preaching. He planned to take his text from John 3:14: "And as Moses lifted up the serpent in the wilderness, even so must the son of man be lifted up." He would tell them of the ordeals of Moses, and of the signs the Lord had given him and all people, that they might know and follow the truth in Jesus Christ.

He put his elbows on his knees, his chin cupped in his hands, a slow inertia seeping into him, the sun warm against his back. He closed his eyes, seeing himself speaking with mighty power before a large concourse of people. It was somehow the Mount Pisgah group but swollen into a throng; people stood outside the doorways and before the open windows in the spring sunshine, peering at him, hanging on his words. And when he ended his exhortation, they surged forward under conviction, acclaiming him a man of God.

One elbow slipped from his knee, and he jerked himself erect. The dream dissolved, and he blinked his eyes, staring down in disbelief and horror into the beady eyes of a mottled rattlesnake coiled between his outspread feet, its long body quivering, its tail waving faintly with the beginning of a death-warning rattle, as though its flattened, scale-like, glistening length were arousing sluggishly into life under the warming sun from a long hibernation.

Breathless, his body as immovable as the stump on which he sat, John stared. The creature blinked its eyes, glittering black beads, and as a forked tongue darted out and was drawn back, and the head wavered, John threw himself backward and to one side in one convulsive, involuntary movement, and fell sprawling into a thicket against his broadax.

Instantly he was on his feet, the ax in his hand uplifted to kill the creature. It was a symbol of hell itself, the biblical embodiment of original sin. He would cut it into a dozen slithering, crawling pieces.

The matted grass before the stump was bare; there was no sign of a snake, not even an imperceptible movement in the underbrush and tangled vines. He struck at the growth savagely, but there was no slimy body anywhere about. The air was suddenly quiet, the only movement the twitching tail of Zeb lazily drowsing in the languorous sunshine.

Cold sweat broke out on John's forehead, and he wiped his face with the sleeve of his cotton shirt. He felt his legs trembling. He stood for a moment, uncertain, and then threw his ax on the ground and went back to his plow. He had been dreaming. But he knew he had not; there had been a rattlesnake between his feet. And it was against all reason that the snake had not struck him. Was it a sign?

He finished plowing the field and unhitched Zeb and rode him back to the barn. He had stumbled upon a sluggish snake that could not strike; such things had happened before. It didn't mean anything. If God sent him a sign at all, it would be a voice calling him in the night, or a vision in the sky, or a word when he lay abed with

Anna. If an angel had been sent to wrestle with Jacob, a sign could be given him of which there could be no doubt.

He told no one of the incident. It would only create amusement, such as he had felt at the story told by the old man who had seen the white yearling calf. But he felt strangely sobered for the next few days, and his evening prayers with Anna the rest of the week became longer and more fervent, although he was abrupt and short with her in his speech and found himself staring at her as though he did not see her at all. Ma would say there was a pox on him. He smiled at the thought.

When he stood to exhort at the church on Sunday, he felt uncertain if he should use the text about the serpent Moses held up. It made him uneasy. But once he had repeated the words, he found himself repeating them with added emphasis, and then his prepared talk faded from his mind and he spoke with such fervency and searching intensity and probing into the secret places of the hearts of his hearers that four people came forward when he finished to give their revealing experiences, among them Anna's brother, Hiram. And when Brother Barrier suggested holding their baptism immediately after the service was over, John was embarrassed when they demurred. The creek water was still too cold, they said, and anyway they would prefer to wait until John himself was ordained and could perform the rite.

"Now you'll have to be ordained," Anna told him happily as they rode home in the jog cart. "You don't need any more sign than that, do you? People wanting you to baptize them? Hiram's been a harum-scarum all his life, and if you could convert him, the Lord's showing you how much you're needed."

John sighed. "It set me to feeling I'm pretty smart. Do you reckon the Lord would use that as a sign?" He shifted his feet uncomfortably. "The Lord's not of a mind to make a man proud-turned. Let me brood on it a while." He flipped the reins and changed the subject. "Elisha Franklin told me a cattle drover was going to hold an auction at his place come Wednesday, and I'm aiming to be there. It'll be a good chance for me to swap that pair of old oxen your pa gave us for a livelier beast. Old Zeb's not strong enough to pull stumps out of all the clearings I'm making; I need a strong young ox. The old pair is plumb wore out."

"You're stubborn-acting," Anna said, "or you're putting worldly things first, like Brother Isaac warned you against. Which is it?"

He smiled and reached out and took hold of her small hand. "You're my conscience, all right, like Brother Isaac said." He shook his head. "I'm not thinking altogether of the auction. I reckon I'm just using it as a reason to put off thinking about my call. I don't rightly know what God wants."

"You expect too much of God," Anna said, shaking her head, her brown curls bobbing under her bonnet. "What are you waiting for, a miracle?"

"Yes, a miracle," he said. "I'm waiting for the Lord to send me a miracle. Do you reckon he'll do it?"

The cattle auction on Wednesday was only tolerable, John grumbled to himself, as he alternately tugged at the reins of old Zeb and turned to crack his long cattle whip about the yoke-shaft of the young ox he was leading home. There had been too much drinking, in spite of Elisha's efforts, and not enough cattle to choose from. But he had done well enough. The drover had been a hard bargainer, as much interested in buying as he was in selling, and the prices he secured were higher than would be heard at the summer auction in Monticello. But John had outtalked him in the swap of his two old oxen for this black young ox with the wide-spaced, spreading horns, almost like a devil's scoop; hard-muscled, and with enough years ahead of him to pull a thousand stumps from cleared ground. Elisha said he'd make a good trade, even when they were having trouble tightening the hempen rope about those wicked horns. He was a mean one, all right, lean and sinewy, and as full of the devil as he was of vigor. John had difficulty holding the guide rope taut as the animal struggled against it, trying to hurl himself into a side ditch. Once, for all the hobble-shaft like a frame about his knees, he had tried to gore the sweating Zebulon, and only by the fierce lashing of his long cattle whip was John able to force him to fall back. The creature had enjoyed his own way too long and had not been broken for steady work. But a firm hand and regular feedings and a little patience would make him a good farm animal, superbly equipped to pull stumps and a plow through the matted roots of cut-over forest land.

Two days later John was not so sure he had made a good trade. The ox had become the terror of the freshening cows in the cow lot and the rooting, fattening hogs. Even Zebulon shied away from him, and all of John's efforts to hitch him to a plow or even yoke him were useless. It was as though in vengeance for his lost potency he dared a man to break him into peaceful ways.

It was the end of the next week that John decided to put a clog on him. The dragging weight would dampen his exuberance and at least make him manageable. He let the animal go without food for a day and then enticed him to feed at the trough. When the thick neck was lowered, John tried to slip the yoke-chained log about it, but the animal lunged at him savagely and, bellowing, raced away. It was then he decided to get Elisha Franklin to help him. The blacksmith had worked with animals all his life, and his strong arm could grapple with any of them.

"He's a black devil, Elisha," John warned him as they stood at the rail fence watching the beast in a far corner beyond the creek. "As Ma would say, I put out my arm farther than I can draw it back when I got that fellow. He's past my ken."

Elisha was close to agreeing after they had worked for an hour. He suggested they lasso the animal first and secure him to a stump where they could hobble him and put the chastening clog about his neck. But the great ox bellowed and raged, tearing about the fenced enclosure, plunging through the stream that bisected the lot, charging at the men and sending them racing for the top rail of the fence. John turned his two young bear dogs into the field, but their lunges at the ox served only to infuriate him further and, fearing they would be gored to death, John soon called them off.

"We'll narrow the enclosure," Elisha said. "You head him toward the shed wall, and I'll barricade him there with them poles and the two wagons."

As Elisha pulled the wagons into place and armed himself with a broadax, John entered the enclosure with his rope and prodding stick, shielding himself behind a clump of wild growth on the edge of the stream. But the ox saw him and with a raging bellow tore toward him, splashing through the shallow water. The mire of the stream bed sucked at the animal's feet, and his horns entangled themselves in the growth of the thicket, momentarily slowing his rush. But for John the pause was enough. He seized the beast by the tender flesh of his nostrils, his grip like a vise. Pa Smith had taught him as a boy in Stockton's Valley how to do it, and the grip on the quivering flesh had never failed to bring an animal into subjection.

But this animal was different. He thrashed for a moment and then threw back his great head, ripping his nostrils from John's hold. With a roar he charged at John's still stooping figure.

As the ox lunged, John leaped across the stream toward him, dodging the lowered head, thinking to gain time in his race for the safety of the fence by forcing the animal to brake his onward rush and wheel around. But his foot slipped on the soft ooze of the stream bank as he leaped across it, and the animal spun about quicker than he had reckoned. As he stumbled to his feet and raced for the fence the animal was upon him, its hot breath on his neck. He felt a quick stab in his hip and a pull on his pantaloons and knew he was impaled on one of the great horns. Then he was lifted off the ground and hurled into the air. He landed on his bottom, closer to the fence than before, but the animal was charging at him again, the black hoofs pounding the earth.

What he remembered later was total, utter helplessness. The breath had been knocked out of him; his legs refused to move; his senses were reeling. There was nothing he could do. But with the acknowledgment of his helplessness he suddenly was aware of a force outside himself, propelling him, flooding him with strength he had never known. In one flying leap, he had vaulted the top rail.

The beast's charge was brought to a sudden, jarring halt against the fence in a frenzy of frustration and rage, and in cool deliberateness Elisha leaned across and struck the wide-spaced head with a calculated blow of his broadax, sending him half-stunned to his knees. In an instant John had looped the rope about his horns while Elisha swung a length about his hind legs.

Anna had been clinging to the fence, her eyes staring in whitened terror, and as the animal was brought under control she slowly crumpled to the ground, her full linsey skirt enveloping her like a billowing cloud.

CHAPTER XIII

THREE weeks later, on the third Sunday in May, 1808, Raccoon John Smith of Horse Hollow was ordained to the ministry of Jesus Christ by Elder Richard Barrier, assisted by Elder Isham Burnet, following the morning sermon at the Mount Pisgah Baptist Church. A torrential rain had fallen for a week before, flooding the roads, damaging the crops, making impassable the narrow trail to Stockton's Valley, and Brother Isaac Denton, already sick abed with a chest cold, was unable to come as he had planned, nor could Ma venture the trip. But Jonathan managed to get through on old Beelzebub who, he said, had enough contrariness in him to defy any storm, and sat with William and Philip and their wives and watched the elders lay their hands on John's head as he knelt by the pulpit stand, setting him aside forever as, so Elder Barrier said, he had been predestined from the beginning of time. Then Elder Burnet offered a prayer, a long, sonorous petition, which ran the gauntlet from iniquity and the Lord's grace to that call to duty which ever hung heavy over the heart and conscience of the Lord's anointed, and which continued until John's knees ached.

The examination which had preceded the laying on of hands was brief, over almost before it had begun, and William told John afterward it was because the elders must have been uneasy lest John change his mind.

"You are acquainted with the *Philadelphia Confession of Faith?*" Brother Burnet had asked him.

"I am well acquainted with it," John had replied.

"Do you adopt the Articles therein set forth?"

"I do," he said after a barely perceptible pause.

"There are no further questions."

After the laying on of hands and the prayer, Elder Barrier charged John with the responsibilities of his new office: he was to preach the gospel unceasingly and without fear or favor; to warn the sinners; to comfort the saved; to conduct the holy ordinances of baptism and the Lord's Supper; and to perform the sacrament of marriage binding unto death according to God and the Commonwealth of Kentucky. Then Elder Burnet charged the members, huddled together for warmth in the dampness of the raw day: they were to uphold their consecrated fellow member in all his endeavors for the Lord. With a final prayer, it was over. John led the group to the creek, swollen by the rain to twice its size, and, bracing himself in the strong current, baptized Hiram Townsend and the other three converts who had awaited his ministrations.

John had confided to no one before the service the sudden, final reason which prompted him to become ordained. Not even to Anna. The decision had come so quickly, and with such finality, he could not put it into words. But from the moment he had picked up Anna from where she had fainted by the cow lot and, carrying her into the house, had learned from the distraught Gramma Jennie wringing her hands by the kitchen door that his wife was in the family way, a luminous quality had enveloped all of life.

He felt he had somehow never completely believed in miracles and suddenly, inexplicably, all life was a miracle. He saw it now in every blade of grass; he experienced it in every incident; it explained his escape from the ox; it transformed his view of life. But the feeling could not be explained, and he did not try. God had a language a man could not translate.

"Maybe it was because you conquered the devil in that black ox," William suggested. "You've broke him into a peaceful farm animal now. Was that what made you decide?"

"It was because you stopped your sinful doubting," Jonathan said in mild reproach. "Now that you've got the feel the Lord's called you you'll never doubt again." His lips curved in bland assurance. "I know nothing could make me doubt. The Lord's called me to preach, and I'm getting myself ordained as soon as Brother Isaac can get around to it."

The heavy spring rains brought a quick fruition, and the heat of summer danced over the hills. Almost overnight, it seemed to John, the corn had tasseled, the peas and beans were swelling in their pods, and the root vegetables were ready for digging. Anna milked the two cows and did what she could in the garden, aided by Gramma Jennie, who was spending more and more time with them. But most of the time she busied herself preparing baby clothes, spinning the flax wheel as Gramma Jennie handled the flax hackle, both of them spending long hours sewing the linen cloth with a fine stitch. John took time from the fields and the care of the stock to fashion her a cradle, a rough, hand-hewn affair, slightly off-center, its rockers unsteady and tilted. But Anna lined it with wool and covered it with printed calico, and Gramma Jennie quilted for it a coverlet, edging it with ruffles. The baby was expected in October, and Anna delighted in telling John it was certain to arrive on his birthday.

"Not every man is given a son as a birthday present," she would say, tossing her curls in a gesture of triumph.

"It's not becoming for a female to be so certain," Gramma Jennie would remind her. "How come you know it's going to be a boy? How come you be so sure of the day?"

But John never questioned her prophecy. He'd be proud to have a son, but a baby girl would pleasure him too. And if it arrived on his own natal day, October 15, he would not be surprised. God's ways were past understanding.

He preached frequently at neighborhood gatherings and once a month at the Mount Pisgah Church, alternating with Brother Barrier. The old preacher had the Ohio fever and was wanting to go north; he was feeling the urge to push ahead of the devil into new settlements, he said, with his Bible and his plan of salvation. He left in late August, and John assumed the full preaching and oversight of the little church, aided occasionally by Elder Isaac Storey, who had moved to the Hollow with his wife, Abigail.

The first day of October Philip came by the house. He was discouraged over the state of the Concord Church, where he was serving as elder. The congregation was dwindling, members were moving out of the county, the preaching was infrequent and irregular.

"What we need is to organize a new church in that section," he told John when he located him in the barn, saddling Zeb for a trip into Monticello. "We've folks all around Bethel who have got no religion at all. They're sitting ducks for the Methodists to come in and claim them. Or the Presbyterians could get them. A Presbyterian, Tom Cleland, was preaching around there last week, and I trembled in my boots that he'd start him up a church. But the Lord took a hand, and he got sick and left. I'm thinking we need to preach some sound Baptist doctrine before he gets back."

John looked at him in mild amusement. "I didn't figure you'd ever be asking me to help you," he said. He laughed and pushed playfully at his brother. "Willy was telling me you doubted I should of been ordained."

Philip grinned, a wry expression on his solemn face. "I did question," he said. "I didn't rightly know you'd had the call." He shifted his feet on the dry earth, stirring up little whorls of dust. "But when I heard you exhort after that ox nearly finished you off, I knew you'd been touched. You're a natural-born preacher, John."

John finished saddling his horse and led the animal out of the barn, walking beside his brother. "I hope you're right, Philip," he said soberly. "I got an urge to preach, but I'm not sure I'll make the Baptists proud of me. I'm not even sure I rightly can expound on Baptist doctrine. I preach around here mainly on the love of God and his mercy to help folks through their everyday agonies. I don't talk doctrine much. But preaching to unbelievers is different. Explaining all that Baptist doctrine," he shook his head, "I don't know as I can rightly do it."

"You can do it," Philip said stoutly. "You're an ordained preacher of the Lord God, John, and you got to do it. People with no religion ought to be hearing the truth."

After Philip had left, and John was on his way to Monticello, he regretted he had promised to ride over to Bethel some time soon and explain the Baptist doctrine to the neighbors Philip would invite to a gathering at his house. It would take a hunk of studying; he'd have to line up arguments for the Baptist position, and he had little hankering for dwelling overmuch on such fine points.

He tethered Zeb at the hitching rail and went to the two-story log courthouse in the center of the public square laid out by Joshua Jones as county surveyor seven years before, where Micah Taul had his office as clerk of the county. John had bought a span of mules the week before from a farmer moving out of the Hollow, but he still had money left from the sale of his corn and hemp, and he had brought it for safekeeping in Mr. Taul's iron chest.

"You've sure been raising hell amongst the yearlings since you were ordained to preach." Micah Taul spoke almost testily as he handed John a receipt for the money. "But you're not banking as much money as you did this time last year." He placed the money bag carefully in the back of the big safe and turned the lock. "Maybe you don't trust my bookkeeping?"

John forced a grin. "I'm busier now, preaching," he said. "I bought me a span of mules with some of my money, but I could of sold another load of seed corn down at Van Winkle's mill if I'd taken it over there last week. But I had to get up a sermon for last Sunday and didn't have time." He looked about the tight little office with its yellow-backed volumes of Blackstone, and Coke's *Institutes*, reading the titles aloud as his eyes roved over them. "It takes a heap of knowing to be a lawyer," he said. "It must pay well."

Micah Taul gave a short laugh. "About as good as preaching, I reckon," he said. He seated himself on the edge of his new roll-top desk, his legs stretched in front of him, his arms crossed over his chest, and smiled at John, his eyes quizzical.

"You know better'n that," John said quickly. "A preacher gets only what people want to give him, and sometimes it's just about nothing. We been taking a collection at Mount Pisgah Church for Brother Barrier, and last month it was not even three dollars. Brother Isaac don't even get that, because they never take a free-will offering at Clear Fork Church. He gets provisions, though, and sometimes some free work with his farm."

Micah Taul eyed him sternly. "Doesn't the Bible say that the laborer is worthy of his hire?" he said. "You got a right to demand some pay, Raccoon John; if you're smart, you'll see you get it."

John shook his head. "I got me a good farm, and I won't take a cent. The gospel should be dispensed without money and without price. The gospel is free."

Micah snorted. "Old man Barrier isn't worth more than three dollars. But you're different; you're a good preacher. They tell me people can sit outside their cabin doors of a still night and hear you preaching two miles away down there in the Hollow. With a little more schooling, you could be one of the best in the county, and I've always said you'd make a good lawyer. You got a legal mind; you try to reason things out."

"It takes more than reason to convert folks," John said. "If that's all it took, the whole world would be Baptists because we got all the reason and logic on our side, and all the truth."

"That means you claim you've got the keys to the kingdom?" Micah Taul shook his head and pushed at his brown hair, thick about his short neck. "People been quarreling for ages over who has them, don't you know that?"

"Yes, I know that," John said shortly. "The Roman Catholics claim they got them; the Greek church claims them; the Episcopalians claim them. The Presbyterians contend they belong to the officers of their church. But I'll tell you where they are—the Lord Jesus Christ has them, also the keys to hell."

"Yet you Baptists claim you got all the truth," Micah said. "What logic have you got on your side?"

John eyed him, wondering if he was serious. "You want I should tell you?" he asked suddenly.

"Don't preach me a sermon." Micah held up his hand in protest. "Just tell me the bone and marrow of your doctrine; boil it down, if you can, without all the thunder and damnation." He went behind the counter and perched himself on his high stool, propping up his knees and clasping his hands across them. It was late afternoon, and the air was drowsy. Few people were on the street, and the low bellowing of oxen and the squealing of hogs in the public pens down by the watering trough came to them faintly through the open window. "Imagine I'm almost a convert; give it to me straight."

John nodded, happy for the chance to clear his own thinking. He could practice explaining the Baptist doctrine on Micah Taul; he was his friend even if he was a scoffer. He straightened and assumed in mock seriousness a preaching stance.

"We Christians, called Baptists after the manner of John the Baptizer, the forerunner of Jesus Christ," he said, "accept the Holy Bible as the inspired and everlasting commandments of God Almighty, and the *Philadelphia Confession of Faith and Discipline* as adopted in 1742 by the Philadelphia Baptist Association, and previously set forth by the Baptists back in London, England, in 1689—we accept that as our guide and practice and statement of our religion before the world."

He paused. He had memorized the statement when he had first been licensed to exhort, and he repeated it by rote. The lawyer's face was impassive, his eyes half closed, and John went on, speaking more slowly, feeling his way.

"All other people who call themselves Christian are wanderers from the truth and are in danger of eternal hellfire and damnation."

Micah Taul's eyes shot open. "You mean you got me in danger of hellfire already?"

"And there you stay," John said firmly, warming to the interchange, "except for the grace of God. Because all men are born dead in sin and can of themselves do nothing to please God. They are wholly corrupt in soul and body, born not only with Adam's guilt upon them, but also they inherit the corrupt nature of the old man. All men, therefore, are utterly indisposed, disabled, and made opposed to all good, wholly inclined to evil. That's the Baptist doctrine of original sin."

Micah gave an exaggerated shudder. "Can't they be justified by their faith, like Martin Luther said? Or by their good works, like the Methodists believe?"

"They cannot, and you know it," John said, his tone so harsh he wondered if he sounded defensive. "Men are saved only by God's grace, which is his undeserved mercy. He singled out those to be saved before the foundations of the world were laid. They are the ones Christ died for, and they are the only ones. And in his own good time God communicates that fact to them through the revealing experience. They know then for certain they are the Elect; all the rest are eternally damned."

"As a lawyer, I'd say that's not equitable," Micah Taul's voice was ringed with sarcasm. "And it's anything but logical. A man doesn't have to do a thing and . . ." He broke off. "I think you're confused, John."

"I'm not confused!" John almost shouted. "If you'd read our *Confession of Faith*, you'd realize a man does have to do something. He has to repent and believe in Christ; he has to understand and obey the Scriptures; he can help the poor and comfort the sorrowing. But the point is, these good works are not in any sense the ground for a man's justification. He's not justified until the Holy Spirit through the revealing experience actually applies Christ to him. And then he can never fall from grace again; he'll persevere to the end and be saved. All others are rejected, and the Holy Spirit can give them neither the disposition nor the ability to do good. Christ did not die for them, so they cannot come to him. Therefore they must perish in their sins."

"Even infants?" Micah asked quietly.

"Yes, even infants." The words shot out before John realized their implication. Micah Taul knew he and Anna were expecting a child;

he had asked the question deliberately, and it angered John. He turned toward the door; he had said enough.

For a moment there was silence in the little room, and then Micah Taul spoke slowly, almost a sadness in his voice. "You'll probably spend your life trying to prove that doctrine, first to yourself and then to the people." He got up and stretched and braced his feet wide apart, a half-mocking, half-serious smile on his face. "I still say it's not logical."

John shoved his battered hat to the back of his head and frowned, his face flushed. "Why do you keep saying that?"

Micah Taul leaned over the counter. "Your doctrine of the Elect and your doctrine of original sin just can't be reconciled, that's why," he said calmly. "If some men are elected to be saved from the foundations of the world, how come they have to be brought under condemnation and conviction of their sin through what you call the revealing experience? Why does the Holy Spirit have to make them feel they are the chief of sinners? And if all men are born in sin, totally depraved, then how can some of them at the same time be elected by God to be saved in spite of their inborn sin?" He shook his head. "You Baptists simply can't have it both ways."

John stared at him, groping in his mind for an answer. But Micah Taul laughed and moved around the counter and opened the door.

"Don't let it bother you, John," he said. "I've asked that same question of preachers before, and they all give me that same look."

"It's to God's eternal glory," John said solemnly, resorting to an answer he had heard Brother Isaac use when confronted by some baffling question, "that no man can understand His mind, nor the mystery of His ways."

He walked out the door without looking back at Micah Taul, and made his way to the hitching rail. When he went to Philip's house to speak to the unconverted neighbors, he would not dwell too much on predestination and the doctrine of the Elect. It might only confuse the people.

CHAPTER XIV

IT was full dark by the time John reached home, and he found Anna in bed.

"I'm hurting, John," she said, reaching out a hand to him, her voice barely audible. "I'm getting feared. What made you be gone so long?"

For a moment panic filled him. "Where's Gramma Jennie?"

"She went back to cook up some food for Pa." She clung to his hand. "I'm not hurting too bad," she said after a long indrawing of breath. "Wait till morning before you get her; nothing's going to happen, I can tell."

He hesitated, doubtful, and sat down on the bed beside her and cradled her head against his shoulder. He should not have left her so long, talking Baptist doctrine with Micah Taul. He pressed her swollen, pear-shaped body against his side, and the security of his arms seemed to soothe her. For a long time he sat, his body almost rigid, fearful any movement would disturb her, until her breathing became regular, and she slept.

Before sunup he left for the Townsend house to fetch Gramma Jennie, and he was back with her by midmorning. To his surprise, Anna was up, mixing hoecakes in the kitchen.

"Just like a man," Gramma Jennie grumbled. "Ain't nothing going to happen. You all get het up too soon."

But to John's relief she took charge of the situation as if she were herself responsible for it, and as the days passed life settled into an uneasy routine. Townsend came over to check on the possible arrival of a grandchild, and to assure them that Gramma had cooked up a large enough passel of food to last the family for some time; that Anna's younger sister Pensy, anyway, was well able to look after her father and her brother Hiram. Willy and Maggie drove over with the children one day, and Maggie agreed to come back later when she was needed.

And she was needed exactly on the day Anna had predicted.

Anna stirred John into tingling, instant awareness before daylight on October 15, his own birthday. "Call Gramma quick!" She reached out for him, stifling a moan as she tried to push her puffed body erect.

John was on his feet before she had finished speaking, his nightshirt flapping about his legs, padding to the door leading to Gramma Jennie's room. Before he could knock it was pulled open, and Gramma's bright eyes peered out at him.

"I heard her," she said. "I'm coming." She pulled a woolen wrapper about her shoulders and pushed John aside. "Get your pants on and get out."

"I'll go for Maggie," he said.

Blindly he began fumbling for his clothes back in the bedroom, his eyes focused on Anna's white face. Gramma Jennie thrust his pants and shirt at him. "Forget about Maggie," she said. "Me and Anna can manage." She bent over Anna, and as John struggled into his clothes, he fought against a rising anger and frustration. The old woman was pulling Anna to a sitting position, pushing her feet to the floor. "Hurting pretty good, ain't it, honey?" she said, almost a pleasuring in her voice. "It'll get worse afore it gets better," she went on cheerfully. She turned back to John. "Get out, like I said. And don't bother none about Maggie. It'll be over afore she could get here."

John stumbled out of the room and into the coolness of the early dawn, pulling the slab door shut behind him. He should go for Maggie, no matter what Gramma Jennie said. But maybe he would be needed more here; he should not leave the two women alone at such a time. He walked uncertainly toward the barn, and for want of something better to do, hitched the black devil ox to the plow, half hoping the beast would rebel and give him a chance to work off some of the tension that gripped him. But the ox only tossed his horn, chastened and broken now to harness, and bent his weight against the new, deep-pronged plow Elisha Franklin had hammered into shape for him, drawing it through the unbroken ground of the cedar thicket on the ridge above the house with such strength and sureness John had trouble holding it. By midmorning he felt the trembles which sometimes plagued him when he was hungry. After a time he unhitched the ox and goaded him back to the barn, leaving the plow in the field.

He pushed open the door, a heaviness in his stomach, and looked in cautiously. Gramma had fanned the banked fire in the hearth into a steady flame, and the room was hot. Anna stood clinging to the edge of the table, her face contorted in agony, her eyes squeezed shut. Gramma Jennie was beside her, wiping the beads of perspiration from her forehead with a heavy towel.

"Keep walking, Anna," Gramma Jennie was saying. "Keep walking. It'll help the hurting."

John stared in horror. "You're killing her! She ought to be in bed!" He grabbed Anna and began guiding her toward the bed, her body almost a dead weight against him, her breath coming in low, moaning gusts of sound.

"You keep out of this." Gramma Jennie placed her hands on her hips in a gesture of disgust. "I know what I'm doing. A woman don't have her young'uns in bed. It's walking as does it." She motioned toward a pallet she had placed against the opposite wall. "That's where she'll drop it, kneeling."

"Like an animal?" John almost shouted, his anger mounting. "Anna's no animal! I'm going to get her in bed!"

Gramma Jennie pulled at his arm, trying to push him away from Anna. "Of course women are animals; men, too. She'll birth her baby kneeling on that pallet; it's easier that way. You get out; it ain't decent for you to be here."

John glared at her. "Why ain't it decent? I'm her husband, ain't I?"

They were standing almost toe to toe, Anna clinging to John's arm, Gramma Jennie shaking her finger under his nose, when suddenly the door was flung wide and Maggie stood within the threshold.

She took in the situation at a glance and, without a word, placed her arms about Anna, her strong, capable, understanding presence enveloping them all in a sudden release of tension.

"I had a feeling it would happen today," she said to John, "just like Anna said. It riles me some, you not coming for me."

"I was feared to leave," John said. "Anna's that bad . . ."

"Anna's coming along fine," Gramma Jennie said. "It's him!" She pointed at John as if he were an inanimate thing. "He's plumb fevered!"

Maggie smiled and nodded. "You'd better get out, John," she said, her arms tight about Anna. "This is woman's work. We'll call you when we want you."

John wiped his face with the back of his sleeve, the sweat suddenly pouring from him, and turned and went out of the door.

It was two hours before Gramma Jennie's shrill voice called to him sitting on the rail fence edging his shearing knife against a pocket whetstone, his ears tuned to catch any sound from the house. Gramma Jennie motioned him toward the bedroom.

"Anna knew what she was up to. It's a boy just like she said. She birthed in bed, after all." She spoke tonelessly, a weariness about her now that it was all over. "But it would of been easier my way."

Maggie had come in from the kitchen, starting into the bedroom with a tray in her hand, a broad smile on her face as she glanced at John. "Hyson tea and vinegar, is that what you said, Gramma?" She motioned to the cup on the tray.

"I told you and I told you," Gramma said in weary reiteration. "It's got to have honey in it, too. And all mixed equal and hot to the tongue." She took the tray from Maggie, and as John went into the bedroom, called from the kitchen in shrill, good-natured grumbling, "I'll get it to her after John's left. Right now she won't have eyes for nothing but showing off her birthday present to him."

John looked down at his birthday present, the miracle of life engulfing him. The red, wrinkled face of his son seemed a symbol of God's hand, shaping man through the ages; the spark of life from an ember God had set aglow in the beginning, a glow that would burn to the limitless end of time. The tiny face contorted in a yawn, and John laughed aloud.

"He looks like an Old Testament prophet," he said and knelt beside the bed, running his hand over Anna's hair in a caress of love and wonder and gratitude. "He looks like the greatest priest and judge of all Israel. We should name him Eli."

The winter passed swiftly. The weather held mild, and the roads were open. John found himself roaming the countryside, preaching at scattered settlements in all parts of Wayne and over into Cumberland County, as far away as Burkesville. In March he rode over to the cabin of Philip and Millie near Bethel and spoke to a gathering of friends in their sitting room. But only two families were interested in constituting a church, and he and Philip decided it would be best to wait another year and let the seed they had sown take stronger root before attempting a harvest.

"Besides," he confided to Philip, "I'm disquieted in my mind a little about some of our doctrine." Briefly he told his brother of his discussion with Micah Taul and of the question the lawyer had raised. Could the doctrine of the Elect and the doctrine of original sin not be reconciled?

Philip's reaction did little to help him. "You're toying with sinful doubt again, John," he said. "Stop listening to scoffers like Micah Taul, even if he is a smart lawyer. All God wants us to know is in his Holy Bible, and he's put it into the minds of wiser men than we are to interpret it for us in the *Philadelphia Confession of Faith.* You leave off tampering with questions you can't reason out."

But John could not leave off tampering with perplexing questions. The baffling dilemma Micah Taul had voiced would not be downed. He rode home slowly, his eyes now and then fixed on the dim outline of Poplar Mountain in the distance. He would get to the bottom of the question, just as he had got to the top of Poplar Mountain when a boy, to see what grew at the summit.

Anna was absorbed with the baby, hovering over it constantly. She had regained her strength quickly, permitting Gramma Jennie to return to the Townsend place, but she did not resume the milking, and not until John turned the garden in early April did she get out in the sunshine, which he knew she needed, and do the seeding. Even then she took the baby with her in a basket, keeping it beside her as she worked.

John delighted in her joy and shared it. Eli was a replica of himself; the baby's light-blue eyes were already focusing on objects with something of John's penetrating gaze, and his almost bald head was showing tufts of reddish hair. But the child dominated all of their times together, and he knew it would be useless to attempt to discuss with Anna such an alien topic as Baptist doctrine. Instead he pored over his books, particularly his *Philadelphia Confession of Faith,* with a relentless probing. Somewhere, somehow, he would find the answer.

He fastened the full strength of his mind upon it as he worked in the fields, sifting facts, sorting evidence, and gradually an explanation seeped into his consciousness, not fully born but taking shape.

As each new facet of truth occurred to him he would stop his work and gaze into the sky, as if staring into the face of God, fearful of losing his hold on the thought by shifting his attention even for a moment. Early in May he felt he was on solid ground.

The next day he was up before sunup, impatient to see Micah Taul. But chores about the place demanded his attention, and it was afternoon before he could get away. A light rain had fallen, and the road was muddy and slippery, and old Zeb had trouble keeping his footing. He rode directly to the courthouse and tethered his horse and went to Micah Taul's office. Micah was on the point of leaving.

"Come on back here," he said to the lawyer, "I got to tell you something."

"It's starting to rain again, John, and Dorothy wants me home to fasten the new glass windows I put in the house last week." Micah frowned. "Can you tell it to me quick? You want to bank some money?"

John sat down on the ladder-back chair beside the counter and motioned Micah to close the door. "This is more important than glass windows," he said. "You remember you said you couldn't understand how the conviction of sin folks got to experience could be reconciled with the fact these same people were not only justified at the time of their conviction but had been justified and saved as the Elect from the foundation of the world?"

Micah let out a long sigh. "You're a fanatic, Raccoon John. You're obsessed, plain, stark obsessed. I got no time to talk that nonsense now." He gave a gesture of disdain and motioned toward the door. "Out with you! I'm closing up the office."

John leaned forward. "You're going to listen, Micah," he said firmly. "I been wrestling for the answer, and now I got it, and you're going to hear it. Sit down." He glared at the lawyer, and Micah glared back.

"Get it over quick then," Micah said after a moment.

"Sit down," John said. "You're going to hear it all." He waited until the lawyer had sat himself gingerly in the chair by his desk. "Sit back and relax. Get out your pipe. You're going to hear this."

Micah frowned, and then in resignation shrugged and leaned back in his chair and pulled out his pipe and filled it with tobacco.

"The answer is," John began, "the Lord made two covenants with his people, and they're not contradictory but successive and supplemental."

"They're what?" Micah Taul asked.

"It's this way," John said patiently. "The first is the Covenant of Works, and that concerns all men. Yet since no man can keep the whole law as set down in that covenant, by it some of them are eternally damned."

"Why aren't all of them?"

"Because some of them are Elect; they are the ones who come under the second covenant, the Covenant of Grace. The Elect, foreordained as saved from the beginning of time, are related to both covenants in that they're condemned by the first covenant, the Covenant of Works, but at the same time they are saved by the second, the Covenant of Grace."

"You think you're a second Moses, come to lead the Lord's people out of the wilderness of Calvinism?" Micah said, shaking his head.

John leaned back, trying to appear casual, his hands laced together at the back of his head, his forced informality unable to conceal the jubilant conviction behind his tumbling words.

"I'm trying to clear the wilderness, yes," he said. "What's wrong about that? We're all doing it, one way or another. People get lost in it, and that's what you've done."

"What part does the Holy Spirit play in all this?"

"The Holy Spirit comes to the Elect during their revealing experience and causes them to realize two things: first, their condition as sinners and their condemnation under the Covenant of Works, and second, the fact they are justified, nevertheless, under the Covenant of Grace."

Micah Taul grinned, a grudging grin of admiration. "You've done well, figuring that out." He pursed his lips. "It must be quite a happy surprise to the Elect to discover after all their worry that they have been saved all the time."

John got to his feet. "Every genuine conversion is in strict accord with the doctrine of redemption." He was not sure whether Micah Taul was being sarcastic or complimentary. "It's as plain as a wart on a hog's nose."

"You play a mighty tune on a few words, Raccoon John," Micah said. "But you haven't told me yet how come God chooses only a few folks to be saved? What's the matter with the rest of the people?"

"Why did he make a doodlebug crawl backward?" John spoke more harshly than he intended and was immediately sorry. "Maybe the Lord prefers to select his associates for eternity just like you do when you invite people to your house and leave the rest of them be. Why don't you give the Lord the same right?" He turned toward the door to leave and then swung back. "You know what I think? I think you're under conviction of sin yourself right now, only you're too stubborn to admit it."

Micah Taul threw back his head and laughed. "I'm under conviction you've got a fair head on your shoulders." His eyes sobered. "You've got a good legal reasoning mind. Why don't you get more schooling? You might go far."

"I am going far," John said shortly. "If the Lord is with me, nothing can stop me." He started to open the door, but Micah motioned him to wait.

"You ever hear of Transylvania College up in Lexington?"

John frowned, nodding. "I hear it's a nest of infidels."

Micah smiled. "You mean it's not a Baptist institution," he said. "But it's still a good school. A man recommended by Dr. James Blythe, Transylvania's president, is coming to Monticello to open a school here. His name is Rodes Garth. He's going to begin teaching soon as crops are laid by this summer right here in the big room in the courthouse until we can raise him a building."

John eyed him. "It'll be a school for the young'uns, won't it?"

Micah Taul shrugged. "Mostly," he said. "But anybody wanting to learn can come."

For a moment there was silence in the room. John coughed and shifted his feet and turned again to the door, opening and then closing it, and then opening it again to peer out into the gathering darkness, the rain coming down now in fine, steady drops.

"I couldn't do it, Micah," he said finally. "I got my preaching and the farm and Anna and the baby, and I reckon I'll just have to content myself studying my fair lot of books."

"That's why a little more instruction would help you; you've got an inquiring mind, a reasoning mind. If you ever wanted to quit preaching you'd make a good lawyer. Henry Clay's going to get himself killed one of these days if he keeps on dueling, and you might take his place."

John gave a short laugh. "I don't aim to quit preaching, no matter how much book learning I get. No, I couldn't do it."

Micah Taul got up and came to the door and looked out. "It's for certain you couldn't ride back and forth to that farm of yours every day. But Dorothy and I would be proud to have you put up at our place. We've got an extra room in the new wing I added last year. You could stay there. I'd be glad to have a burr-picking mind like yours to argue with nights, if you'd talk something else than your Baptist doctrine sometimes." He jammed his broad-rimmed hat on his head as they stepped out into the rain. "Think it over, John. You could make arrangements for the care of your stock after crops are laid by. It'd pay you well in the long run. Talk it over with Anna."

Work on the farm consumed the summer months, and John's preaching appointments increased. In July he again visited Philip, and a church at Bethel was constituted with nine members after John had preached a rousing sermon on the doctrine of the two covenants. John agreed to pastor the church, preaching for it once a month, and Philip was chosen as the church clerk. He preached on the same doctrine at the Burkesville Baptist Church in the Cumberland Association, and Brother Isaac insisted he preach it at the Clear Fork Church, declaring John to have had a revelation, indeed, when he had conceived the doctrine, placing him among the minor prophets and anointed ones of the Lord.

John disclaimed such distinction with a tolerant smile, but the acceptance of his clarification of the troublesome Baptist doctrine of redemption whetted his appetite for more learning, and in October, when he celebrated Eli's first birthday by taking Anna and the baby with him into Monticello to bank his corn and hog money with Micah Taul, he looked with unconcealed interest at the new log schoolhouse the town had constructed during the summer on the rise of the hill above the town creek. He tied Zeb to the hitching rail and helped Anna and the baby out of the wagon and walked with them to Joseph Beard's store, and then went into Micah's office and deposited his money. It was court day, and the place was crowded, and he had no opportunity to speak with Micah about the school. But after he had left the courthouse he wandered up the plank sidewalk past a circle of men watching a cock fight and stared at the new two-story structure.

They were riding home when Anna surprised him by mentioning the school herself.

"I was talking to Mrs. Taul in the store," she began, looking at John intently. "Her brother, Ben Gholson, is clerking for Joe Beard, and he showed us some bargains."

"You're a canny one, Anna," John said, patting her knee. "What bargains do you mean?"

"Why didn't you tell me Mr. Taul wanted you to go to that new school they've got in Monticello?"

John slapped the reins hard on old Zeb's rump. The horse was getting old; his eyesight was failing, and his ambling gait sometimes drove John to distraction. But he loved the old horse, and after the animal's first startled reaction to the unaccustomed slapping, he let him resume his slow plodding. "I didn't think it was that important," he said briefly. "I don't need any more schooling."

"Then why are you studying all the time?" she prodded. "Why are you all the time bringing home papers and pamphlets folks give you at your preaching places?" When he didn't answer, she looked down at the baby asleep in her lap. "It's because you think little Eli and me need you at home, isn't it, John?" Her tone was more a statement than a question. "You feel sort of tied down with us."

John smiled and put his arm about her. "Now I should hope you'd be needing me; every man wants to feel needed by his family. But that's not all the reason. I got my farm work and my preaching, and it's about all I can say grace over, I figure."

She was thoughtful for a moment and then, as if dismissing the subject, showed him the calico and the iron skillet she had bought at Joe Beard's store for a bargain.

But that night, as John was on the point of blowing out the candle after evening prayers, she stopped him.

"I want you should go to the school, John." She spoke quietly, sitting on the bed in her shift, braiding her hair. "I been thinking it over, and I want you should go. I figured how we could manage." Simply, concisely, she outlined the plan that had been forming in her mind: her brother, Hiram, could come over and stay nights and look after the stock. He was fifteen and restless at home, fretting under Gramma Jennie's grumpy ways, and he needed to get away. It would give him a chance to practice his reading with John's books; it would help him. John could stay at Mr. Taul's house in Monticello, riding home for Sunday preaching at Mount Pisgah Church, and once a month they would all go to Bethel when he preached there.

John listened at first with the air of resigned patience he often assumed at Anna's chatter, and then with growing interest. Anna was serious; the plan might work. By the time the candle had spluttered to a mass of soft tallow, John had agreed the plan was feasible. If he was going at all, Anna insisted, he should enter at once.

The next morning he found old Zeb dead in the cow lot directly across the creek from where the devil ox had made his fierce stand. John had missed him from his stall in the barn when he went to attend to the morning chores at daybreak but not until he had finished milking did he look for him. It was almost like finding a member of the family dead. The morning dew still glistened on his coarse, roughened brown hide, and only the limpness of his head betrayed the fact that he had stumbled in his half-blind state and broken his neck, bringing the end with merciful swiftness.

The loss of Zeb left him with only the pair of mules. They pulled well in harness, but neither was good for a saddle, so on the following Monday morning he set out to walk the fourteen miles to Monticello rather than attempt to break either of them to the saddle for so important a journey.

It took him a little over three hours, but they were not wasted hours. He planned two sermons as he walked; and he let his mind linger on Anna's almost naive delight in the prospect of his becoming a learned man. He would soon know as much, she said, as the great Henry Clay. Hiram had come over and was already dipping into John's books, and Mr. Townsend, as well as William and Maggie, had agreed to ride over at every opportunity. As a final precaution, he had made Anna practice in loading and firing his Dechard rifle, and he smiled as he recalled how she never failed to squeeze her eyes shut when she pulled the trigger, and of her tendency to fight against the gun stock with the discharge rather than to roll with the recoil. But the one constant danger which threatened every wilderness family—fire—was not mentioned between them. After all, he reassured himself, the house chimney was of rock and stood two feet above the roof, and the fall rains had prevented any tinder dryness. He gave a sigh of relief as he thought of it, and lifted his face to the light snow that began to fall; and then hastened his steps almost to a run. He had never met the new professor, Rodes Garth, and he would rather not be soggy wet and chilled to the bone when he presented himself.

But he was dry and pleasantly warmed by his walk when he entered the schoolhouse. And Mr. Garth was all that he might have expected, he told himself, if he had known what to expect: a hawk-nosed, thin-faced man of about thirty years, who said frankly that he expected to read law on the side while operating the Academy. The school had been opened three weeks, and already thirty-nine pupils were enrolled, with the prospect of fifty before Christmas.

John was not surprised to learn he was the oldest pupil by ten years and, as Robert Ferrill had done in Stockton's Valley school, the new professor asked him to assist in keeping order, hearing him recite after the others were dismissed. And although Rodes Garth was as thorough a schoolmaster as ever Robert Ferrill had been, and perhaps a better one in his general supervision, John felt almost from the first day that the man was not the lover of books Ferrill had been. But he made up for it by his ability to teach orthography and pronunciation.

The writing as well as the meaning of words was basic to all learning, John remembered Ferrill had often said, and their correct pronunciation, especially in public discourse, was equally as important. Already John had noticed that the pronunciation of men he occasionally encountered from northern Kentucky was different from his own, and he was happy to start at once practicing precise and distinctly syllabic utterance which, Garth told him, would in time make him stand out among public speakers as a sunflower among the daisies. His other studies would embrace ancient and Roman history, the Scriptures, arithmetic, and a wide range of reading in mythology, the elements of philosophy, and English history.

But it was in the company of Micah Taul that, as the first week passed, he felt he was receiving the greater education. He had been welcomed into the home with genuine warmth, although Micah's wife, Dorothy, had her hands full with a sickly baby, a girl named

Louisiana, but she merrily called him one of the schoolchildren, along with her two small sons, Thomas Paine Taul, proud of the fact he was seven-going-on-eight, and Algernon, a year younger. The tide of history was ever rolling westward, Micah said, as he guided the fireside talk in the evenings. Specific Baptist doctrines were not mentioned, except in passing reference, as the talk ranged from the day's assignments to the fields of general religion and national politics, and on to the destinies of Colonel Richard Johnson of Georgetown and the eloquent Henry Clay of Lexington, one of whom, Micah declared, would some day be President of the country. Sometimes the talk turned to the increasing troubles of President James Monroe with the arrogant British who, in their wars with Emperor Napoleon of France, seemed to respect no rights of others, least of all those of their former American colonies. And then would come talk of the great orators, as Micah brought out volumes of orations of Caesar and Cicero and Demosthenes and Pericles, and of Edmund Burke and William Penn.

The first week was gone almost before it had begun, it seemed to John, as he trudged back to Horse Hollow on Saturday. He would never have time to learn all that lay locked in the writings of Plato and Aristotle, and of Plutarch and Seneca; or in the law books Micah had let him handle—his Blackstone and Coke, and Kentucky statutes, and a volume of decisions of the great John Marshall of the United States Supreme Court.

Anna had missed him, he knew at once, more than she would admit. Slowly, piecemeal, the week's events were related. Hiram had failed to fasten the rail gate, and the black devil ox had got out; he had been missing for two days before he had wandered back again, hungry, and with a wicked gleam in his eye from the taste of his almost forgotten liberty. One of the cows had calved, and prowling wolves had made off with some chickens and two of Anna's choice geese.

But she insisted he return to the school. She could manage, she said again and again, with a fierceness that betrayed her need to be helpful. To bolster her confidence he assumed a cheerfulness which did not offset his own misgivings, and went back to spend a second week in Monticello, drinking up what knowledge he could, the conviction growing in him that it would not last long.

And he was right. The moment he saw Anna on his trip home the next Saturday, he knew he could not leave her again. Her face was white and strangely drawn, and he noticed for the first time a middle thickness about her.

"Why didn't you tell me?" he said accusingly as he held her at arm's length, studying her.

Her face crumpled into sobs, and her frame shook as he held her to him. "I'm not due until maybe April, I figure," she said when he had quieted her. "You could keep on with the school until then."

But John never returned to the school. "To everything there is a season, and a time to every purpose under heaven," he quoted to William when he and Maggie came over the next week. "My duty is here at home now. It's plain as daylight."

On April 10, 1810, at ten o'clock in the morning, the baby came quickly and easily, a healthy girl.

"I mean as easily," explained Maggie as she laid the squirming bundle in John's arms, "as such things go." She had delivered the baby alone. Gramma Jennie had feebled during the winter and could do little more than sit and scold and give directions, but her tart tongue was silenced, and her flashing, quick-darting eyes grew misty when Anna announced from her bed that the child's name was to be Jennie.

Despite his disappointment in leaving the school, John felt as the weeks passed and summer came that he had never been happier. The work on the farm was endless, but he managed somehow to attend to it in addition to answering calls for preaching from settlements near and far, amazing himself with his ready sermonizing, loving the work with a growing passion. And in July it took little urging from Brother Isaac to convince him he should attend the annual meeting of the Cumberland Baptist Association the last of the month at Somerset in adjacent Pulaski County.

CHAPTER XV

NIGHT was thickening in the hollows when the final sermon of the three-day meeting of the Cumberland Baptist Association at Somerset drew to its sweltering close. Many of the people were staying the night at the camp grove near the Baptist meetinghouse, but John swung his saddlebags over Saul, the bay gelding he had bought to replace old Zebulon, anxious to be on his way.

The Cumberland Association had been formed out of the Tate Creek Association the year before, to bring the dozen or more Baptist churches in the river country into closer fellowship, but as John mingled with the brethren he had more a feeling of alienation. The feeling made him uneasy. Was he getting proud-turned because of his studies and his reading and his success in the pulpit? These were good men, steeped in sound doctrine, sacrificial, humble men for the most part, ready to quote copiously from either the Holy Bible or the *Philadelphia Confession of Faith* at a moment's notice. But too many of them were suspicious of secular learning as the devil's bait. They stared at him blankly, or even in resentment, whenever he mentioned books or events not directly connected with orthodox Baptist matters. They were rousing preachers, most of them, and the souls who fell slain before them were their trumpets in heaven, but their sermons had seemed to him vengeful, filled with the demands and the threats and the wrath of a jealous God, with never a word of his redeeming love. Only a few of them, he knew, were men of studious habits or inclinations; many could do little more than read and write, or figure beyond the rule of three. They depended on the Lord to put the words of truth in their mouths, firm in the conviction they were among the saved, the favorites of heaven, and sin was not in them.

He rode along the narrow trace, thankful for the solitude, grateful for the darkness. He felt a sense of shame; he was tinctured with the devil's stain of self-righteousness. Some of those preachers were the salt of the earth, chosen stewards of God, saints like Isaac Denton and Richard Barrier and Isham Burnet and Jeremiah Vardeman. He smiled in recollection of the towering, big-boned Vardeman, and then he squirmed uncomfortably. The sermons of this man, whose thunderous voice, it was said, could awaken a thousand echoes, had saved the meeting from being a waste of time for him. Jeremiah Vardeman was one of the best-known and most influential Baptist preachers in Kentucky, and a man to reckon with in any encampment of the saints. He had brought his enormous bulk, three hundred pounds well distributed over a six-foot frame, with his pink moon face and stentorian voice, to the meeting for only the first day, and the next morning had gone on to other appointments, hurrying away to mighty deeds. But he had stayed long enough to hammer the Association into a tight, cohesive group of almost fanatical enthusiasm, and to leave the imprint of his dominating personality upon them all. And he had unwittingly, perhaps, planted within John seeds of discontent; holy seeds, John told himself, considering their source and their predicted fruit.

He had recognized Vardeman immediately as the young fiddler in the gay coat and the yellow velvet breeches he had first seen at Crab Orchard Tavern when he had gone to Horine's Mill on the Dix River as a boy of twelve to grind his father's corn during that first hard winter in Stockton's Valley fifteen years before. There was the same ease and grace of movement; the same self-assurance and charm for the women; the same broad, florid, smiling face, topped now by a mass of whitening hair over deep-brown, glowing eyes which could grow stern or limpid; the same full, resolute smiling lips. Bulk had been added, and the clean-shaven features had coarsened and grown stronger, an impetuousness and a smiling impatience now about them accountable by his reputation as an orator and mighty prophet of the Lord; a broad, earthy humor, tolerant and understanding, and not too demanding, John felt, upon sound doctrine. He had not remembered the boy as John Smith, Vardeman admitted, but he recalled the occasion, his short, fat fingers strumming the strings of an imaginary fiddle. All was changed now, Vardeman said, as they reminisced together under a white oak tree before Vardeman preached his final sermon that night from Romans 6:23: "The Wages of Sin is Death." He had not even touched a fiddle in a dozen years except for the glory of God. He laughed a bit ruefully, it seemed to John, as he explained that as a boy he had come under the influence of the worldly Colonel William Whitley, a true patriot of the Revolution but a good example of those who had been ensnared by the writings of the deist, Tom Paine, and the even more unholy teachings of the French philosopher François Voltaire. The result, he said, was that as a young man he had been excluded from the church at Crab Orchard. He had even attended dancing school in the Colonel's home, and for many years had been a scandalous example of sinful frivolity at every neighborhood frolic. But the Lord had touched him at the age of twenty-five, and he had put worldly things away. He had listened to the voice of God, and it had led him, he admitted with disarming candor, to become the greatest preacher in Kentucky.

"You have the gift, too," he told John as he rolled a leaf of thick, brown tobacco between his palms. John had preached that morning on the last verse of the twenty-fifth chapter of St. Matthew: "And these shall go away into everlasting punishment; but the righteous into life eternal." He knew Vardeman had been impressed, because he had praised John later, when he had risen to preach, although he had whispered to him as John took his seat, "You could have borne down more heavily upon the horrors of hell; thus are the saved brought more quickly to revelation of their happy state."

"You could go far," he told him later, "but you must get away from the woods. You must go to the cities where the people are, and the money." He placed a little wad of tobacco leaf inside his cheek and put the remainder carefully away in the tail pocket of his black alpaca coat. "I've heard of you, although I did not know it was the thin, wild-eyed lad who dogged my heels when I was a lost fiddling sinner back at Horine's Mill." He paused, his eyes brightening in recollection. "The Lord was letting me wander then in Gomorrah so I might be able later to warn the people of the venality of sin."

"You've heard of me?" John asked, incredulous.

Vardeman nodded, his attention diverted for the moment by others pressing on them to shake the great man's hand, to bask for a moment in his smile. "Yes, you are well spoken of by many of the brethren, not only because of your gift for words but because of your insight into the true doctrines. Someone related at the last meeting of the North District Association your doctrine of the two covenants. The man who can explain in such clear fashion predestination so that even the dead in Christ can accept it should go far."

John glowed with pleasure. He shifted his feet self-consciously and waited until the big man waved on another group of well-wishers with an imperious motion of his hand. "The Lord has blessed me beyond my deserving," he replied. "Yet I'll admit there are times I'd like to move on," adding hastily, "if it is foreordained, I mean. I'd like to get better advantages for my children." He studied a twig he had picked up and then snapped it in two. "But I'm not trained for the north; I've got no real education; I don't know city ways."

"You're a student," Vardeman said, "and a self-educated man is often the best educated if he keeps on studying like you seem to be doing. Your talents are needed in the bluegrass region, and a man's talents will always make room for him and lead him into the presence of the great." He stopped to shake hands with another group of people, and John started to turn away, but Vardeman called after him, "If you get a call from some church up there, will you come?"

John smiled and shrugged and, without waiting for an answer, Vardeman turned back to a man pulling at his sleeve.

Now John shifted uneasily in his saddle at the recollection, and hastened Saul on with a pressing together of his knees. He had not talked to Vardeman again, and he felt intuitively that the great man had said all he had to say; maybe he felt he had even said too much. What had he meant when he asked if John would come to the north? He shook himself, aware suddenly of his weariness. He had ridden for hours; it would soon be daylight. He brushed his hand across his eyes as the first shimmering rays of light broke through the darkness, filtering through the trees like shafts of light from the throne of God. He would be home in another hour. Anna would not be expecting him so early. He would bag a squirrel or two to take her for his breakfast.

With the advance of summer, rumblings of war began to filter into the mountains of Wayne. England, in its wars with Napoleon of France, was impressing American seamen into the British navy on the trumped-up charge that they were deserters; her frigates, so Micah Taul and Joshua Jones reported, haunted American shores from New England to Florida, stopping and boarding vessels at will and impressing into the King's service not only thousands of American sailors in direct violation of international law but hundreds of other nationals who were obviously never British seamen. But the struggle seemed remote and alien to the interests of the mountain people, the happenings long over by the time they passed by word of mouth through the hills, and the news stirred only dull resentment and loud threats of vengeance after the second dram. There was no declared state of war and no call for volunteers, and although John attended with other young men the monthly musters of the militia under the instruction of Joshua Jones and Micah Taul with zest and much loud talk, his busy round of meetings and preaching appointments and the gathering of the harvest occupied most of his time, and war talk finally died down to little more than threats against the British whenever men gathered to drink and talk.

And then in late August he received a letter from Jeremiah Vardeman inviting him to visit his churches in Montgomery County. There would be a love offering, Vardeman said, which would partially pay his expenses, and he would be housed in the homes of the brethren. There would be the chance to visit Lexington and see for himself the wealth and culture of the bluegrass region, and the opportunities there for a young man of his talents. He owed it to his God and to his family to visit where the harvest was heavy, and the pay was good.

Anna had not been enthusiastic about his going but had conceded it might be the leading of the Lord, and John had ridden away on Saul, his saddlebags filled with fresh clothing and new sermons. He was back in eighteen days, a week sooner than he had expected; a little fatter about his neck and middle, Anna told him, but with a chastisement about him and a gleam in his eyes she had not seen there before.

"I'm not ready for that country, Anna," he confessed. "It's almost a modern Babylon. Lexington has all of nine or ten thousand people, and more pouring in all the time. It'll be the biggest city west of Philadelphia. It's on the town fork of the Elkhorn with a three-story red-brick courthouse right in the center. Long, wide streets run at all angles, all lined with stores and shops: Main Street, Mill Street, Water Street, Cheapside, they all got names. There's a factory where they make cloths and a shop for making women's hats run by a woman named Julia Logan; and a silversmith's place where a man named Samuel Ayers can make anything out of a little silver coin. They've got four big taverns, and one night Brother Vardeman and I stayed at the biggest one, Postlethwaite's Tavern, just to see how the big rich act; and a public place called Vauxhall, all lit up with different-colored lamps every Wednesday night for dancing and play-partying." He paused and shook his head.

"Sounds like they need preaching." Anna said. "Did you do any?" She looked at him closely. "You wasn't too took in with the fancy things you forgot to preach, was you, John?"

"Of course I preached," he said defensively. "I preached at all of Brother Vardeman's churches in Montgomery County—at Spencer's Creek and Lulbegrud and Old Bethel and Grassy Lick. And once I even preached in Lexington in a meetinghouse on Mill Street." He stared at her, his face solemn, his eyes darkened. "But I didn't do so well, Anna. I could tell that. The people didn't seem to warm up none to my preaching. It's my hill talk; I think I even stuttered a little."

She put down her mending and came over and ran her hand through his hair. "The Lord is never absent when you preach, John. I know you done well enough."

He pulled her into his lap. "Brother Vardeman said nice things about me, but I took it he was being kind. He said I showed lots of promise, and several people told me they'd help me find a church up there." He looked at her intently. "Would you like that, Anna? The houses there are prettier than any down here, all lined up back from the streets, three or four hundred of them, and slaves everywhere, all waiting on the white people. And four big churches, all made of weather boarding and brick, and three newspapers and a public library full of books. And you should see the carriages; everybody rides in a carriage."

"I'd druther walk," Anna said, and got up from his lap and began putting away her mending. "My mother's family had fancy things, but they're not befitting church folks, Brother Isaac says, and I wouldn't know what it was to ride in a carriage with slaves waiting on me. I'm trying to be a Christian, John; I wouldn't know how to act with all that finery."

"And there's Transylvania College," John went on, lost in his own musings. "I could maybe go there if we lived thereabouts. Henry Clay taught law there. I walked right by his office with Brother Vardeman, and we'd of spoken to him if he'd been in town because Brother Vardeman knows him. But he's in Washington City now, a member of Congress and a Whig. There's talk he's for war with England; he's saying we could take Canada easy as a man could catch a skunk that robbed his hen roost. I'm a Henry Clay man, I reckon."

"You're God's man," Anna corrected him.

The next year war drums again echoed through the Hollow. A United States frigate, *President*, had been fired upon by an English sloop of war; the English were enlisting the aid of Indians in organizing attacks against the Americans. On the opening day of County Court at Monticello on the first Monday in December, 1811, Judge Nichola Lloyd reported that a month before, General William Henry Harrison had defeated the Shawnee Indians at Tippecanoe in nearby Indiana Territory and had discovered that the guns and powder used by the Indians had been supplied so recently by the English that the wrappings were still on them. "It is high time," the Judge shouted, as John stood in the crowd about the Courthouse, his hand cupped behind his ear to catch the news, "that vigorous young leaders such as Henry Clay, the rising star of the West, take over the nation's affairs from the aging leadership of the Revolutionary fathers and bring both the British and their Indian allies back to their senses."

But within a week great convulsions of the earth drove away even the thoughts of war, for a time at least. According to the recollections of those telling it afterward, there were only a few tremors in the Little South Fork country. But as travelers returned from the market places of Lexington and Louisville and St. Louis, and visiting preachers arrived whose word could not be doubted, and fearful settlers passed through the Hollow seeking safe and solid ground, it soon became plain, as Brother Richard Barrier said, that the fearful earthquakes were a long, overdue, and just punishment of a vengeful God against his wicked people. When the tremors and quakes continued, and were felt as near as Logan County, it served to increase the fear and forebodings of the people, and for weeks afterwards, and well into the summer of 1812, the churches and the prayer meetings in the homes were filled with the lamentations of the fearful, and there were many revealing experiences and conversions, and for a time the scoffers and the scornful dwindled almost to insignificance.

It was Joshua Jones and his brother James who brought the first authentic, detailed news after a hurried visit to New Madrid in the Territory of Missouri, where the earthquakes centered, when they went to rescue their cousin, Aaron. According to Joshua, the wrath of the Almighty had been fearfully evidenced there, and the fright of the people was beyond all description. A violent shaking and thundering of the earth had occurred shortly after midnight on December 16, with sulphurous vapors defiling the nostrils of saints and sinners alike. Hell had opened its dreadful caverns, and the town and all its people had dropped fifteen feet toward the everlasting fires. The Mississippi River had become a tidal wave scouring the countryside, receding as rapidly as it had arisen and stripping the land of all its possessions. Hot sands and burning embers from the brimstone fires had been scattered far and wide. In the unsettled Indian country across the river in west Tennessee, a declivity had been formed a hundred miles long and at some points six miles wide, reaching down to the tip of hell itself. By the grace of God the space had filled with water, making a great lake where dry land had been before. For a time the Mississippi River had even reversed its course, it was said; it had raced upstream beyond the new city of Louisville before the hand of the Almighty had looped it in lightning rings and sent it back again on its established course.

A second tremendous shaking of the New Madrid area occurred on a night late in January, 1812, sent to remind both the sanctified and the damned, Philip told John after talking with a traveler from the region, that the vigilance of the Lord was unending and his vengeance lasted forever. The earth had continued to shake for a solid week, weaving under the feet of the terrified people, and everywhere the penitent were loud in their cries for mercy, and only the most hardened sinners stood resolute against the clear manifestation of God's wrath.

Stories of the disaster were told about every fireside, but not until Brother Isaac, spending the night with John and Anna, related the experience of a Methodist preacher in the holocaust did John find solace he could communicate to the people in the Hollow.

"The gude man told it on himself," said Brother Isaac, "in solemn ignorance that it illustrated as nothing better could do the selfishness and spiritual blindness of souls doomed by unsound doctrine and blissfully on their way to torment."

The man was a tolerable preacher, even considering his Methodist doctrine, according to Brother Isaac. Tobias Johnson by name, he had been asleep with his wife of forty years at the time of the second great quaking and had jumped from his bed like a good Methodist on the bishop's reception committee. Clothed only in his long cotton nightshirt flapping about his shanks, he had run out of the house with the joyous shouts, "My Jesus is coming! My God, my Jesus is coming!"

Behind him came his wife in her own nightgown, the preacher's pants in her hand. "Oh, Mr. Johnson, here's your pants!" she cried. "Wait for me, Mr. Johnson; here's your pants!"

"It's Judgment Dee, and my Lord is here," he called back. "I canna wait for pants or ye!"

"A man shows his real nature, all right, at such times," John commented after the laughter had subsided. "The least the old brother could do would be to put on his pants for the Lord."

The earth tremors gradually subsided and, with the coming of spring, passed into legend. But not so the talk of war. The eloquent Henry Clay of Lexington was the acknowledged leader, so it was said, of the "War Hawks," a group of younger men in Congress demanding war against England unless peace would be had with the self-respect and dignity which befitted a sovereign nation. Since memories were still green of the long war for independence, it was easy enough, John reflected, to stir up war fever against the British, even if the cause against them had not been just. Young men volunteered in increasing numbers for the monthly musters and drills of the Wayne County militia under the spirited leadership of Micah Taul as captain. Instruction was furnished by Joshua Jones and Reuben Coffee and Abraham Hurt, all old enough to have had experience in the first war with England, and now in prime seasoning for another fight. Pa Smith, John remembered, had fought the Redcoats for five years as a matter of duty and religious practice. But Pa had been a single man, Brother Isaac reminded him when John sought his counsel; he had not been a foreordained minister of the Lord sent to tend his mountain sheep in Kentucky. Jonathan and Henry, young and single and vigorous, could represent the family when the need came. But the need had not yet come, Elisha Franklin pointed out when John mentioned the matter to him; there had been no war declared yet; no call for volunteers. And it did seem the Lord had other plans for him, John had to admit, or Anna would not have gone again into the family way at such a time, disturbed and oppressed as she seemed by the warnings the Lord had given in the earthquakes and by the talk of war; a war that could leave the women and small children helpless against wandering ruffians and roving Indians already being inflamed by the British against the people.

When the baby was born on May 30, 1812, another little girl, Anna was left weak and despondent. She seemed almost obsessed, John thought, by fear of Indians now beginning to be seen occasionally filtering through the mountains, although most of them were said to be friendly Cherokees. But when Anna announced that she was naming the baby Elvira, after her own mother, who had passed to heaven when Anna was a child of ten, Gramma Jennie, barely able to hobble about, sat down in the rocker by Anna's bed and said firmly it was a sure sign Anna herself was not long for this troubled world. John scoffed and made light of the remark, but he detected, indeed, that a change had come over Anna. Although she had always been gentle and quiet, she appeared much weakened, almost listless as the weeks passed; her talk became concerned with religion; her free time was spent in reading the Bible.

It was a full week after war against England was declared on June 18, 1812, that the news reached Wayne County. Congressman Richard M. Johnson of Great Crossings proposed to raise five hundred volunteer Kentucky fighting men and go to the immediate aid of General William Hull, holding the fort at Detroit; there were rumors Henry Clay would resign his position as Speaker in the House of Representatives in Washington City and become general of the army; and the muster ground at Monticello began to echo with the sounds of marching feet. Micah Taul, who had been campaigning for Congress against the veteran politician Thomas Montgomery of Lincoln County, lost his race by a majority of sixty-two of the twelve hundred votes cast, and marched away as captain of a company of Kentucky volunteers to join the army of General William Henry Harrison in the Indiana Territory, taking with him Rodes Garth and James Jones. Henry and Jonathan were mustered in at Burkesville, but Jonathan was found to have a weakness in his lungs which made him unfit for military service and was honorably discharged. Henry, sound as a hickory nut, marched joyously away to represent the family in the army of General Winchester, going to the relief of General Hull at Detroit. If the Lord wanted him to go, John reasoned, the Lord would let him know. Men were needed at home to protect the women and children and to raise crops to feed the fighting men; but often, hearing the war talk, he had to fight the impulse to sign up. It would be pleasuring to sit on the golden stairs in heaven some day with Pa and swap tales of how they fought and whipped the British.

The urge to enlist increased when Micah Taul was commissioned as colonel of the Seventh Regiment, offset to a degree by word that the great Shawnee Chief Tecumseh had been killed by Colonel Richard M. Johnson of Great Crossings during the victory over the British and Indians at the Battle of the Thames. War was a fearful business.

"Tecumseh was an enemy, I realize," he told Brother Isaac, during a long walk while on a visit with his mother in Stockton's Valley. "But he was an honorable Indian, fighting for the rights of his people as he saw them. Nevertheless," he paused, groping for words to express his own inner conflict, "it was better to have died like Tecumseh, even in defeat, than never to have fought at all. Even my old schoolteacher Robert Ferrill has volunteered, Ma told me, although he's beyond the fighting age."

Brother Isaac let his blue eyes probe his young friend's face. "I detect a mark of sinful envy in that remark; a sinful pride that aches for glory and power. You should give prayerful thanks unto the Lord that he has shown you your duty, where you will labor in humble, unceasing toil for his name's sake." He walked a few paces in silence. "With all your sanctification, I fear you are still nursing worldly ambition, my boy. If your desire is purely to serve your country, well, the Creeks and the Shawnees are rising over the land, inflamed by the British, and there is wide talk of an Indian confederacy. That means it may soon be safer for a man to be in the army than to remain at home. Your duty is clear. You are needed here."

"Now, Brother Isaac . . ." John began.

"You should be ashamed," Brother Isaac went on as if he had not spoken. "It is all very well for Robert Ferrill to sell what he has and go south to join our great Indian fighter, General Andrew Jackson. But Ferrill is a heretic, God rest his soul, and you are an ordained minister of God, with a family and a flock that needs you."

"Now, Brother Isaac . . ."

"The Indians may again make of Kentucky a dark and bloody ground. With all our young men joining the armies, and many of them seeing no fighting at all except with the bottle, there is great need for men at home to guard the hearths. I'm an old man myself, but I'll do what I can, and here's my thumb on it."

"Brother Isaac, I'm not going!" John spoke desperately, without pride. "I was only thinking..."

"Then you quit nourishing your ambitions and take up your cross. The Lord does not favor a complainer. It is ever the humbler paths that are more difficult, not the glory road. And remember this, my boy"—the broad face broke into a smile at John's genuine discomfort as they stood facing each other in the narrow path—"the Lord in his jealous wrath wreaks just punishment upon the sinful, and he rewards the righteous who follow his words."

For a moment they stood, and then resumed their walk toward the house, a serenity of spirit, an inner glow of peace upon them both which had been absent before.

Brother Isaac was proved right. The dread of marauding Indians or, even worse, of degenerate whites, their blood lusts unleashed by the war, descending upon unprotected households, stalked the land and haunted every cabin. Every Kentucky musket was oiled and primed and placed at the ready over the hearth. And although Henry Clay talked of victory against the British in Congress and Governor Isaac Shelby sent out reports that dwarfed even the exploits of the Revolutionary heroes, and Colonel Richard M. Johnson, credited with killing the great Tecumseh, became a national hero, victory seemed far away. The long-heralded invasion of Canada dwindled into a fiasco, and the Creek Indians in the south, encouraged by the British, captured Fort Mims, a stockade near the junction of the Tombigbee and Alabama rivers, in Mississippi Territory, and massacred over five hundred people.

But then came word of victories at sea. The exploits of the mighty frigate, *Constitution*, and the capture by Commodore Oliver Perry of a British squadron on Lake Erie cheered all hearts. And in April, 1814, the news came that General Andrew Jackson of Tennessee, with the aid of friendly Cherokee Indians, had virtually annihilated the Creek Nation the month before at a battle on the banks of the Tallapoosa River at a place called Horseshoe Bend. As Elisha Franklin said, men could hold up their heads again and be proud they were Americans. The war was the same as won, he said; there would be other battles and other losses, but with the Indians crushed and scattered, the final end could never be in doubt.

A wave of optimism, which could not be overcome even by the burning of Washington City by the British in August, swept the West, and when the government threw open the choice lands of the banished Creeks in Georgia and in the Mississippi Territory to settlers at a patent of $1.25 an acre, and only ten dollars required for every hundred acres entered, the balance payable in four years, a rush of settlers like a swarm of locusts was predicted.

The news fascinated John. The discontent which had been upon him since his encounter with Jeremiah Vardeman was fanned into a new restlessness, and when John Francis, the high sheriff of the county, gave him a closely printed public document describing the lands, he read the entire sheet aloud to Anna. The soil was a heavy loam, the brochure said, rich in limestone, suitable for either cotton or grain. A growing settlement called Huntsville, just below the Tennessee line, boasted an academy where a man's children could receive a finer education than their parents ever had. Anna listened and smiled but said little, and John went to William with his dream.

"I got a feeling it's the Lord's hand," John told his older brother. "The settlers are going to swarm in there, and they'll need preachers."

"And get prosperous?" William smiled at him in understanding. "You got a right to get rich, I reckon, John, like anybody else. You go if you've a mind to. Pa moved from Virginia to Tennessee, and then here to Kentucky."

"If you'd go too, we could maybe enter ten thousand acres together," John said.

William shook his head. "The Lord has called me to be a poor man, and it satisfies me. I got no itching foot like you. You ponder the matter and do what you think is right."

The rest of the year and well into spring, John pondered the matter. He dropped discreet inquiries among friends here and there, feeling them out, seeking advice from only a few. That there was no overt opposition, even from Brother Isaac, he took as a good sign, and Anna's lack of enthusiasm he attributed to the sudden death of Gramma Jennie, who was found dead in her bed one morning in February. The old lady was staying at the cabin with them and had ventured into the cow lot to tend a sick calf in a driving winter rain the week before, and neither he nor Anna had thought much of the slight cough she had developed. Upon Anna's insistence, she was buried in the Mount Pisgah Church burying plot, even though she was not a member. "She was a believer," Anna said. "People have different ways of being believers."

When the news reached Wayne County during the heat of August, 1814, that Henry Clay had been appointed by President Madison as one of the High Commissioners to meet the British High Commissioners at Ghent, Belgium, and arrange the terms of a peace treaty, John knew the war was over at last, and his plans to move into the new country crystallized into a decision. William was rightly settled, as he had said, but John was different. In the new country he could still preach, but he could also farm, maybe thousands of acres; he might actually become rich. His children would have advantages denied them in Wayne. Eli was almost seven, and Jennie was four, both lively youngsters, their restless energy already taxing his ability to satisfy their inquiring minds. Elvira was now two, and then, as though to cap the argument, another baby was born in June, a girl they named Zerelda Ann for the Irish fairies.

It had been a drought year; the pastures were brown, the grass dry, and they had gathered only shriveled nubbins of corn, as he pointed out to James Townsend when he told him of his decision. He had lived in the Little South Fork country for nine years; he owned a leasehold of two hundred acres of fair land, seventy acres of it cleared and arable. He had accumulated a herd of over a hundred beef cattle; his hogs and sheep numbered twice that. The house with the big barn and outbuildings were in good shape. By disposing of the land and some of the stock, he figured he could realize enough to enter five, maybe ten, thousand acres of land in the new country. Townsend agreed it might be a good move; he himself had the Ohio fever and was thinking some of going north. Night after night John and Anna sat by the kitchen table, figuring, planning, dreaming, John's enthusiasm eventually overcoming all misgivings. The Lord was leading him; they would move at once.

By early fall the farm was sold, with some of the stock, and John found himself in possession of fifteen hundred dollars in hard cash. It was an exhilarating moment. A sense of well-being and importance stayed with him for days. At William's urging he placed one thousand dollars of it in the leather pocket of a locked oaken strong box disguised as a tool chest which William made for him and kept only five hundred dollars in his money belt. "That way," William said, "it will always be with you if you need it all, but what's in your money belt will be enough to get you started, and the rest is safer in case of Indians." John secured the promise of Isaac Storey, the Baptist preacher who had come to the region, to take over the Mount Pisgah and the Bethel churches, and Anna's father agreed to allow her brother and sister, Hiram and Pensy, to accompany them on the journey. They could benefit from the experience and could help with the work.

The future was as bright as the promises of God.

CHAPTER XVI

A LIGHT frost covered the ground the morning in late October when they pulled away from the warm cabin of William and Maggie, where they had spent the last night, and headed south. John had packed the jolt wagon only with the essentials needed to start life in the new country, leaving room for a hassock for Pensy and the two older children on the wagon floor. Anna sat in a chair in the rear of the wagon leading a pack horse on which John had fitted a saddle with leather thongs with which to tie on bundles of cooking pots, and across which he placed two creels with hickory withes in the fashion of a crate, one on each side, to carry bedclothes and a baby in each. He drove the team, sitting on a narrow plank, and Hiram rode John's horse, Saul, acting as drover for the fifty head of cattle and eighty-five hogs John had decided to take along.

They followed Little South Fork down to Wolf River, fording it at a narrow bend, and by nightfall were within sight of the Tennessee line. John left the Indian trace and turned into the head of a hollow to make camp, mindful of rumored Indian raids. They rested the next day; the children foraged along the trace and returned with a basket of wild berries and grapes sufficient for all of them. The next morning they entered Tennessee and joined the Kentucky Road; the country cleared somewhat, and a scattering of houses and settlements began to appear. But before nightfall it had grown hilly, almost mountainous, and two days later they descended into the fertile land that surrounded the village of Sparta. Black locusts, hickory, and towering oaks had edged the road, and the hogs, John knew, would fatten on the acorn mast.

The sky was threatening when they pushed out from Sparta, and by noon the rain was coming down in torrents. The road swerved to the east, and they ferried Caney Fork with a pig-tailed man named Rock Martin. Before nightfall they crossed Collins River, swollen into a surging torrent that reached the planking of the narrow bridge, and were grateful for the shelter of a tavern at the settlement of Shellsford. All night the rain hammered against the walls of the two-story log house, and the next morning they lingered until it slacked somewhat while the dish-faced proprietor, Christian Shell, ground corn for them at his mill and entertained them with stories of bear hunting in nearby Ben Lomand Mountain.

Two days later they crossed Looney's Trace and by nightfall were in McMinnville. All day the road had been sheeted with rain, and they welcomed the warmth of Marbury House, staying the following day to give John and Hiram a chance to grease the wagon wheels from the tar bucket swung underneath the wagon. John had filled it with pine resin before they left, and now he rubbed the tar liberally on the hickory axles and oak hubs, covered solidly with a coat of mud.

By morning the sky had cleared; the air was sharp. Eli and Jennie were happy as larks to be freed from the confines of the wagon. "Don't step on any spiders or it'll bring on more rain," Anna cautioned them as they ran beside the lumbering wagon jolting along the rutted road, exploring the heavy growth of reeds that outlined the widening trace, marveling at the wild sunflowers that lined the banks of Elk River. They ferried the river and took a buffalo trace to the settlement of Winchester, camping for the night in a grove of beech and black locust, the leaves rustling in the night air. The next morning John picked up information about the Mississippi Territory, now less than twenty miles distant. Three hunters were returning from the region, and advised him to go into Madison County just across the Territory line in what was beginning to be called Alabama country, and enter his claim at Huntsville. Nearby was Hickory Flats, they said, where a blockhouse provided protection in case of Indian attack.

A day's journey and they camped at Beatty's Spring, entertained that night by a troupe of performing bears, and the next morning John rode down the single planked street of Huntsville, leaving Anna and the children at the campsite with Hiram in charge of the stock, and went directly to the new brick courthouse. He would enter no claim as yet, he had decided. He would take his time and look about, studying the country. Meanwhile, he would seek shelter for the family in a rented cabin.

The red-haired county clerk eyed him shrewdly, adjusting his cartridge belt slung across his hips. Yes, there were cabins to be had, and land to be worked, provided a man had a will to do it. Five miles east near Hickory Flats, he said, a house that seemed to fit John's needs could be had for a reasonable fee. They followed his directions and found the place after an inquiry at a two-story log house at the second fork.

"The cabin is only a couple of miles over the rise," said the lean, soldierly man who answered John's call from the road. He came to the wagon and extended his hand. "My name is Archibald Woods," he said. "The cabin belongs to my daughter, Mrs. Anna Miller, widowed last year." He looked the family over with friendly interest. "You all light and stay the night. Plenty of room here, with only me and my daughter left to fill it. We would be your nearest neighbors, and it would pleasure us to get acquainted."

John thanked him but demurred. It was still early afternoon; they could reach the place and be settled by nightfall. They were on the point of leaving when a woman appeared around the corner of the barn, pushing her sunbonnet to the back of her head, holding her voluminous, sagging apron gingerly by the corners. "Anna's been gathering eggs," Mr. Woods said by way of introduction as she came to the wagon and surveyed the group with welcoming eyes.

"We'd be mighty proud to have good neighbors," she said, smiling at Anna. "It would seem good to have a woman about. That cabin's been empty since my man Timothy was killed by Indians last fall. We lived there happy for most a year and planned on fixing up the place. It ain't much, but it's got two pole beds and a wall table that will come in handy." She looked in frank curiosity over their belongings. "You all take some of these eggs; they'll make good eating for a day or two until you get some fowl of your own." She peered into the wagon for a container. "You sure got no extry pots! Here!"

She pulled off her bonnet and filled it with eggs, handing it to Anna. "When you run out, just ask for more. You can get me the bonnet back any time."

Woods returned with a bucket of water from a well by the fence. He handed a gourdful in turn to each member of the family. "Best water in the county," he said. "Better even than the water over at Anna's place. Send your boy up for a bucketful now and then."

It was with a comfortable feeling that John headed the little procession on to the cabin. They had fallen among friends; Archibald Woods and his daughter, Anna Miller, would make good neighbors and good landlords.

A narrow lane, scarcely more than a footpath, led over a slope, and within an hour they came in sight of their new home. The four-room cabin, they found, was full of dust and cobwebs; the only flooring was hard-packed earth. A wide, wooden chimney almost filled the end wall of the main room; the window openings, covered with paper smeared with bear grease, were not shuttered. But the chinking was solid, and the place would give shelter. A fenced pen and a shed secured the stock. By nightfall the wagon was unloaded, pallets made on the pole beds and on the floor, and Anna had a stew of squirrel meat steaming in the iron kettle on the open hearth.

Life settled into a pleasant routine. The weather held mild for November, and John made frequent trips into Huntsville for supplies, and for possible land to file for entry.

"Best public land is to east of the settlement," the clerk told him. "Some folks living over there was in here couple days ago. I told them you was looking, and they wondered was you related to old George Smith who used to live on the Holston over in east Tennessee."

John smiled his delight. "He was my father!" he exclaimed. "I'd pleasure to know them. Who would they be?"

"Old man Guy Groton and his wife Nell," the clerk said. "They got a place southeast of here, ten or twelve miles. He was doing some preaching for the Baptists around about, but he's getting too old to do much shouting now. He's a purty good man."

John nodded. He had heard Pa speak of Guy Groton. He had been among those emigrating with the Smith family from Virginia into the valley of the Holston, but he had traveled on still further, penetrating into the interior of the Free State of Franklin. Pa had heard from him by way of travelers a few times; of his fights with the Indians; his exploits in fighting bears. And then nothing more.

"I'm journeying over that way to see him," John said when he related the news to Anna. "There's a Baptist church thereabouts needing a preacher, and I can stay over Sunday and give them a sermon."

Christmas came and went, with only a visit from Anna Miller and her father, Archibald Woods, to mark the day as different from any other. They sat about the hearth, recalling early days of Indian fighting, discussing crops, speculating with John on possible land nearby to mark for entry.

"We're a poor country now," Woods said, "but just wait. The land here is rich and full of promise. Give a man like yourself a couple of years, and you'll be lord of your surroundings. You get a good parcel of land and build yourself a big house; the land will support you plenty. You can even get yourself some slaves, Smith."

John shifted uncomfortably. "Don't know as I'd ever do that," he said.

"Timothy was all set to buy one," Anna Miller said. "And what with the good home we'd provide him, he'd be better off than being sold down the river. A body like you, Mr. Smith, would be doing a black a good turn to buy him."

"I reckon there's something to what you say," John admitted. "But only if there was no other way to keep a farm going, only then would I consider it. And even then, it don't seem right."

But the idea took root, and two weeks later, as he started out on Saturday morning to look up his father's old friend, he let his imagination toy with the possibilities the future might hold. The January morning was crisp, and the blood raced in his veins as he pushed Saul into a gallop. The world seemed his for the taking; his cup was running over. In a few years, as Archibald Woods had said, he could possess a thousand acres, with a house as big as that of Joshua Jones. Slaves would do his bidding, happy, carefree in his benevolent care. His children would never know the privations he had endured; he would sponsor schools everywhere, and his preaching would go on and on until the countryside rang with his good name and his good deeds. And the Lord would bless him like Jacob and his brethren.

The dream lingered with him as he visited with his father's old friends. He found the Grotons in comfortable surroundings, their cabin warm with the life of forty years. Nell Groton was a toothless, withered little woman, hobbling about, bent almost double, but she took delight in ladling out hot soup as they sat about the kitchen hearth, and hearty helpings of wild turkey and slabs of venison. They sat talking far into the night, and when John slipped under the bear-skin rug on a pallet in the far corner of the family room, he fell instantly asleep, happy in the confidence this was only the beginning of the good things to come.

A heavy beating against the outer wall of the room woke him. Sleepily he opened his eyes. It was not yet light, the black shape of the block table by the wall looking like a huge bear in the darkness. Slowly he located the sound. It was a pounding on the door.

Guy Groton was on his feet now, his nightshirt flapping about his ankles as he slid the heavy bar from its cradle and loosened the door. The door swung open and John sat upright.

In the opening, outlined against the first streaks of dawn, was the towering figure of Archibald Woods. John saw his eyes rove the room and come to rest on him.

"I've come to fetch you, Smith," he said, his voice edged with excitement. "I've bad news! You're needed at home."

John stared, speechless. Was he having a nightmare? "Bad news?" he echoed. "What bad news?" He pushed himself to his feet and thrust his legs into his breeches.

From the pole bed on the far side of the room Nell Groton's high, cracked voice called out. "Bad news travels too fast," she said, climbing from the bed. "Wait until I fix you gruel afore you tell it."

"No waiting!" Woods said hoarsely. He came into the room and suddenly, as if collapsing, sank into the high-backed rocker.

"What happened?" John asked, his voice strangely quiet. "Tell me, Mr. Woods, what has happened?"

Woods turned and looked at him, his face ghostly in the half-darkness of the room. "Your cabin burned," he said, his voice thick. "The wooden chimney caught fire and the place burned."

John felt frozen, unable to move. "Anna?" he found the voice to say at last. "The children? Anna got them out?"

Archibald Woods stood up slowly and held on to the back of the chair. "Mrs. Smith had gone to be with a neighbor in sickness," he said. The ominous calm of his voice sent a tremor through John, and he reached out and clutched his shoulder.

"The children?" he demanded. "The children were saved?"

"Two of the children were saved by the boy Hiram and his sister. The other two . . ."

The words were left dangling, the thick silence of the room broken only by the wheezened breathing of old Nell Groton. John never remembered Woods finishing his explanation; he never knew how he got out of the house and on his horse; he remembered nothing of the unrelenting wild ride over the half-frozen slush of the muddy trace of a road.

It was midmorning when their lathered horses came to a stop before the still glowing embers of what had been his cabin. Neighbors were grouped about, some poking in the ruins, others morbidly curious, most of them staring in silent sympathy. Hiram and Pensy, wide-eyed in shock, were standing near Anna, sitting on a tree stump holding the baby, Zerelda, partly covered by a blanket someone had placed about her, one arm about Jennie. She was staring in glazed, stupefied disbelief at the ruins.

Horror beat against John's brain. Only charred remnants of the cabin remained; not a stick of their furnishings, not a wisp of cloth. Only smoldering heaps of embers, crazily stacked, small wisps of smoke drifting into the limitless blue sky of the January morning.

Anna looked up at him as John laid a hand on her shoulder, her eyes vacant. "Eli and Elvira are gone," she said tonelessly. "Eli and Elvira were burned to death."

It was not until the next day that John found the courage to sift in the ruins. He found a small, ragged lump of silver, the residue of his coins, but when he turned up three charred bones he turned in horror from the task. Silently, Archibald Woods took the forked stick from him and motioned him away. The next morning Woods showed him a handful of coins which had somehow remained intact.

"I also found a few more bones," he confided to John when Anna was out of hearing. "But I thought it best . . ."

John nodded. He had no wish to see them.

Late that afternoon, Guy and Nell Groton drove up in their gig, and in the glory of a brilliant sunset the old man conducted a simple funeral service over the pine box which contained all that was mortal of the two children. Burial was beside a young white oak which would live a hundred years, the preacher said, reminding generations to come of the unfathomable design of the Almighty God. And although the neighbors found release in tears, Anna remained locked in her grief, a blank, unheeding rigidity about her.

John gratefully accepted shelter for the family in a loft room of the Woods house. Although Anna gave way to her grief after the first terrifying few days, it did not lessen. Instead her sobs pulsated through the house, her anguish fed by self-reproach. She should not have left the children the night of the fire; she had been careless in caring for them. John consoled her as best he could, sitting often with her in the brisk open air on a log near the edge of the clearing wrapped in a bearskin rug.

"Jesus has reclaimed his own," he repeated over and over. But the words were awkward, like strange, unwieldly instruments in his hands. Slowly they etched in his own mind a gnawing doubt. How did he know the children were reclaimed? Were they of the Elect? He tried to persuade himself that only the Elect would be taken so young, that God in his infinite mercy would want only his own, but there was little reassurance in the thought. The children had not been baptized; they had not received the revealing experience. How could he be sure they were in heaven? The relentless doctrine of the Elect became unbearable. Could his innocent children, the pride and hope of his life, be at this moment suffering the torments of the eternally damned? It was unthinkable!

He determined at whatever cost to save Anna from the agony of his doubts, but to his astonishment and relief, she never questioned their heavenly destination, although, as the days wore on, her distress and self-abasement deepened, and nothing he could say could comfort her. Helplessly he watched as she became hollow-cheeked and remote, sitting for long periods in the kitchen with Anna Miller, staring sightlessly at the wall in brooding melancholy.

"I'd best file a claim for some land right away," John told her at the end of the week. "It will be good for us to go about normal things again. It is the Lord's will."

Plans for the future began to take form. They would stay at the Woods home until a place was secured; Anna would be able to care for the two children, and Hiram and Pensy could return to Kentucky. "I can raise a cabin in no time, once I get some land of my own," John said to Archibald Woods. "And Anna can busy herself with the furnishings; it will do her good to have something to do. All the stock has been saved, and I can farm and preach and take up my plans again."

His plans? He paused at the thought, but Woods was nodding in agreement. The future could still hold wonderful things; the land was there, waiting to yield its riches. "God's still in his heaven." Anna Miller cheerfully reminded him.

In February he rode into Huntsville, driving a dozen sheep and hogs to the market, accompanied by Hiram and Pensy in a two-wheeled cart on their return to Kentucky. They would carry back more detailed word of the tragedy than John had been able to write to the family, and take assurance that life still held hope and promise.

But no suitable claims were available, John found, and although he made frequent trips into Huntsville in the following weeks, and pored over the big record book in the courthouse, he postponed making a decision. He helped Archibald Woods with his spring planting and looked after the stock, hopeful that the spring weather would bring a surge of new life to Anna. But February slipped into March, and she did not respond. He talked cheerfully with Woods and Anna Miller of his dreams for the future, but in the darkness of the night, sleepless on his pallet in the loft-room corner, his mind increasingly centered on a torturous unwinding of the circumstances that had brought on this horror. Step by step he retraced his disastrous course. Somewhere along the way God had receded behind the beckoning lure of worldly gain. At such times he would slip from under the covers and stand for long minutes at the window, pushing its shutter ajar to stare into the night. Was this retribution?

He was still groping his way to an answer when Anna sickened early in April. As he watched over her, he realized with the clarity of remorse that she had never possessed the lusty earthiness of other pioneer women. There was no coarse, tough fiber of strength in her. She was soft and tender, full of gentleness and goodness, but with little resiliency to the blows of fate. She lay in a stupor for four days, scarcely breathing, her body growing gradually rigid, her staring eyes without expression. She died at the week's end.

Archibald Woods and a neighbor dug a grave near the ruins of the cabin. Again Pa Smith's old friend, Guy Groton, was summoned, and conducted the funeral service, a reverent, brief service, humbly unquestioning of God's ways. The pine box was lowered in the dark, soggy earth as John stood with his arms about Jennie, and Anna Miller held the baby, Zerelda. Rain had started to fall, and a biting wind whistled through the leafing trees. That night John had his first chill.

The next day he was fevered, and the chills were frequent and more severe. Anna Miller secured the services of a passing physician, who pronounced John afflicted with the cold plague and offered little hope for his recovery. The world became vast and formless, time without beginning or end. Pain racked his body and yet seemed remote. At times he could make out the shadow of leafing branches on the bare floor when the sunlight beamed through the window, and knew it was spring, but the days and nights ran together, and life held no meaning. As the days grew hot, his fever-racked body cried for water, but the doctor had forbidden it, Anna Miller told him, her voice sounding afar off as she gently ministered to him, and he could sense Archibald Woods bending over him in solicitous sympathy in response to his piteous pleas.

It was early in June that Archibald Woods spoke in grim determination, after looking at John's pinched face and bloated, purplish lips. "If a man has to die, he shouldn't be forced to die in agony like this," he called to his daughter in the kitchen. "Fetch me some fresh well water, Anna. And fetch it quick!"

A minute later John felt a wet, dripping gourd pressed to his lips. He tried to open his eyes, but the effort seemed too great. Feebly he fastened his teeth about the edge and gulped. The water burned his parched throat and trickled down into his body, through his bowels, tingling into his very toes. Frenzied, he opened his eyes, begging for more, and Woods again held the cool gourd to his lips.

"You've killed him," Anna Miller whispered hoarsely from the doorway as John's head fell back, his ravished body exhausted. "Pa, you shouldn't have done it!"

Archibald Woods shook his head. "I don't care what that doctor said. I can't believe pure well water can hurt a thirsty, dying body," he said. "It's the water of life."

John heard the words from a distance. A relieving drowsiness enveloped him. He was dying, he knew it now; such relief as he felt could come only by death. His body seemed no longer to ache;

the burning throb of pain was eased. His mouth fell open, and he slept.

By the end of June John was able to sit in the shade of the maples back of the house. His body was empty of all strength, sucked dry by the plague. His nerves were shattered, and his arms shook with palsy. But as the days passed he began easing himself out of his chair, tottering about on crutches at first, talking with the children who had been well sheltered and cared for by generous neighbors during his long illness, examining the garden plot. Slowly, imperceptibly, strength seeped into him. Energy would come, and then it would go; but always it returned with renewed force. And with it his will to live deepened, and grew strong.

One course only was clear to him. He must rally his resources for the greatest battle of his life. He must retrace his steps back to Kentucky, back to the moment in time when he had relinquished his soul to the lure of riches.

Book 2

". . . but now mine eye
seeth thee."

CHAPTER XVII

JOHN felt the sun on his closed eyelids, warm and penetrating. He let his thin fingers slide along the edge of the woolen blanket of the corner-walled bed, exploring, identifying his surroundings. "I'm home," he thought. "I'm not dreaming; I'm home again!" He turned to move on his side, but a sharp pain in his neck stopped him. He heard a door creak on its leather hinges, and then a movement in the room. A wet cloth was laid on his forehead. Slowly he opened his eyes.

The sun was streaming in the room through the open window above him, falling across the worn puncheon floor, dancing in shattered lights against the stone hearth. Against the edge of the bed, distorted by the closeness to his eyes, he made out two brown-stained, moccasined feet, a strength in their immobility. He moved stiffly, and his eyes traveled up the voluminous linsey skirt that met the ankles, past the sack blouse, up to the shrewd, kindly, anxious face that bent above him.

He moved his head again. The crick in his neck was not so painful now, and he raised his hand and pulled away the cloth on his forehead.

"Ma, don't look so scared. I'm all right."

"I know you are. You're tough, John, just like your ma." She smiled, her gray eyes crinkled in quick relief. "But the Irish pookas almost got you this time. You been sleeping like you was dead."

He stirred and tried to sit up.

She reached down and tousled his hair. "Get your pantaloons on and come sit on the doorstone. It's high noon. Jonathan went to meet the postrider; he'll be back soon. I'll get you some breakfast."

He watched her bustle out of the room through the plank door that led to the shed kitchen, and lay still until the door settled into place and the sound of eggs sizzling in a skillet of bacon grease reached him. Then he swung his feet off the pallet and pushed himself slowly upright.

He pulled on the breeches he had thrown against the cane-bottom chair, ran his socked feet into his mud-splattered moccasins, and went into the kitchen. Ma was bending over the crane in the hearth, flapping hoecakes, and he patted her on the back as he pushed past her and went outside.

"You and Jonathan are making out real handy, Ma." He dipped a gourd of water from the wooden bucket by the door and splashed it against his face. "Jonathan fixing to marry?"

"He's thinking some of it," she said. "With Henry and Jane and Fancy Mae married and gone, he pretends he has to look after me. But I can make out; either Jane or Fancy Mae or any of the others would be glad I should come to help with their babies. Jonathan's too sobersides; he needs you to rile him up some, John. He's old before his time."

"He's most two years younger'n me," John said. "But I'm thirty; that's getting along, Ma." He ran a quill comb through his shock of hair and took the wooden platter of eggs and hoecakes his mother poked out the doorway, and sat down on the doorstone, his legs stretched in front of him. The platter shook on his knees, and he put it on the ground beside him and pulled his legs back, tucking them under him. "I've got a trembling, Ma, from my sickness, but the doctor I saw in Huntsville as I came through said it would pass." He grinned cheerfully in answer to her questioning eyes, a new sense of vitality surging through him.

She sat down on a log bench beside him. "Tell me about it, John; tell me about everything."

He picked up a hoecake as though studying it before he spoke. And then the Creek Indian country sprang to life as he lived again in the retelling the days of hope and promise, the nights of hardship and dread, until they flowed together in the tragedy of the fire and the weeks when he lay suspended between life and death, his bones aching, his mind in torment.

His mother listened without comment. When he had finished, she stood up and took his empty plate. "The Lord's vengeance is always certain, John. The wages of sin . . ." She paused, her eyes misty. "You was seeking sinful riches, and you a born preacher. Preachers got no call going off after such. Lusting after the flesh, that's what it was." She looked at him, reflecting. "You think you can get your place back over in Wayne?"

John shook his head. "I wouldn't want it; it's too remindful of Anna, and it's too big. But I wrote Willy a while back to keep an eye out for a smaller parcel, maybe fifty, sixty acres nearby. As soon as I get it, I'll start farming, and do some preaching again. I want to get my two girls back soon. I'll ever be grateful to a neighbor woman for looking after them. But they're mine."

"You should have brought them with you," Ma said. "I could've looked after them." She studied him, her eyes suddenly glowing. "Why don't you settle right here in Cumberland County? Mr. Townsend's gone to Ohio with his two young'uns, and there's no call for you to go back to Wayne. Jonathan and you could farm together." She hesitated and then went on, "You could help him with his preaching."

John grimaced. "Jonathan and me don't see eye to eye, Ma; you know that. He talks too much hell and damnation, too much about folks being foreordained before the foundation of the world." He stopped abruptly, his face suddenly lined with thoughts of his tragedy. "I'm better off being near Willy over in Wayne. Besides, I like the farming over there; this here land is corned to death."

A shout from the cow pasture, and Jonathan came into view, waving his arm in greeting. John watched him splash through the creek and ride up the slope to the yard and swing from the saddle.

"Your vittles are ready, Jonathan," Ma called to him, and then said to John, "Know he's about starved; he's been gone since sunup."

The lean, hard-muscled figure hobbled his bay mare and came toward them, a faint smile about his eyes at sight of John. "I figured you was that wore out last night when you come in, you'd be sleeping in today," he said. He sat down on the bench and took off his straw hat and fanned himself. "You make eating sound too important, Ma. Man does not live by bread alone."

John gave a short laugh. "You got Scripture for everything, haven't you, Jonathan?" he said. "What does the Book say about trying to live without bread?"

Jonathan ignored the thrust. He reached into the wallet of his linsey shirt and pulled out an envelope. "This here's for you, John."

He handed John the envelope and looked at his mother. "Reckon the girls are all right, or they'd have written."

Ma nodded to hide the disappointment in her face. "Leastways Fancy's time is not here yet. I figured it wouldn't be till last of this month." She turned to John. "Fancy's having her first young'un, and I promised to go over soon as she lets me know. She and Jason bought forty acres from Tom Stockton back of Clear Fork, but the postrider goes within couple miles of their place, and she can get me word easy." She glanced curiously at the letter in John's hand.

John slit open the single sheet of paper and read the finely lettered script through twice before he looked up. It was from Jeremiah Vardeman.

"Brother Vardeman wants me to come to Crab Orchard next week," he said. "It's a meeting of the Tate's Creek Association."

Ma looked her pleasure. "You go, John," she said. "It's the Lord's leading. He's a big preacher; you do like he says."

Jonathan leaned forward, nodding agreement. "It would help you to get back into preaching, John," he said.

John frowned. "I was planning on going back to Hickory Flats as soon as I'm rested and get my little girls."

"I been aiming to see some of that country," Jonathan said quickly. "I could go easy, following your trace. I'd be proud to go and bring them back."

John rubbed his hand over the stubble of beard on his chin and looked out over the slope to where Poplar Mountain reared its head. The noon heat was on the land; the air shimmered in waves across the cow pasture. "I don't know, I don't know." He spoke slowly, crushing the letter in his hand. "They're mainly town preachers in the Tate's Creek Association. They're sort of highfalutin. I've been trying to improve my speech, and I've kept up my studying and reading, but I don't know if I should mingle with them yet. And besides..." He looked at Ma standing in the narrow doorway that led to the kitchen, fanning herself with her apron. "You won't like this, Ma. Brother Vardeman says some of the brethren heard of my affliction and have taken an offering for me." He watched his mother narrowly. "Like as I should take it?"

Ma looked at him, her eyes troubled, and then looked at Jonathan. But Jonathan's face was stolid, giving no sign. Jonathan would not take it, John knew she was thinking. Jonathan was proud-turned.

She wheeled about and started to hone some knives on the whetstone before she spoke.

"Charity's bitter bread," she said finally, "but you brought it on yourself, John, and you must pay for it. You could use the money."

"Christians should help one another," Jonathan spoke suddenly, his words surprising them. "And a real Christian will allow as how he could let other folks help him. You're thinking only of yourself, John; it'll do those high-toned preachers good to have a body like you to help."

"But they don't know I brought my troubles on myself being worldly-minded. I don't know as how they'd be so glad to help if they knew."

Ma turned the whetstone vigorously. "None of them preachers are saints. Look at Brother Isaac . . . even he's not so sanctified he couldn't be better. He got himself two more parcels of land hereabouts lately. He's got notions . . ."

Jonathan lifted his hand in protest. "Now, Ma, don't go rattling off like that. Brother Denton is a man of God if I ever seen one. Who picks on him picks on me."

"Jonathan's fixing to preach for him next Sunday," Ma said to John. "He and Brother Isaac are real close." She started into the house and then came back. "Get off those pantaloons and fetch me that cotton coat you had on when you rode in last night," she said. She tugged at an iron kettle behind the door and handed it to Jonathan. "Fill it with creek water and put it on that fire block. I can wash those clothes in no time." She motioned John toward his feet. "Scrape the mud off them moccasins, and they'll be fitten; you can take Jonathan's new wool socks for Sunday preaching."

"Brother Isaac's been like a second father, a sort of Baptist saint to all of us," John said. "I think I'll be riding over to see him tomorrow."

"Isaac Denton is maybe as good a man as most people think he is," Ma said, a glimmer of a smile about her lips. "He'll be good for you."

As John rode over to Brother Isaac's the next afternoon, his spirits lifted with every mile of the rugged, familiar roadway he had known and loved since boyhood. He found the aging preacher, now past sixty, his sturdy body leaned with the buffeting of the years, shelling corn in the shadow of his barn.

"I knew you'd be over," Brother Isaac said after the greetings were over. "Jonathan said they were expecting you, and I knew you'd come see me right off." He motioned to the wooden tub of corn. "I'm shelling corn to take to the mill. You want to help me shell?"

John laughed and sat down on the bench and picked up a handful of ears. "You're always working, aren't you, Brother Isaac? I figure you even work at something in your sleep."

"Aye!" Brother Isaac agreed. "Sometimes I work out my sermons in my dreams. Maybe that's the reason my people act like sleepwalkers." He chuckled, a low, throaty sound. "Where is the Lord leading you, John? Back to Stockton's Valley? I could use a fine young preacher to help me here."

John shook his head. "The Lord would not be putting a saint into bed with a sinner. And a sinner I am. I lusted for the fleshpots, and the Lord dealt with me."

"Thank his holy name!" said Brother Isaac reverently. "For whom the Lord loveth he chasteneth, and scourgeth every son whom he receiveth. The Lord loves you, John."

"I know," said John. He tossed the stripped cob into a trough and picked up another ear to shell. "And the Psalmist said, 'Blessed is the man who thou chasteneth, O Lord, and teachest him out of thy law.' I know that Scripture, too. I learned my lesson. I'll never go lusting after riches again. All I got left is a little money and my wagon and one mule and my two little girls. All my cattle and hogs wandered away or got stole while I was sick, even my pacing horse, Saul. I can stand the loss of all that, Brother Isaac, but Anna and the two babies . . ."

"We'll not talk of it now," Brother Isaac interrupted firmly. "Let's talk of your friends, the angels the Lord caused to stand guard over you. Let's talk of . . ."

"It was way last January," John went on as if Brother Isaac had not spoken, "but it seems like yesterday. It was Saturday night when it happened, the seventh day of January, and . . ."

"And it was the next day, January 8, if I remember rightly," Brother Isaac broke in firmly, "that the Lord permitted General Andrew Jackson to give the British a beating at New Orleans, a sound beating they'll never forget."

"I never thought you was much interested in war talk," John said, crossing his legs, his tension easing. He began shelling the ear of corn he was holding, rubbing it against his palms. "That is, unless it was war against the devil, or in self-defense."

"The British represented the devil in this case," Brother Isaac said. "And it was a war of self-defense. Henry Clay had already signed the peace treaty over there in Belgium, but Jackson didn't know it. Anyway, both Clay and Jackson are heroes now; with proper prayer, either of them, or maybe both of them, will be President some day. I'd be pleasured to vote for both of them."

"Me, too," John nodded, relaxed, smiling at the old preacher's stratagem in changing the subject from his tragedy. "Although I favor Clay some, him being a Kentuckian."

"Indade, and so would I, and for the same reason," said Brother Isaac, "although there are human frailties in the man. I recall he was the leader in a state lottery to raise four thousand dollars to build a house of public worship in Frankfort. And it not even a Baptist meetinghouse. I would never preach in such a place. Nor would any man consecrated of God."

"Aye, 'tis a shame," agreed John, smiling, falling into his way of speech. "It will take much prayer, and many long sermons to rid the place of the devilish smell of it. But at least 'twas for a holy purpose, and there is hope."

"And there is hope for General Jackson, too," Brother Isaac went on. "I na misdoubt he has seen the error of his ways, gaming and dueling as he was wont. Both vices are abominations in the sight of God."

"The Dickinson duel was an affair of honor," explained John. "Lawyer Dickinson had made slurs about the General's wife, Rachel, as I heard it. And the General even held his fire until Dickinson had given him a bullet which he will carry to his grave."

"But it was still a duel," insisted Brother Isaac. "And it all began over gambling debts, horse racing, that idle pleasuring of the rich. There are other ways to settle disputes. 'Vengeance is mine, saith the Lord'; that's why I leave my enemies to the Lord for punishment."

"I'd never want to be your enemy," said John. "I know no man who has the ear of the Lord more than you."

"You're my Timothy," said Brother Isaac gently. "And Jonathan, too. He is to preach for me Sunday at Clear Fork. And the following Sunday, would you preach, John?"

John shook his head. "I've been asked to attend the Tate's Creek Association meeting at Crab Orchard," he said, and pulled out the letter from Jeremiah Vardeman.

Brother Isaac read it slowly, nodding in agreement. "Go, by all means. Be yourself. There is but one Raccoon John Smith, and there will never be another. Let the spirit lead you, and be ever gracious in His sight."

It was Saturday afternoon a week later before John reached the clearing that surrounded the Baptist meetinghouse at Crab Orchard. It had been a dusty trip of three days' steady riding on the new bay gelding he had bought from Tom Stockton; the weather hot, with rumblings of distant thunder. He slept one night in the shelter of a hollow sycamore and the other night in the canebrake, eating as he rode along, the corn pone and slices of turkey breast Ma had wrapped for him in moist, soft deerskin. The trace led up the Dix River Valley, the bottom lands covered with red haw and clover, the silence broken only by the chatter of birds and the distant cawing of crows. Twice he had stopped to gather wild grapes, but his horse had run strong and easy, and most of the time he had pushed steadily ahead.

As he entered the clearing he looked curiously at the log fort, peopling it with the early settlers who had built it as a refuge from Indian attacks. He let his horse follow his head to a stream bordering a grove of poplars that shaded the meetinghouse a quarter mile farther on, and waited until the animal drank his fill. Then he slid off and hitched him to a sapling and looked about.

The afternoon meeting was about to begin. Men milled about, walking along the pathways toward the meetinghouse; they wore rough clothes, but they were clean; a few had their womenfolks with them. John tugged at his faded, striped cotton coat Ma had washed, now again dusty and clammy with the sweat of the trip. He should have worn his buckskin breeches and hunting shirt, as Ma had said, and saved his clean pantaloons and coat for the meeting. "Be yourself," Brother Isaac had said. "There is but one Raccoon John Smith; let the spirit lead you." He almost laughed aloud as he thought of Brother Isaac's gentle words, a lightness of spirit upon him he would not have thought possible a week before. He rubbed his hand across his bristling chin; he almost had a beard. He should have had Jonathan clip his hair; it straggled over his neck, almost to his shoulders. He straightened and adjusted the hat Jonathan had given him; its scissor bill made him look sharp as a raccoon caught in a tree, Jonathan had said. He grinned at the thought; he had never particularly liked his nickname, nor disliked it. He started to whistle, hastening his steps. The big speakings were about to begin.

Three boys blocked the path ahead, laughing, eying him; long-legged splinters of boys in the morning of life, with never a thought of the struggles ahead. As he reached them, they stepped aside.

"Good morning, Father Abraham," one of them said soberly, while the others doubled in laughter. "We wish you good day."

"Good morning, boys," John said. He forced his face into a gravity he did not feel.

He heard the scamper of feet behind him, and then a crashing through the undergrowth as the boys circled him and went on ahead. At a clump of walnut trees they waited, bowing low as he approached.

"Good morning, Father Isaac," another one said. "We wish you good day."

Gravely, John bowed in return. "And a good day to you," he said.

Again the scampering of feet, and beyond a bend in the path ahead, the three again awaited him.

"Good morning, Father Jacob," the tallest boy said, his high-pitched voice forced deep in his throat.

John stopped and faced them, as grave as though about to pronounce a benediction. "Good morning, boys," he said, his voice deep in mild reproof. "But you are mistaken. I am not Father Abraham, nor am I Father Isaac nor Father Jacob. My name is Saul, son of Kish, and I was sent to search for my father's three lost jackasses. And lo, I have found them." He reached out as if to grasp them, but the boys, startled for a moment, wheeled and raced away as though pursued.

John looked after them, his face crinkled in laughter he made no effort to restrain. It was good to be alive and to feel young again. They were smart boys and knew the Scriptures. They would make good Baptists.

At the door of the meetinghouse he joined the group standing about and looked in. A high pulpit stand of puncheon logs faced the rows of backless benches, already well filled. People crowded past him, the men taking seats in the center, the women grouped across the aisles on either side. The meetinghouse was too small for the group; people were spilling over into the aisles and against the walls.

A large, florid-faced man behind the pulpit stand began intoning a prayer, his thick brows drawn together in concentration over keen black eyes which opened with the final words and cast an appraising glance over the assembled group. John looked about for Jeremiah Vardeman, but the crowd pressed against him, and he had difficulty hearing the speaker. He touched the shoulder of a man standing beside him.

"Who's that talking?" he whispered.

The man stared at him, surprised. "Why, that's Jacob Creath. Everybody knows him." He looked at John in curiosity. "Did you catch what he said? Seems he's asking us all to get out, the place is too crowded. The meeting is to be held in the grove." John nodded and turned silently toward the door as the crowd started to move, but the stranger grasped his arm.

"Would you be Raccoon John Smith?"

John's eyes widened. "I am that," he said. He was puzzled for a moment, and then he grinned. "And I heard you preach at Clear Fork once–you're Brother Tom Hansford!"

Brother Hansford pumped his hand warmly, and in genial welcome threw an arm across John's shoulder. "I was delegated to keep an eye out for you," he said. "Brother Vardeman was detained and won't be here. He said I should get you to preach for us; the session this afternoon is given over to hearing the visitors."

John grimaced. "With all these preachers here? No, Brother Hansford, I'm not ready to preach. I just rode in, and I'm dirty; I've been sick and . . ."

"I know of your affliction." Hansford shook his head in understanding. "But trouble makes great souls all the greater. The Lord chastises those whom he loves." He looked about as he steered John out the door and toward the stand being carried from the church to the grove. "Two smart young fellows are lined up to exhort, but I'm not sure they can hold the crowd." He fished in a leather pouch slung across his hips and handed John a small cloth bag tied with a draw string. "Brother Vardeman said to give you this," he said.

John fumbled with it, and poured out the contents of coins in his hand. Slowly he counted them—fifty-five dollars and twelve and and a half cents. He felt the blood rush to his face. Misery filled him. "I'm not stone-broke, Brother Hansford. I've got me a stake left, and I've got my pride. I've never taken charity in all my life."

Hansford slapped him on the shoulder. "Christian love is not charity; it's God's way of working through men. We fulfill his purposes when we give it and when we receive it. That's the way Brother Vardeman meant it."

"Maybe I can preach for it then," John said, drawing the string on the bag and thrusting it in his shirt pocket. "But I warn you"—he shook his head—"I'm not like you northern Kentucky preachers. I'm trying to mend my speech, but I'm plain from the hill country. If those two young educated fellows can't preach to suit the people, you can't expect them to listen to me."

The crowd had gathered on benches and split logs placed before the stand, and John could hear murmurings of disappointment that Jacob Creath was not to preach. Next to Vardeman, Creath was the best orator among the Baptist preachers in all Kentucky. But a polite silence fell as two young men in store-bought clothes mounted the stand. For almost an hour they expounded their themes, one following the other, their solemn, pretentious speech a monotonous rhythm of obviously memorized words.

John sat on the grass near the stand. He could see Jacob Creath on the front row in a cane chair someone had brought out for him, his shoulders slightly stooped, his proud head with its shock of black hair rigidly erect. He gave the impression he was listening closely, but at the conclusion of the second discourse John heard his resonant voice, toned with music, boom out on the opening line of a familiar hymn as if he knew the need to hold the crowd. And there was need for it, John could see; people were beginning to drift away in twos and threes and in groups.

Prompted by a sudden compulsion, John got to his feet. "Stay, friends," he called, "and hear what the great Augustine said!" He jumped upon the stand. People moving to the edge of the crowd turned, puzzled, curious at the sound of the new voice. He waited a moment and then his voice, imperative, rang out over the crowd. "Augustine said he wished he might have seen three things during his lifetime: Rome in her glory and purity; Paul on Mars Hill; and Jesus in the flesh." He looked down and caught the eye of Jacob Creath, staring at him in open-mouthed wonder. For a moment their gaze held, and then the great preacher's face broke into a wide smile, and he nodded vigorously. "Will you not stay?" John called again. "Stay, and hear what the great Cato said!"

Movement at the edge of the crowd ceased, expectant faces were turned toward him, and men cupped their ears the better to hear.

"Cato," he said, "repented of three things before his death: that he had ever spent an idle day; that he had ever gone on a voyage by water when he could have made the same journey by land; that he had ever told the secrets of his bosom to a woman." A ripple of laughter ran through the crowd.

"Come, friends, and hear what the great Thales thanked the gods for! Three things: that he was endowed with reason and was not a brute; that he was a Greek and not a Barbarian; that he was a man and not a woman."

John noticed a man near the front nudge his companion, his eyes fixed on John in sudden recognition. "He's Raccoon John Smith from down on Little South Fork." The man's hoarse whisper was plainly audible.

"Yes, I'm John Smith from the rocks and rills of the Cumberland in Stockton's Valley," John called out as if in answer. "In my country saltpeter caves abound, and raccoons run in packs. On that wild frontier we had neither schools nor many books when I was a boy; consequently, I stand before you today as a man without an education except in the hard school of experience. But, my brethren, even in that ill-favored region, as the world would call it, the Lord in his good time found me. He showed me his wondrous grace and called me to preach the everlasting gospel of his son. Redemption! Redemption!" He let his voice ring out with the warmth of his conviction. "He sent redemption to his people; he hath commanded his covenant forever, holy and reverend is his name."

He paused as the crowd seemed to sway forward, and then he swung into a sermon on redemption, realizing, as his words rang with compelling vibrancy, that it would forever be his favorite theme. "Let the redeemed of the Lord say so!" he cried as memories of his own temptation and fall and punishment and redemption flooded his mind. For an hour he spoke, his audience barely moving, his words bringing to life and new meaning the nature of redemption through the sufferings and death of Jesus, and the saving grace of the resurrected Christ in the preservation of the saints.

The sun was casting long shadows in the grove as he finished. He stood for a moment as the lowing of a brood cow came from the clearing behind the meetinghouse and the smell of wood smoke drifted toward them. Then, explosively, the silence was broken.

"Glory to God in the highest!" came a shout from the audience. Like the rolling of a drum the shout was taken up by others. "Hallelujah! Amen! Glory be to God!"

John jumped from the stand. Perspiration was streaming from his face, and he mopped his forehead with the sleeve of his striped coat. He felt an arm about his shoulders, gripping him, and turned to find himself in the embrace of Jacob Creath. For a moment they stood speechless, the older man's eyes beaming into his, an understanding between them deeper than words. And then the people swarmed about them.

CHAPTER XVIII

IT was a week before John returned to Stockton's Valley. The brethren attending the Tate's Creek Association at Crab Orchard had insisted he preach again before they adjourned on Monday, and he had been urged to stop on the way down the Dix River country at several homes. At each place he found neighbors assembled, good people, earnest and hard-working, who made up the bone and sinew of the church. He sat with them about the cabin clearings in the cool of the long dusks, pouring out his heart on the theme of God's redeeming love, and their hungry attention, their genuine response amazed him.

A sense of confidence began returning to him, and with it a sense of wonder. God had chastised him and now was ready to use him. Yet he was no different from other men; God chastised every man in some way. And he could use every man. Every man, that is, who would let God have his way. Martin Luther, he recalled, had said that every true believer is his own priest. The words had meant little to John when he had first read them, but now they struck him with force. That was the only call to preach a man needed. Suddenly his voice broke the stillness of the rugged trail. "All right, Lord," he cried out. "Use me! I'm your man!" The words echoed against the dense undergrowth and the high cliffs edging the narrow road winding along the bank of the river. "Use me!" But where?

He pulled on the reins sharply, recalling his promise to Jacob Creath to visit northern Kentucky. He had been drawn to Jacob Creath, his admiration increasing as their friendship had developed during the remaining days of the meeting. He was a great preacher, and John could learn from him, if only he could be with him, preach alongside him. He attempted a gesture he had noticed Creath affect, and aloud he repeated the twenty-third Psalm, imitating the stentorian tones of the man, pulling himself up in the saddle with Creath's erectness.

As he entered the clearing at Ma's place, he saw the wagon he had left in Hickory Flats pushed against the rain barrel, and he knew Jonathan was back with the girls. The reunion was warm and tender. They had both grown, he decided, studying them at arm's length, even in the several weeks since he had left them. Jennie was five, a serious, thin child, resembling Gramma Jennie in her appearance but with a warmth and affection about her that reminded him of her mother. Zerelda, a little over one year old, was robust and lively, toddling everywhere, plain talking. Both of them were a handful for his mother, he could see, but her affection for them was genuine. He was glad he had brought some calico from Crab Orchard as well as a sack of meal and some lead and a pound of salt.

The next day William rode over from Wayne County with good news. Isaac Storey, the preacher who had taken the pastoral oversight of the Mount Pisgah and Bethel churches when John left for the south, was willing to sell John eighty acres of his holdings.

"It's north and some east of your old place, and a good twenty miles from my parcel," William explained. "But pretty fair land, pasturewise. North Fork runs plumb through it, providing water, and I figure what with your preaching, you'll go in more for hogs and cattle than pure farming. You can raise enough corn in the bottom land, anyway, to feed out."

John's inspection of the land bore out William's words, and within a week he had paid four hundred dollars to Isaac Storey for the land, the last of the money he had left, and was in receipt of an official-looking deed from the preacher and his wife Abigail.

He tried to puzzle out the document as he entered it for filing with John Chrisman, Micah Taul's nephew, who had succeeded him as clerk of the county court at Monticello. Slowly he read: "... beginning at the black oak and sugar tree of the south side of 1 degree fork in Benjamin Atkin's line running thence with said line N 9 E 109 poles to two hickory and poplar trees, thence N 34 W 155 poles to John Parmley's line ..." He shook his head. Legal descriptions baffled him, and he wished Micah Taul were still around to explain them, or even Rodes Garth. But Professor Garth was now a lawyer and a Wayne County representative in the state legislature up in Frankfort, and Micah Taul was in Washington City, a congressman now, elected while John had been in the Alabama country and still proud, so Jonathan said, that he had defeated Judge Montgomery of Lincoln County at last for the office by over twelve hundred votes. "I didn't figure there were that many folks took time from crops to go vote," John said. He smiled at the recollection of Micah Taul and his manner of talk, but he liked the man. He would ever be grateful to him for his encouragement and his friendship.

A two-room cabin was on the place, and early in September John moved his few belongings over the twelve-mile road and set up housekeeping by himself. Ma insisted on keeping the two little girls. "For a while," she said as he prepared to leave. But she looked at him, a knowing, shrewdly appraising glance, and bluntly added, "I mean, until you find yourself a wife."

"Don't know as I ever want another wife, Ma," he answered, and walked quickly out of the house. It wasn't just rebellion at the thought of anyone taking Anna's place. He was uneasy in his mind. Jacob Creath had said about the same thing, but he had also added something about the rich widows in the bluegrass region. He swung his loaded pack over his horse and scrambled up on the saddle. Maybe he did need a wife, but to marry a woman for worldly gain would be his final, unforgivable sin before the Almighty, especially after all that he had done. He had to look sharp; the devil was ever ready to tempt a man at his weakest.

All of September he worked about the place, clearing space for a garden in the spring, building quarters for the stock he would eventually secure, making ready the cabin for the children; investing the place with his mark until he felt a sense of belonging; almost compulsively forging it into an anchor which would hold him to the hill country.

Isaac Storey had taken charge of three other churches further east and was glad to relinquish Mount Pisgah and Bethel to John's ministrations. He preached at both places on alternate Sundays, rousing, compassionate sermons on God's all-embracing love, and with no mention of Baptist doctrine. He admitted to himself that he questioned some of it, and it worried him; to stress it, insisting on its full acceptance by others, seemed less than honest to him. Yet to air his doubts would serve no good purpose. Instead he cried again and again with Isaiah, "Come ye, and let us walk in the light of the Lord!"

Several evenings of every week were spent at neighborhood gatherings, social warmth and prayer times mingling so thoroughly that the nature of the occasions was indistinguishable. His sermons at such times were both rollicking and heartwarming, filled with a new tenderness, Maggie told him. "You got the spirit of God about you someway, John," she said. "It's like your trouble's made him more real to you."

Elisha Franklin's house was open to him as often as he could use it for the religious instruction of the children of the community. John Parmley owned four slave families now, the only slaveholder in the Hollow, and several times he asked John to preach to his blacks in a grove back of his sprawling house, an experience which always left John with a sense of exhaustion as he closed his message in the name of their Lord and Saviour, Jesus Christ.

Joseph Hurt's two-story house, closer by, was the scene of more lighthearted gatherings. Joseph Hurt's wife had died while John was away, and his daughter Nancy was keeping house for him and her two younger brothers. William and Maggie drove over frequently, bringing eggs and fresh milk and kettles of soup on which he feasted for days, and the brothers exchanged help in the fields as each needed it. William had made a new clearing the winter before, but one thing and another had prevented the logrolling in the spring. Now, on the last day in September, the neighbors were assembling for the event.

John left his cabin early and had ridden the twenty miles by a little after sunup. It was a brisk morning, cool with little wind, and Chinker, the hound Jonathan had given him, ran ahead of him, sniffing out rabbit nests, baying, eager for a hunt. But John whistled her back, and the dog zigzagged in and out of the underbrush that lined the steep downgrade trail. Most of the other neighbors were already there, the men surveying the felled logs, the women busying themselves with preparation for the noonday dinner. John hobbled his horse and swung his felling ax and handspike over his shoulder as he made for the group of men.

The logs were large, some of them twice the height of a man, none of them under three feet across. It was a wonder William had felled them so clean. William and John Parmley directed the men as they lined up, five or six to a side of the bigger logs, inserting their handspikes underneath, and slowly, as William shouted the count, heaving them up by main strength and staggering with them to the log heap. It was burdensome work, but the men were all muscle, and John felt an exhilaration as he matched his steps in rhythm with the other men. Two logs were close enough to be rolled, and he and Joseph Hurt heaved, tugged, and swung them into place for the burning. Between each effort there was loud laughter and happy talk, and John relished the friendly banter and led in the songs, full of rhythm, tuneful, that punctuated the day. All morning they worked, and by early afternoon the logs were in place and the burning started, and John found himself beside Joseph Hurt in the circle of men around the fire as the women served them heaping wooden plates of food.

Nancy Hurt was among them, a slender young woman of twenty-two. The other women wore sunbonnets, but Nancy had pushed her bonnet back until it hung between her shoulders and her molasses-colored hair, braided tight about her head, glinted in the sun. It made a pretty sight, John thought, but he paid her no special mind until he saw the other women glancing at them as Nancy brought him a platter of corncakes baked on the hot stones and a choice piece of broiled venison steak. Her voluminous linsey skirt swept his knees in passing, and he frowned, annoyed at the thumping in his breast. The chattering women were witches; tongue-waggers who couldn't let a widowed man alone. He shifted closer to Joseph Hurt as if for comfort; and then he realized Hurt himself was a widower, and together they were sitting ducks for gossip. He grinned and poked furiously at the food on his plate. When Nancy came again with a helping of corn pudding, he sat cool and easy and looked directly at her. Her eyes were amber, darker than her hair and almost brown but with the same glint of gold in them. They were seeing eyes, he thought, honest eyes that would betoken a sharp mind and a strong will. Rachel Parmley giggled across the circle and, after finishing his corn pudding, he rose to his feet.

"I'm getting back," he said to no one in particular. "Can't stay the night." He turned to William standing near the burning logs. "I'm promised to go north next week."

He surprised himself with the statement, but in a manner of speaking it was true. He had written Jacob Creath to expect him within the fortnight, but the decision seemed to come impulsively, and he felt the quick tightening of interest in the little circle. And then Elisha Franklin called out.

"Don't let them bluegrass people lure you away, John; we need preaching here just as bad."

"Couldn't be those rich widow women thereabouts have anything to do with your going, could it now?" John Parmley said, and a chorus of laughing banter arose.

"John, don't you fail to come back." Maggie turned with a tray of food she was taking back to the house and looked at him knowingly. "We need you here. Now don't you go fooling around!"

The talk was general for a few minutes, and then he went around the circle, his lean, lanky figure moving quickly, passing a quip here, pressing a hard calloused hand there. A trip was not taken lightly by these friends, and the fabled bluegrass region beyond the Cumberland River was a land unknown to some of them; the city of Lexington on the other side of the world.

He came to Nancy, standing at the moment beside her father, and could almost physically feel in the back of his neck the eyes of the others on him. They were well-meaning, warm-hearted friends, and their interest was only human. Nancy alone seemed oblivious of it as she solemnly shook his hand and said, her voice clear and distinct for every listening ear, "Do you want I should miss you, Mr. Smith?"

He felt his face flush, but he returned the look of her steady eyes. He had been right; she did have a fresh, almost an alarming candor about her. He started to give a half-joking reply, but something in her manner stopped him. "That I do, Miss Nancy," he said, his voice clear and firm. "That I do."

The early morning fog in the bottoms had not yet lifted from the fields of cane stubble when John rode away three days later. An extension of the old Tellico Indian trace, now called the Jacksboro road, had been cleared the year before to reach the salt wells in Wayne, and John took this trace, crossing South Fork at Long Springs, and going on to Tatesville.

He rode slowly, savoring the beauty about him. The trees were turning to gold, some of them yellow as butter, and cast an amber haze through which the sun filtered. The hillsides were alive with red sumac, and flocks of wild geese flying south now and then darkened the sun.

From Crab Orchard he went to Logan's Station and pressed north through Danville, and entered Jessamine County. For a full day he rode along the palisades of the Kentucky River, marveling at the sheer walls of limestone rising three hundred feet from the river bed, extending all of seventy-five miles in both directions, farther than the eye could see.

He had written Jacob Creath he would meet him at Nicholasville, but as he neared the town apprehension filled him. Suppose Mr. Creath should be disappointed in him? How would his homely sermons compare with those of the great preacher? He rode past Todd's Tavern twice before he stopped and tied his horse at the hitching rail between two stagecoaches. Their drivers were on the boardwalk in front of the Tavern playing bottle ante, flipping their long whips at coins on the top of whiskey bottles, attempting to knock off the coins without upsetting the bottles. He watched them for a moment and then went inside.

Jacob Creath was waiting for him in the common room. "I've made appointments for you to preach in almost every settlement around here!" He spoke with pleasure rippling in his deep, almost musical voice, his dark eyes flashing in the warmth of welcome. "It will take a couple of months itinerating. Can the folks in Wayne spare you that long?"

John laughed. "I don't have that many sermons, Brother Creath. I'll run out of thunder." And then he sobered. "But I reckon we all preach mainly one sermon after all," he went on, "the love and mercy of God. We just serve it up in different words."

Creath smiled. "You're given to joking, I can see. It's a healthy habit; I envy you."

"Well, old John Calvin himself said that the chief end of man is to glorify God and enjoy him forever," John replied. "A lot of folks need to be reminded of it; they forget to enjoy him."

"But they're good people, just the same. You'll be preaching to good people up here."

"You mean they think they're good. I'd rather be preaching to those who think they're damned," John said. "They're more ready to listen. But I reckon they all need to be converted."

They reached the room assigned to them, and John dumped his saddlebags on the floor and started to unpack. His linen coat would be badly wrinkled. Mr. Creath removed his cravat and poured water from the ironstone pitcher into the washbowl. He scrubbed his face and hands vigorously and dumped the water into the high wooden jar before he spoke.

"They need to be converted, but to convert them to the gospel alone would leave them wide open for any sect to come in and claim them." He was drying his face with the rough towel from the rack, and his voice was muffled, and John turned to listen. "We want to be sure they're converted to the Baptist faith."

John reflected for a moment, and then pulled his shirt over his head. He needed to wash up. "You mean I should stress our Baptist doctrine as set out in our *Confession of Faith?*" he asked cautiously.

"The inroads the Methodists and Presbyterians are making are pretty heavy," Creath said. "We Baptist preachers have to proclaim the truth. And next to the Bible itself our *Philadelphia Confession of Faith* is the greatest depository of truth ever given to the people."

John stared out the half-opened window beside the washstand. "I often think now of what Paul said to Timothy," he said quietly. "What we preach is not ourselves but Jesus Christ as Lord."

But Jacob Creath's gentle warning stuck in his mind. The service that night in the Baptist meetinghouse in Nicholasville found John filled with admiration for his eloquence. Never had he heard such diction, such persuasive pleading, such euphonious phrases; it was oratory at its best; it was the way he yearned to talk. By comparison his own style, improved as he had tried to make it, would appear ludicrous; beside Mr. Creath's dignity of bearing his own gangling awkwardness would be humiliating. But as the sermon developed, he squirmed uncomfortably. He just couldn't hanker after stressing such fine Baptist points; it was almost unseemly. Brother Isaac believed that way, but he wasn't all the time preaching it. It was as if church folks up in this fancy bluegrass region were, as Mr. Creath had intimated, more in competition with each other than with the devil.

John cleared his throat and walked with assumed dignity to the stand when his sermon was announced. In unconscious imitation of the deep tones and precise enunciation of the great Creath, he read his text from the tenth verse of the first chapter of Second Corinthians: "Who delivered us from so great a death, and doth deliver."

The people looked tired now, he thought, almost listless, although Creath had preached only a half hour. It was as though his natural eloquence had drained them and left them empty, unready just yet to accept the homilies of lesser men. He repeated the text, and suddenly he felt again his own struggles at dawn in the spicewood thicket, the hope that came like a gleam of starlight, delivering him from so great a death. He pushed to the back of his mind his desire to emulate the great preacher; he fell into his natural speech, his guileless sincerity illuminating one after another his homely illustrations, until he knew he was imparting his own profound conviction that the power of God as men discovered it for themselves in the Holy Bible and in the lives of the saints was the only power that could help in this life and save from the death eternal. But as he spoke he kept one eye on Jacob Creath; the other, he hoped, was on the Recording Angel.

Even before he sat down he knew the people had responded. Jacob Creath, he knew, had felt it too.

"You're a breath of fresh air, Brother Raccoon John," Creath told him as they walked back under the stars to their lodgings, leading their horses. "You preach with the passion of a redeemed man." He shook his head. "God knows we need such preaching."

For a moment they walked in silence, and then the older man went on, measuring his words. "But you need to be careful. Urging people to read the Bible is fine, but to interpret it for themselves, well, that could lead to trouble."

In the darkness John frowned, but his voice was light when he spoke. "Maybe," he said. "But I'm the kind that has to sort of reason things out for myself, and I'm beginning to get the notion any man's got the right to examine the sacred writings and exercise the sense God gave him. He doesn't have to believe a thing just because the church believes it, and in exactly the same way the church believes it; he ought to use his God-given reason to find the truth the Lord ordained for him, and once he finds it, to act accordingly."

"Not so loud, my boy, not so loud." Creath sighed gently. "Maybe in God's good time men will be given the wisdom to do that, but today . . ." He leaned closer to John's ear. "That's heresy!"

From Nicholasville the trip became a blurred succession of chicken dinners, preaching appointments, new faces. In homes, in store buildings, in open clearings lighted by pine torches, in rudely constructed meetinghouses and in fancy church buildings the two men preached. By unspoken agreement each supplemented the other: Mr. Creath stressed the peculiar Baptist doctrines, and John expounded on the simple gospel. They penetrated the remote areas of neighboring counties, swinging south and then west, and after six weeks again turned east and entered Fayette County. Twice Creath had nudged him when handsomely dressed widows had lingered after services, chatting, urging attentions on them with pointed interest, but John had given no acknowledgment, and the matter of his widowed state was never mentioned.

"Isn't Cane Ridge meetinghouse hereabouts?" John asked Creath as they were riding along a tree-lined roadway in Fayette County. "I'd give a plenty to see the campsite of that revival."

"It's in Bourbon County to the north," Creath said. "I've appointments set up in Lexington for tomorrow, and we'd best hasten on. Could be we'll run across the Cane Ridge preacher, Barton Stone, in Lexington. He's a good friend of mine even if he is a heretic. He started one of his peculiar churches there this year and preaches for it once a month."

"I'd be pleasured to see that preacher again," John said. He told of their encounter years before in Logan County. "The last I heard of him, the Presbyterians had expelled him."

Jacob Creath shifted in his saddle. "They didn't exactly expel him," he said. "Stone left of his own accord when he felt he could no longer subscribe to their creed. That's the long and short of it. He went to Tennessee for a time, but he's back now, starting churches all over the state which will never amount to a thing." He coughed uneasily, and then went on. "That's why I warned you, Brother John, not to trifle with the Baptist doctrine in your preaching. Keep your doubts to yourself; airing them will only lead to loss of power and influence, as it has with Barton Stone. He's a fine man and a good preacher, but he's a heretic of the worst sort."

The biting cold of mid-November was turning the red and gold of the autumn foliage into a brown, dry brittleness. John had brought leather breeches for rough trips but only two tow-linen shirts and a single cotton coat. He hugged the coat now about him tightly; he would have to buy a woolen garment. He felt the coins in his wallet. At most points a free-will offering had been given the men; his share would be enough to buy a shawl.

It was not quite noon when they crossed the wooden bridge of the Town Fork of Elkhorn Creek and found themselves on Main Street in Lexington. The brick sidewalks seemed to John thronged with people; the planked streets more heavily crowded with handsome carriages than on his first visit five years before. The market house on Cheapside had been enlarged; and nearby was a new auction block for slaves, and a whipping post. He pulled in his horse and stared, and started to ask about them, a revulsion in him, but Jacob Creath was pointing out the log library building on the corner of the public square. Jordan's Row, between Main and Second Streets, he reminded John, was where most of the big lawyers like Henry Clay had their offices, and farther up Main Cross was the celebrated Transylvania College.

They stopped at the Sheaf of Wheat Tavern on the south side of Main Street between Jordan's Row and Mulberry. It was less costly, Creath explained, than the more fashionable Postlethwaite's Tavern up the street, where John had stopped before with Jeremiah Vardeman. They secured lodging for the two of them for half a dollar, with a twenty-cent charge for stabling and pasturing their horses.

No preaching appointment had been scheduled for that afternoon, and after freshing themselves at the tavern they walked down Main Street. Jacob Creath was well known, and their stops were frequent as high-hatted men and fashionably dressed women greeted him, their eyes veiled with polite curiosity as he introduced John. At Ayers Alley a jovial man called to them from the doorway of the silversmith shop John had noticed on his first trip, and John was introduced to Samuel Ayers, a prominent Baptist. Inside the shop his eyes widened at the array of silver articles. He had never before handled anything of real silver except money, and he lingered before the showcases as the silversmith displayed his wares.

"Have you any coins about you, Brother Smith?" Ayers asked. "I could melt you a set of teaspoons for your lady with a few."

John looked to Jacob Creath for objection to such vanity, but the older preacher nodded his approval. "It's an excellent way to save your money," he said. "The coins will be soon spent, but the teaspoons could last your life."

John hesitated. He needed a shawl, but he had an extra pair of wool socks Maggie had given him; he could wrap them around his neck if it got colder. He pulled out his wallet and counted out the coins: three silver dollars and four two-bit pieces.

"The three silver cartwheels will do it," Ayers said, and John slid them across the counter. "I'll have six spoons ready for you by week's end."

The Baptist Townfork Church, recently constituted, met in the chapel of Transylvania College, a square-shaped, spacious building with chairs instead of benches, some of them, John noticed with astonishment, even cushioned. For a week, John and Jacob Creath preached every night and on three afternoons, but as the days wore on, John felt a vague, deepening depression instead of the exhilaration he had experienced at the other places. He missed the simple piety of the hill people; the warmth of the smaller settlements. Here the people seemed too comfortable somehow; they had no noticeable expectancy of a mysterious grace. He met the families of James Trotter, William and Walter Warfield, Matthew Elder, Gabriel Tandy, William Poindexter, and liked them all. But while they listened politely to his sermons, he sensed an impatience about them.

Other things were demanding their attention. They had chosen as their pastor a former Presbyterian who had recently embraced the Baptist doctrine, Dr. James Fishback, a learned man whose salary would be four hundred dollars a year. It was a big sum to John, but the church people seemed to think nothing of it; they were prosperous and were planning to erect a handsome brick church building with a gallery, more commodious, Gabriel Tandy told him, than any church building Lexington had yet to offer. But their attitude baffled John. He felt they sensed deep down that they still needed God, and they willed their minds to be receptive. It was their hearts they had closed, a crack at a time. The realization troubled him. Was this what would happen to all Kentucky, to all America, as prosperous living and culture moved across the land?

He asked himself the question again as he called at Ayers' Silversmith Shop and picked up his teaspoons. That night he had an uneasy sense of guilt as he looked at the spoons in his room, studying the curved line of the thin handle, running his finger along the fine line of the bowl. They seemed a symbol of an unreal yet a threatening world. He rolled them hastily back in their brown paper wrappings and tied securely the hempen cord.

"I'd best be getting back to Wayne," he told Jacob Creath two nights later as they finished their last preaching service and prepared to leave the chapel. "These people are interested in religion from the head up, not the neck down." He shook his head. "I don't know as it's wrong. I'm a man myself who has to be convinced in his head. But with these folks it never gets beyond their head, and head faith isn't enough; you got to have heart faith."

They made their way along the cindered sidewalk. It was a full minute before Jacob Creath spoke. "They're accustomed to sermons on dogma; they think they've served the Lord when they win a convert from Methodism." He took hold of John's arm. "We need you up here, Raccoon John Smith."

His words were confirmed the next day as the two men sat in the sitting room of the Jeremiah Vardeman home near David's Fork, and visited with the bulky preacher. Mrs. Vardeman plied them with hot milk and corn bread. She was a frail woman, her face pallid, her voice weak, and although she and her husband urged them to stay the night, they declined. But John promised to preach for Vardeman's church at David's Fork on Sunday.

"He'll give them a rousing gospel sermon," Creath said, and John thought he detected a wistful note in his tone, but then Creath went on in almost mild reproof, "I fear he's weakening a little on our Baptist fundamentals."

Vardeman's voice boomed in laughter. "Maybe we could do with a little less doctrine on occasion. Sometimes I fear we're getting lost in a thicket of theology. That's all we talked about at the Elkhorn Association last month."

"We're good Baptists down in Wayne," John said, "but we're not all the time talking about it. I explain our doctrine to folks who want to know what we believe, and then forget about it."

"That's because you've been influenced by the Separate Baptists," Creath said. "They settled all through south Kentucky and there's a batch of them up here."

"The four churches you preached for in Montgomery County when you were up here before," Vardeman said to John, "differ so much I have to carry water on both shoulders. Two of them, Spencer's Creek and Bethel, are made up of people who moved here from south Kentucky and reflect the views of the Separatists; they don't hanker to sermons on Baptist doctrine, but they don't want to make a fuss about it. The other two, Lulbegrud and Grassy Lick, why, I've got to preach the *Philadelphia Confession of Faith* every sermon, or they think I'm a long-gone heretic." His large frame shifted in the cane rocker. "They're all four in the North District Association, and that's why we don't dare talk much theology in our annual meetings. Too many Separate Baptist folks would kick over the traces, and too many Regular Baptists would be glad to see them get out. It would split us wide open."

"I sometimes wonder," Jacob Creath mused aloud, "if all this doctrinal preaching we do doesn't have its origin in pride." He rubbed his hand over his eyes. "Pride is the snare of the devil."

For some reason his sermon at David's Fork the next Sunday gave John a reassuring sense of kinship with the people. It was as if they reached across his loneliness, accepting him as one of them. He took his seat at the conclusion of the discourse and bowed his head with a warm sense of gratitude. Jeremiah Vardeman, with uplifted hand, was starting to pronounce the benediction.

But it was not a benediction Mr. Vardeman was voicing. John's head jerked erect. The man was asking for donations to help the unfortunate preacher from the country of the raccoons and the salt-peter caves who had suffered such severe affliction. John felt his cheeks burn. He sat stiffly in his chair, mortified, humiliated, staring straight ahead as, slowly at first, and then more rapidly, the members came forward and laid coins upon the stand.

"Of course I'm grateful, Brother Vardeman," he said as they parted at the door. "I know you meant well. But somehow I don't feel it's a disgrace to be either poor or unfortunate. I can overcome both with the Lord's help." He reached for Vardeman's hand and, surprised at his audacity, poured into it the collection of coins. "Keep this for folks in need; I'm doing right well, thank you."

Vardeman's heavy face underwent a gauntlet of emotions. "You're spunky, Raccoon John," he said finally, pocketing the coins. "I'm going to keep you in mind. Yes, I meant well, but I guess I was wrong."

John smiled in quick sympathy and appreciation. It was not easy, he knew, for this big man to admit he was wrong. He pressed the stocky hand with warmth as they parted.

Jacob Creath agreed he had done the right thing when he recounted the incident to him that night in their room. "As you say, Vardeman meant well," he said. "But he is inclined to place money reward pretty high in his values. It is a symptom of the times."

John was pulling off his boots, preparing to remove his linsey trousers and pack them in his saddlebags. He would be leaving for home in the morning and would wear his leather breeches on the rough trace. "I once had ambition for riches, for the power of money," he said slowly. "I know how he feels. And I'm not above craving the good things of this world now. But a man is supposed to work for his rewards in life, not have them given to him. Brother Vardeman has some blind spots, I'm thinking."

The older man chuckled. "You sound like a heretic again, Brother John. I fear for you."

A knock on the door. Creath opened it, his long nightshirt flapping about his heels, and peered cautiously out. And then his booming voice rang through the room. "What's this? Speak of heretics, and here they are. Come on in, friend, and greet an old man in his nightshirt!"

John rose from the low bench on which he had been sitting as a tall, balding man with a thin, kindly face and smiling gray eyes entered the room and embraced Creath. And then the man's hand shot out in greeting.

"John Smith!" he exclaimed. "The lad I met long ago in Logan County! *Canaly* John! I heard you were in these parts, itinerating with my old friend here. You're in sound company."

John stared. It was Barton Stone. He grabbed his loosened trousers and swung the rope suspenders back over his shoulders. "It's like the Judgment Day. You've most caught me, sir, with my pants down."

For two hours the men sat, talking of the intervening years, of the things of the Kingdom. Barton Stone was living in Lexington now, married to his first wife's cousin, glad to be back in the bluegrass region after a couple of years in Tennessee. But the farm he had sold for twelve dollars an acre when he left in 1812 he could not buy back for twice that amount now, he said, so he was living in rented rooms, teaching school, preaching at Cane Ridge and Concord and at his new church in Lexington.

"You mean a Presbyterian church?" John asked.

Jacob Creath laughed. "You know better than that, John. This man is a heretic. He wrote the famous document, 'The Last Will and Testament of the Springfield Presbytery,' and buried the remains, even though he had helped organize it. But the Presbyterians still love him."

Stone gave a wry smile. "They have a queer way of showing it if they do," he said. "A member was disciplined the other day because he asked me to speak at his mother's funeral."

John pushed a chair toward the visitor, and as Stone sat down and Jacob Creath seated himself on the edge of the bed, hugging his nightshirt about him, John leaned against the washstand.

"If it isn't a Presbyterian church, what is it?" he asked.

"It's a Christian church," Stone said simply. "We recognize every sect whose head is Jesus Christ as Christian, and we see no reason why we should call ourselves by any other name."

John's eyes widened. "And you still allow all sects their own opinions?" he asked, frankly puzzled.

"Of course," Stone said. "The Scriptures nowhere command that men should be of one opinion in religion. On the contrary, Christians are commanded to receive one another without regard to them."

"Now, Barton, be honest," Creath said. "You won't accept our creed, and you know it."

"If we all took our religion directly from the Bible there would be no need for creeds," Stone said. "Jesus Christ is our creed; there should be no other."

"But our creed, our Baptist *Philadelphia Confession of Faith,* is taken straight from the Bible," John said.

Stone smiled. "If you believe that, then we must grant that the message and the intelligibility of the Bible is relative, depending as much upon the state of mind and heart of him who reads it, and the method he pursues, as upon the Book itself." He tilted back his chair and ran his fine, sensitive fingers over his face. "You see, my Cherokee friend," he said to John, "there is no essential difference between the Presbyterian's *Westminster Confession of Faith,* which once held me in spiritual bondage, and your own *Philadelphia Confession of Faith.* Both are based on the dark teachings of John Calvin, both are alike in their doctrine of total depravity and in their decrees of election and reprobation. The Apostle John said that God is love, but that is not the God of John Calvin."

"It makes me uneasy to hear talk like that," Creath said, frowning, "even from Barton Stone. You disturb the minds of people. You're a heretic."

"Whatever I am, I'm not a Calvinist," Stone said. He got up and came over and stood beside John. "Calvinism is among the heaviest clogs on Christianity in the world. It's a dark mountain between heaven and earth, the most discouraging hindrance to sinners in seeking the kingdom of God. Its influence is felt throughout the Christian world, even where it is least suspected."

"You're too severe," interrupted Creath, his hands crossed about his knees as though restraining an urge to rise and end the discussion. "The doctrine of election is the pure teaching of the Bible, it is . . ."

"You mean it's the teaching of the creeds," Stone broke in. He came back and sat down again in his chair. "I once believed that, too, that men were so totally depraved they could do nothing acceptable to God until by some physical, almighty, mysterious power he had quickened and enlightened the heart. If God did not do this for all men, we concluded that it was because he chose to do it only for some, depending on his own sovereign will and pleasure." He ran his hand again over his face, and shook his head. "For years I was appalled by such a doctrine, though I forced myself to believe it."

"How did you . . ." John paused, groping for the right words. "How did you finally escape from it?"

Jacob Creath arose slowly to his feet like a mountain of growing wrath in his white nightshirt. "You're a good man, Stone," he said, "but you and your kind have an upsetting influence. You should hearken to the Scriptures and resolve your doubts."

Stone laughed and waved him to sit down. "That's just what I did," he said. "I went back to the precious Word of God, and in reading it I became convinced that God does love the whole world, that the reason he does not save all men is solely because of their unbelief." He shrugged and threw out both hands. "It's really very simple, once you cut through the maze of theology. The gospel is God's power unto salvation, and if the sinner will but believe, and obey, he will be saved."

John gave a short laugh. "I can see, believing that way, you were sort of uncomfortable in the Presbyterian church." He grinned. "When did the Presbyterians put you out?"

"The church didn't exactly put me out," Stone said. "There were five of us preachers who were feeling this way, and we voluntarily seceded from the Synod of Kentucky and organized a presbytery of our own, the Springfield Presbytery we called it. But we didn't withdraw from the Presbyterian church. We felt at the time that would only be causing another division in the body of our Lord."

"But you did cause another division," Creath said. "You didn't last any time as a separate presbytery; you cut all strings and started another sect. Tell John the truth, Barton."

"He's right," Stone said, smiling. "The exact date was June 28, 1804. We broke away entirely and buried our new presbytery, even writing what we called 'The Last Will and Testament of the Springfield Presbytery.' " He fumbled in the inside pocket of his coat and pulled out a document, soiled from much handling. "Here, read this as you have time. No, keep it," he added, as John started to speak. "I always carry extra copies; it sums up our belief about as well as any human document can, I suppose. But don't trouble my friend Jacob with it." He got up and slapped the older man in friendly fashion on the knee. "No man so steeped in Calvinism as Jacob Creath can stomach it; it gives him spiritual indigestion."

"You're right about that," Jacob Creath said, getting to his feet, pulling about him a blanket from the bed. "I pray for you, Barton. You are an apostate, a heretic, yes, even an Arminian, offering God's salvation to all men."

"I try to be a Christian, Jacob," Stone said mildly, "even as you try to be."

As the door closed behind Barton Stone, Jacob Creath shivered under his long white nightshirt and padded to the bed and crawled in, shaking his head. John leaned against the wall beside the tall tallow candle on the table and flipped the pages of the document Stone had handed him. He scanned the first paragraph and then, as though in response to the restless movement of the figure in the bed, he read aloud:

> "We will that this body die, be dissolved and sink into union with the Body of Christ at large; for there is but one Body and one Spirit, even as we are called in one hope of our calling.
>
> "We will that our name of distinction, with its Reverend title, be forgotten, that there be but one Lord over God's heritage, and his name one.
>
> "We will that our power of making laws for the government of the church, and executing them by delegated authority, forever cease; that the people may have free course to the Bible, and adopt the law of the spirit of life in Jesus Christ."

"I have read it, I have read it," Creath said impatiently. "It's rebellion; plain heresy. Some say that Richard M'Nemar wrote it, and some say Barton Stone. Neither will deny nor affirm it. They're ashamed of it, that's why."

John waited a moment and then read on:

> "We will that the people henceforth take the Bible as the only sure guide to heaven; and as many as are offended with other books, which stand in competition with it, may cast them into the fire if they choose; for it is better to enter into life having one book than having many, to be cast into hell."

John folded the document carefully, running his finger along the creased edge. "He speaks his mind," he said after a moment.

"And the devil will speak for him later if he clings to such heresy."

Jacob Creath spoke wearily. He turned on his back and folded his hands across his chest.

"What's so sinful about being a heretic?" John asked suddenly, stooping to unlace his boots again. "Wasn't Jesus a heretic?"

Jacob Creath yawned. "If you'd study your Bible in one hand and our *Confession of Faith* in the other, such things wouldn't bother you," he said shortly. And then he sat half-upright, propped on his elbow. "Maybe this will answer you," he said in sudden triumphant recollection. "Of the five Presbyterian preachers who formed that so-called independent Springfield Presbytery, you know what happened? John Marshall and John Thompson went back to the Presbyterians, and Richard M'Nemar and John Dunlavy became so befuddled they forsook their wives and their children and all their property and became Shaker missionaries. Only Barton Stone was left. That's what happens to poor, misguided heretics; they don't think straight." He sank back on the bed and grunted and turned his face to the wall, and before John could get in bed, he was gently snoring.

But sleep did not come as easily to John. For hours he tossed restlessly. Yesterday he had been almost convinced his future lay in the mountain country. Now he was not so sure.

CHAPTER XIX

IT was warm for early December when John reached south Kentucky and left the trace to follow the winding banks of Little South Fork in Wayne County toward his cabin on the narrow ridge in Horse Hollow. The stream was quiet in spots, then leaped over rocks, roaring, churning, tumbling. He pulled in his horse and looked back toward Poplar Mountain, a spur of the great Cumberland Range that dominated the area, dwarfing the nearer Little Pilot and Big Pilot. He had passed close to its base an hour ago when the peak of the mountain seemed to penetrate the rim of Stockton's Valley, which curved and curled about it, hugging it, embracing the old home where Ma still lived with Jonathan, and where his two children were now awaiting him.

He sighed, a deep, lingering, indrawing of breath as he thought of the children. Ma was getting old, and they were a care for her; they were his responsibility. They were developing into fine little girls, and needed to be with a woman. He ran his hand over the stubble of beard on his chin; he had not shaved since he left Lexington four days ago. That's what mountain living did sometimes to a man; he grew careless.

He looked back toward Poplar Mountain again, rearing its head a thousand feet, seeming to touch heaven itself. A man could rise, too, in these parts, high above the rock and stubble and undergrowth of things, high as he wanted to go. All he had to do was take hold of the hand of God and be pulled up. He had a sudden urge to climb Poplar Mountain as he had done as a boy, to see if the three chalybeate springs at its summit were still bubbling. He could taste the sweet, health-giving water, and he could see the winding trail that led from the springs almost three miles to the foaming, perpendicular falls formed by Indian Creek, and hear the roar of the water cascading in its plunge to the valley. For a moment he sat, lost in the past, and then turned abruptly and urged his horse on.

Two hours later he rode into the clearing surrounding his cabin. It was almost dusk; the sun shot a last ray and hid behind the hills, but the soft glow seemed to bring the cabin alive. It was turning cold; the smell of snow was in the air. He bedded his horse and pushed open the door. The cabin held a hard coldness, and he lighted a flatwood torch and went to the shed to get firewood from the down trees. Only a few thin limbs were in the shed; outside were big logs, too big for the hearth. He looked about for his ax, and then he remembered; he had taken it to William's to help in the logrolling.

He gathered what wood he could and heated some squirrel soup Maggie had made for him and which had kept well covered in the coolness of the stone lean-to. He had ridden eighteen miles and was tired. He drank the soup and pulled off his boots and breeches, slung the shot pouch and powder horn from around his neck, and crawled under the bearskin rug on his mattress of corn-shuck ticks.

Snow was piled against the door when he pushed it open the next morning. It must have snowed all night, but now the air was clear with the hard cold of winter. He stomped his feet and slapped his hands to keep warm. It must have dropped twenty degrees, he reckoned. He cut off a piece of jerked meat and ate it as he pulled on his buckskin breeches and moccasins with their long leggings, and slipped on his leather jacket and adjusted his coonskin cap tight on his head. He would have to ride over to William's cabin for his ax in order to cut himself some firewood.

He crossed the frozen creek and was climbing Little Pilot when he noticed the curling smoke of the two-story Joseph Hurt cabin near the thicket of spruce pine. He could borrow a whittling ax there and get his own later.

Nancy Hurt was already at the spinning wheel; he heard it hum even before her father led him into the big kitchen, warm and fragrant with bacon bakings. Joseph Hurt was a hearty man, and John liked him. The two boys, Amos and Joshua, younger than Nancy, were on the point of leaving for squirrel hunting with their hounds, and John stopped at the door to admire the dogs as they trudged out in the snow. Slender and frail-looking, they must have resembled their mother, he thought, buried now in the plot next the Mount Pisgah Church. But Nancy had the robustness of her father.

For two hours he sat with them. Joseph Hurt was making bullets. He had shaved a bar of lead into an iron pot hanging over the fire, and John watched him ladle the sliding stream of hot, melted lead into the soapstone molds, reciting, as he watched, his adventures in the bluegrass country, his errand almost forgotten. Nancy pushed her spinning wheel aside and piled creamed eggs and milk gravy on hot biscuits, and he ate as though he were starved. Then she set the wheel to turning again, her brown eyes now and then on John as her hands kept the tension right so that the wool, stretching and twisting and winding itself into yarn, filled the spindle evenly.

"I'm not being bold, Mr. Smith," she said when he rose to leave, "but that small cabin of yours is no place for two little girls, least not in winter. It's a wonder of earth if you could manage." She paused and looked at her father as if for confirmation, and then turned to John, meeting his gaze straightforward. "We got two loft rooms up that ladderway, using them just for storing root vegetables and like. They'd make comfortable rooms for those little girls, and I'd pleasure to keep them."

John swallowed and fumbled with his cap as silence filled the room. Then he looked at her for a long minute. Her taffy-colored hair was braided securely about her head, but some strands had escaped in curling wisps about her face and peeked from under her crisp white cap. Her brown eyes looked at him in complete candor, intelligent and unafraid, a glint of humor about them. He twisted his cap and then loosened it and raised his eyes to meet those of her father's. Slowly Mr. Hurt nodded, a half-smile on his face, and rubbed his chin, a knowing gesture. Life was elemental in the mountains; talk was sometimes of necessity straight. They both knew what Nancy meant. A house needed a woman; children needed a mother; a woman needed a man; a man needed a wife. And Anna was gone forever.

"You're purely asking for trouble, Miss Nancy," he said gently.

Her face broke into a quick smile. "Nothing's trouble that needs doing, Mr. Smith," she said briskly. "It would pleasure me a lot."

They were married in the sitting room of the Hurt house on Christmas day, with Isaac Denton performing the ceremony, and John and Nancy and the two children moved into the two loft rooms of the house. He and Joseph Hurt would farm together, they had decided, raising maize on the richer soil of the Hurt place, feeding out the corn to hogs and cattle which could range on the thinner blueberry-pine soil of his eighty acres.

As the winter passed, they grew into a compact family unit. Nancy encouraged his quick interest, his curiosity, his eagerness to learn, his desire for knowledge. But when he speculated on points of doctrine that bothered him, she remained undisturbed. She ignored rather than condemned doctrine with which she disagreed, protesting only when some church member criticized John's sermons for emphasizing the spirit of tolerance rather than the letter of the Mosaic code.

She loved pretty things, he discovered, and held no truck with the church's admonition against vanity. Her full-skirted practical dresses of linsey were always brightened with an apron of gay colors, and from her variety of ruffled petticoats she was soon making lace-edged pantaloons and swishing skirts for Jennie and Zerelda to wear on Sunday. She gave the girls a pair of brushes and a looking glass, and helped them brush and braid their hair until it shone like silk before setting them down each morning to work the churn, or taking them with her to drop seed in the garden John turned for her as soon as frost left the ground.

Her brown eyes grew big as John laid a long, narrow box in

rough wrapping tied with a hempen cord in her lap one evening early in March as they sat about the hearth after putting the two girls to bed.

"Your wedding gift," he chuckled. "I almost forgot about it. I had it tucked away in my old saddlebags ever since I got back from up north. Seeing you rub the pewter things so hard today, it came to me the Lord must of had a hand in me getting it."

Joseph Hurt stopped his whittling of a buckeye bowl and the boys, sitting cross-legged before the fire with their Dilworth spellers, crowded about her as she untied the hemp string and lifted the paper lid. Inside were the six silver teaspoons John had allowed the silversmith Ayers to make for him from the coins in his pocket that day in Lexington.

Nancy lifted them out one by one, rubbing her fingers along their thin edge, tapping them, her handling almost a caress. "They're silver," she said, her voice full of wonder. "Look, Pa, they're silver."

Gingerly, Hurt examined them. "They're silver, all right," he said. "Don't know as I ever saw real silver eating tools before. Nancy's mother used to tell how her grandmother back in England had silver knives, but she never mentioned silver spoons." He looked quizzically at his son-in-law. "Reckon folks'll think you're taken with worldly riches, John?"

John frowned. "No reason for folks in these parts not to have nice things, just as nice as they do in the bluegrass."

"That ain't the point," Hurt said. "Church folks in no place are supposed to hanker after show of finery."

"Well, I'm proud to have them," Nancy said firmly. "Prouder than I can say."

By April the cattle and hogs were ready for market, and with Joshua and Amos and their hounds, John drove them to Stanford, up past Crab Orchard, where traders were coming in increasing numbers. It was a pleasant trip. The gorges cut by swift-flowing streams were alive with dogwood and redbud, and the dogs raced up and down the slopes and tore through the thickets. On the rocky ledges mountain violet and Indian pink grew in profusion, and along the smaller creeks were anemones and wild poppies. The hillsides were a riot of mountain laurel and cucumber. Once they saw a long line of wild deer racing toward the cane, and as they neared the flatter country of the Dix River Valley, John pointed out to the boys their first sight of three yoke of oxen for each plow, turning the black, rich earth. They managed the stock well, and the hogs and cattle proved good travelers. They grazed along the way on the abundant grass and rich mast and increased in weight, bringing better prices than John had expected. By early frost, he knew, they would be in the eastern markets. It was going to be a good year; the summer would bring a rich harvest.

But spring did not turn into summer. The air held a chill, and July brought a frost. In August of that year, 1816, for the first time in Joseph Hurt's memory, he said, a backlog of gum kept a fire blazing night and day in the big hearth of the Hurt sitting room.

John preached twice a month on Sundays at Bethel, where Philip was still serving as clerk, and twice a month at Mount Pisgah. The meetinghouse at Bethel had been erected hurriedly when John first organized the church, and it still had its original earthen floor with a few puncheons for him to stand on when preaching, and a couple of forked sticks pushed into the ground with a crosspiece for his hand-board.

"It's a disgrace to the Lord," Nancy announced forthrightly after attending preaching there for the first time with John. "A meetinghouse ought to be more fit."

John agreed, and the next time he was there he mentioned it to Philip after the service.

"The gospel don't need fancy trimmings," Philip said. "This house is plenty good enough. Just see your preaching is as good, John."

Nancy had walked on with Philip's wife, Millie, and John was glad she had not heard the implied rebuke. Philip was beginning to detect, he knew, an unsoundness in his preaching. Like Jonathan, he was a hill man; stolid, unquestioning, rooted like an oak in the *Philadelphia Confession.* John looked at him now half-amused, half-annoyed, recalling how Philip had sat that morning in rigid disapproval as John had declared that Christ had tasted death for every man; that the gospel provided for the salvation of all. The others, too, had stared, uncomprehending, reflecting the same hostility to their cherished dogma, even after he had patiently explained such belief was not entirely contrary to Baptist doctrine as held by the Separatists.

"I'm a questioning man, Philip; I just can't help it," he said now as they walked together toward their wagons. He started to tell of his encounter with Barton Stone in Lexington, and of his heretical views, of the new winds blowing through the whole field of religious thought, but he dismissed the matter from his mind; Philip would never understand. "I had a hard time convincing myself I was saved, and I still got the scars from my battle. Maybe that's why I'm having a hard time believing other folks, just as good as me and some a lot better, aren't saved just because they can't prove it."

"That's unsound doctrine, John," Philip reproved him. "The folks here won't stand for it."

"I don't remember folks around here being so set in their thinking when I preached for them before," he said.

"It's you who's changed," Philip said. "They are just as they were."

John frowned, reflecting. "I reckon you're right," he said slowly. "I reckon it was what happened to me in Hickory Flats. That experience shook me up more powerful than I realized at the time. Up to then I figured knowing about God was enough, but it's not. A man's got to know God himself. It makes a heap of difference. Losing Anna and the babies made me wonder about a lot of things; it shook the dust out of my brain." He looked at Philip steadily. "It cleaned the cobwebs out of my courage, too. I'm beginning to have the grit to say what I think."

"You got Ma worried, John," Philip said, "and Jonathan and Brother Isaac, too."

The year flew by. In November the boys shot a deer, and John helped jerk the meat, drying it on a low crosspiece over a slow fire. It dried better than buffalo meat and would be good eating all winter. The girls needed shoes, and with deerskin aplenty, he made shoes for the whole family, tanning the skins carefully to retain their pliant softness. He had secured a new pegging awl in Stanford, and he used it now to make holes, binding the seams with rolls of whang leather. On the shoes for the girls, he left the hair untouched to go inside for warmth, and made the uppers unusually long to allow secure wrapping around their thin legs. The snows were frequent and heavy, and he made them sleds, with runners cut from a curved sourwood tree.

It was after hog-killing time, with sausage meat abundant, that Nancy invited to the house the ladies from both the Mount Pisgah and the Bethel churches for a quilting bee. She set up the quilting frame in the big room, and John tied the ropes to the four corners and attached them to the roof of the room so she could regulate the frame to the height of the women sitting about it. She decorated the house with red haw and cedar, and spread the kitchen table with her best woven cloth.

By nine o'clock the women had arrived. Dinner would be at noon, and they would leave by the middle of the afternoon to reach home before the winter dusk invaded the mountain slopes. It was a happy, laughing day. Nancy had carded the batting, cut and sewn the pieces together, and made the lining, so the women gave all their time to their flying needles and their talk, and by going-home time the wedding-bell pattern Nancy had wanted was emerging. The abundant dinner served at noon had been a success, crowned by apple pudding and sassafras-root tea. It was then, biding her time, Nancy had proudly brought out her silver teaspoons.

The effect was all she had hoped for. The women crowded about to see them as she laid them beside the pewter cups. Wooden spoons were common; many had bone and pewter, but real silver was unknown among the church folks in the Hollow. They studied the curved edges; they tested the thin metal for bending; they tapped them against their teeth.

"You do beat all, Nancy," Rachel Parmley said as she tied on her bonnet, preparing to leave. "John Parmley has never yet brought me nothing like these. How come a preacher like Brother Smith took such a notion?"

Millie, Philip's wife, looked thoughtful. "John shouldn't of done it," she said quietly. "The elders won't like it. You wait, they'll say it's sinful extravagance. John got tainted with worldliness up north."

"The church discipline warns against vanity," Polly Eads said. "It leads to levity."

"Fiddle-dee!" Nancy laughed. Polly Eads was recently widowed and could be excused acting solemn but not the rest of the church people; mostly they were only pious-acting. "Church folks think they can frolic and fidget other times, but the password to heaven has to be given with a long face by the preacher. I don't hold with such."

Within a week repercussions began sounding through the hills on the Little South Fork. "Sinful extravagance," was the verdict of the elders of Mount Pisgah, led by John Parmley and quoting, Nancy was convinced, his wife. "Pride in worldly things," Philip told John, speaking for the folks at Bethel, "is the first step toward hell." And on Saturday afternoon before Christmas, when the Bethel members assembled for their monthly business session, the innovation was taken in hand.

"Nancy Smith has been guilty of grave offense in setting an example of sinful extravagance," the elders said in public reprimand.

John was indignant, but Nancy brushed it off. "Reckon I should feel chastened," she said, tucking her hand under John's arm in the wagon, riding home in the late twilight, "but I'm not. I got a feeling for pretty things, and I don't feel sinful about it at all." She brushed her cheek against the shoulder of his buffalo-skin jacket. "You're a preacher, John; shouldn't you of warned me I was on the road to hell?"

"Don't speak so, Nancy," he said. "Maybe they're right; could be it is sinful extravagance. But I'm more guilty than you. I had those spoons made apurpose."

"But that's not what they say is sinful," Nancy said. "Rachel Parmley told me herself, sort of bragging, that she had tucked away some gold earrings her grandmother had, only she had more religion than to show them. And everybody knows Hannah Todhunter Jones has a silver water pitcher she brings out when she thinks no church members are about. Is it according to the gospel that church folks can have their sins but they best keep them hid?"

John sighed. "Not the way I read it," he said. "But I reckon I'm reading it more with my heart here of late than with my head."

Someone blew a fox horn. It floated against the hills in the frosty air, and the hills gave back the sound, low and mournful.

Nancy snuggled against him. "I've something that will be read by your heart," she said. "We're going to have a baby. Do you think the elders will say that's sinful extravagance?"

The baby was born in early May. A tiny girl, she joined her two half-sisters, with Granny Wilson from Pea Ridge serving as midwife. They named her Eliza Blaze, after Nancy's mother, but the baby was delicate and sickly, and it was June before Nancy was up and about the house. As soon as he felt it would be safe to leave her for a day, John rode over to Stockton's Valley for a reassuring visit with his mother.

As Philip had said, Ma was worried about his doctrine. But he found her bubbling with her usual good spirits, eager for news of Nancy and the new baby, full of family talk. Jonathan had gone to Burkesville with Tom Stockton for supplies, and Fancy Mae and her baby were visiting her husband's folks on Stubbins Creek. George was on a trip back to Christian County, thinking of settling there again. It was not until they were sitting in the yard under the big locust, eating the noon meal of corn pones and ham slices, that Ma suddenly looked at him, her eyes intent on his face.

"You true to the faith, John?" she said.

He smiled. "I love the Lord and fear him," he said, "and keep his commandments."

She pondered a moment. "Seems a body couldn't do more," she said, and the old feeling of understanding comradeship returned to them both, and his preaching was not mentioned again.

He left early in the afternoon, heading north to go the longer route home by way of Monticello, where the postrider was due later in the day on his twice-monthly trip. He was jogging past the Clear Fork Church when Brother Isaac Denton hailed him, and he reined to a stop. It would be good to talk with his old friend for a little. He dismounted and led his horse to the creek for watering, and whistled for his hound. Brother Isaac followed him and, as the animal splashed in the water, the old man eased himself down on the bank and motioned John to a place beside him. Clear Fork, swollen with spring rains, was higher than John had seen it in some time, gurgling, foaming as it raced among the tangled mass of vines, the riot of clover and anemones and bloodroot that lined its banks.

" 'Twas about twelve years ago I baptized you, John, right where that horse of yours is standing," Brother Isaac said, musing. "You still true to the faith?"

John sat down beside him. "That's what Ma asked me," he said. "You're hearing things, aren't you? But you needn't worry, Brother Isaac. I'm true to the faith as . . ."—he paused and picked up a small stone and skimmed it across the water—"as I see it."

"That's not the same thing, John."

"A man can only be true to himself, Brother Isaac," John said. "If you mean, am I true to the Bible or am I true to the *Philadelphia Confession of Faith,* I can tell you plain wherever there's a difference between them, I'm true to the Bible."

"But they're one and the same, practically," Brother Isaac said.

John shook his head. "I'm beginning to think, Brother Isaac, that ever since the day the first creed was written, teaching the commandments of men as if they were the doctrine of God, all creeds and creed-makers are anathema to the Lord. They're the root of all our bickerings and divisions and bitterness. All we need is the Bible, shed of men's opinions about it." He paused and looked over the valley. His hound was fox hunting, picking up a scent, and he listened for a moment to the long, baying cry. "Reckon the Lord thinks I'm a hound, Brother Isaac." He smiled at the old man. "Reckon I'm sort of a hound of God. He's put it into me someway to run down the little foxes, the little foxes that spoil the vines, for our vines have tender grapes." He turned to Brother Isaac, his eyes seeking, almost pleading for understanding. "There's such things as the love of God and his redeeming mercy we should be preaching; the Lord's depending on us to do it. The fruit of the spirit is love, joy, peace, long-suffering, gentleness, goodness and faith, meekness and temperance, against which there is no law. They're the tender grapes of the gospel; but here we are, letting the little foxes of men's opinions destroy them."

Brother Isaac stared at him sorrowfully. "You're going off on strange paths. What's taken possession of you, son?"

"We're all on new paths in this country," John said, and jumped to his feet. "New paths through our thinking as well as our thickets. I reckon it's the future that's got hold of me." He tightened the belt that circled his hunting shirt, tucking in the folds that crossed his middle. He called to his hound, and stood for a moment, patting the animal's head. "Take a long breath, Brother Isaac. It's free, free as the gospel, and as pure." He laughed and put his hand affectionately on the shoulder of the stooped figure, and then glanced at the sun. "I'd best be off. I promised Ma if the postrider brought any word from George, I'd see it got over to her. He's off again in Christian County, and I've no mind to go get him again if there's trouble."

"There'll be no trouble there any more," Brother Isaac said. "The Lord has put the terrible Harpes out of their misery."

John smiled. "The Lord didn't do it alone," he couldn't resist saying. "As I heard it, it took a few bullets." He slapped Brother Isaac playfully on the back. "Like I said, the Lord needs us."

They shook hands soberly for all John's banter, and as he rode away he felt Brother Isaac's probing, questing gaze following him. He loved Isaac Denton, more than he could say, more probably than the old man realized; he was like a father to him. But there was little use arguing with him now; the years were too many; his mind was rigid-set.

John reached Monticello in time to watch the postrider gallop up before Roger Oatt's Tavern adjacent to the jailhouse and blow his horn. A crowd had gathered, and he dismounted and mingled with the town people, calling greetings, exchanging farm talk. And then he heard the postrider call out his name.

He took the letter handed him and studied the sealed sheet. The postage was ten cents; it had come at least a hundred miles. It was not from George; yet the small handwriting was somehow familiar. He got on his horse and passed the town spring and headed for the south trace. He rode a full mile before he slid loose the flap and spread the single sheet out on the smooth pommel of his saddle. He read slowly at first, his eyes scrutinizing the scribbled words. The letter was from Jeremiah Vardeman.

His wife had died, Brother Vardeman said, and he was wanting to go itinerating, preaching all over the state as a balm for his loneliness. Would John come up and take charge of the four churches which had been in his care in Montgomery County? John read the letter through three times, the reins hanging loose, before he thrust it into his wallet and dug his heels into the horse's flanks.

But it was not until he and Nancy were in the privacy of their bedroom that night that he had a chance to tell her of the letter. Mr. Hurt wanted to talk farm; the children needed help with their ciphering. Nancy put the baby in the underbed and came and sat beside him, reading the letter with him by the light of the spluttering bear-oil lamp on the wide hickory block pressed against the far wall.

"His wife looked sickly when I was there," John said, "now I recollect." Roughly he brushed the back of his hand across his eyes as if to blot out remembrance of his own sorrow. He had related the tragedy to Nancy only once and then, by tacit understanding, it had never been mentioned. But Nancy was absorbed in reading the letter again.

"What four churches is he talking about?" she asked.

John pondered. "Seems one was Grassy Lick and one was Lulbegrud, and I can't recollect the others. They're small but all within easy riding of each other. I do know he said some of them were tainted with Separate Baptist views." He read aloud from the letter: "We have had a glorious outpouring of the spirit in all of them." He paused, his eyes twinkling. "Now, doesn't that sound preacherish?" He wagged his head. "What he means is that they're full of good folks, Nancy, folks hungry for the gospel."

She got up and loosened her hair, and started brushing it. "What about Pa?" she asked after a moment.

John considered. "Maybe he would go with us; maybe we could all move there."

Nancy pursed her lips. "Pa was born on this land; he'd never leave it." She sighed deeply. "We can't leave him, John, leastwise I don't see how we can. Amos and Joshua could get along; they're young and can adapt. But Pa needs a woman about to look after him. He's most sixty."

John got up and put the letter on the table and took off his hunting coat and shirt and reached for his long cotton nightshirt before he spoke. "We'd best talk to the Lord about it, Nancy," he said finally to the silent figure already in the pole bed against the wall. He blew out the lamp and sank to his knees beside the bed.

John carried the letter from Vardeman about with him for a week. He read it as he rested at his plow at the end of the sinuous row on the west slope of the ridge; he stopped in the middle of a long furrow and pondered on it as he watched a rabbit hop along between the furrows; he kept it in the pocket of his cotton coat as he preached on Sunday at Mount Pisgah on the power of God, quoting from Paul's letter to the church at Rome: "For I am not ashamed of the gospel of Christ for it is the power of God unto salvation to every one that believeth."

"That power is available to everybody," he heard himself saying, "not just to a few of the Elect."

The people stared at him, a hurt puzzlement in their eyes, and he had a sudden twinge of conscience. Was he justified in tearing down a cherished belief? He knew he was right, but what proof did he have? The conviction that God's power and mercy and guidance could be claimed by all men filled him with an almost suffocating certainty; but he couldn't explain it. He brought the service to a close and joined the people in the grove for dinner under the towering pines. No one spoke of his sermon, and as he heaped his tin plate high with ham slices and fried chicken and hominy, he felt an estrangement, almost a loneliness, he had never experienced before. He had brought the church into being based on a creed as clear as ice, and just as cold. He wished Elisha Franklin were there; he alone of all these good people was conscious of God's great, all-embracing care for all men. But the hearty blacksmith was in Burkesville on a buying trip. John put his plate on the stump of a cedar tree beside Nancy and the baby sitting on a buffalo rug on the ground, and felt of the letter in his breast pocket. Somehow God would guide him in answering it.

He looked up to see his father-in-law, Joseph Hurt, making his way toward them. The widow, Polly Eads, was beside him. She was a slight woman with a clinging, helpless air, widowed now a year. Her farm adjoined the Hurt's on the other side from that of John's. Her lace-edged bonnet was pushed to the back of her head, her face flushed, her eyes veiled, fluttering in a becoming modesty as she greeted John and Nancy. Joseph Hurt took the bearskin rug she was carrying and spread it beside that on which John and Nancy were sitting, and helped her sit down.

John took a swift bite of ham and glanced at Nancy. She was smiling in happy surprise at her father.

Two months later, on September 15, John performed the marriage ceremony for his father-in-law and the Widow Eads in the tidy cabin of the widow. The couple planned to stay in that cabin until John and Nancy moved north.

John had written Vardeman as soon as Joseph Hurt's plans to marry were revealed, accepting the oversight of the four churches in Montgomery County. Swiftly, arrangements were made for the move. The Mount Pisgah and Bethel churches were again put into the pastoral hands of Isaac Storey, and John conveyed title to his eighty acres to his father-in-law for four hundred dollars. He disposed of his stock, accepted the offer of Nancy's younger brother,

Joshua, now seventeen, to go north with them and, on October 22, 1817, he loaded his little family in the flatbed wagon, hitched to it a fine team of new bay mares given them by Mr. Hurt, and drove away.

CHAPTER XX

IT was a leisurely trip in the wagon. John had made a top for the vehicle of six rows of bent hickory, covering them with twill, and Nancy had sewed a puckering string at the back by which the end could be closed. She sat with the baby on the wagon floor on the two feather beds she had insisted on bringing, piled between mounds of their belongings. Much of it, John knew, they could secure in Mount Sterling, Montgomery's county seat, but Nancy wanted her own things—her piggins and churn and sugar box of rived cedar, shaped by her father with a froe and drawing knife; her keeler for washing dishes and her buckeye bread tray. She had even brought her hominy block. John tried to draw the line at her loom and spinning wheel. "There's stores up there with yarn aplenty," he had told her, "and like as not you won't do any weaving anyhow as there's yard cloth to be had cheap."

But Nancy would not hear of it. She had made the loom herself, of stout white oak beams, and her foot was used to the treadle and her hands to the shuttle. A house didn't look right, she said, without a loom.

They took a trace on the Big South Fork to the Great Lakes Trail. At Smith's Shoals they crossed the Cumberland River, frozen in spots and whirling below the shoals. For three days they pressed through canebrake in the Rockcastle country on a prong of the road that hugged the mountains, the great Cumberland Range which crossed Kentucky's south and eastern lands. From those great heights, John pointed out to Jennie and Zerelda, sitting wide-eyed between him and Joshua in the driver's seat, all the rivers in the state—the Kentucky, the Dix, the Big Sandy, the Licking, the Green—began their sources, feeding the state in all directions.

The land had a roll, and then it would level; at such times the canebrake seemed impenetrable, rising twice as high as a man, shutting out the light, whipping them as it rebounded from its bending. But it seemed a protecting wall at night as they camped in it, snug in bearskin rugs, and listened to the wind moan and sigh high along the ridges among the pines. The third morning the fog was thick, then turned to a drizzling mist, and for two days it rained, and they took shelter in a rock house, no more than a shallow cave under rock ledges.

John entertained them as they rode along with stories of the Indians, still seen but now peaceful. "No Indians ever lived for long in Kentucky anyway," he told them. "That is, since back almost a hundred years. Too many of them claimed it: the Iroquois, the Chickasaws, the Shawnees, the Chicamaugas, the Cherokees, the Creeks, and others. They fought all over the place, first the animals and then each other and then the white men—that's why it's called the dark and bloody ground." He waved his whip as they passed dense growth. "Kentucky is still mostly a wilderness; still a baby state, but it's growing fast. Some day it will be a great country. It's got mountains, hills, rivers, plains, fertile valleys, everything." He mused for a moment and then quoted, "Where every prospect pleases . . ."

Jennie's quick mind took up the phrase. ". . . and only man is vile," she prattled. "Mama read that to me in my reader. Why is man vile? What does vile mean?"

"I didn't say that," John protested. "Men are not born vile; they're all children of God."

Buffalo crossed the trace twice; red and gray foxes raced, squirrels chattered, cottontail rabbits darted from the cane, startled, and retreated. Above Renfro Valley they came to a toll gate, but John avoided it by taking a shun-pike a mile above it, scarcely more than a widened path through the cane which scraped the wagon on both sides. In a sycamore grove they spotted the gay plumage of two parrots, and as they emerged into the clearing at its edge, ruffled grouse and prairie chickens and wild turkeys crossed and crisscrossed the rutted road, and the crack of Joshua's rifle brought them good eating of fresh meat.

"The trees," Nancy marveled, peering into the countryside from over their shoulders, "we don't have such trees in Wayne."

"We've scrub trees there," John said, "because the soil is thin with rock and sandstone and shale. But the valley soils up here are different; they're deep and rich, and in the bluegrass region there's plenty of limestone."

"Why do they call it bluegrass?" Joshua asked suddenly.

"Wait until spring, and you'll see," John said. "There's a little blue tip forms, and a whole field of that gives the grass a blue tint. It grows only in deep limestone country. Some people call it June grass." He pointed to a distant sycamore. "See that tree? It's ten feet across, I'd say, and there's plenty more like it up here."

"Look at that oak!" Nancy said. "And that yellow poplar yonder!" They knew the yellow poplar; it grew in the hills, an aberrant member of the magnolia family. Nancy loved it, and had shown the girls how to gather the dainty green and orange chalices in the spring and press them between stones for keeping, and in the fall how to make strings of the crimson seed cones.

"They call it the tulip tree up here," John said. "They grow to be giants."

Seven days after leaving Wayne County, they crossed the Red River branch of the Kentucky River, camping on its banks, and the next morning just before noon entered Montgomery County. It was one of the largest and oldest counties in the state, John told them as they looked about, older even than Wayne. It had been formed in 1796, but in 1811 a slice had been taken away to form adjacent Bath County, and now there was talk of dividing it up still more. But it was good soil, finely watered and well timbered.

The road led up Spencer's Creek and turned sharply to the west, skirting a dense growth of cane, and then resumed its meandering course north, passing an abandoned stockade.

"That's probably what's left of Morgan's Station," John said in answer to Joshua's excited view of his first fort. "And Fort Baker is somewhere around here, another old stockade. The Indians did a powerful try to keep us out of this region. There's salt wells around here they wanted. We can't be far from Mount Sterling."

Another stream crossed the road, flowing into Spencer's Creek, and at the juncture the paddles of a grist mill sputtered noisily. John called to a man standing with a meal sack beside the chute.

"How far be it to Mount Sterling?"

"You still got the mountains in your mouth, John," Nancy said in a hoarse whisper from her seat behind him. "You don't go calling out to folks in these parts. And you don't say, 'How far be it!' Shame on you!"

The man cupped his hand behind his ear, and John called again, ignoring her. "How far be it to Mount Sterling?"

"Just over the rise," the man said. He came forward slowly, limping, wiping his hands on his pantaloons. "You strangers?" He stuck out his hand to John. "This is Hodges' grist mill. I come out here to get my meal ground because they don't use slave labor. Name is David Barrow."

John grinned, studying the man. Tom Stockton, he remembered, had mentioned David Barrow, the man who was fighting slavery. He looked at the lean, sensitive face, the skin tightly drawn over high cheekbones, showing marks of suffering. "Glad to make your acquaintance, Mr. Barrow," he said. "I'm John Smith from Wayne County, coming here with my family to take charge of four Baptist churches."

Barrow's face brightened. "We've been expecting you, Brother Smith. I'm a Baptist preacher myself, preaching for the church in Mount Sterling. Brother Vardeman told me you'd be around soon." He peered into the wagon, and Nancy leaned forward as John introduced her.

"We're pure sightly, we are, Brother Barrow," she said, trying to adjust her shawl, brushing Jennie's hair back from her face, straightening Zerelda's neckerchief. "You'll have to excuse our appearance."

Barrow smiled broadly. "You're a kindly sight," he said. "This community needs Christian folks like you."

"Your church is in North District Association then, same as my four churches?" John said. "We'll be seeing much of each other."

The preacher shook his head. "Not as much as you think. North District has excluded my church at Mount Sterling from fellowship." He dug his heel into the soft dirt by the wagon and studied it as John looked his embarrassment, sorry he had asked the question.

But David Barrow was unabashed. "For preaching emancipation. I'm outspoken against slavery," he said frankly.

John twisted the reins in his hands. "We don't have slaves much in Wayne," he said, his voice hoarse. "I've not had much occasion to study it. But things are different up here, I reckon."

"God's word is the same everywhere," Barrow said. "And God's children are equally precious in his sight. The man who preaches such truth, however, must court not the favor of the world, nor fear its frown." He smiled and stepped back and bowed. "You'll find Mount Sterling just over the rise," he said. "I imagine you'll be taken in charge by Judge James French. He's a member of your Lulbegrud Church and is serving as clerk of North District Association. One of the biggest lawyers around here, and our county judge. I pastored the Lulbegrud Church a while back," he went on, "but when Judge French got wind of my stand on slavery, he had me put out. You'd best not tell him you've met me; no use prejudicing him against you at the start."

John watched him turn and trudge back to the mill before he clucked to the horses and the wagon lurched forward.

Fences began snaking across the fields, and soon a scattering of cabins lined the pike, thickening as the road became rocked. A peddler's wagon jingled to a stop before them at a cabin entrance, and the girls stared as the man hung out his glittering wares. John drove slowly; they were in the settlement of Mount Sterling, a village of about six hundred people, the seat of Montgomery County, a raw newness about it that reminded John of Monticello. And yet, there was a difference. In Wayne the land seemed to resent intrusion, and the people sided with it, clinging as if for comfort to the old ways of a fading past. Here, the very contour of the earth seemed as open as a friendly hand eager to be grasped; the half-cleared fields impatient for growth; the clusters of buildings sprawling in every direction seemed to cry out loud for help in shaping the life that centered in them.

At the intersection of the rocked pike with a wide cross street, they passed a story-and-a-half brick building, beside it a log house with barred windows. John pointed it out as the courthouse and jail. Diagonally across the intersection was Payne's General Store.

John drove the team and wagon to a hitching rail in front, handed the reins to Joshua, and climbed out. The store was a two-story building of logs and white frame; along the front ran a covered porch, and on the bench which ran its length several men lounged, farmers from nearby, taking their ease, airing their views.

Inside, John looked in amazement at the clutter of goods piled and heaped and stacked and strewn from the sawdust-covered floor to the smoky ceiling. Joe Beard's store in Monticello had nothing like this. In the center was a table supporting ironstone chamber pots, earthenware bean pots, boot scrapers, bellows, and butter-ball paddles, while on either side were counters filled with hickory-smoked cheese, candle snuffers, balsam soap, beeswax, licorice gum-drops, pie baskets. Overhead an array of iron swing-bracket lamps dangled from the rafters.

Two loungers near the whiskey barrel to the right looked up at the sound of the tinkling bell as he pushed open the door and scrutinized him briefly. He lifted his hand in a gesture of greeting.

"Mr. Payne hereabouts?" he asked. The storekeepers in such villages, he knew, were sources of general information to the whole community.

One man motioned with his thumb to the rear, and John went toward the partition and peered behind it into the counting room. A man seated at a wide table near the window looked up and got to his feet.

"I'm John Smith," John said, extending his hand. "You be Mr. Payne?"

"Buckner Payne," the man said, grasping his hand. He was tall and balding, slightly stooped, his eyes deep-set and probing. "You're the new Baptist preacher, I take it." John nodded, and the man went on. "Judge French is expecting you. He . . . why, there he is now."

At his words John turned to see a thick-set man with gray side whiskers standing in the doorway, a tall hat shading a dour face set in a thin smile, his claw-hammer green frock coat reaching to his knees. During the introduction, John recalled from his previous trip that Judge James French was not only the most prominent lawyer in the community, as David Barrow had mentioned, and the county judge, but one of the most powerful Baptists in the state. Mr. Payne's manner was casual toward him but deferential, and John felt there was a lack of heartiness in the relationship that spoke of no affection.

Judge French spoke with a hurried, almost an absent-minded air. "I saw your wagon from my window in the courthouse," he said. He pulled out a gold watch and studied it. "I have a place for you to stay until you look about some. It's part of a tract of nine thousand acres I patented on Slate Creek. It's got a good enough cabin for the time to shelter your family."

Within a few minutes Judge French and Buckner Payne had met

the family in the wagon, and the Judge mounted his horse, riding ahead of them to lead the way to the cabin.

"He's a stiff-necked man but a good one, Nancy," John said as they followed the erect figure down the rutted roadway. It was thoughtful of the man to provide shelter for the family, and John felt a twinge of guilt that his first impression had been unfavorable. "The sort of man I somehow feel who will give you anything but his love. But I'm grateful to him; he's charging us only thirty-eight dollars for the use of the place for a year while we look around for a farm of our own. And he seems pleasant enough, always smiling."

Nancy nodded. "It was thoughtful of him, all right," she agreed, "but I'd never warm up to him. I'd trust a man who wears a frown quicker than I would one with a fixed smile."

It was almost nightfall when the little company reached the cabin, two miles from town. Slate Creek furnished water for Mount Sterling and ran close by the house. Judge French bade them a hasty farewell and had ridden away before they discovered he had stocked the cabin with provisions enough to last several days.

Within the week the family routine was established; and as November slid into December, and then into the new year of 1818, John found himself settling into the life of the community. He and Joshua secured some stock and fowls; they bedded in sand the gifts of root vegetables and other provisions supplied by neighbors, and planned the spring planting. The weather held mild, and as he could spare the time from home duties, he covered all of Montgomery County and rode far beyond its confines, his natural friendliness, his good humor, and ready wit gradually making his wiry frame a welcome figure among the twenty-one Baptist churches with their fourteen hundred members which comprised the North District Association. Although the Mount Sterling Church had been excluded from the Association, as David Barrow had told him, he visited the venerable preacher whenever he had occasion to be near his church, his respect for the man and his unswerving stand against slavery increasing with each encounter.

He and Nancy put their membership in the Grassy Lick Church, received cordially by the families of James and Peter Mason, William Ralls, and Reuben McDonnold, all eager to make them feel at home. It was here, he was told, that bluegrass had first been identified, and it was here that one of the oldest churches in the state, a Methodist group, had been organized in 1794, erecting the small building he passed at a fork in the road that led to his own church.

The church at Bethel, he found, had fewer than a dozen families holding membership, surrounded by a sparsely settled area, but at Spencer's Creek he found a vital, stimulating group of more than fifty families, led by Thomas Mosely and Joe Bondurant, energized by their roots in the Separate Baptist movement, attaching little importance to the fine points of Calvinism. Jacob and Jane Coons opened the doors of their small cabin to him whenever he was in the vicinity, and although neither were members of the church, it became his habit to drop into their home, often accompanied by Nancy, to hold prayer meetings and to counsel with them and their friend, Absalom Rice, on their problems, and to discuss in the free atmosphere of their home his own developing views. Young people he met there and in other homes were attracted by his happy banter, and he was called more and more frequently to perform marriage ceremonies.

But the Lulbegrud Church was a different story. It was as equally firmly rooted in austerity and in the *Philadelphia Confession of Faith*, rigid in its interpretation, intolerant of innovation. Dominated by Judge James French, it had erected the most imposing of all the church buildings in the area, a frame-and-log structure containing twelve corners, representing the twelve apostles, and from the high pulpit stand as John preached what he called his "thinking" sermons, he could sense the stony attitude of the very proper families of Matt Davis and John Treadway and John Fletcher sitting stolidly behind the Judge in the front row, and he held in check more than he liked his own dissentient views.

John was bedding down straw in the barn early in April when he looked out the door to see four men approaching, one from each of the four churches. He wiped his hands on the sides of his breeches before he shook hands all around. It was a committee, Judge French said as spokesman, come to say they were pleased with his ministry and wanted that he should settle permanently among them.

John did not conceal his surprise. "Why, that's what I intended to do, brethren," he said jovially. "I didn't know I'd been on trial up to now."

"Not on trial exactly," Judge French said, shifting his feet. "But there's been unrest, as you know, in North District; the churches don't all see alike, and not every preacher can please them all. He has to . . ."—the Judge paused, his thin set smile seeming like a crack in his long face— "Well, temper the wind to the shorn lamb, as the Scriptures say. And you're doing that, Brother Smith."

John frowned. "I don't exactly take that as a tribute, Brother French. I've no liking for feeling I'm not free to speak my mind."

Judge French held up his hand in protest. "Nothing of the kind intended. You are free to speak, but naturally," he cleared his throat, "as we all know, all things that are lawful are not always expedient." He looked at John solemnly. "You seem to realize that, and that's why we like you. We've come today offering to help you buy a farm." He looked to the others for confirmation. "We're proposing that you look for a place for sale, and when you find it, if you make the down payment, the churches will endeavor to keep up the succeeding payments for you."

It was a fair proposition, John thought. No mention had been made of any payment when he came, and he was not eager to accept a salary. He could manage to support himself if he had a farm, but he would need help in buying one at the outrageous prices land was bringing in northern Kentucky.

Hearty handshakes all around sealed the understanding, and as he trudged with the men toward their horses and watched them ride away, John rubbed thoughtfully at the stubble of beard on his chin. The Judge had him troubled; did he consider John Smith a compromiser? He grimaced, despising the thought. He had been too cautious when preaching at Lulbegrud with James French in the front row.

"I'm a little disquieted in my mind, Nancy," he said when he returned to the house and related the encounter. Nancy was heating the smoothing iron, pressing ribbons for the girls' hair; the children were in the lean-to, shelling bread corn. "I've not a mind to cause any more trouble than North District already has, but I'm not sure I'm doing right, trying to steer a middle course; it's against my nature. And it's not being honest with the people. There's right, and there's wrong, and a man has to take a stand."

Nancy stopped pressing, holding the iron in midair. "But who's to say what's right and what's wrong? Like this ribbon; both sides are pretty. I favor one side showing on the girls' hair, and they favor the other." She resumed her ironing. "But I know what you mean. The women got to talking last week at the Female Sewing Society at Bertha Mason's house about you visiting so much with Jacob Coons and Absalom Rice down at Spencer's Creek, and them not even church members. The women from the Lulbegrud Church didn't think it was right; they said it should be brought before the North District at its next meeting."

John sank down into a chair in exasperation. "Brought before North District!" he cried. "That's just the trouble up here, the Associations have too much power. I always took it for granted a church had to have a governing body, but I'm beginning to wonder. It creates a hierarchy and assumes power it shouldn't have. I could see that at the midwinter meeting of North District; it was the first one I'd been to, but I could see right off it was deciding matters that rightly should be left to the churches. Like ousting the Mount Sterling Church because it kept David Barrow as pastor—that was a matter strictly for that church to decide, and North District should have let it alone." He got up and paced the length of the stone floor of the kitchen. "At that meeting the Association even went on record declaring it's wrong for Baptists to belong to the Freemasons. Judge French proposed it and said it was because the Masons are a secret society, but I asked him right out if it wasn't because he thought the Masons were in competition with the churches, and we're jealous of them. He got mad as a wet hen when I said if some of our folks are joining them it's because people needing help can't find it in the churches, that we're so busy fighting each other we haven't time to fight the devil. Shame on us!" He glared at Nancy for a moment. "And same's true of the reason the Shakers are making headway among our people."

Nancy laughed. "Molly Higgins was telling me how you ran the Shakers away from their house the other day." She shook her head. "John, you do beat all. Did you deliberately make one of those visiting Shaker men mad to prove to Moses Higgins he wasn't as good as he claimed?"

John smiled at the recollection. It was true. He had encountered a team of touring Shakers at the Moses Higgins' home, one of the Grassy Lick Church families, and, to counteract their claim that they were the people of the resurrection and as such had put away their wives and become angels, he had taunted two of them into anger. "A mad Shaker! A mad angel!" he had cried, routing the men in confusion from their efforts to proselyte the Higgins family. But it would take more than that, he knew, to rout them from the inroads they were making all over the state with their queer doctrine. It would take the full power of the gospel.

It was late in the summer, and the broad leaves of the corn had yellowed in the garden plot John and Joshua had planted next to the rented cabin before John located a farm for sale. Two miles east of Mount Sterling, the place was owned by two women, Grace Forbes and Elizabeth Dozer, who would accept $3,150 for their 107 acres. It was good soil, watered by a cold, clear spring, its source hidden in a rock ledge in the grove. Another deep well was on the far edge of the five-acre clearing back of the house. John had hoarded the four hundred dollars he had secured from Joseph Hurt for his eighty acres down in Wayne, and with another one hundred dollars he and Nancy had saved since their marriage, he paid five hundred dollars down on the place, secure in the knowledge the churches would keep up the twice-yearly payments.

The fall was deep in grayness, the sky granite-hard, with a cold, thin rain falling the first day of November, 1818, when they moved in. Nancy was pregnant and could do little to help except keep the three children out of the way, but Joshua herded the stock, now grown to six cows and twice as many hogs and sheep, across back fields to the new location and had them penned in the barn pasture by the time John completed the two trips with the wagon containing the belongings they had accumulated.

The rain increased in intensity. By nightfall it had become a torrent. They built a roaring fire in the kitchen hearth, and Nancy located the iron spider and kettle from among the boxes and barrels they had hurriedly pushed, helter-skelter, into the rooms, and fried corn cakes and ham slices and made onion stew. They ate ravenously, their only light that of the fire and a single candle; and then John led them in fervent prayer, and they crawled into whatever pallets Nancy could throw together out of the confusion of bearskins and blankets and buffalo hides.

But it was a good house, John decided, as he lay listening to the rain on the roof. The logs were daubed with clay and straw, the clapboards of the roof bound together by long poles. The floors were puncheon; the jambs and backwall were of stiff mortar, and the chimney was also of mortar, John thought thankfully, remembering that the fire at Hickory Flats had started in the timber chimney. John and Nancy would have their bedroom at the rear of the lower floor, the front half reserved as a sitting room, separated by a dogtrot from the kitchen, while overhead the loft, extending over the dogtrot, was partitioned into four square rooms for the children, reached by an open stairwell leading up from the dogtrot. And it was so handy to the road the children could watch the wagon trains heading west.

The rain turned to snow in the night, and in the morning the sky, a dull gray, seemed to be emptying itself. John and Joshua cleared a path to the barn to feed the stock and to get wood. They could not get to the well, a good quarter-mile from the house, so John brought in pails of snow to melt, and then Joshua carried the snow water to the stock. Sadie McDonnold had given Nancy a setting of goose eggs, and Nancy insisted John bring her single goose into the house as well as the baby chickens, and penned them all in the kitchen after pouring warm water down their throats. By nightfall the trees, the fence railings, the barn roof were layered with ice-covered snow; branches of trees snapped and groaned.

The third morning the sky cleared, and a thaw set in, and by week's end John and Joshua had hollowed out some tree lengths and hitched them together to form a split-log flume to bring water to the oak trough near the barn. Nancy insisted they run another close to the house for her use.

The next week Joshua left, lured by the promise of riches in Ohio, and life settled again into a routine. When John rode into Mount Sterling early in January to pick up supplies at Buckner Payne's store, he was happily surprised when the friendly merchant presented him with a white-oak plow with iron points. "It's a housewarming present," Mr. Payne said.

"There'll be housewarming in heaven," John said, thanking him, "when you give yourself to the Lord. I can't understand how, with all the rascals that have edged themselves into the church, a good man like you has been kept out."

"It's because Eliza and I could never decide which church was right; maybe we don't care," Buckner Payne said, laughing. "The

Methodists and Presbyterians and Baptists all have good points; give or take a little, any of them would suit us."

John eyed him thoughtfully. "You mean the points on which they differ mean nothing to you?"

"That's about the sum of it," Mr. Payne said, snapping his fingers. "They don't mean that. So don't ask me to subscribe to your peculiar Baptist doctrine. I'll take my chances on getting to heaven on my own."

"You may beat us all there," John said as he left. "God knows!"

He picked up several recent copies of the Lexington newspaper, the *Kentucky Gazette*, at the store, and as he read them that night at home the news disturbed him. Kentucky had chartered forty-six state banks, allowing them to issue paper money totaling, he read, over twenty-six million dollars. He felt the two crisp new bank notes in his pocket. These notes were being viewed with suspicion, the editor said; some business houses were refusing to accept them. Even the new banks, called by the editor "the Forty Thieves," would not accept notes from each other. Business failures were rampant in Lexington, several great trading places, their names familiar to John, were bankrupt. Homesteads, he read, were being mortgaged, and business generally was stagnant.

But the land was still in the care of God, he reminded himself as the months raced by, and he preached with increased fervor. And the four churches responded. Lulbegrud increased to 135 members; he baptized fifty-seven new members into the Spencer's Creek Church and thirty at Grassy Lick. But the people were poor, and when the first note on his farm became due in April, 1819, he knew only the more wealthy Lulbegrud Church would be able to pay its share of the amount due.

Without mentioning the matter to anyone, he drove six of his hogs into Mount Sterling the day the payment was due, and sold them to meet the obligation himself. It meant they would not butcher, come fall, but Nancy could manage somehow, and Lulbegrud's payment would help.

It was not until he ran by chance across Judge French in the bank that he realized Lulbegrud, too, would not pay its share. The Judge saw him, but his eyes passed over him, and assuming absorption in some papers in his hand, the Judge walked by him and out the door.

John looked thoughtfully at the long green coat flapping about the Judge's knees, at the glint of sunlight on the gray side whiskers as the Judge reached the street and turned and stalked down the plank sidewalk. A sickening surge of certainty tightened in his stomach. It was not a matter of Lulbegrud's lack of money. There were other reasons. He had been less cautious lately in his preaching; the Judge was becoming suspicious of him.

CHAPTER XXI

SPRING was lamb-dropping time, and three ewes were dropped the day Nancy's baby was born in May, 1819. It was an easy birth; Nancy had awakened John in the night, and he had given her black-pepper tea and quinine to hurry the pains before he rode over for Granny Whelen. As the toothless midwife laid the baby in his arm, John scrutinized the red, wrinkled face. It was a boy, the first son to take the place of the son he had lost in the fire.

"He looks like Jonathan," he said as he placed the baby beside Nancy in the feather bed. Her eyes widened, and then she smiled, understanding. His name was Jonathan.

With his new white-oak plow John turned the garden, showing Jennie, now nine, and Zerelda, almost five, how to drop the seed, putting a bit of lime in now and then to fertilize, and within a month after the baby's birth, Nancy was beside them, helping with the hoeing, responding to the stirrings of life in the earth. Eliza Blaze, two years old and sickly from birth, toddled after her, and it was when they paused one day to listen to a flock of wild geese honking that Nancy first noticed her listlessness. She felt the child's forehead; it was burning hot. She doctored her for three days with quinine and molasses, and the fourth morning John rode into Mount Sterling to fetch Dr. Ennis Combs. By the time they returned in the early afternoon, the little body was in convulsions. She died that night.

The burial took place in the Grassy Lick burying plot, and Nancy and John shared their first grief. For a week they lived in a daze, but life pressed them on, and they were thankful for its absorbing, healing demands. Their days became a race with planting and harvesting. Nancy, grounded in mountain lore, insisted they plant the rooted things in the dark of the moon lest they go to all vine, and the beans and corn in the full moon. No sooner had they gathered the early garden peas than the corn was ready; turnips and beans, pumpkins and yellow squash ripened in quick succession. The gourd seed Nancy had planted became vines, their thick pods swelling, and she snapped them off and dried them to make dippers and noggins. Three cows freshened and, to relieve Nancy, John took over for a time the twice-daily milking.

But the demands on his time were increasing. The churches were growing, and his sermons before the North District Association were spreading his fame. People called on him for funerals as well as marriages, comforted by the joy with which he seemed to push open the gates of heaven and usher the loved one into the very presence of God. Absalom Rice appeared one day with his sister Polly, to arrange for him to perform Polly's marriage ceremony to Joseph Smith; the next day his neighbor, Edward Sallee, secured him to officiate at the marriage of his daughter Patsy to Henry Brothers. Both were large, fashionable weddings, and he wore the new store-bought black broadcloth suit Nancy had urged him to buy from Buckner Payne. Often couples dropped by the house to be married, when Nancy would serve as the only witness, and frequently he was asked to perform the ceremony in rough cabins with only the families present. He became known as the "marrying preacher," and each marriage brought a fee of some kind: a quart of preserves, a gallon of whiskey, sometimes a dollar or two. "I do it because it's a holy work," he told Nancy, "but the gifts come in handy."

It was the following year on Friday, July 2, that John made his usual weekly trip into Mount Sterling for supplies. It was a warm day and, riding home, the wagon filled, he slowed the horse to a walk and opened the copy of the *Kentucky Gazette* he had purchased. The news was exciting.

"Listen to this, Nancy," he called as he entered the kitchen. He stood within the light pouring through the door and read:

> "The President of the United States is expected in town today. A procession of the citizens and uniform companies will be

> formed on Short Street, back of the public square, at the third beat of the drum, where the citizens are respectfully requested to attend."

Nancy stopped her loom to listen, and her brown eyes grew round with excitement. "President Monroe himself!"

John nodded. "And General Jackson will be with him."

"You should be there to see him, John," Nancy said. "It isn't every man in his lifetime gets to see two such bigwigs. Change your breeches and put on your linen shirt. You could be there by late afternoon."

John considered, tempted, and then shook his head. "I'm preaching tonight at Goshen, and tomorrow I promised to visit Bath County; then Sunday is preaching day at Grassy Lick in the morning, and in the afternoon I'm preaching at Mount Sterling for Brother David." He folded the paper and laid it on the table. "But I'm sorely tempted. I've never seen a President."

"How long's he to be hereabouts?"

"Until Tuesday, the paper says."

"Then you go over to Lexington on Monday. You could leave before sunup and be there in time to see whatever doings are scheduled."

John looked at her as she sat bending slightly over the yarn in her lap, letting it flow through her fingers, testing it, winding it. "Why don't you go with me?" he said on impulse. "You need to get away; you work too hard."

Nancy's eyes brightened. "It would pleasure me, all right," she said. "I could wear that new ruffled petticoat I made under my blue skirt; it fluffs it out pretty. And I got that white shawl and . . ." She got up and shook herself. "Shucks, what am I thinking of?" She pushed the cluster of yarn balls and the loom aside and went to the cradle and picked up the baby. "I can't go any place much just now," she said, settling herself in the rocker and opening the front of her dress. "Men never seem to think of such things, but I reckon that's nature." She laughed softly and pressed the hungry baby to her breast.

When John rode into Lexington the following Monday he found the streets crowded. It was his first visit to the town since his trip there with Jacob Creath five years before. And the town had changed. He slowed the horse to a walk as he went down Main Street to the public square. The wooden market house which had stood on Cheapside, close to Short, had been torn down, the market moved to a brick building on Water Street. The library building, too, on the public square was being abandoned; relays of Negroes were carrying books to the confectionery shop of the Frenchman, M. Giron, on Mill Street. Lexington was growing, despite rumors its best days were over since steamboat travel was taking folks to Louisville; it was still the meeting place of the cultured and the learned and the gay. But the whipping post on Cheapside and Main still stood, and close to it the auction block for slaves. Coming into town he had passed the slave jail, averting his gaze from its high walls crowned with spikes. But now he pulled in his horse and stared, feeling the full force of the silent rebuke of this national sin. The courthouse in the center of the public square now boasted a clock in its cupola that worked, and the hands stood at thirty minutes past nine o'clock. He had made the thirty-mile ride in a little over three hours. At Main Cross he passed the new Masonic Hall beginning to take shape, replacing the building on Market burned in March. He rode past Main Cross to Spring Street and turned toward Water Street, passing Usher's Theater, and stopped at Hugh's Livery Stable and left his horse.

A public dinner was scheduled for noon at Keen's Tavern, and as he started walking back down Main Street he could see a crowd already assembling about the front entrance. But the big men would not be arriving, he knew, until just before the festivities began. He would have time to walk about and see the town. He turned at Main Cross and walked toward Gratz Park, and stood at the rail fence and stared at the cupola that topped the three-story building which was Transylvania College, now calling itself a university, recalling the week he preached in the chapel with Jacob Creath. The little Town Fork Baptist congregation that had met there was now the First Baptist Church with a brick building of its own, pastored by the liberal-minded preacher James Fishback, a great friend, so it was rumored, of the controversial Horace Holley, president of the college. Together these two men were challenging all sorts of cherished dogmas, things he scarcely understood; but they were profound scholars. He looked at the glass windows of the college, reflecting the sun; all the learning of the world was contained in that building. Almost wistfully he turned away.

He walked over to Jordan's Row, hoping for a sight of Henry Clay. His offices were close by at 132 Short Street, and John stood for a while in front of the green door with its huge brass knocker. But Mr. Clay was probably not around; he would not be attending anything that Andrew Jackson attended if he could help it. John grinned. Henry Clay was his man; he liked his stand on every issue; he stood for things that would fulfill the country's promise.

He made his way toward Keen's Tavern. It was almost noon. People were milling about the entrance as he elbowed his way through the crowd and found a spot near one of the new oil street lamps, and leaned against it. Jeremiah Vardeman would probably be attending the dinner, and maybe Jacob Creath. They were big men and had been to Washington City and knew everybody. But he did not see them, and after a time he pulled out of his pocket the turkey breast slices and hunk of corn bread Nancy had insisted he bring along. The food tasted good; he was tired. It was hot in the sun, and the crowd was restless. He wiped his forehead with the back of his hand and thought of the coolness of the grove at Grassy Lick, and then for some reason the pulpit stand at Spencer's Creek came before him; he could almost feel its edge, rubbed to satiny smoothness by hands that had preached there. He closed his eyes and imagined the shaded lanes of Montgomery County, the dappled sunlight coming through in great patches; he could hear the birds, and the cattle lowing. He shook himself and stood erect. God was in the cities, too; it was just harder to hear him.

He had finished the last crumb when a face in the crowd attracted his attention. For a moment he stared, puzzled. The man's hat was drawn low, shielding his eyes, but there was no mistaking the generous mouth and the firm chin. It was Barton W. Stone.

"You're like balm in Gilead," he said, catching Stone by the sleeve. "I don't know as how I want to hang around just to see a President and a General when I can talk to the author of 'The Last Will and Testament!' How are you, sir?"

"There's danger here," Stone laughed. "You might become a heretic. Why haven't you been to see me? I heard you were in Montgomery County."

"I was fixing to walk by your church here later on," John said. "I been wanting to talk to you."

"It's a good thing we met then," Stone said, smiling in welcome. "Because I'm riding on to Georgetown right away. I've bought a farm near there and have organized a church. I'm also teaching at Rittenhouse Academy there."

"And you've given up the other churches?"

"Not at all. I'm still preaching here in Lexington once a month; that's why I'm in town today, I preached here yesterday. I'm also still preaching at Cane Ridge and Concord once a month."

A stir in the crowd, and several carriages drew up before the tavern, escorted by an infantry and rifle company. Salutes were fired, and John, standing beside Stone, watched as former Governor Isaac Shelby stepped gingerly to the ground, his aging frame assisted by Governor Slaughter, followed by a robust, disheveled man in a crumpled suit with red vest and flaming red cravat.

"That's Colonel Richard M. Johnson," Stone whispered to John. "His father, Colonel Robert, was a big Baptist over near Georgetown at Great Crossings; the Colonel's been in Congress and is headed for the Senate this fall, they say. He's reported to have killed Tecumseh, the great Indian chief, in the Battle of the Thames back during the war with England. He and General Jackson are good friends."

"They must be a very fine family," John said. "Brother Creath told me another son, John T., is in the state legislature."

"And that's Colonel James Morrison," Stone went on as a tall, dignified man stepped from the next carriage and stood in the forming semicircle, ignoring the crowd, staring straight ahead. "He's to give the speech today; he's a close friend of Dr. Horace Holley, the president of Transylvania. And, yes, that's Dr. Holley just behind him, with Judge Bledsoe."

A cheer from the crowd, and John saw the gaunt, emaciated figure of General Andrew Jackson emerge, vigorously waving his tall hat with his one good arm, his shock of white hair standing upright, a frame for his strong, deeply lined face. Another cheer, and the stocky figure of President James Monroe stepped from the carriage. He stood in the center of the semicircle, a frozen smile on his face, lifting his hand in a half-wave as mingled boos and catcalls began to mingle with the cheers.

"They're mostly Clay supporters here," Stone said. "The boos are for the General. Henry Clay is the idol of Lexington, and his friends are not likely to let Andrew Jackson, or the President either, forget it."

With hurried strides the President led the group toward the tavern door, and they were swallowed in the surging crowd.

John was glad it was over. "Well, Old Hickory was a great Indian fighter," he said. "And he did work with Governor Sevier in getting the Chickasaws to cede their claims to those seven million acres of land in Tennessee and Kentucky to the government." He turned to Stone. "Let's get out of here," he said, dismissing the subject. "I've seen my fill."

Stone nodded. "Mine, too. Politics will never redeem society. Greatness isn't won by political office. A man is great only to the degree he does the thing God wants him to do, be it in high places or low places."

"But God needs somebody to fill the high places," John protested mildly. "Who's going to run the government?"

Stone frowned. "Politics is a school of corruption and demoralization. I question if Christians should even participate in political life."

John looked his surprise. "Why?"

"In politics, whether church or secular, a man has to defend his cause whether right or wrong," Stone said. "This develops into a habit of mind that undermines his integrity, and eventually it shows in hundreds of little ways. I was struck with this when I attended the meeting for these distinguished men at Transylvania Saturday morning. President Holley's remarks far outshone, for instance, the remarks of any of the others, even President Monroe's speech. We have a brilliant man in Dr. Holley." He shook his head. "It's a pity there is so much agitation against him by the conservative Presbyterians on the college board."

"I've been hearing he's liberal-minded," John said. "Some of our preachers are saying he doesn't even believe in God. Is that true?"

Stone's lips tightened. "He believes devoutly in God," he said stoutly. "He just uses different words to explain his belief. I sometimes fear," he went on, a tinge of sadness in his tone, "that the churches are in some sort of conspiracy against the growth or even the mere expression of a spirit of inquiry or tolerance in matters of religion."

"I don't see your point about Christians not engaging in politics," John said, "but I do agree with you that folks seem to be getting more fond of their own way of saying things all the time, and less inclined to listen to the way the other fellow says it. It's a bad thing for the country as well as for the church."

Stone glanced at the courthouse clock. "I promised Celia I'd meet her at the farm by midafternoon to decide on a horse a man wants to sell us. Why don't you ride on to Georgetown with me? It would be out of your way a little, but we could visit, and you could see the town."

All things work together for those who love the Lord, John mused as the two men jogged down Main Cross and out the pike. Just to visit with this dedicated, thought-provoking man would make any day worth while. And they had much to talk about. John had never been north of Lexington, and the countryside was more populated than he had imagined. They passed at least twenty houses in the ten-mile stretch between Lexington and Georgetown, large two-story houses, some of brick with high, white columns, all of them set in the midst of rippling fields of bluegrass and gardens, surrounded by horse corrals and huge barns and low stone fences Something in the limestone soil produced excellent grazing conditions, Stone told him as they rode along exulting in the beauty of it all, and although horse racing had been suspended for the last few years, fine horses were still raised and shown. "I don't frown on such worldly display," Stone said. "I just consider it meaningless."

Georgetown itself boasted seventy houses, and a mile or so north was Great Crossings on the Elkhorn River with more houses sprawling about the big estate of Colonel Richard Johnson, Stone pointed out.

"There's your Baptist Church," he said as they passed Pratt's Hotel on Court Street dissecting Main Street, and paused in front of a low brick building, square, with a plank door. "The church belongs in the Elkhorn Association which pulled out of your North District Association because of a squabble."

John laughed. "I'm not surprised; North District has a history of squabbles."

"The Baptists used to meet in the courthouse, but they got out a few years back and put up this building. Rittenhouse Academy, where I'm teaching, bought the old courthouse."

John twisted around in his saddle and looked at the imposing two-story brick structure in the center of the public square. His eyes widened. "You mean we Baptists are strong enough here to need that big courthouse?"

Stone laughed. "That's not the building. The one they used was a frame structure, and the Scott County Trustees wanted to get rid of it. So last year Rittenhouse Academy bought it for a bit over a hundred dollars and had it moved to a place over yonder," he motioned with his whip, "called Science Hill. That's where I teach now. It's near the Christian Church I organized last year. I want you to see my church."

They rode slowly, past Gaines General Store, bigger than Buckner Payne's store in Mount Sterling, John thought; past a carding works and a nail factory, and stopped in front of a small brick structure built, Stone said, on the former burying ground given to the town by an old Baptist preacher, Joel Craig. They sat for a while on their horses, silent.

"I can't get it right in my mind about there being a church that's not connected with a sect," John said after a moment, staring at the name over the door. "Christian Church. It sounds too good to be true." He turned in his saddle. "Will it work, having no creed at all, I mean?"

Stone shrugged. "I've no objection to creeds if they're just a statement of what men believe. In a way, they're good things to have, to inform the world of a man's beliefs. But what I object to is making them a test of Christian character, or a term of Christian communion."

"And you have no governing body, either," John said. "Who makes your rules? What body has authority to legislate?"

"That's part of the invisible structure. Jesus Christ is the one and only lawmaker," Stone said. "He will save those who obey his laws and punish those who disobey them. There is no need for any other lawmaker in the earthly church, nor of any additional laws."

"No disciplines? No calling a member to account?"

"Only a man's conscience before God," Stone said soberly. "The church was governed only by God's commandments as interpreted by Jesus Christ for a hundred and fifty years. When men began adding their own set of laws and rules, well, it was then the trouble started, and the church began to divide. My aim is to restore the apostolic simplicity of the early church."

John was silent, absorbing the words. Then he looked up, his eyes twinkling. "Some folks say you ran out of Babylon so fast you've run right past Jerusalem."

Barton Stone smiled. "I know they do. It's my fault, too, because I'm unable to explain to some people. They have legalistic minds; they have to have a precedent for everything. They can't see the original church restored because we have no exact description of it, and no one ever attempted it before. They have to have a reason or an example for everything."

John looked thoughtful. "I'm sort of that way. Maybe too much that way." He was silent a moment. "But I'm beginning to see that there's a place where reason shuts the door, and the spirit takes over." He squirmed in his saddle. "But I still think you'd done better to stay with the Presbyterians and reform them. One man alone can't give history much of a turn."

"One man and God can," Stone replied quietly. "And there's more than one of us devoted to restoring that unity of the church for which Christ prayed."

John repressed as somehow irreverent the impulse to remark that all followers of Jesus would again be united if they would only return to the one true faith of John the Baptist.

"There's a new wind sweeping over the earth," Stone continued. "We are not alone. For the first time since the apostasy, men are arising here and there denouncing human creeds and urging a return to the teachings of Jesus as set forth in the Holy Bible. It is such a simple way to salvation that many men, blind fools, reject it; but there are some—a few—who understand. Did you know"—he turned to John in a note of triumph—"that under our Springfield Presbytery, short-lived as it was, fifteen congregations were established? There were seven in Ohio and eight here in Kentucky. The people will respond, once creeds and theology are brushed aside."

John frowned, puzzled. "Then why did you dissolve your Springfield Presbytery? How did it happen that you're the only one of the five preachers who started it, to stick with its principles?"

"It only goes to prove what fools we mortals be, after all," Stone replied, shaking his head. His horse was getting restless, and he reined him in sharply. "Yes, two of our men went back to the Presbyterians, and two ran off with the Shakers. It was because we organized too hastily and hadn't thought our way through. We got together when Richard M'Nemar was brought to trial by the Kentucky Synod in Lexington back almost seventeen years ago now, on charges of preaching the everlasting love of God. Arminian views, they called it. Four others of us were implicated in the same charges, and so we simply withdrew together. We had no wish at the time to leave the Presbyterian Church, so we just organized an independent presbytery, making it clear that we renounced all creeds but the Bible and no longer believed in the total depravity of man or the doctrine of the Elect. We issued what we called our Apology in an effort to throw new light on the ancient gospel. That's why many call us 'New Lights' now." He laughed quietly. "We did convince a number of people but not the Synod of Kentucky. The others thought we were fighting a losing battle, but I never gave up hope and stuck with it."

"But why did you dissolve your presbytery?" John asked. "You were changing people, converting them to your way of thinking, you say, some of them pretty smart folks. I'm told that a legislator, David Purviance, even quit politics to preach your New Light gospel. You were doing pretty well, I'd say."

"David Purviance was one of the witnesses to our 'Last Will and Testament of the Springfield Presbytery.' He was strong in the gospel and as firm against slavery as David Barrow. Now he's an Ohio legislator; a lawmaker and a preacher, like the prophets." He pushed his hat to the back of his head. "We dissolved the presbytery because, as we stated in the Address which we sent the Synod at the same time we sent the 'Last Will and Testament,' we finally agreed we wished to repudiate all divisions and parties and all human creeds and organizations as without precept or example in the New Testament, and would call ourselves, and act, simply as Christians. We would still unite, we said, with all other Christian brethren in the glorification of our Lord, but we would not be Presbyterians or Methodists or Episcopalians or Catholics, or members of any church parties. No, nor Baptists either!" He smiled at John. "We will not be called Baptists even though we eventually realized that immersion is the only scriptural baptism, and we all became immersed."

It had grown late, and John took a bearing on the sun. "I've a far piece to ride," he said. "I'd best be pushing on."

"I wish you had time to stop by Cane Ridge and see my church there," Stone said. "It's on the edge of the town of Paris, some out of your way, but I'd like you to see it."

"I'll come there to hear you preach some time," John said. "That is, if you'll come hear me. You're on your way to becoming a Baptist. I have hope for you."

"I'll let you try to work on me if you'll give me a hearing, too. It's a fair exchange."

"Exchange heresy for orthodoxy?" John grinned. "I'm not so sure about it."

He waved in farewell and rode away swiftly in the thickening twilight. The air was pungent with the odor of smoke from burning shives of hemp stalks, and figures of the black workers silhouetted the fields. It would be good to hear Barton Stone preach at Cane Ridge, but as for now, he had heard enough. What the man had done was wrong. But maybe a man had to do wrong sometimes; not to do so could be even more wrong.

CHAPTER XXII

HARD times were again on the land. John found he could secure only twelve and a half cents a bushel for his corn when he drove a wagonload into Mount Sterling market in September, and although Nancy churned every day, the going rate for her butter was only six cents a pound. But the three fresh cows were producing more than enough milk for the family, and she enjoyed making the rich, golden butter. "But we're not selling the eggs," she said definitely. "They're bringing only three cents a dozen, and they're worth more than that to us as food."

The children did need them; they were growing rapidly, active and intelligent. Jennie was ten and tall for her years, and Zerelda was six. Jonathan was going on two, toddling everywhere, into everything. Nancy didn't hold with idleness. Both the girls had their house duties when they weren't hoeing in the garden or gathering papaws and persimmons, walnuts and hickory nuts, and when Nancy was confined early in December, Jennie and Zerelda proved the value of her training as they helped John keep the household on an even keel. Jennie had learned to make rabbit scrapple, and John kept her supplied with rabbits which she boiled until the bones worked out and then kneaded the meat with corn meal and pepper, and sliced into the big iron skillet for frying. Until Nancy was able to cook, they depended on the dish for all meals, and the turkey Nancy roasted at Christmas tasted, John said, like manna from heaven. The baby was another boy.

"He puts me in mind of Willy," Nancy declared when the baby was a week old. "He's not given to crying fits and sort of seems to take life as it comes."

That night John wrote William of the arrival of his namesake, and two days after Christmas a reply was received: a long letter with surprising family news. Jonathan was getting married, William wrote, and would bring his bride, Rachel Derby, to live at the old home place with Ma, but only until the place was sold. Then Ma would go to live with Betsy and her husband, Ezra Matlock, across the Tennessee line, and Jonathan would move to the bluegrass region.

Nancy looked dubious when he relayed the news to her. "It'll be nice having some of the family about," she said, "but somehow I wish it was Willy and Maggie moving up here instead of Jonathan."

"Jonathan means well," John said, "he was just born old; that's his trouble. He was born set in his ways, like Philip." He read the letter again. "I'm glad Ma's going to sell the old place; it was too much for her, trying to keep house, and she's better off with one of her own daughters, like Betsy, instead of with Jonathan's wife."

The winter rains set in, making many roads impassable, and as the new year of 1821 advanced, business conditions worsened. The banks collapsed, paper money flooded the state; farmers were in trouble, and interest rates were high. The churches paid John nothing on his farm debt, and only by scraping together every piece of hard money he could obtain did he keep the interest paid.

"Pity you didn't get that agreement down in writing," Nancy said. "Business is business, even between church folks."

"Christians should be able to trust one another," John replied.

"I didn't say anything about Christians," she said tartly. And then her tone softened. "But I don't feel unkindly toward the Spencer's Creek folks and them at Grassy Lick or Bethel, either; they're poor, and we know it, and they do what they can, sending us provisions. It's the Lulbegrud crowd I can't figure out; they're plenty able."

But as if to remind the country that wealth did not consist only in banks and trade and interest payments, the summer brought an exceptionable harvest, fed by the heavy rains. John was working with a bull calf in the front pasture, trying to break it to wear a yoke early in September, when a gig stopped at the stile.

"I hear you're the marrying preacher around here," a hearty voice called.

John wiped his hands on the sides of his linsey breeches and pushed his straw hat to the back of his head, squinting against the sun, peering at the big man clambering out of the buggy. Slowly he grinned. It was Jeremiah Vardeman, all three hundred pounds of him, he thought grimly. A woman was seated in the gig, and as John went forward to greet them, he noticed her push herself further back into the corner of the seat.

Vardeman's voice again boomed out. "How's my young Timothy faring these days?"

John almost instinctively shrank from the grasp of the powerful clasp on his outstretched hand across the fence. "You're a sight for sore eyes, Brother Vardeman," he said. "My first sight of you since Nancy and I met you at the first North District meeting we attended up here. Where've you been? We've been to every meeting of North District since, and all we hear is that you're off itinerating some place or other."

"That's right," Vardeman said. "I've had the itching foot, but I'm settling down again for a spell. I kept my farm over near David's Fork, and I'm back there, preaching a half-dozen places nearby and staying close to home"—he waved toward the buggy—"since I married."

John pulled off his wide-brimmed straw hat and gravely bowed as Vardeman formally introduced the woman in the buggy. "My wife of six months, formerly Miss Elizabeth Bryant."

The woman smiled and inclined her head, and John noticed she pulled the rug closer about her although the day was warm. Instantly he realized she was in the family way.

"Won't you light and stay for dinner?" he said hurriedly, sharing her embarrassment. "Nancy would pleasure to have you; she often asks about you, Brother Vardeman. It's near noon, and she's got a mess of turnip greens cooking. I know because I did the picking." He anticipated the refusal even before it came. Vardeman had an afternoon wedding at David's Fork, and they had better be pushing on.

John smiled. "I know how it is. Seems I'm hurrying somewhere half the time for a wedding." He turned to Vardeman. "Yes, I do a heap of them. Big ones and little ones; sometimes they come to the house, and it takes place in the kitchen; other times I'm called to the big houses along the pike. Seems folks around here think if I can hitch them they'll stay hitched."

"And each one means a fee, of course." Vardeman leaned across the fence and poked him knowingly in the side.

"Maybe," John said, not responding to the sally. "Maybe a dollar or two—sometimes a basket of provisions. It helps out."

"You're a shrewd one, Raccoon John," Vardeman said. "You're building up the four churches too, I hear. They doing well by you?"

"If you mean are they paying me," John said sharply, "the answer is no. Times are pretty hard. I'm having to keep up the payments on the farm myself although our agreement was they'd do it."

Vardeman frowned. "James French at Lulbegrud could pay your whole debt himself and never miss it," he said.

"Judge French and I don't see eye to eye," John said, wondering how much to tell this friend, how far to seek his advice. "He's a pretty rigid Calvinist, and I've not entirely concealed my doctrinal doubts. He runs the Lulbegrud Church, and it's a bastion of Calvinism." He kicked at a clod of earth. "But I try not to rile him."

"That's the way to do, my boy." Vardeman spoke with emphasis. "We can't get out of step with our Baptist brethren." He laughed heartily.

"But that's just the point—a preacher has to do more than just keep step," John said. "He's supposed to be a leader."

Vardeman nodded. "And rightly so. The clergy must dominate the church."

"I didn't mean that," John said almost harshly. "Only God should dominate the church. I meant a leader in searching out God's will." And then, as if he had said too much, his voice calmed, and he went on. "I'll keep step, of course, but I'm still trying to think through some points that disturb me. I'm working my way out of the woods, just as I had to do when I was converted. Some men make decisions easy; I don't."

"Well, don't do your thinking out loud. We have to temper the wind to the shorn lamb. Give in a little here and there to please the brethren; it's a matter of expediency."

"You've got me wrong, Brother Vardeman." John spoke more sharply than he intended, but he could feel his temper rising. "Whenever I'm sure of my views, whenever I'm convinced that some of the things that are troubling me should be corrected," he paused and looked Vardeman steadily in the eyes, "well, I'll speak my piece. My conscience is an article that I've never yet brought into the market."

The woman in the gig leaned forward. "We really should be leaving, Mr. Vardeman," she said. "I think there's a storm coming up."

Vardeman laughed. "John does sound like he's bent on talking up a storm." He reached across and slapped John on the shoulder. "You remind me of Philip Fall, Raccoon John," he said genially. "He's a young man about your age I licensed to preach at Forks of Elkhorn couple of years ago. I took him along on a trip last year into the Tennessee country and got him to help me organize the Baptists in Nashville." He climbed back into the buggy. "I thought he was good Baptist preacher material, but he got hold of a sermon by Alexander Campbell, and it gave him ideas."

"What sort of ideas?" John asked, curious. "Who is Alexander Campbell?"

"Campbell's a young preacher up in Virginia, about your age, I'd say. A Scot raised in north Ireland who came over here ten or twelve years ago as a Presbyterian, but he soon saw the light and had his whole family rebaptized by immersion. Now he's one of our up-and-coming Baptist preachers like you, and making a name for himself as a debater. He defends our scriptural position on baptism by immersion, and he cut a Presbyterian by the name of Walker to pieces in a debate last year." He looked thoughtful. "But I'm not sure he's sound. Some time back he preached a sermon he called 'The Law,' and it was way off center. He claimed Christians are no longer under the law of Moses but only that of Christ. If that means anything it means a man wouldn't even have to know the Old Testament teachings in order to receive the gospel."

John leaned over the fence, listening closely. "Sounds like some of the thinking I've been doing lately," he said, half to himself.

Vardeman snorted in disdain. "You and Philip Fall—you'll both go hungry if you're not careful. Philip's helping Jacob Creath over in Frankfort now, and I hope Jacob straightens him out. Independent thinking is all right so long as it stays within the *Philadelphia Confession;* when it goes off limits, it's heresy." He eyed John, reflecting. "But you'll straighten out. Campbell came by his notions naturally; his father, Thomas Campbell, jumped the Presbyterian traces more or less like your friend Barton Stone. He wrote a document favoring Christians all getting together and called it 'The Declaration and Address,' and young Alexander took it up. The Presbyterians put them out, and they've organized what they call the 'Christian Association,' and have even set up a separate church at Brush Run up in Virginia. When they got themselves all rebaptized by immersion, our Baptists in Virginia took them in, thinking they'd eventually fall in line with the rest of our doctrine, but they haven't."

"You ever met them?" John asked. "They sound real interesting."

"I met the old man, Thomas," Vardeman said. "He came down here and ran a school for a time over in Boone County couple of years ago. But he gave it up and moved back up near Buffalo, Virginia, where Alexander lives. He's a good teacher but impractical; too visionary." He leaned across the dashboard and spoke earnestly. "You know what he did down here? He preached to a group of blacks without a white man present, and that's against the law. When folks told him it was unlawful he got all upset and packed up bag and caboodle and moved back to where he said his children could breathe the air of freedom and where religion could be taught unfettered, or some such nonsense."

"Maybe he had a point," John said. "I see more wrong than good in slavery myself, and I'm finding there are plenty of good men in Kentucky who are against the whole system."

But Vardeman acted as if he weren't listening. "He's impractical. Of all people, a preacher has to be practical. That document he wrote, 'The Declaration and Address,' shows how visionary he is. Some of it is pretty good, and I agree with a few points he makes in what he calls his thirteen propositions. But the first one is this: 'The church of Christ upon earth is essentially, intentionally, and constitutionally one.' Now, doesn't that sound more like a poet than a hardheaded, realistic preacher?"

"I like poetry," John said stubbornly.

"Then read your Psalms," Vardeman said and laughed again in exuberant good humor and picked up the reins. "There's poetry there enough for any preacher." He cracked his whip sharply above the head of his patient horse, and the buggy spurted forward.

John watched uneasily as the vehicle rolled down the lane and turned into the pike. Mr. Vardeman was a big preacher, a powerful figure in the Baptist stronghold, and he meant well. He was a good man. He could fling his thunderbolts in the face of a transgressor and shake the soul of a stout-hearted sinner by holding him over the fiery lake and making him listen to the groans and agonies of those in endless despair, but for some reason John could not feel as kindly toward him as he felt he should. The man set him on edge. But those Campbells, Thomas and his son Alexander, they sounded like people he'd like to know. Maybe, some time, when he was talking with Barton Stone...

"Why didn't you ask him to light?" Nancy interrupted his thoughts, calling from the house, shading her eyes with her hand, her apron billowing in the breeze.

He went toward the house slowly, and her eyes searched his face. "That was Brother Vardeman, wasn't it?" she said. "You should have asked him to light and stay for dinner." When he didn't answer, her knowing eyes twinkled. "The Bible says to entertain folks, and never mind about wanting them all to be angels."

John took hold of her arm and pinched it, laughing. "You do beat all, Nancy," he said. "He has a new wife, and she's plain in the family way. We shouldn't think ill of the man." The leaves of the yellowing maples sifted the sunlight, making a pattern on the hard earth about the kitchen door. John sniffed. "Smells like those turnip greens are begging to be eaten," he said. "I'd like dinner; because I'm riding over to Cane Ridge. I feel a need to talk to my friend, Barton Stone. It's Wednesday, and he's there getting ready for midweek prayer meeting."

It was almost three o'clock in the afternoon and rain was starting to fall when John reached the Cane Ridge meetinghouse. He had ridden a narrow trace through heavy cane, the ground rising steadily until it formed a ridge between Hinkston and Stoner Creeks, and after a sharp turn, he came unexpectedly upon the church. He pulled his horse in, and sat looking at it, in imagination peopling the spot with scenes of the Great Revival as Thomas Stockton had described it now almost twenty years ago. The structure was set well back in a full two-acre clearing, adjacent to a burying plot on the west, a grove of poplars and horse chestnuts and elms shielding it on the east. Three horses were hobbled in the grove, and he dismounted and hitched his own horse near them and made his way toward the building. It appeared to be almost fifty feet square, of rough-hewn logs, its roof more than twice the height of a man. There was no chinking between the logs, no glass at the window openings, no chimney; only a ladder extending to a small opening on the far side.

For a moment he stood in the doorway, his eyes growing accustomed to the dimness. A single aisle ran down the center leading to a boxed pulpit which loomed above the rows of backless benches, reached by four puncheon steps. Three immense girders, hewn with a broadax, tied the log walls to the clapboard roofing, held in place with wooden pins. The floor was of puncheons, and over all a gallery encircled the room on three sides, its only entrance, as far as John could see, the ladder he had noticed outside.

Straddling one of the backless benches at the front, Barton Stone was in earnest conversation with two young men. They all glanced up as John entered, and Stone jumped to his feet. The greeting was cordial.

"Such a collection of Johns," he said, introducing the two other men. "John Rogers and John Allan Gano. I baptized both of them."

John instantly liked the two young men. John Rogers, a stocky, round-faced youth of perhaps twenty, he learned, was a cabinetmaker, but since his baptism two years before in Hinkston Creek had been also preaching in the courthouse in Carlisle on Sundays. Now Barton Stone was taking him on a preaching tour of the state, starting early in October.

"We're planning it now," John Rogers said, "because I must be back by year's end."

John Allan Gano laughed. "Tell him the reason, John."

John Rogers flushed. "I'm to be married," he said. "It's to be a double ceremony with William Morrow to two sisters. I'm marrying Eleanor Hildreth, and Will is marrying her sister Maria."

"Two of my brothers married sisters in a double wedding," John said, smiling. "You're in for a bad time." He turned to Barton Stone. "What about your church here at Cane Ridge while you're gone?"

John Allan Gano's thin, sensitive face brightened. "That's what I was just asking him," he said. He glanced up at the pulpit stand. "It's the dream of my life to some day preach from that pulpit," he said, his voice almost wistful.

Stone smiled. "And that's my dream for you, too. But you're not ready for it yet, John Allan, not quite. You're a fledgling." He turned to John. "John Mulkey and Francis Palmer will preach here while I'm away. John Allan is not yet nineteen and has been studying with me at Rittenhouse Academy over in Georgetown. He's reading law, but he's more and more inclined toward the ministry. His family are Baptists."

"Then you're a Baptist, of course?" John's tone was that of a question, although he had not intended it to be.

John Allan Gano shook his head. "I was brought up to think I was one, and I've been about excommunicated by my family for leaving it. But I can't see the Baptist doctrine, or maybe it's just that I see more clearly Mr. Stone's position. I like to think I'm just a Christian."

Stone laid his hand on the young man's arm. "He's such a Christian he almost converted Jacob Creath to our stand this past summer. Seems his two older sisters became so concerned when he joined our movement, they sent for Creath to come over from Frankfort, riding seventy miles in the August heat last month, and talk to him." He turned to John Allan. "You talked almost all of one night together, didn't you?"

John Allan Gano smiled. "That we did. And I almost convinced him, at least to the extent he admitted he was seriously disturbed about the rightness of preaching under any other authority than the Bible itself." He shook his head. "But what I can't understand is how he could then go on being a Baptist. He's a fair-minded man, but for all his patient willingness to listen, he went over to Great Crossings the very next day and baptized one of Colonel Robert Johnson's sons into the Baptist Church."

Stone nodded. "It was the son who has just been elected to Congress, John T. Johnson," he said. "A fine man even if he is in politics, and a close friend of Creath's nephew, Jacob, in Washington City."

John studied the puncheon floor. "It was probably because he thought it wiser to stay in the Baptist Church and reform it than start another sect," he said. "That's the way I feel."

"Trouble with reforming anything," Stone said, "is that you have to reform again and again. That's the history of every reform movement. Instead of reforming the existing church parties, I suggest we restore the church as it was in New Testament days, rooting it firmly in the pattern set by the early disciples. With its roots there, it can sway and bend to adjust to the times, but fundamentally it would always be the same. A strong tree is still a tree whatever winds blow, and the church would still be the church despite men's opinions blowing about it."

"Did you ever hear of a Baptist preacher in Virginia named Alexander Campbell?" John asked suddenly.

"Indeed, yes." Stone's face brightened. "I met his father, Thomas Campbell, when he taught a school over in Boone County at Burlington a couple of years ago, and he gave me a copy of his 'Declaration and Address,' a powerful document he'd written urging the restoration of the unity of the early church. His son, Alexander, preached a sermon on 'The Law,' which has been having a tremendous influence. Their thinking is much like mine; so much so I see no essential difference between us, although they call themselves Baptists."

"Maybe it's because they don't want to form another religious party. You didn't want to either, but folks are calling your people New Lights and Stoneites."

Stone shrugged. "I know it, and I don't doubt but that in time those who follow the thinking of the Campbells will be called Campbellites. That's the calculated risk we run. Paul rebuked the church at Corinth because some of the members said they were of Paul, some of Apollos, some of Cephas, and some of Christ."

"I'd like to read that sermon on 'The Law,' and the 'Declaration and Address,' too. They must set a fellow to thinking," John said.

"That they do," Stone said. "I'll see you get copies of them. These two young preachers have already read them and agree with every word."

John Rogers nodded in agreement, and John Allan Gano said, "It struck me that Thomas Campbell sums up better than anything I've ever seen the basic rule on which all the churches could unite."

"What is that?" John asked.

John Allan thought for a moment and then stood up as if in acknowledgment of his respect for the words. "He said, 'Where the Scriptures speak, we speak; and where the Scriptures are silent, we are silent.' He called it simply The Rule."

John pondered the words as the young man resumed his seat, and then John Rogers spoke.

"What good would it do if the early brotherhood were restored?" he asked. "Suppose all the religious parties united into one church, would the world be any better off than it is now?"

"That's what I'm wondering," John said. "Would the gospel be any more effective?"

Stone arose and walked toward the pulpit stand, his face thoughtful, and then turned to the three men watching him.

"It would make all the difference," he said, his voice heavy with conviction, "all the difference in the world." His eyes took on a burning directness. "By what means has God ordained to bring the world to believe in his Son? I answer, The unity of believers. Tremendous thought! Yet we believers are nullifying the divinely appointed means by living in disunion." He paused, visibly agitated, and then went on, his voice deepening in intensity. "Since God will save none but believers in him, and by our disunity we are preventing men from believing, we are therefore instrumental in plunging the world into eternal ruin. The strife of Christians is the food of infidelity and the sport of hell."

For a moment there was silence in the room. Then Stone walked back to the bench and stood facing them. "The trouble is this, the want of the spirit of Jesus. The want of that spirit is the grand cause of division among Christians. And this spirit, restored, will be the grand cause of union."

For an hour longer the men talked, and when John walked with them toward their horses, the unrest he had felt since his encounter with Jeremiah Vardeman had turned into a curious elation. The rain had stopped, and the setting sun streaked the sky with a vividness of red and gold he had not seen before. The elation increased as he rode toward home, turning over in his mind Barton Stone's words. An urgency filled him to examine the barriers that divided Christians. Their disunity was indeed a tremendous stumbling block to the conversion of sinners. God would not hold men blameless who persisted in it.

The heat simmered on the brown earth as late as October, and each day found John in the saddle heading for a preaching appointment, gone sometimes for a week at a time. Nancy assumed much of the farm work, and her days were filled to overflowing, leaving her exhausted. With November a hard crispness came into the air, and one morning they awoke to find a heavy frost. John discovered Nancy took the sudden change in the weather as a personal affront.

"There's still corn that isn't picked," she said at breakfast, watching him rub off his saddlebags. He had returned home only the day before after an absence of four days. "Why can't you get it picked for me before you go out preaching again?" Her voice was tired, edged with exasperation. "The devil won't run off with the world while you're doing it."

"I wasn't going preaching this morning," he said, and was annoyed because he knew he sounded defensive. "I heard when I came through Mount Sterling yesterday that David Barrow is sick, and I feel I should go see him."

"Well, he can wait until afternoon," she said. She shoved a bushel basket toward him with her foot. "There's only two or three rows; won't take you long."

John took the basket and went to the patch. In a few minutes he was back. "The rows have been stripped," he announced. "Foxes did it sure; I could see their tracks."

"Foxes?" Nancy echoed, incredulous. She came to the door and peered out into the winter morning. "You must be fevered. This is no wilderness."

"A country doesn't stop being a wilderness just because people live in fancy houses," John said as they examined the damaged stalks. "Nature's just waiting to catch man asleep, and she'll reclaim all he thinks he's won. Same's true of the devil; that's why I've got to go on preaching."

"Makes a body mad, doesn't it?" Nancy said, ignoring his remark.

"Not too mad," John said mildly. They went back into the house, and he slipped off his leather jacket and again put on his woolen coat. "It's part of God's plan."

Nancy eyed him, plainly irritated. "You mean like the devil's abroad all the time? It's part of God's plan you should always be gone from home fighting him?"

John turned away to hide his amusement. Nancy was good as gold, but she was tired. He would see David Barrow and then come back and help with the work. "Yes, if I may say so."

"You may say so," Nancy said. "And I may say if you can't get the corn for me, maybe you can get me some honey. There's a dead sycamore back of the thicket near the creek, and I was fixing to smoke out the bees with this heaping of moss. Do you think nature and the devil will stay quiet long enough for you to get the honey? We could use some sweetening."

John's jaw tightened, and he started to give an angry retort. But there was no use holding speech with Nancy when she was in one of her moods. He slipped again into his working jacket. He could see David Barrow later. He took the bundle of moss and the pail, and let the door slam behind him as he headed toward the dead sycamore. He was back by noon with a great slab of the golden sweet. Together they ladled it into a wooden tub by the shed door. It would do them all winter.

It was in the middle of the night that John awakened. There was a stirring among the stock. He lay still, listening in the darkness. A slight stirring, and then the hound's barking, an excited note in it. In an instant he was out of bed, moving silently in the big room in his bare feet, his hands reaching for his rifle on the antlers over the hearth. He slipped out into the dogtrot and stood in the back opening. The moon was behind a cloud, and he stood silently, his eyes adjusting to the half-darkness, listening to the hound tethered to the hitching post, barking now in panic.

A shapeless form moved against the shed, and then John heard a peculiar sniffing, a sound he had not heard since he had last gone bear hunting in Wayne with William. He rubbed the back of his hand across his eyes, unbelieving. A bear in these parts? He crouched against the door and raised the rifle, and a shot rang out. The creature seemed to weave from side to side, whining, and then a snarl. Another shot, and the body lurched and whirled, groping, sprawling; as it fell John made out the tub of honey clinging to its broad paws.

Nancy, awakened, was at the door with the lamp. Together they inspected the beast. It was a half-grown brown cub, shot squarely behind the ear. They dragged it into the cooling shed and barred the door. The next morning they skinned it and quartered the meat. The haunches would make juicy roasts, and Nancy planned to render the feet for grease. The rest of the meat John hung on a crosspiece in the barn, away from the hound, to be jerked.

"Maybe I should slow up some in my preaching trips," John said to Nancy as they finished and he wiped his hands on the towel by the back door. "The farm does need attention; it's too much for you. God's hand is behind this, showing it to me. I reckon I might be doing his work just as much by keeping the wilderness from reclaiming the farm as . . ."

"You might, and you might not," Nancy interrupted him with a finality that forever closed the subject. She laid down the iron skillet she was greasing and came over and stood beside him. "If God's hand is behind this, it's a long way behind. Nature's persistent, that's all, and the devil's far worse." She reached up and tousled his hair. "You look after one, and I'll see to the other."

CHAPTER XXIII

CHRISTMAS brought the news that Jeremiah Vardeman's wife had died in childbirth. A letter from Jonathan said the old farm had been sold; that Ma had gone to live with Betsy and her husband in Tennessee; that he was moving to Bath County in northern Kentucky adjoining Montgomery County. And in March, as John was preaching at Spencer's Creek, he startled himself with a declaration that changed his life.

"He that believeth and is baptized shall be saved; he that believeth not shall be damned." He had quoted the familiar Scripture passage from St. Mark times without number in his sermons, but this time something stopped him. The words struck him with new, startling clarity. He stared unseeing at the upturned faces before him. Here was the reasoning based on Scripture for which he had been groping, and it had been before him all the time. In this familiar, simple passage was all the proof he needed that there was no validity in the doctrine of the Elect.

He gripped the pulpit stand for a moment, hesitating, and then, abandoning his prepared sermon, plunged into a bold, complete, unequivocal renunciation of the cherished doctrine. "Suppose the Elect should not believe," he said, his tone ominously calm, "would they be damned? Of course they would. Therefore the doctrine of the Elect is false. It is inconsistent. It is based on the dogma that only the Holy Spirit can reveal to a man that he is saved; yet God made man able to think and reason; made him able, if he reads and studies and listens to the word of God, to save himself. He is not necessarily damned if he has no mystical experience revealing that he is among the elected saints."

It had happened. He had at last, publicly and without qualification, broken with an essential dogma of the Baptist church.

Yet there was little comment on his sermon. "It's because most of the folks at Spencer's Creek don't hold with the Calvinist doctrines anyway; they're Separate Baptists," he told Nancy as they drove home. "And same's true at Bethel. Grassy Lick won't like it, though, but I think they'll hear me out." He flicked the reins, hurrying the horse. "That's more than I can say about Lulbegrud. James French is just waiting for something like this to fire me."

Nancy sighed. "Getting too stirred up about such can make a preacher lose track of what he started out to do," she said. "Why don't you just enjoy your religion and let folks think what they please about all these doctrines?"

"I reckon it's because I feel a responsibility to contend for the truth." John spoke solemnly, his eyes glazed in memory. "I was in torture for years trying to come by what's true religion, and now it's coming to me like the light of day. I'll be struggling toward it the rest of my life, I reckon." He paused, recognizing a need to purge himself of bonds that had fettered his soul for years, and squirmed in his seat. "You take this doctrine of the Elect," he went on, "I never did feel easy about it. It holds that God not only deprives a man of the means of salvation but holds him accountable, nevertheless, for his failure to achieve it, and then inflicts his helpless creatures with a damnable hell of torment forever and forever. And as for infant damnation . . ."

"I'll not listen to another word of such slander on my heavenly father, not even from you, John," Nancy said briskly. "You hush that kind of talk."

"Christ came into the world to save that which was lost. God is love. The truth was there before me all the time," he said as though he had not heard her. "But I wouldn't see it. I was blinded, just like a lot of folks in the church. Do you think now that I got hold of the truth, I should keep quiet at Lulbegrud about my views?"

She pondered a moment and then looked at him with open-faced directness. "I got a queer feeling when you say you got hold of the truth. What you really got hold of, John, is God." A smile crossed her face and as quickly passed. "I never figured that God reveals himself to cowards."

As John anticipated, the Lulbegrud Church dismissed him with chilling directness when he announced his denunciation of the doctrine of the Elect, and immediately secured Thomas Boone as its pastor.

"You're a fanatic, Mr. Smith," Judge French told him. "I've suspected it all along."

John shrugged. "No more than you, Judge," he said. "And I'd rather be a fanatic for the truth than for the status quo."

Judge French's tight smile grew tighter. "There'll be a Judgment Day, you know."

"Life is full of judgment days," John replied.

The Grassy Lick Church was divided in its reaction, but John remained as pastor. Spencer's Creek and Bethel swung quickly over to his views, and other churches in North District, weary of Calvinism and already infiltrated by the Separate Baptist liberal views, embraced the innovation and welcomed him into their pulpits. He reacted as a flower to the sun. His sermons took on new depth; he became charged with holy zeal; he baptized scores. Spiritually starved lives were changed, and a noticeable atmosphere of Christian tolerance began to pervade the church meetings. On the last Saturday in July the North District Association met, and John was not surprised that it took no notice of a letter from the Lulbegrud Church complaining of his heresy. God was preparing the minds of the people for his truth.

In late September John started for Mount Sterling to secure a roll of hemp to rope two fractious young bulls. He was jogging along the road in the early afternoon when two riders overtook him and pulled alongside. He turned to pass the time of day and stared, recollection flooding him. One of the men was Peter Cartwright.

Eighteen years had passed since they had last met. They leaned across their horses and shook hands in warm affection. Peter was riding the Cumberland Circuit and was returning with another Methodist preacher from a Methodist conference in Lexington.

"I hear all sorts of things about you, John," Peter said genially after the greetings were over and they continued their ride. "You're getting so far out from the Baptists you'll be joining the Methodists next."

John laughed. "Not as long as you wrap the pure gospel about with your creeds and disciplines, and blunt it against your mourning benches."

"Hear, hear!" Peter cried. "There's nothing wrong with our mourning benches. You have water baptism; we have mourning benches. They're both designed to bring the sinner to salvation. What's the difference?"

John felt again the irritation he had known before at Peter's sarcasm. "The difference," he said shortly, "is that one is from heaven and the other from the sawmill."

Peter and his friend laughed uproariously, and John felt ashamed of his outburst. "The only way I've departed from the Baptists," he said when they reached Mount Sterling and were hitching their horses in front of Meadows Tavern, "is to denounce the belief that God made up his mind before man was even created as to who would be damned and who would be saved. In that I reckon I'm like the Methodists, but that's all."

"John, you need something for your liver; you're seeing spots." It was beginning to rain, and Peter turned John into the doorway of the tavern. "We're staying the night here," he said. "Come in and visit a while. We're weary and worn and need a bit of relaxation."

John demurred. "I've got two young bulls I've got to pen before nightfall," he said. "It can only be a minute."

Inside several loungers sat about the stone hearth where a fire played fitfully against the chill of the early fall, and behind the long mahogany bar Jim Boothby, a member of the Bethel Church, stopped wiping the counter long enough to wave a greeting to John.

"A little wine for the stomach's sake, preacher?" he called. "It'll warm your insides, and it'll be on the house."

"Maybe I need something," John said. He leaned against the counter, pushing his hat to the back of his head. "I'm wrangling with two Methodist circuit riders, and it's worse than wrangling with the devil."

"There's nothing wrong with a Methodist circuit rider," Boothby said grinning, "that a shortage of riding horses wouldn't cure."

In the general laughter John introduced the two men. He pushed toward them the glasses which Boothby set on the counter, looking at them inquiringly. "Your Methodist discipline hasn't come out flat-footed yet against a glass of cherry bounce, has it?"

"It hasn't yet, but time's coming it will," Peter said. He eased himself onto a stool. "Strong drink and religion don't mix. I'll have none of it."

"If it's only cherry bounce," the other preacher said, "I'll have a small glass." He turned to Peter, staring in puzzled good humor, and went on as if in explanation, "I have a slight chill. But I'll have it, Brother Smith, only on condition we follow the plain injunction of the Lord that in all things we should give thanks."

John gave a short laugh. "You're being too pious," he said. "It's not the habit of believing Baptists to make a public show of their holiness." He picked up his glass and emptied it.

Peter frowned. "Well, it's an old Methodist custom to remember the Lord on all occasions, and no Baptist is going to change it for us." He put his elbows on the counter and covered his eyes with his hands. "A petition for forgiveness would be in order," he said to his friend, and the man began intoning the familiar, mumbling cadence of a prayer, his face tight as if in pain, his eyes shut.

John glanced about the room. The men near the hearth had stopped talking and were watching them, half amused. Such a public display of piety was plainly not advancing the cause of the gospel. John grinned at them and picked up the man's glass and in one swallow emptied it.

He was staring solemnly ahead when the man closed his prayer and Peter pronounced a loud and fervent amen, and they both opened their eyes. The friend reached for his glass and stopped. Peter's sharp eyes took in the situation at a glance.

"This is some of your mischief, John Smith," he said with mock sternness. "It's downright sinful."

John's eyes widened in innocence. "It's a lesson in biblical discipline. You two Methodist preachers forgot that the Good Book says ye must watch as well as pray!"

For all their scrimmages, John's encounter with Peter left him in a genial mood as he went toward Buckner Payne's General Store to get his hemp. The little bell tinkled invitingly as he opened the store door, and Payne, sitting in the rear smoking a Powhatan pipe, its bowl resting on his knees, looked up and beckoned to him.

"I was hoping you'd stop by," the merchant said. "I want your opinion on this. The postrider brought several of them, addressed to me for distribution." He pulled a small folder from his pocket. "Take it home and read it. It sounds like sense to me."

It was late, and John stuffed the folder in his pocket to read when he got home. But it was not until he was preparing for bed that night that he remembered it. Nancy was already asleep, and the house was quiet. He glanced at the title: "Prospectus of *The Christian Baptist*." He laid it on the bed and continued pulling on his flannel nightshirt. Then he picked it up and turned a page. The Betty lamp was dim, and he blew it out and went into the kitchen. A few embers still glowed beneath the ashes in the hearth where he had banked the fire for the night, and he poked them into a flame and sat down in Nancy's high-backed rocker and turned up the bear-oil lamp beside it, pulling his nightshirt closer about his lean body. Slowly he read:

> "*The Christian Baptist* should espouse the cause of no religious sect. Its sole object shall be the eviction of truth and the exposing of error in doctrine and practice. The editor, acknowledging no standard of religious faith or works other than the Old and New Testament, will oppose nothing which it contains and recommend nothing which it does not enjoin. Having no worldly interest at stake from the adoption or reprobation of any article of faith or religious practice, having no religious emolument to blind his eyes or to pervert his judgment, he hopes to manifest that he is an impartial advocate of truth."

John read the words again. What kind of writing was this? He looked at the editor's name. "Alexander Campbell," he read aloud. "Well, Mr. Campbell, I've heard of you," he mused as he turned out the lamp. "Be ye heretic or be ye saint, I'll be subscribing to your new paper."

Jonathan and Rachel, and their three-month-old baby girl, drove by the house on the first day of the new year, 1823. They had arrived in adjacent Bath County in November and were comfortably settled on a small farm of thirty acres on Slate Creek. It was a happy reunion. Rachel was small and fragile-looking, a shrinking, timid girl of twenty. Nancy fluttered over her like a mother hen. Jonathan was thinner than John remembered him, his face long, his eyes solemn. But he was wiry and tough, John thought, in his mind as well as his body. All day the families visited, exchanging news, reliving old times, enjoying the midday dinner of hog jowl and black-eyed peas. No mention was made of religion until they were preparing to leave and Jonathan remarked he planned to do some preaching in Bath County. John hesitated, and then showed him the "Prospectus of *The Christian Baptist*."

Jonathan frowned. "I've heard of that man, Alexander Campbell. A wild-eyed preacher from Ohio was telling Brother Isaac about him. He's worse than the Separate Baptists, stirring up all kinds of trouble north of the Ohio. I wouldn't have his paper in my house."

"You can't judge a man just on hearsay," John protested. "His new paper won't be out until July. Wait and read it; I'll see you get a copy."

"No, you don't, John." Jonathan shook his head, adamant. "I don't want to have any truck with it; and you'd best leave it alone, too." His eyes narrowed. "Brother Isaac said he'd been hearing you were preaching it don't matter what a man believes; and that you're getting some off Baptist doctrine."

"If I am it isn't because I feel it matters less what a man believes but because I feel it matters more," John said, trying to keep his voice calm.

"It's got Ma worried," Jonathan went on, ignoring his remark. "She asked me to have you write her that you were true to the faith; it'd set her mind at ease."

John changed the subject. No use spoiling the day by telling Jonathan of his heresy. He would hear of it soon enough.

In early August John received a copy of the pamphlet Barton Stone had promised him, labeled "The Declaration and Address," by Thomas Campbell. The day was rainy, and he stayed indoors reading the closely printed pages, his wonder and delight increasing as the document unfolded its message.

"Listen to this, Nancy," he called repeatedly. "This is what I've been thinking all along!" He read aloud:

> "Our desire is that, rejecting human opinions and inventions of men as of any authority, we might forever cease from further contentions about such things, taking the divine word alone for our rule.... Let us come fairly and firmly to original ground and take up things just as the Apostles left them, standing upon the same ground on which the church stood at the beginning."

Nancy was standing in the kitchen doorway, drinking a cup of hot venison broth. She was pregnant and plainly in no mood for religious discussion. "Did a Baptist actually write that?" she asked absently.

"He claims to be a Baptist," John said, "both Thomas, the old man, and his son, Alexander. But I misdoubt they're Calvinists. Listen to this:

> "The Church of Christ upon earth is essentially, intentionally and constitutionally, one; consisting of all those in every place that profess their faith in Christ and obedience to him in all things according to the scriptures, and that manifest the same by their tempers and conduct, and of none else as none else can be truly and properly called Christians."

He skipped ahead, eagerly scanning the closely printed pages. "Here's where he explains how Christians can really unite:

> "Although the church of Christ upon earth must necessarily exist in particular and distinct societies, locally separate one from another, yet there ought to be no schisms, no uncharitable divisions among them.... In order to do this, nothing ought to be inculcated upon Christians as articles of faith, nor required of them as terms of communion, but what is expressly taught and enjoined upon them in the word of God. Nor ought anything to be admitted as of divine obligation in their church constitutions and managements, but what is expressly enjoined by the authority of our Lord Jesus Christ and his Apostles upon the New Testament Church, either in express terms or by approved precedent.... The New Testament is as perfect a con-

> stitution for our worship, discipline and government of the New Testament church as the Old Testament was for the worship, discipline and government of the Old Testament Church."

He folded the pamphlet carefully, running his fingers along the edge. "No wonder Barton Stone admires the Campbells so much," he said. "And Jeremiah Vardeman does, too, even if he doesn't agree with all they say. They're thinking for themselves. They're not afraid to state the truth; they . . ."

"I don't think Brother Isaac would like all that you just read," Nancy said, "or Jonathan, either. You best be careful, John."

"If they don't like it, it's because they're both given to Baptist-thinking, and these men are given to truth-thinking, let the chips fall where they may." John exploded indignantly.

Nancy wiped the back of her hand over her mouth and came in and sat heavily in the cane rocker. She picked up her knitting and began to rock slowly, an abstracted, faraway look on her face. And then she looked up at him as if suddenly conscious that a reply was expected of her.

"I'd druther be given to God-thinking," she said shortly. "You be certain you're doing that, John, before you jump the fence too quick!"

Three weeks later, at the yearly meeting of the North District Association at Goshen, John found the preachers in a furor of bewilderment over the views of the Campbells. What were they trying to do? Start a new sect? Were they really Baptists? Jeremiah Vardeman contended they were. "Alexander Campbell is a powerful speaker," he said, "and the Baptists should claim him, even if he is a bit off-center on some things. He'll come around. He's coming to Kentucky in October to defend our position on baptism in a debate with W. L. McCalla, the Presbyterian preacher in Mason County, and he's asked me to be his moderator." He strutted a little. "He'll tear that man apart, and we should all be there to glory in the triumph of our Baptist cause."

John had not seen Vardeman since the death of his wife in childbirth in December, and offered his sympathy. "Thank you, Brother John," Vardeman said. "I was deeply grieved. But God does not intend man to live alone." He paused a moment. "I'm getting married next month to Miss Lucy Bullock, daughter of Thomas Bullock, moderator of our Elkhorn Baptist Association."

When John relayed the news to Nancy, she pursed her lips. "I didn't think he was a man to hitch his horse to one post," she said.

John ignored the remark and told her of the coming of Alexander Campbell to the state in October to debate on baptism with the Presbyterian. Nancy studied him, her eyes reflecting. "There's just nobody you want to meet like that man Campbell, is there?" she said. "You go, John; you plan to go."

But John did not get to the debate. Nancy was confined on the day he planned to leave; her labor became difficult, and John rode into Mount Sterling and brought back Dr. Ennis Combs, and, although the baby was born that night, the doctor stayed with her until morning, shaking his head.

"She'll pull through, but she's got a touch of milk fever, and it's bad," he said.

The baby was another boy, and they named him Joshua after Nancy's brother, and Nancy forgot her suffering in the joy of fondling another baby, although it was a week before she was able to sit up and a month before she could walk about.

But as if the Lord had given one child only to reclaim another, within six weeks little William, not yet three years old, died suddenly in a convulsive sickness. It was the second grave Nancy had stood beside in the Grassy Lick burying plot, and she was still weak, John realized with groping tenderness as he held her arm. The November rain dripped from the trees, and before the brief service was concluded a strong wind had sprung up, scattering the bunches of late fall flowers the neighbors had strewn on the small mound of earth, making little eddies of water on the rutted, brown ground. Slowly he and Nancy walked back to the gig against the wind, bending their strength into it.

He tried to push the grief from his mind as he went about his farm duties, staying close to home. Three weeks later he drove a team into Mount Sterling to have the two horses shod at Jeremiah Davis' blacksmith shop. It was one of the meeting places of the town. Andrew Jackson of Tennessee had been elected to the United States Senate, and the talk would be lively. Jeremiah Davis was a popular man in the community; he had been sheriff for years, but now he was slated for the state legislature and his son, Amos, had been elected sheriff in his stead.

As John drove the team into the yard another son, Garrett, a gangling boy of twelve, took his horses in charge, and John went into the shed. Kenaz Farrow and John Williams were there, talking with Dr. Ennis Combs and Mr. Davis. They turned as he entered, and Dr. Combs was the first to speak.

"You've heard, have you, Brother John?" he said quietly.

"Heard what?"

"David Barrow died last night."

John took off his woolen cap and sat down heavily on the wood box near the fire. He felt an almost physical shock. "He seemed better, last time I saw him," he said after a moment. "What caused his death, Doc?"

Dr. Combs shook his head. "As far as I can determine," he said, "it was trying to do the impossible."

For days after David Barrow's funeral, John could not shake off a feeling of depression. The man had been persecuted, tormented, ostracized, but what troubled John was the realization the treatment was not for his views on emancipation. Most thoughtful people in and out of the church deplored slavery and wished to see it end. Slavery was as much an evil as murder or adultery. But slavery was a political issue, and discussing it in the church disturbed the peace of Christian people. That had been David Barrow's crime. He had tried to make the people put their preachments into practice; and the power of the whole church hierarchy had been brought to bear against him. North District Association had not only ousted him and his church, but had gone on record, as Judge French had pointedly shown John one day in the minute book, advising "that any minister that should propagate unsound doctrines or views, pernicious to peace and good order, might be suspended."

John was asked to assume the pastorate of the Mount Sterling Church to succeed David Barrow, and as he stood the first Sunday morning behind the pulpit stand and ran his hand over the wood, worn smooth by the sensitive fingers of the earnest, fearless old preacher, he cried in exultation, almost in defiance, "May this church never be robbed of its character or have its glory dimmed by transferring its freedom to speak the truth to a human, man-made governing body!"

Let the North District Association of Baptist Churches make of his stand what it would.

CHAPTER XXIV

IN March word came that Alexander Campbell was again to visit Kentucky. He would be in Flemingsburg in two weeks, and then come on to Mount Sterling.

"You should maybe ride over to Flemingsburg to meet him," Nancy said. She was feeling the responsibility of serving as the minister's wife of the Mount Sterling Church, the largest church in Montgomery County, and was punctilious in her duties. She attended most of the District meetings with John, and entertained visiting brethren gladly, her natural friendliness endearing her to them all. "If he's such a great man, it would be the polite thing to do. I'll stay here and have things ready when you ride back with him."

John considered. Spring planting was under way; the stone fence at the back forty needed rebuilding; two brood cows were about to calve. In addition, preaching appointments were scheduled for almost every night in nearby small communities, and he hesitated to disappoint the people. They would come streaming in from every direction, their paths through the woods lighted by their hickory-bark torches, anxious to hear the word of truth.

But was he preaching the full truth? The question had been haunting him ever since reading the first issue of *The Christian Baptist*. Copies of the new magazine had been distributed at the McCalla debate by Mr. Campbell himself last fall, and it was creating a ground swell of clamor all over the state; preachers and lay people alike were confused, groping, feeling their way to a fuller understanding of this new interpretation of the whole body of Christian doctrine and practice. John shared their bewilderment.

"It would give me a chance to know the man," he said, reflecting.

"I'd like nothing better." Nancy was churning by the kitchen door, and he picked up a recent number of *The Christian Baptist* from the table in the sitting room and came back to the kitchen, thumbing through it. "Here's this article on experimental religion," he said. "I've read it twice now, and I think I know what the man means, and I agree pretty well with him. Some folks say it shows he doubts the Lord's will is ever made known to a man through a revealing experience, let alone the fact that he's saved, and they feel that proves he's unregenerate and no Baptist at all." He walked over and stood by the kitchen window to read better the closely printed pages. "I'm not sure myself what religious party he belongs to, but I don't agree he doubts the Lord makes his will known to men. What he denies as coming from God are the visions and the voices in the woods and the Saviour appearing in the treetops and the white yearling calves standing on the ridges at break of day, and I agree with him. He says we have to use reason. Listen to this: 'Open your Bibles and harken to the voice of God, which is the voice of reason.' That's what I've been feeling all along, that God reveals himself to us if we read our Bible and use our God-given reason." He folded the magazine and rubbed his hand over his eyes. "I've got to hear him, Nancy; he's my kind of man, maybe even more than Barton Stone. I've got to find out if a man can believe like this and still be a Baptist."

"Maybe he's a reformed Baptist," Nancy said crisply, "or a Christian Baptist, like his paper says. Or maybe he's just a plain Christian like Barton Stone and me and Willy."

The sky had been overcast the morning John left home for the ride to Flemingsburg, but by the time he had ridden the twenty intervening miles the sun was pouring its radiance in full measure upon an earth bursting with promise of renewed life. He stopped beside a creek on the edge of the town to eat the sandwich Nancy had fixed for him, and then rode up to the door of the Baptist meetinghouse and dismounted.

William Vaughn was tethering his chestnut mare to the hitching rail. John had met Billy Vaughn at several meetings of the North District Association, and liked him. The man had been a tailor, he had learned, flaunting his infidelity until converted by Jeremiah Vardeman. He had entered the ministry and was now living in Mason

County, and preaching for four nearby churches, wholly dedicated to the cause of Christ as decreed by Baptist doctrine.

"Why the grin, Brother Billy?" John asked as the two men clasped hands. "You met the great man?"

Vaughn's thick-set body shook with silent laughter. "I've been riding with him for eight days through Bracken and Mason counties, and I've been thinking of the puzzlement he's going to throw all our people into. We're going to be like a swarm of bees, sailing off in forty directions, landing nowhere." He shook his head. "I tell you I still don't know whether the man's a Calvinist or an Arminian, or an Arian or a Trinitarian."

John grinned at him. "He has you hexed," he teased. "Let me listen to him an hour, and I can tell you. I've been studying all the 'isms,' and there's not one I can't smell a mile away." He threw his arm across Billy Vaughn's shoulder as the two men turned toward the church. "I've been reading every word of every copy of his paper, just like all the other preachers, and I'm uncertain, too, in my mind about him." He paused, doubtfully. "But if he means what I think he means, Billy," he said slowly, nodding, "well, that's what I mean, too."

The meetinghouse was too small to accommodate the crowd, and a group was assembling in the adjacent churchyard, where a speaker's stand had been erected against the wall. John looked about. Most of the people were preachers he knew. David Chenault from Cane Springs greeted him, and John Rogers, the young man he had met with Barton Stone, grabbed his hand. Rogers was now married and living in nearby Carlisle, he reported, introducing a slender, bushy-haired man about John's age.

"This is Philip Fall," he said. "He's so taken with Mr. Campbell's views he's ridden for three days clear from Louisville to hear him today."

"I can understand that," John said as they shook hands. "I'd have done it myself. But Brother Vardeman has spoken of you as being in Frankfort, helping Jacob Creath."

Philip Fall nodded. "I was there, but Mr. Creath left when Dr. Silas Noel returned, and I left too." He laughed shortly. "Dr. Noel feared I had become too imbued with Mr. Campbell's views. For that matter, so do Mr. Creath and Mr. Vardeman. I'm becoming *persona non grata.*"

"What do they object to?" John asked.

"Their latest complaint is that I'm not convinced the first concern of the Baptists should be their own preservation and success," he said, smiling. "I'm calling my church in Louisville Reformed Baptist, and that's a bitter pill to some of our people, to intimate we need reforming. I'm hoping next year we can live up to the name by voting out the *Philadelphia Confession of Faith* and start guiding ourselves by the Bible alone."

John looked at him closely. The man was in earnest. "You ever hear the word 'heresy'?" he said, half-joking. "There's a place assigned in the hereafter to such as you. But I may be asking you to move over and make room for me pretty soon. Who knows?" He moved on. He would like Philip Fall.

Near the stand he saw Jeremiah Vardeman and Jacob Creath talking with a stranger who was taking off his sherryvallies. John stared at the man. He was taller than average, his face slender and sensitive; his blue-gray eyes deep-set under bushy brows; his nose, John thought, leaning a little to the north. He made his way to the stand with Billy Vaughn.

"Mr. Campbell," Vaughn said, "I want you to meet Brother Raccoon John Smith."

Someone was limning out a hymn, and John had a chance to clasp the extended hand only a moment before Campbell mounted the stand. The benches were almost filled, and John stood uncertainly for a moment and then hoisted himself up on the floor of the platform. He wanted more than an introduction; he wanted to be close to the man, to sense his physical presence, study his face, his speech, his manner of thinking. Alexander Campbell was leading many souls to the brink of a great decision. What motives, what reasoning lay in the depths of his mind and heart? Was he right, or wrong?

John crossed his legs and rested his arms on his knees, and sat, his eyes glued to the face of the great Alexander Campbell as he discoursed on the allegory of Hagar and Sarah in Paul's letter to the Galatians; his artless, simple manner of speaking, his clear logic, his matter-of-fact reasoning moving John into a realm of thinking that left all his concern for pinpointing any theological position forgotten. He was still sitting, lost in thought, when Billy Vaughn tapped him on the shoulder. Mr. Campbell had stopped speaking, and the meeting was breaking up.

He stretched out his legs and found them cramped, and then he swung himself to the ground. "It's a shame, Billy," he said fretfully, "to ride twenty miles, as I've done, just to hear a man preach thirty minutes."

Vaughn laughed. "Look at your watch, John. Brother Campbell spoke for two hours and a half. You were entranced. Did you discover what he is?"

John stared at him in amazement, and then laughed at himself ruefully. "No, and I don't care," he said. "Be he devil or saint, all I know is that he has thrown more light on that Scripture than I have received in all the sermons I ever heard before."

"Well, you'll have a chance to probe a little deeper," Billy said. "He's riding on toward Mount Sterling, spending the night with Jason Cannon; you can join the group riding with him. Brother Creath and Jeremiah Vardeman are inclined to his thinking, but I'm frankly suspicious; it would ruin the Baptist church."

Within an hour John found himself in a group of riders on the Mount Sterling road. The other men held back, hesitant, diffident, as Mr. Campbell took the lead and rode ahead. "Get him starting to talk, John," some of them whispered, prodding him. "You know how to fend with him; find out if he's really a Baptist."

John frowned. He rode in silence for a while, studying Campbell's erect carriage, his proud head; watching him drink deep the soft spring air, his eyes roving the countryside, missing nothing. Then he urged his sorrel mare forward and pulled up beside him.

"It's only fair to tell you, Mr. Campbell," he said, "that some of the brethren hereabouts are a mite suspicious of you, religiously speaking. I'd like to ask you a few questions."

Campbell laughed. "What's worrying you?"

"Well, sir," John began hesitantly, "there are folks who say you are an unregenerate sinner, that in spite of all your fine words you have no real heart-religion."

Campbell slowed his horse to a walk, his head cocked to one side, a sudden soberness about him. He started to speak but then closed his lips tightly and nodded to John as if he wanted to hear more.

"For instance, in your March issue of *The Christian Baptist,*" John said, choosing his words with care, "you had quite a piece criticizing what we old-time Calvinistic Baptists call the revealing experience, meaning that experience that reveals to us God's will whether we're saved or damned. You call it 'experimental religion.' Does that mean you never had a Christian experience of your own?"

"My father gave me a scolding for publishing that piece." Campbell laughed as though in apology. "He said the people were not ready for it, but I think the time has come for men to realize that becoming a Christian is relatively simple, and that no man need pass through some morass of terror and despair before he can believe. Jesus told us how simple it is. 'He that believeth and is baptized shall be saved; he that believeth not shall be damned,' is what he said. He offers us a *believer's* salvation, and belief is of the mind. That is all the experience multitudes had who heard Christ and the apostles gladly, and understood and believed. Today we should do the same, but we've become imprisoned in our separate warring sects by our creeds, and the clergy who formulated them, until we lose hope and are willing to accept any mumbo-jumbo the clergy offers to escape that everlasting torment they talk so much about."

John nodded. "I was in mental torment for years, and I sometimes wonder yet if I'm saved. I've never had a real vision."

"Perhaps you are like I am; you are still a Calvinist sometimes in your thoughts," said Campbell, studying him. "If you are lost, my friend, it will be by your own will, or your lack of it."

"But you did have an experience?" John persisted.

Campbell jogged his horse a little and then drew back sharply on the reins, riding high in the saddle as though lost in memory. "My father wanted to make a clergyman out of me, good Presbyterian that he was, and always kept me near him. From the time I could read the Scriptures, I believed that Jesus was the Son of God, and was convinced I was a great sinner and must obtain pardon through him, or I was forever lost. This caused me great distress of mind and much working of a guilty conscience because I, too, experienced no apparitions or miraculous signs and heard no voices calling to me from the treetops or the gullies. But I was conscious more and more of God's care, and my conviction firmed that Jesus was his Son and the Christ. I put my sole reliance in him, and I have never been disappointed. That is my experience."

"You were then a Calvinist, a Presbyterian?" John asked.

Campbell continued as if he had not heard, for the moment staring straight ahead. "As a strict Seceder Presbyterian, like my father, baptized by sprinkling when an infant into the *Westminster Con-*

fession of Faith, so to speak, it had not yet entered my head to search the Scriptures on the subject of baptism or the doctrine of the creeds. After I came to the United States, I began to think seriously about baptism when my daughter Jane was born, and through study of the teachings and example of the Saviour as set forth in the New Testament I was led to the truth, not only that baptism is a believer's baptism, which thus ruled out forever the hideous doctrine of the Elect and infant damnation, but that baptism by immersion is the only scriptural mode. Both my father and I, with our families, were then rebaptized by immersion. Now I feel that, as for myself, the scriptural commandment has been obeyed, and I'm now a Christian."

"That's why you left the Presbyterian church?" John asked.

"My father and I left the Presbyterians, or rather, we were put out, when Father Thomas was censured for daring to offer the Lord's Supper to some Presbyterians in western Pennsylvania who were other than his own splinter sect of that denomination about fourteen years ago. You must realize that my father was then a preacher of the Old Light Anti-Burgher Branch of the Seceder Church of Scotland, and when he wrote the 'Declaration and Address,' all doors were shut to him in that church forever. His first proposition in that document, that the church of Christ on earth is essentially, intentionally, and constitutionally one, was alone sufficient to send him to the gallows. But to the restoration of that doctrine upon this earth, Friend John, I have dedicated my life." Unconsciously he slapped his reins against his horse's shank, and the spirited animal began to canter along the narrow roadway as Campbell rode loosely in the stirrups, leaning slightly forward, his coattails flapping, his tall hat set firmly on his head as his angular figure bobbed uncertainly in the saddle.

John grinned and looked at the other men, who had followed closely, listening intently to the conversation. He surmised their thoughts. Alexander Campbell was a fearless and original thinker, and a great leader, but none could say he was a graceful horseman. John closed the gap between them and pulled alongside him.

"But you became a Baptist," he said as their horses slowed to a walk. "Why was that? We've a man down here in Kentucky, Barton W. Stone, who thinks much as you do. He left his church, the

Presbyterian, but he didn't join any other. He calls himself just a Christian."

"I know of Barton Stone," Campbell said, nodding. "And I plan to meet him. There seems to be no essential difference between us. But I have a feeling he made a mistake dissolving his Springfield Presbytery so soon; perhaps he might have started a reform movement within the Presbyterian fold where we had failed, although I rather doubt it. We became Baptists because our little group of followers at Brush Run was invited to enter the Redstone Baptist Association in Virginia after we had accepted the scriptural baptism of immersion, and we had no desire to stand apart and form another sect."

"From what I've heard you are none too comfortable with the Baptists," John said, and then he grinned and leaned closer to Campbell's ear, "nor am I."

Campbell nodded, an understanding smile on his face. "I'm afraid our orthodox Baptist brethren are as much creed-bound by their *Philadelphia Confession of Faith* as the Presbyterians by their *Westminster Confession*, or the Lutherans by their *Augsburg Confession*, or the Episcopalians by their Thirty-nine Articles, or the Methodists by their Disciplines. It appears the theologians feel they must make the road to salvation as difficult as possible in order to keep control of the people. But I haven't given up hope. We are all priests before God."

"Where the Scriptures speak, we speak; and where the Scriptures are silent, we are silent," John quoted. "Your father, Thomas Campbell, was inspired when he gave us that rule. I'd like to meet him some time."

"He is a great man," Campbell said simply, "a scholar and a saint. And the rule is good, although some men heed only the first part of it. The silences of the Scriptures are to be observed, too; they are not an invitation for man to speak where God has not. Another good rule for Christians to remember is one first pronounced by Rupertus Meldenius of Germany four hundred years ago: 'In essentials, unity; in non-essentials, liberty; in all things, charity.' That sage advice has saved me from many a hasty action."

John mulled the words over in his mind as for a few minutes they rode in silence. "I'm an uneducated man, Brother Campbell," he said finally. "I never went to college. My schooling has been limited to a few months, but I've been a reader since I can remember, and a few men have stimulated my thinking and guided me to books. Two of these men, Robert Ferrill, a wheelwright and a teacher, and Micah Taul, a lawyer, were great admirers of Thomas Paine and his philosophy. Micah Taul even named his oldest boy for Tom Paine. They called themselves free-thinkers or deists, like Paine, although I reckon some folks would call them infidels. I've read most of Paine's books, and although a lot of people seem to interpret his writings, especially his *Age of Reason*, as an attack on the Bible, I don't. I figure him as a really religious man, but he was off-center; he was superficial in his religious thinking and too much a literalist. But his influence is still widespread because he appeals to reason, and we've got to meet it. I know there's a place where reason ends and faith begins, but don't you think the church has to recognize that men want a religion that is logical?"

" 'For now we see through a glass darkly but then face to face,' " Campbell quoted, " 'now we know in part but then shall we know even as also we are known.' I have met many of these so-called deists; they cling to reeds, and they know it. That's the reason they are generally so belligerent, as Tom Paine was. Paine, like his master Voltaire, made no allowance for the symbolic meaning and appeal of the Bible. He took no account of the essential poetry in things of the spirit that is more basic to many people than demonstrable fact. Yes, we should preach a logical religion, for there is no conflict between reason and God; they are one, just as God and love are one." He leaned over and put his hand on the pommel of John's saddle. "Don't bemean yourself, my friend. I've heard fine things of you; you are unique among us preachers. If ever there was a preacher who would have been spoiled by a college education, it is you, Brother Raccoon John."

John shifted in his saddle, embarrassed, and cleared his throat, canvassing his mind for a rejoinder. "Thank you, Brother Campbell," he said. "If I may say so, you're a right smart chunk of preacher yourself!"

Alexander Campbell laughed heartily, leaning back in the saddle, and the others in the group joined him, the tension gone, a comradeship now upon them all which loosened their tongues and buoyed them to ask their own questions. And as the horses slowed again to a walk, Campbell answered, readily and without equivocation, simple, clear statements; explaining, interpreting, clarifying; his replies revealing to John no diabolical conspiracy to overthrow religion but a deep desire for a clear approach to God through a restoration of the simplicities of the New Testament Church.

The talk continued after they reached the house of Jason Cannon, through the dinner at the long trestle table in the yard and into the night as they sat about a hearth fire that warmed the chill of the spring night air. At last Mr. Campbell stood up, weary and in obvious need of rest.

"I've been talking most of the day," he said. "Won't one of you gentlemen please lead the evening devotion? Then we can retire."

An awkward silence fell on the group, a sudden reticence at leading the divine worship in the presence of so renowned a religious leader. John squared himself and stood up.

"I'll lead the devotion," he said. "If Brother Campbell is the Christian I think he is, he'll make allowance for my imperfection; but if he be a poor, unregenerate sinner, I don't care what he thinks."

For three days John lingered with Alexander Campbell as he spoke in Mount Sterling and nearby churches, feasting on his logical thinking, his penetrating insights, his incisive search of the Scripture and man's struggle for salvation. When they parted he was convinced that the man was right. He had proclaimed, with quiet certainty and unanswerable logic, the principles based squarely upon the Scriptures toward which John had been groping all these years. More clearly even than Barton Stone he pointed the way to that unity of Christians for which Jesus had prayed. But how could he make others see that? Habits do not change easily; the minds of men grow slowly, he knew. To hasten them unduly brings defeat of the very purpose.

He brooded about the problem for weeks, tempering his preaching with caution.

"Don't throw away the old bucket," Nancy admonished him, "until you know the new one holds water."

"I don't want a new bucket," he said. "I want to mend the old one. Forming a new sect is the last thing Brother Campbell has in mind, and I agree with him." Like a man on thin ice, he scrutinized each tenet of the Restoration doctrine with care, avoiding offense, testing his new concepts by experience.

The summer brought an abundant harvest; corn was shucked and stored in the bins to later feed the young cattle and hogs; sheep and hogs were driven to Mount Sterling to join the cattle drover to the eastern markets. Nancy canned and stored fruits and vegetables; her spinning wheel and loom hummed every evening, for store-bought yard goods were out of the question. John had given up all hope the churches would resume payment of the farm debt and was attempting not only to meet the interest but make payments on the principal. It took all the hard money he could get, and Nancy turned old clothes and remade garments for herself and the children, and patched and relined his worn pants and his preaching coat.

And then the gray of November settled on the land. As 1824 drew to a close, unrest filled not only the Baptist churches but all of Kentucky. The state's favorite son, Henry Clay, was tottering on his pedestal. As a candidate for the Presidency, he had stood only fourth in electoral votes. Neither of the two top candidates had a majority, so the election went to the House of Representatives where Clay, despite instructions to the contrary, had cast the deciding vote for John Adams over Andrew Jackson, and stories of intrigue were rife. He had betrayed the people, it was charged, to gain a seat in Adams' cabinet as Secretary of State. He was a worldly man, a winebibber, given to following the races, approving of lottery. The attacks became bitterly personal.

John read the accusations with a sinking heart. He believed in Henry Clay; the great statesman had not been intentionally deceitful but, driven by his ambition for high office, had he wavered in his trust to his people and himself? A man must stand by his convictions, be the cost what it may.

It was Jonathan's visit at Christmas that confirmed his nagging suspicion that he was more guilty than Henry Clay in his own wavering. He should stand openly for his convictions; he should be fearless in his preaching, whatever the penalty.

Jonathan and Rachel and their child, now a toddler of two, spent Christmas Day at the house at Nancy's insistence. The children kept the atmosphere lively, but the talk among their elders was stilted.

There was a restraint among them that bothered John; he felt as if he were watching helplessly as a gulf widened between him and his brother. The talk skirted any mention of John's heresy, but the thought of it was there, smoldering, in the minds of them all.

A light snow had fallen during the day, barely covering the ground, and dusk came early. Jonathan insisted on being at home before full dark, and John's lantern glinted on diamonds of frost as he led the way to the barn. Nancy threw a shawl over her cap and came along, stomping her feet and slapping her hands to keep warm, tucking the robe about Rachel and the baby. They were standing beside the wagon when John extended his hand in farewell.

"Don't know as I should shake hands with you, John," Jonathan said. "I only shake with honest men."

John and Nancy stared in amazement. "What on earth do you mean?" John asked, his voice hoarse, gripping the side of the wagon.

"You're not being honest, trying to wreck the Baptist church under pretense of being loyal to it. Even if you are my brother, I can't be friends with such a man." He clucked to the horses, but John held to the sideboards.

"Jonathan!" he cried. "Explain yourself!"

"It's not that you differ with me," Jonathan said. "I can admire a man that differs, but I want him to show his real colors. You're not a Baptist any longer; you're just a plain Campbellite, and you won't admit it." The wagon lurched forward. "You're a wolf in sheep's clothing," he called back.

John stared at the wagon disappearing down the lane in the dusk, as Nancy bristled with indignation beside him. "He's either stupid or ignorant or blind," she said. "Which is it?"

John turned toward the house, his mind in a whirl. "Maybe he's none of them, maybe he's talking the truth," he mumbled. "Maybe he's right."

Long into the night they talked, and when they knelt for bedtime prayer both John and Nancy were agreed he should give his full time to preaching. God had been preparing him for the truths revealed by Alexander Campbell, and he was not ashamed of the gospel they proclaimed, for it was the power of God unto the salvation of his church.

But leaving Nancy again with the care of the farm worried him. A visit with Buckner Payne early in February crystallized his decision to get help on the farm. Payne knew of a Negro couple who were looking for a place to live.

"They're free blacks," John explained to Nancy when he got home. "A man and his wife. They'd work on the place as needed if we gave them space for a cabin and a piece of ground to cultivate. Payne said they were church-going Baptists."

Nancy nodded, only half listening. A change had come over her since Jonathan's outburst; a protective, almost a fierce, loyalty to John burned in her. She stood straight and easy, her eyes sparkling, and John knew she was waiting to say something. But she went about it in her own way, teasing him.

"Mr. Payne figuring on joining the church ever?" She spoke so casually he knew there was meaning behind the question. "Pity for a man as good as that to go to hell!"

John turned sharply. "Who said he was going to hell?"

She picked up a hickory pole she was shredding to make a broom, and began tying with hickory splints the fluffy shreds about the end. "Jonathan," she said. "He came by today while you were in town, pretending to get a recipe Rachel wanted, but actually I think he had it in mind to apologize to you for what he said. But I didn't give him much of a chance."

"What did you tell him?" John asked.

Her lips tightened. "Plenty," she said, drawing out the word.

John sighed. "Nancy, things are bad enough. You didn't . . ."

She waved him to silence. "He did so much talking I didn't have time to get in all I wanted to say, so don't worry. He said he was quit doing business with Buckner Payne because he wasn't of the Elect. I asked him what happened to people who weren't of the Elect, and he said plain out they was going to hell."

John sat down at the kitchen table and looked at her smooth hair, parted in the middle and braided in buns over her ears and topped by her crisp cap. Nancy could always do what had to be done. She was light on her feet and swift in her movements and quick to laugh, and a new contentment shone in her eyes. "I know you're joking about all this, but you know it isn't just funny business. It means a great deal to people like Jonathan; they're sincere, and they mean right."

She put down the pole and turned to him, her eyes sobering. She had changed, John thought again, more than he had realized. And it was not only toward him. Gradually, imperceptibly, a spiritual discernment, an awareness had been taking place. "I know it, John," she said. "That's why I can't figure out why you can't just preach the gospel as you see it and leave the Baptist doctrine be. If people like Jonathan want to act up about it, let them."

"I know it's hard to understand." He put his elbows on the table and for a moment covered his face with his hands. Then he picked up a glass of water on the table. "Nancy, I'm a mite hungry. Would you give me a glass of milk?"

She came over and took the glass and started to pour the water in the kitchen basin.

"Don't do that!" he cried.

She turned, startled. "What do you mean? You wanted milk, didn't you?"

"Yes," he said, "but give it to me in that glass just as it is."

"Are you fevered? The glass is full of water!"

His brows shot up, and his eyes crinkled in amusement. "It is?" he said innocently. And then he laughed. "Just so it is you cannot fill a man's heart nor his head with new truths until you get rid of the old errors. That's the reason I don't want to leave the Baptist church. I want to empty the minds and hearts of my Baptist brethren of their unsound doctrines and fill them with New Testament truth."

Within two weeks the Negro man, Hep, and his wife, Robbie, were on the Smith farm. A cabin had been raised in a clearing near the creek a mile from the house, and their belongings moved into it. John agreed to let them farm the five acres surrounding the cabin in return for help with the field work and, on the advice of Buckner Payne and with a loan from him, he increased his own holdings by buying twelve acres adjoining his land from Joshua Sander, and then reselling six acres of it to his neighbor, Edward Sallee, at a profit sufficient for him to repay Payne. "I feel like a big moneyed man," he told Nancy, laughing, "handling that transaction. But it was Buckner Payne that steered it; he knew what was coming, with Sallee wanting some of that land, and he wanted me to get the benefit."

Nancy gave him a shrewd, smiling look. "You're not getting the urge to get rich again, are you?" she said, tilting her head to one side, appraising him.

Fragments of his early ambitions stabbed his memory. And then he grinned ruefully. A man's soul was laid naked in Nancy's presence. "It wouldn't be honest to say no. But it's an urge I can conquer now, praise the Lord!"

All of February and into March John roamed the state, returning home only to preach at Grassy Lick and Mount Sterling and Spencer's Creek, and once a month at Bethel, and to get a change of clothing. Nancy was pleased with the work of Hep and Robbie; Hep looked after the stock and worked the garden for spring planting, and Robbie did the milking and churning, relieving Nancy so she could make white muslin dresses for the girls for Easter and twill suits for the boys. Jennie and Zerelda, dressed in crispy aprons, attended school at James Mason's place, and sometimes little Jonathan, now almost six, trudged along with them, leaving her with the care of Joshua, a laughing, good-natured toddler of one and a half years. She made bright-colored rugs for the floor, and each bed now had its piece-work quilt.

But each time John stopped she had clean clothes ready for him, a peace in her eyes that quieted his occasional twinges of guilt at leaving her so much. He discovered she was calling on the sick, a warmth about her, folks told him, that was better than medicine. She never prayed with them, or read Scripture, but she had only to put her hand on the bed coverlet, they said, and they felt better. She counseled with young people who came to the house seeking John to perform their marriage ceremonies, and kept his appointments straight. She took especial delight in the arrangements for one couple—Micah Taul, a nephew of John's old friend from Wayne County, who came one morning with a pretty young girl, Mary Oden. Although they were Methodists, they wanted John to marry them. John was expected home that night, and Nancy kept the excited boy and girl busy all day, decorating the house, preparing a wedding supper, helping the girl pretty her hair, until John arrived and the ceremony was performed.

"It was the least I could do," she told John when they had left, "knowing how grateful you are to Mr. Taul."

The rain was falling in sheets the last morning in March when John left after only one day at home for a series of appointments. He was bone-tired, but he had written to the brethren in several settlements of his itinerary, and he knew that notices would be posted in the taverns and at the watering wells. He reached Hinkston Creek at noon, and that afternoon preached in the home of Merton Bland. The storm had increased, but despite its severity more than fifty men and women were there, listening earnestly to his sermon, plying him with questions at its close. It was after five o'clock before he could get away, and dusk had fallen. The next morning he was due in Bracken County and, although the rain was showing no slackening, he insisted on riding on his way.

He cut through the woods, taking a short route he thought he knew. He planned to stay the night at the Jason Welton cabin, but after riding an hour he became confused in the darkness and decided to locate the meetinghouse and take shelter for the night there. He rode for a while along a slope, thickly wooded on one side, the overhead branches, heavy with rain, whipping his face. Suddenly the air stilled, then a sharp flash of lightning, and John was deafened by the thunder that instantly followed as before him a giant sycamore split in two and crashed through the heavy undergrowth. The horse's legs stiffened in fright, and John was thrown over the animal's head, sliding down the slope, the horse sliding helplessly after him. He came to a stop in a deep mire, half-buried in mud, and the horse slid over him, its forelegs across his chest. Then all was darkness, and he lay still.

When he came to, the rain was coming down in torrents, the mud thick about him, the horse's legs heavy, pinning him down. He reached out and groped his hand along the wet earth, searching for a whip to arouse the animal but could feel only soggy vines. He slapped at the horse with his hands. The animal's head thrashed about, but the ground was deep in mire, and every effort seemed to push them both further in the mud. He tried to yell, but his nose and mouth were filled with the sticky ooze, his lips cracked and bleeding, and the wind tore at his lungs, sucking the breath from him, flattening matted leaves across his face. The rain came in sheets.

This was the end, he thought; the end of his dreams, the end of his work; the end of his life. *God! Help me!* Alternately he slapped at the horse and prayed as time became meaningless in the dark and the wet and the cold.

He felt the animal struggle and in a sharp flash of lightning could make out his flaying hind feet breaking loose of the mire. Then the weight of his front legs left John's body, and he could sense the animal standing beside him. He lay still for a moment and then rolled over and slowly pushed himself to his knees. His hand struck his saddlebag, thrown against a pile of wet leaves, and he pulled it to him, pressing against it for support as he felt of himself. The wind had been knocked out of him, and he was sore and bruised, but there were no bones broken. He grabbed the horse's tail and slowly, shakily, pulled himself to his feet.

The saddle was still in position on the horse but was thick with mud, and he scooped it off as best he could and clambered up, groping for the bridle. The horse lurched forward. He held on to the mane, oblivious of direction, giving the horse his head. The rain drenched his face, running in streams of mud down his back and chest.

He never knew how long he rode, numbed, before the rain lessened and he recognized a familiar shed. They were crossing the back pasture of his next-door neighbor, Edward Sallee. The horse had found his way home.

CHAPTER XXV

THE next day John had chills and fever. He was in bed three days. Nancy was glad for the enforced rest it gave him, and doctored him with tart bark and a blistering plaster.

"You've been doing too much huffing and puffing, John," she said, running her hand over his forehead, studying him. His face was becoming lined, and deep furrows were forming between his brows; his hair was thinning, and white streaks were showing. "That accident was a warning from the Lord; you've got to slow down."

He nodded, but on the fourth morning he insisted on getting up, sitting with a heavy blanket about him in the high-backed rocker near the kitchen hearth, poring over a translation of the New Testament Alexander Campbell had just published. All day he read it, comparing it with the King James version, critical of it in spots, commending it in passages. Nancy was glad for his absorption; and she piled beside him his books, his commentaries on Baptist doctrine, copies of *The Christian Baptist*, and copies of Barton Stone's new paper, *The Christian Messenger.*

But by the end of the week, completely recovered, a restlessness seized him. Churches were showing definite signs of strain over the Campbell reform movement; a mood of bickering was developing, he sensed, that could invite trouble. David Chenault of Cane Springs had told him at the last North District meeting that he was creating dissension, that his views were anathema. John had written a Circular Letter to all the neighboring associations in an effort to combat the dissension, pleading for patience. But the document had met with silence. Now, in the mail Hep had brought from an early morning trip into Mount Sterling, an answer had come from the Licking Association. John studied it and then read it aloud to Nancy.

" 'Who tells you that Christ died for the sins of all the world, and who says that he has Christ and salvation to offer you on the condition of your obedience, faith and repentance only, set him down as a blind guide.' " He read the words aloud twice, almost unbelieving, as Nancy stared at him, indignation flushing her face.

"There's more yet," he said after a moment. "Listen to this: 'Avoid such; have no fellowship with them; receive them not into your house, neither bid them God-speed.' " He laid the paper on the table and got up and walked to the window and stared out into the April morning. "God knows I have no desire to break fellowship with our Baptist brethren. Or to divide them. I want only to help lead them on to greater truth so we can all become better witnesses for the Lord."

Nancy's face reflected her compassion for his hurt, but she said nothing, bending over the bowl of corn she was shelling for hominy.

"If a separation comes," John said, his voice low as if he were speaking to himself, "they'll do the leaving; it won't be me."

In the following weeks he preached with heightened zeal, organizing new churches, baptizing scores, among them the two young men he had met when he first came to Montgomery County, Absalom Rice and Jacob Coons. "I reckon I'm baptizing them into the Baptist church," he told Nancy, "even if some folks call them Campbellites. Alexander Campbell is still a Baptist, so that makes me one, too. They're going to have a hard time pushing me out. I got a feeling Barton Stone sometimes wonders if he didn't make a mistake, leaving the Presbyterians instead of staying in there and fighting for his views. I got a mind to ride over to Georgetown and talk to him; he refreshes my soul even when I don't agree with him."

Nancy nodded. "And you could come home from Georgetown by way of Lexington. I was reading in the *Gazette* the great Frenchman, Lafayette, is to be visiting there day after tomorrow; you could watch the doings."

But Barton Stone was not in Georgetown, John found when he rode up to the Christian meetinghouse in the little village; he was in Ohio, expecting to be gone the rest of the year. John sat down on the bench in front of the courthouse and ate the turkey slices and hard-boiled eggs and corn bread Nancy had packed for him, wondering if he should ride on into Lexington that night. It was early twilight, and a light rain was falling, and he decided against it. Instead he would go over to Great Crossings, only a mile or so away. The Great Crossings Church was in the Elkhorn Association, and rumblings in the organization against the reform movement had been increasing. Maybe he could clarify some points with the brethren there.

He rode slowly along Big Spring branch; Elijah Craig, the pioneer Baptist preacher, had started his paper mill here, and John looked at the place with interest. He crossed Stamping Ground pike and pulled in his horse to stare at an immense house with rock chimneys that loomed in a clearing of rippling bluegrass on a knoll overlooking the creek. This was the home, he knew, of the Johnson family, one of the oldest families in the state, said to own at one time one-third of Scott County. Old Colonel Robert Johnson, now dead, had come to the region as a surveyor with Daniel Boone, staying on to help forge Kentucky into a state, and had given it nine sons and daughters, all of whom were prominent in public life. He and his wife Jemima had been devout Baptists, founding the Great Crossings Baptist Church, but only one son, John T., so it was rumored, carried on their interest in religious matters. John recalled seeing another son, Richard, in Lexington at the time of President Monroe's visit. He was a flamboyant man, now a United States senator, with ambitions to go higher, it was said.

He rode on to the Baptist meetinghouse behind a thicket on the other side of the creek, a low-roofed log structure on ground given by Colonel Johnson. A midweek prayer service was being held, and a scattering of people were seated on the backless benches as John entered and took a seat on the side. The service had started, and he glanced about. A lean, pleasant-faced man turned on the adjacent bench to look at him, the hint of austerity in his erect carriage dispelling as he extended his hand.

"Welcome, brother," he whispered. "My name is John T. Johnson."

John smiled and nodded. This was the son of the prominent Johnson family. A young man he did not recognize was conducting the service, limning out a hymn, and under cover of the responding voices he replied, "I'm John Smith from Montgomery County."

Johnson's eyes widened in quick recognition. "Raccoon John Smith?" he said, smiling. "I've heard of you."

As the service proceeded John listened with growing interest to the young man behind the pulpit stand. His voice had an unusual resonance to it, a lingering quality that made John feel he had heard it before. The man's smooth skin bespoke his youth; he was not over twenty-five years, John judged, with finely chiseled features, his brown hair thick over brows that protruded above quick gray eyes. Yet he spoke with maturity, and although an intensity in his tones revealed strong passions, his closing prayer was tender, filled with compassion.

"Who be he?" he said to Johnson as the service ended.

"Jacob Creath," Johnson replied. At John's surprised expression, he went on. "He's a nephew of the well-known Jacob Creath, so to avoid confusion he's called Jacob Creath, Jr."

"I knew that voice had a familiar ring," John said when Johnson introduced them. "You've got a bit of your uncle in you. When did you come to these parts?"

"Just a couple of months ago," Jacob said. "Mr. Johnson and I were close friends in Washington City while he was in Congress, and he and Uncle Jake persuaded me I was needed here. I'll be preaching for a time here at Great Crossings."

John T. Johnson shook his head. "His uncle did most of the persuading," he said. "He thought at the time young Jacob would help defend the Baptists in Kentucky from the inroads of Campbellism, but both Jacob and I are for it. We're convinced of the imbecility of all human devices to bind Christians together; only the word of God can do it."

"Shake hands again," John said heartily.

Jacob laughed. "I've read your Circular Letter," he said to John. "You hit the nail on the head. And I read the disgraceful reply of the Licking Association. If that feeling spreads, and they refuse to fellowship with us, I'm wondering if it will mean a split?"

"We'll absolutely not split here in Great Crossings," Johnson said with conviction. "There are some in this church who object to Mr. Campbell's views, and that's all right with me. I am not insisting they change; they have the right to private judgment. But I ask that for myself, too. I keep in mind one of the great landmarks of the King of Kings—when you are reviled, revile not again."

"Actually," Jacob said, "the Baptist church originally stood for much that Campbell is now advocating. Take his stand against the domination of the clergy, why, the Baptists stood for that; it's only of late years the clergy has got such a hold on the church. The first Baptist church in the United States, back in 1636, advocated equal participation of the laymen. In fact, a layman named Ezekiel Holliman baptized Roger Williams himself, and then Mr. Williams turned about and baptized Mr. Holliman."

John nodded, his eyes gleaming. "Of course we must stay together. That's the only way we can get the Baptists back on the road they started on. That's what Mr. Campbell thinks, too." He had spotted a copy of *The Christian Baptist* on a block table at the back of the room where they were standing, and he picked it up. In the light of the pair of flickering candle-lamps near the door he flipped its pages. "Listen to this: 'The Baptist system is capable of being reformed or brought back again to the constitution of the Kingdom of Heaven; it carries in its bosom the means of its purification. The foundation needs to have the rubbish cleared away; the constitution is essentially of divine construction.' "

Jacob blew out the candles, and they wandered out into the churchyard, talking, warming to their common view of the church. The Elkhorn Association, Johnson said, was becoming sharply divided on Campbell's teaching, but Jacob said his uncle, Jacob Creath, Sr., was beginning to weaken in his stand against the reform movement. "Uncle Jake is fair-minded," he said. "He sees merit in Campbell's points, but he's opposed to dividing the church. He thinks many of the reforms Campbell is advocating can be brought about gradually. But I'm not so sure."

The rain had stopped, but clouds skittered across the sky, and the wind had sharpened. Johnson pulled a scarf from his pocket and tied it about his neck, tucking the ends up under his tall hat.

"You'll stay the night with me, won't you?" he said to John. "My wife Sophia and I are living at the big house above the rise, and there's room aplenty."

"There's room in my loft room, too," Jacob said, placing his hand on John's arm. "And I need someone to talk with. He can stay with you some other time, Mr. Johnson."

"It's not much but adequate for an unmarried man like me," Jacob told John after Johnson had ridden away and John had stretched himself comfortably on a pallet in the corner of the lodgings in the loft of the meetinghouse. Long after Jacob had blown out the candle and settled himself beside him, the two men talked, a bond of understanding and lasting friendship forging itself between them.

The streets of Lexington were aswarm with people, John found when he rode the ten miles into town the next morning. He tethered his horse at the courthouse hitching rail and walked down Main Street. A boy was hawking sales of printed programs of the day, and copies of *The Kentucky Miscellany*. John thumbed through a copy the boy handed him. He had heard of it, a collection of poems by a man named Tom Johnson, "O Rare Tom Johnson," the Robert Burns of the West, the editor of the *Kentucky Gazette*, John Bradford, called him. But the poems were rowdy and not to his liking, and he handed the copy back. Revolutionary soldiers, aged in years but young in memory, paraded in faded uniforms with the still fresh-faced veterans of the War of 1812, as people lined the street, most of them wearing Lafayette badges, eager to welcome the great General Gilbert du Motier, Marquis de la Fayette on his fourth and probably his last visit to the United States, accompanied this time by his son, appropriately named George Washington. Companies of infantry, artillery, and cavalry with fife and drum and bugles marched by, including a procession of Royal Arch Masons gathered to welcome their fraternal brother. After all the marching would come welcoming addresses and responding speeches, John knew, and the musketry salutes, and then a great banquet and ball in the new Grand Masonic Hall, despite the fact it was still unfinished. John made his way to the corner of Main Street and Main Cross and looked at the building, and then wandered in. The walls of the banquet rooms were framed with portraits of Washington, Jefferson, Lafayette, and Henry Clay. A giant transparency of Daniel Boone, made by the artist Matthew Jouett, stood between the doors leading to the great upper rooms, and all about were flowers and gay bunting and the national colors and flags of the United States and France.

John pictured the scene the banquet and ball would provide. His own homespun costume would be out of place among the elegant waistcoats and satin breeches and the lace and sprigged petticoats of the evening. He left the building and went back on the street. It was not yet noon. The General, so it was reported, had spent the night at Versailles, five miles west of Lexington, at the home of his old friend and fellow-soldier, Major John Keen, and was now proceeding slowly, accompanied by his military escort, through cheering groups of citizens to Lexington in a decorated carriage drawn by four bay horses.

Quite suddenly, and for no logical reason, John felt an aloneness, a separateness. All of this pomp and power represented something for which the Lord had chastened him, and sent him reeling back from the Hickory Flats country; it was not for him. Yet it represented also something of which he was forced by time and circumstance to be a part. It symbolized the slow penetration of a new refinement into what only yesterday had been a wilderness. And just as the buckskin jackets and homespun suits and coonskin caps were giving way in this bluegrass region to the sights and sounds of an advancing culture, so must the church be forged to fit into this new, developing climate. In the face of rising secularism, there was more need than ever for the church to hold fast to its essentials, but the ancient traditions of right and wrong, the sublime fact of God, the saving power of Jesus—all these fundamentals would be lost unless translated into terms the emerging society would find vital. Slowly he pushed his way through the crowd back to his horse, and turned the animal's head toward home.

The year raced by. Joseph Desha had been elected Governor of Kentucky on the "relief" ticket, defeating Christopher Tompkins, the anti-relief candidate, and political tension was lessening. Better feeling was developing among neighbors, money flowed more freely, and Henry Clay again became the idol of the people as he toured the state, attending great burgoo gatherings and parties, his popularity only slightly dimmed by word that came later of his duel with John Randolph in the nation's capital. For the first time since 1812, horse racing was resumed in Lexington.

A sense of expectancy was abroad in the land, a feeling of impending change, as if an era were passing, John thought as he rode up the rutted lane to his barn late one afternoon the next June and slowly eased himself to the ground. A new day was coming to birth, and resistance to it could bring only futility and remorse. He unloosened the horse's cinch and slid off the saddle. The hill shadows were creeping down; it was almost dark. He had been gone since sunup. He was weary, but it was a good weariness, a blessed tiredness. He had preached four times that day, each preaching followed by a baptizing in flowing streams, the cool waters of the June day sweet and refreshing.

So far this year, he figured, nearly nine hundred people had been brought into the churches of North District, the greater number of whom he had himself baptized. People liked him; he was successful. He was pleased with his acceptance, but the knowledge also humbled him. There was danger in success. The mill stream, he remembered, always drove the wheel most vigorously when a flood was starting to sweep the mill to destruction. Another visit to the state by Alexander Campbell had stimulated his followers to unshackle the church further from its creeds; and John had organized five new congregations on the basis of the Bible alone instead of on the *Philadelphia Confession of Faith*. They were all called Reformed Baptists, and many of the older groups who had come over to the Campbell movement were now going by the same name. But they were still tolerated within the Baptist framework. North District now numbered twenty-five churches with more than two thousand members.

He had started toward the cabin with his saddlebags stuffed with his wet baptizing clothes before he noticed Jonathan's horse and wagon at the far side, hitched under the big poplar. He smiled. He had not seen Jonathan since he had organized two churches a month before in Bath County, near Jonathan's place, and he had noticed his brother in the crowd at the baptizing which followed in Slate Creek. But Jonathan had left without speaking to him when he had begun to baptize Colonel James Mason, one of the big lawyers in the area, who had said he had no "experience" to give. "There is nothing in the Bible that requires a sinner to tell all the workings of his guilty conscience," John had announced, plain out. "All he has to do is say, Colonel Mason, as you have done, that he believes in the Lord Jesus Christ as the Son of God and accepts him and obeys him." It was then Jonathan had left.

He went on toward the house and dumped his saddlebags outside the kitchen door, and went in. The house smelled good. Three apple pies stood on the new Empire stove he had given Nancy last year after the baby, Maria, was born. He ran his thumb under the pies' ridged edges, tasting the rich juice. It would be pleasant to have a visit with the family. Jonathan meant well; his mind was just rigid-set. He pushed open the door into the sitting room.

Nancy was in the straight ladder-back chair, erect and unsmiling, facing Jonathan and Rachel standing awkwardly near the table. He called a greeting and slapped Jonathan on the shoulder and then turned to Rachel and playfully pinched her cheek. Rachel was almost pretty, he thought, but her eyes, wide and gentle, seemed also uncomprehending, and her sweetness was tempered by a whimpering habit that both annoyed and amused Nancy.

"You're feeding him well, Rachel," he said. "The man's getting some flesh on his bones."

"They've come to tell us trouble's brewing, John," Nancy spoke up, coming to the point at once. He turned to her. "North District's planning to censure you."

For a moment there was silence. "So?" John said, and shrugged. "In a way that's a compliment. They're after me because I'm successful. I've got the devil on the run."

"It's because you're a plain heretic, John!" Jonathan's face flushed with anger. "Don't try to make light of it. You brought it on yourself, chasing off after that Campbell doctrine. That man's a wrong-doing man, trying to start his own church."

John held himself in check with difficulty. "What on earth do you know about the Campbell doctrine, as you call it?" He faced his brother, his hands clenched. "Did you go to hear him preach even once? Have you read one word in his paper?" He went to the wooden box at the far end of the room in which he kept his books and papers, and pulled out a copy of *The Christian Baptist*. "Here, read this before you pronounce judgment." He held the paper out, and when Jonathan made no move to take it, he thumbed through it and then read aloud: " 'I have no idea of adding to the catalogue of sects; I labor only to see sectarianism abolished and all Christians of every name united upon the one foundation upon which the Apostolic Church was founded.'" He looked up. "Does this sound like he's trying to start another church? He's trying only to restore the original one; what's wrong-doing about that?" When Jonathan didn't answer, he said more quietly, "You think I'm wrong-doing too, organizing Baptist churches on the basis of the New Testament alone like I did over in Bath County?"

"Your conscience ought to tell you that, John." Jonathan stared at him soberly. "You got all the folks in Bath County upset; the good regular Baptists there don't know what's right any more; the churches are all mixed up on this thing. I'm plumb ashamed of you, baptizing like you did the other day."

"Ashamed of me!" John said, exasperated. "For baptizing a man on his honest, heartfelt confession of faith in Jesus?"

Jonathan shook his head. "But you did it without any sign from God he'd been saved, with not even a hint of a revealing experience. That's wrong-doing, and any good Baptist will say so."

John turned to Nancy quietly. "Didn't I see some apple pies?" he said. "Jonathan needs something to chew on besides me."

Rachel turned toward the door. "We left the baby with the Rigdon woman," she said, "and we'd best be getting back."

Jonathan followed her toward the door. "They're planning on censuring you at the North District meeting at Cane Springs in July, John," he said solemnly. "Are you going to the meeting anyway, now that you know?"

Before John could answer, Nancy's voice rang out from the kitchen. "He'll be going, Jonathan." She came and stood in the doorway, wiping her hands on her apron. "You can tell all the brethren he'll be there. Your brother's not the kind to run from trouble."

When John rode into Mount Sterling the next week for supplies, Buckner Payne confirmed Jonathan's warning. The community was buzzing with charges and countercharges, all aired freely in the general store. James French was openly soliciting messengers from the North District churches who would back him up at the Cane Springs meeting in denouncing John for heresy and apostasy; folks from the Licking Association were against him to a man, although their vote would not count at the North District meeting, but the votes of members of Lulbegrud, Goshen, Howard's Creek, Cane Springs would count, and they seemed solidly opposed to him.

The news distressed John more than he would admit; its significance was ominous, its implications could be far-reaching. But he tried to push it to the back of his mind as Mr. Payne went on talking. A change had come over the kindly merchant; his eyes shone with a respect and a sympathy and an understanding for John.

"All this talk has set me thinking," he said. "Eliza and I have been friendly with all the churches hereabouts, but we've never joined any, because while they all seem to have a beautiful theory, they've set a miserable example." He paused as John smiled and nodded in agreement. "So we concluded we'd just be good citizens and do what good we could and let the churches sort of rock along without us."

"And you've found that isn't enough?" John said.

"That's it," Payne admitted slowly. "Reading *The Christian Baptist* has something to do with changing our idea, but it's mainly watching the way you work, John Smith. I can see a lot more is required of a man; he can't ignore God. Eliza and I have come to realize it isn't enough just to believe in yourself; a man has to believe in the divine Lord. It isn't enough to just do good, a man has to do the will of God. You're the only preacher in the North District who relies on the revealed will of God as your sole authority; you're not adding to it or subtracting from it. And the brand of Christianity you're preaching now is not something vague and full of theological dogma; it's not merely a way of doing certain things. It's a way of living a life. If that's Campbellism, as folks call it, then let's have more of it!" He motioned John toward the back of the store, and for an hour the men talked. And when John left he knew he had won a major ally for the new Restoration Movement. Buckner Payne was a highly respected citizen, useful in the community, his influence a factor in every circle in which he moved.

But Buckner Payne would not be at the North District meeting in July at Cane Springs to help defend the Reformers' views. Many who were committed to it would be there, but able men were scarce. He wished young Jacob Creath could be present. But Jacob had gone to New Orleans, sick at heart over the dissension that was rocking the Great Crossings Church. John T. Johnson could be an able advocate and defender, but he was busy as judge of the new Court of Appeals and was in Frankfort for the summer.

He got on his horse and slowly jogged toward home. For the first time the possibility of a break with the Baptists seemed a real threat. He had no stomach for it.

CHAPTER XXVI

IT was on the Fourth of July, as John finished reading the Declaration of Independence to his family, seated about the trestle table in the grove by the house, that little Joshua first complained of chest pains. The next day he was delirious, and two weeks of anxiety and fear came and went as his fever surged and ebbed. On July 20 John held in his arms the white, still body of another son.

Nancy came back from the burying plot beside the Grassy Lick Church and sat in the rocker in the shade of the maples, and put her apron over her head. Little moaning cries escaped her, the hurt too hard for tears. This was the third child the Lord had taken from her tender in years. John sat beside her, silent, his hands thumbing his Bible, his eyes comforting her. The hill shadows crept closer; a heifer lowed in the back pasture, a whippoorwill called, and fireflies began playing in the stubble.

"Troubles all get ripe at the same time, like beans," John said quietly. "This means I won't be going to Cane Springs next week. I wouldn't feel right, leaving you at such a time."

Nancy stiffened. Slowly she pulled the apron from her face. "You'll be going," she said, after a moment. "And I'll be going with you."

The Cane Springs Baptist Church was in Madison County, south of the Kentucky River, nominally outside the bounds of North District, but it had been received into the Association as early as 1805, before the lines were firmly drawn, and still retained its membership. The log meetinghouse was on the farm owned by David Chenault, its minister and the moderator of North District Association.

"I met David Chenault at the first North District meeting I went to when we first came up here," John told Nancy as they drove along the dusty road in the gig. "But I never have felt close to him. Maybe it's because he's rich. He owns about twenty slaves and is proud as Lucifer." He shook his head. "And he's hard as hickory on Baptist doctrine, won't concede Jesus Christ himself wasn't a Baptist."

They passed a long, low stone fence bordering the road and turned into a wide lane leading to a wagon gate. John pulled on the hemp rope suspended from a hickory arm dangling above them, and the gate swung open.

"David's father bought this place from a brother of Daniel Boone back in '86 or so," he said. "And David inherited it. That's why he's rich. A man with a farm like this couldn't help but make money."

"Seems strange for a preacher to be rich," Nancy said, adjusting her new chip bonnet. "Folks might suspect it gets in the way of his religion."

John shook his head. "Not with David, it doesn't; he's a hyper-Calvinist if I ever met one."

"That's not the same as being religious," Nancy said.

The lane forked sharply, one road leading up between tall trees to the big house of cut lumber that topped a gentle slope, the other toward a grove surrounding a clearing where the log meetinghouse had been erected. As they drove up to the hitching rail, John saw Thomas Mosley, Jacob Coons, Joe Bondurant, all good friends who had embraced the Restoration Movement walking toward the building. He helped Nancy out of the gig and followed them, waving a greeting.

The church was almost filled as they entered. Peter and James Mason from Grassy Lick were there with their wives, along with William Ralls; they were his friends and supporters. But there were others who opposed him. Near the pulpit stand he saw the group from Lulbegrud, Matt Davis, John Treadway, John Fletcher, their heads together, talking with James French. They were sincere men, John thought; he bore them no ill will. They had been reared to believe in the rightness of their views, and his own inquiring mind was foreign to their way of thinking.

He looked about for others who might support him. Jeremiah Vardeman was nowhere to be seen. Had he stayed away on purpose? Vardeman had been cordial to Alexander Campbell on his visits to the state, but John had noticed he had been cautious in openly endorsing Campbell's views on the restoration of the New Testament church unhampered by human creeds; he had preferred to listen and let others storm the Baptist citadel. And now he had even more reason to be cautious. He was preaching for the Calvinist remnant of the fashionable First Baptist Church in Lexington left when the liberal-minded Dr. James Fishback had split the church, taking a following of free-thinkers to form what he was calling a "Church of Christ." John's eyes clouded. Jeremiah Vardeman could not risk exposure of his stand to a vote.

Nancy slipped into a seat near the rear, and he sat down beside her, accepting condolences as women from neighboring churches and sturdy, God-fearing men came up to press their hands in sympathy.

David Chenault was mounting the narrow rostrum. John looked somberly at this good man who was moderator of the North District Association, at his black eyes and hair, his slender frame, his olive complexion, his thin lips drawn now in a tight line as his high voice started limning out a hymn, motioning for William Markell to vibrate his tuning fork for the key.

Markell was a good man, too, John thought, watching him. He smiled as he recalled the singing school the young man had organized in the Grassy Lick Church, assembling the children on Saturday afternoons under the great maples and elms in the churchyard while their elders were in the business session, disciplining the back-sliding members. John had often been tempted to listen to the high, sweet voices of the children singing "Primrose" or "Pisgah," and even the rollicking "Dublin," instead of to the discipline charges. He had no liking for such business. The church was made up of people of the earth, earthy; many of them, he knew, as basic in their needs as the soil they worked, but as clean. There were sinners among them, scarlet sinners maybe. But wrestling with elemental instincts, they could be doomed to a frustrating succession of failures by insistence on the rigid, puritanical standards of conduct set by some of their more fortunate, protected fellow members.

Now Markell was attempting to get the group to sing in parts—bass, treble, tenor, and counter tenor—each deciding for himself what part to sing. After listening a moment to the resulting babble, John let his clear tenor ring out.

"You're singing too loud," Nancy nudged him. "And you're doing it on purpose."

He looked at her and winked. "It'll be my last chance before they chop my head off," he whispered.

And John was not mistaken. David Chenault drove the meeting forward with the skill of a politician, calling the roll of the churches, receiving their formal reports.

"They're supposed to be called in alphabetical order," John said, "but he's holding the Lulbegrud Church until the last. I can see his strategy; it's Lulbegrud, which means smiling Judge French, who is going to be hatchet man."

And he was right. One by one James French read off charges against him as he stood to represent the Lulbegrud Church: using Campbell's translation of the New Testament; changing the words used in the ordinance of baptism; not breaking the communion bread into small pieces but allowing each communicant to break it for himself; intimating that the *Philadelphia Confession of Faith* was merely the opinion of men instead of the inspiration of God. John listened closely.

As Judge French finished, William Markell shouted from the side of the room, "What evidence do you have to sustain these charges?"

Immediately John was on his feet. A hush fell over the little room, the only sound the heavy breathing of bewildered men. "My brethren from Lulbegrud need not feel the least concerned for evidence to sustain their charges," he called out. "I plead guilty to them all—and many more."

The meeting was thrown into an uproar. Calls of "Shame! Shame!" were drowned in heavy applause and cries of "Bravo!"

John waved the people to silence. "If you give me a chance," he cried, "I'll promise not to expose more than thirteen additional errors in our Baptist doctrine, and the people can then without difficulty discover the rest for themselves." He waited for the ripple of laughter coupled with a rumble of disapproval to quiet, and then went on, his voice calm, his tone deliberate. "But, my brethren, you mistake the reforms I seek for innovations; with you, every dissenting view is considered heretical. You confuse the freedom to think and the desire to return to the simplicity of the early church with apostasy. To no such charges do I plead guilty."

For almost an hour the meeting continued, charges flying right and left. The restoration views of Alexander Campbell were challenged, and were in turn defended; the effect of the "Ancient Order of Things" on the Baptist churches was deplored by staunch Calvinists, and as warmly acclaimed by others.

"They're outshouting us," John whispered to Nancy, "but I can see David Chenault is afraid they won't be able to outvote us." And he was right.

When the confusion subsided, the weary Moderator ruled that any vote to censure John Smith for his heretical preaching would be postponed until the next year, when North District would meet at Lulbegrud, giving time for said John Smith to think it all over.

As if it had been a signal, the tumultuous meeting of North District fanned into open flame the smoldering dissension in almost every other association in the state. It became a time of ferment and passion, argument and debate. The state's Baptist paper, *The Recorder*, long suspicious of Alexander Campbell, now openly labeled the whole movement to restore the teachings and practice of the New Testament Church as a Campbellite conspiracy to wreck the Baptist church. Some associations refused John recognition as a messenger from North District, and on some preaching appointments he found the churches locked against him. At Stony Point he was ordered out of the pulpit by the elders of the church and, in defiance, he shouted, "I come to you bringing the Apostle Paul's doctrine, but since you will not hear me, I shall follow his advice and shake off the dust from my feet as a testimony against you." Suiting the words to action, he dramatically, recklessly, shook first one foot and then the other in the faces of the startled elders, and stalked from the building. A few days later he found that his adherents at Mount Pleasant had hauled two wagonloads of planks and benches to a grove in preparation for his visit as the church was closed to him. But on the morning on which he was to preach, they were found burned and the grove a shambles. "It's the work of the orthodox," an outraged adherent, George Elley, told John. "They are venting their spleen and holy indignation against the presumption of those of us who would prove all things and hold fast to that which is good. Well, let the wicked rage! As fire burned these benches so will fire burn away the chaff, and the wheat shall be garnered."

John deplored such public display of the Baptist controversy, but he noticed it was attracting to his meetings curious members of other sects. A scattering of Presbyterians was in every audience, he discovered, and one or more of them came forward for baptism by immersion after sermons in which he emphasized that distinguishing feature of Baptist doctrine. But immersing the Methodists was his special joy. The vitality of his preaching seemed to meet a natural response in the hearts of these emotionally attuned people, and he seized every opportunity to shed light on the tenets of their different beliefs.

In passing a Methodist camp meeting one day in September he stopped to watch a young Methodist preacher baptize a howling, rebellious infant by sprinkling water on the squirming body. When the service was concluded, he stepped to the front of the crowd and, identifying himself, took the preacher firmly by the arm and attempted to lead him toward the creek a few yards away.

"What are you trying to do, Brother Smith?" the young preacher protested. "Are you out of your mind?"

"What am I trying to do?" John affected deep surprise. "Why, sir, I am going to baptize you by immersion into the death, burial, and resurrection of our Lord Jesus Christ, according to his commandment."

"But I have no desire for such baptism. I know of you; you are called 'The Dipper.' But you are not going to dip me. I'm a Methodist; let me go!"

John tightened his hold on the man's arm while the crowd watched, some in apprehension, others in amusement. "That is a scoffer's blasphemy of a holy ordinance," he said sternly. "Are you a believer?"

"Of course I'm a believer," the preacher said indignantly. "But I'm not willing to be immersed. It would do no good for you to baptize me against my will. It would be wrong!"

"I don't understand," John said. "Only a few minutes ago you baptized a helpless baby against its will, although it screamed and kicked. Did you get its consent first? Come along, sir, we will have no more of this foolishness."

The crowd broke into open laughter, and John gave the young preacher a quick pull toward the creek, and then as suddenly released him. He waved to the people for silence.

"Brethren and friends, I shall be in the neighborhood for a little while visiting among you; let me know if this poor, misguided man ever again baptizes another without his consent. For you have heard him say that it would do no good, that it would be wrong.

"And now, since there will be no interference with my brother's discourse, as he has concluded his service, hear me out! Let me tell you something of the Lord's plan of salvation as revealed in the Gospels, and the Christian mode of baptism as practiced by Christ and certified to us by the Holy Bible. Water in itself has no power to cleanse from sin but immersing in it is the symbol of the washing away of our guilt by Christ's death and resurrection. We must ourselves first experience faith and repentance, then we are ready for baptism and the remission of our sins, which is followed by the gift of the Holy Spirit and Eternal Life. 'Know ye not,' as Paul said, 'that so many of us as were baptized into Jesus Christ were baptized into his death? Therefore we are buried with him by baptism into death; that like as Christ was raised up from the dead by the glory of the Father, even so we also should walk in newness of life. For if we have been planted together in the likeness of his death, we shall be also in the likeness of his resurrection.' "

For almost an hour he talked, the people listening closely, only a few of them seeming to note that the young preacher had stalked toward the hitching rail and mounted his horse, riding away in a cloud of dust. When John extended the invitation, seven young people, all from Methodist families, responded, requesting baptism by immersion. He led them to the creek and performed the rite, a sense of triumph filling him. But it was short-lived. As he concluded the service and stepped back on the bank in his wet clothes, an excited, indignant mother pushed her way through the crowd, confronting him.

"You are a demon," she cried. "When you led my innocent young daughter into that water, you led her that much further toward hell."

For a moment John stood in shocked surprise. Then he reached out and patted the woman's arm, soothing her. "My good sister," he said quietly, "when you read your Bible more and your Methodist discipline less, you will learn that people do not go to that place by water."

John knew his sermons divided families, and he was troubled by it. But he knew they also changed lives. They confused many people, he realized, but they enlightened more. And eventually, he felt in his heart, the air would clear as after a storm and the Baptist church would emerge a stronger witness to the majesty and mystery of the gospel.

His regular charges at Grassy Lick, Spencer's Creek, Bethel, and Mount Sterling continued as he alternated among them. Dissension was increasing at Grassy Lick, but the others were solidly behind him, and his position with the Mount Sterling Church was made more firm when Buckner Payne and his wife Eliza came forward one Sunday, claiming allegiance to the Bible alone, throwing the weight of their wide influence into the battle for the reformation.

The calls on his time seemed endless. He performed twenty-four marriages in June the next year, and conducted seven funerals in one week. Sick people in and out of the churches pleaded for visits from him, and Nancy loaded them down with fresh corn and jars of pickles and crocks of hominy when she and John left.

"You've learned to love God," Matt Treadwell's wife told him when he visited her injured child.

"You don't learn to love God," he told her. "You soak it in through the pores of your skin."

The summer heat was mercifully mild in 1828. It had rained every day for three months in the spring, and as late as April a three-inch snow had fallen in Mount Sterling. The last Saturday in July he was glad to put on the tow-linen coat Nancy had ironed for him to wear to the North District Association meeting at Lulbegrud.

"I may have to take it off," he told Nancy as he slipped his arms in the sleeves. "They've got more ammunition this year, and they'll make it hotter than last time. But at least the coat feels good now."

The atmosphere in the twelve-cornered meetinghouse where he had once tempered his sermons to woo the unbending James French, was tense, charged with the heat of angry messengers from Howard's Creek, Goshen, Cane Springs—all again accusing him of increased heresy, apostasy, innovation, their strategy strengthened now by adroit maneuvers by which he was prevented from speaking in his own defense. But his supporters had increased in both numbers and conviction, and as the day wore on he realized that David Chenault sensed they were not only so strong they might be able to vote down a censure, but they might even be able to vote the loyal Calvinists as being, themselves, in disorder. Chenault's own Cane Springs Church, represented as vocal in its opposition to John by a few noisy members, was showing signs of weakening as a group and, as James Mason whispered to him during a recess, it might even swing into the ranks of the Reformers. John shook his head almost sadly. "That would break David's heart," he said, "I don't know as how I could rejoice in it." He looked with compassion on the stern face of the Moderator as he brought the meeting to an abrupt close, ruling again that all matters of doctrinal discipline be held in abeyance until the next year's session.

It was again a victory, a victory that was beginning to form a pattern.

John took time in October to help store food for the winter in the stone cellar beneath the kitchen. Cabbages, turnips, potatoes were buried in creek sand; apples, beans, pumpkins were hung on rafters for drying. He went into the field with Hep, the Negro man, and cut the tobacco he had planted for the first time that year; bending, slashing the ripening stalks, followed down the rows by Nancy and Robbie and the older children, stacking the cut stalks. The acrid odor pervaded the countryside. Hog-killing time followed, and while Hep and Robbie salted and smoked the meat, he helped Nancy make soap, filling the V-shaped ash hopper with wood ashes, drenching them with boiling water to form lye in which they boiled the hog entrails.

He had made a preaching appointment for early November at the home of Sam Muchols near Versailles, and it was while there he learned Jacob Creath, Jr., had returned to Kentucky. The next afternoon he rode into Versailles, a leisurely town of several hundred people, its cluttering of houses dissected by a single street crossing the Lexington pike. He passed Watkins Tavern, run by the mother of Henry Clay, and went west of the crossroads to Rose Hill, where the Baptist meetinghouse stood. Beside it was the rambling log cabin of Elder Jacob Creath, its pastor.

John tied his horse at the stile and climbed over and went to the door and let the brass knocker clang twice. "I'm begging shelter for the night," he said, grinning, to the short, stout man who opened it. "How are you, Brother Creath?"

The older man embraced him. His frock coat was baggy, and his white cravat was wrenched to one side, but his black eyes still shone with quiet wisdom. John had not seen him since the last meeting of the Elkhorn Association a year ago, when John had been bitterly denounced. Jacob Creath, he knew, had been in only partial sympathy with the Reformers, but he had championed John's stand that day, and it was now rumored that, although he was still in full fellowship with the Baptists, he was inclined more and more to accept the principles of the Restoration Movement as outlined by Alexander Campbell. "Young Jacob is here, and we're discussing the things of the Kingdom," he said heartily. "Come on in!"

"If you can call it a kingdom," a young voice called from the next room. "It's more like a caldron just now."

John followed Creath down the wide hallway and turned into the sitting room. Before the fire young Jacob stood, feet apart, hands on hips, quickly extending an arm as John entered.

John grinned at sight of the impetuous young Jacob Creath, so like and yet so unlike his uncle. His thick patch of brown hair now stood almost upright, and his gray eyes flashed, bespeaking his fearless, high-strung nature.

"I heard you were back in these parts, Jacob." John shook the offered hand vigorously. "I came over on purpose to see you. I thought you'd bring a wife back from this trip."

"It's high time," Mr. Creath chuckled. "Jacob is all of thirty years; a wife would settle him some."

Seated about the fire, warming his feet, drinking a bowl of hot soup, John listened as Jacob recounted the story of his journey south, of his visit to Andrew Jackson at his homestead, The Hermitage, near Nashville, more beautiful even than Henry Clay's Ashland. He told of his visit with Philip Fall in Nashville, of the swing toward the Reformers young Philip had started all over Tennessee. Young Jacob had been so inspired by Philip's stand he had preached without restraint as he went on through the south, pleading for all sects to return to the Bible alone, explaining the Restoration Movement, and in Natchez, Mississippi, he had so enraged the Methodists, Episcopalians, and the Presbyterians as well as the Baptists by his doctrine of "Bible-alone churches," a group of irate members had burned him in effigy. A bout with yellow fever followed in New Orleans, and then he had returned by way of Bethany, West Virginia, where he had visited, and been again inspired by, the great Alexander Campbell.

"And now I'm back, preaching at Versailles along with Uncle Jake, and at Cane Run, South Elkhorn and Clear Creek—and making them all mad," he finished.

"Mad but wiser, I'm observing," the elder Creath laughed.

John smiled. "Campbellism seems to do that," he said.

"Campbellism?" Mr. Creath frowned. He leaned back in his rocker and placed the spread finger tips of his two hands together. "Campbellism is a term used only by people who cannot conceive of Christianity in any other light than as an 'ism.' "

John nodded, accepting the gentle rebuke, and then Mr. Creath went on. "Neither you nor Jacob are so blinded, and neither am I. But if we are to lead others who are that blind, we can't get too far ahead of them; we must maintain contact. Young Jacob is getting too far ahead."

"I know what you mean," John said. "We should remain one body, otherwise we defeat our purpose."

"Exactly," Mr. Creath said. "And it can be done. Philip Fall did it with the Louisville Church and has done it at Nashville; Benjamin Allan has done it at Bear Grass. At Harrods Creek, at Chenoweth Lane, at Pond Creek, at South Elkhorn—the majority of members have disavowed the *Philadelphia Confession of Faith*, yet there is no formal separation from those who cling to it; they're remaining in fellowship."

"But for how long?" Young Jacob spoke impatiently. He dropped down on a low hassock, extending his feet to the fire. "They think we're lost in the fatal delusions of Alexander Campbell, and when they give up all hope of rescuing us, they'll separate from us. You know what they've done at Clear Creek?" He turned to John. "They've turned us Reformers out, literally out in the cold. They deny us the use of the building, and we're meeting in a grove. That's where I'm preaching, in an open grove in this weather."

"Don't make yourself a martyr, Jacob," his uncle said mildly. "You probably don't get as chilled as your listeners. I've preached in groves many times in the dead of winter."

"And you'll probably have opportunity again," young Jacob said. "The church here at Versailles is about to turn us both out. They're planning to bring charges when the Elkhorn Association meets next

August." He jumped to his feet from the low hassock. "You've heard what the Great Crossings Church has done?" he asked John.

John's eyes widened. "What do you mean?"

"The great Silas Noel, the arch-Calvinist from Frankfort, has been over in Georgetown helping to get a college started there to combat the Campbell heresy, as he calls it, and the Great Crossing Church got him to preach for it while there. He has literally uprooted every seed I planted in that church. I received a letter from the church clerk yesterday, asking me to give an accounting of the doctrine I preached there. It sounds like they're planning to try me."

The visit with the lively Creaths had refreshed him, John thought as he rode away the next morning. But their news disturbed him. Conditions were more acute than even he had realized; the attacks had widened. He was no longer alone in suffering the attacks of the opponents to what was being called the Restoration Movement. It was comforting to have company, but it boded no easy solution. And his anxiety was well founded; rumblings of dissent continued all winter, and broke into open warfare as spring and summer brought the annual District meetings.

It was the called session of the Great Crossings Church to "try" Jacob Creath that decided John to go to Frankfort and storm the citadel of the great Silas Noel himself. Dr. Noel was a learned Baptist preacher, respected and able, but as John sat late the next August in the little meetinghouse at Great Crossings, it struck him that the great arch-Calvinist had sown to the whirlwind when he had dared plant distrust of Jacob Creath while preaching for this group. The meeting was not a formal trial in the usual sense; no formal charges were brought. They were made by innuendo; by subtle thrusts hard to grapple with; by suggestions of apostasy that could not be openly countered. The people were confused; fear of something they did not understand was in their faces. They had loved young Jacob Creath when he served as their pastor, but they had the vague, uneasy feeling they had been preached a false doctrine; they had been betrayed. One by one they now arose to denounce any adherence to that doctrine, to reaffirm their loyalty to the Baptist faith.

"This is a case of people being in religious bondage," John said to John T. Johnson, sitting beside him. "They are both bound and blinded by their sectarian shackles, and they refuse to think their way loose. Jacob's great crime is that he tried to get them to think for themselves."

Johnson nodded, a flush of anger mounting his face. "Absolutely," he said. "If they don't leave Jacob alone the stones of the street will cry out against them."

When the last man had spoken, the group looked expectantly at Jacob, sitting on the other side of Johnson. He hesitated for a moment, and then got up and went to the pulpit stand and looked over the upturned faces. These people were his friends; he had visited in their homes, comforted them in their trials, consoled them in bereavement, buried their dead. He began quietly in a low, vibrant voice to quote from Paul's defense before King Agrippa, ignoring any reference to the attacks on his doctrine.

"I was not disobedient to the heavenly vision," he said simply as he concluded. "Having therefore obtained the help of God, I continue unto this day, witnessing both to small and great. And I would to God that not only thou but also all that hear me this day were such as I am." He bowed his head, and in the silence the people began filing out, some sobbing, others stony-faced.

"I'm ashamed of this church," Johnson said as he stood with John and Jacob beside their horses at the hitching rail. "I'm leaving it."

"Where will you go?" John asked.

Johnson shook his head. "God alone knows," he said. "I've been talking lately with Barton Stone over in Georgetown. He was in the same dilemma when he left the Presbyterians. In order to have fellowship he organized like-minded people into his Christian Church, and his movement is growing. I may organize just such a group here in Great Crossings, based only upon the teachings of the Scriptures; there would be only a few of us but at least we'd be Christians."

"And have Silas Noel come along and wreck it for you?" Jacob said almost bitterly. "Somebody should turn the tables on him."

When John told Nancy of his decision to go to Frankfort and challenge Silas Noel's preaching, she looked dubious. "You remind me of David, taking on Goliath," she said.

"If I don't go," he replied, "I'd remind myself of Jonah, fleeing from his duty."

She had started out of the room, but at his words she turned and came back and laid her hand on his shoulder, her eyes probing him.

"You're right, John," she said. "You don't have to be a great man to be used of God; you just have to be willing."

But John did not leave immediately for Frankfort. The next day word reached him that the Calvinists in the Grassy Lick Church were insisting on drawing apart. John learned of the decision almost with dismay. The church had voted out the old covenant, and he knew there was an undercurrent of dissension among the members, but a formal separation had never been discussed.

"If I am the bone of contention," he announced at a called meeting of the church the next week, "I will resign as your preacher." He laid an arm about the shoulder of Reuben McDonnold, the leader of the Calvinists. "My wish is to live with you in peace. But do not separate!"

"Your resignation would not remedy the situation," McDonnold said sadly. "Should you leave, a worse might be called in your place, and to be candid, we would rather have you here than any other preacher of your sort. No, we insist on a complete separation."

"But this building, these grounds?" John looked about him. "Which group shall possess them?"

For a moment there was silence. John looked over the group. More than a hundred of them, by far the majority, had taken their stand with him. They would have legal right to the property. But would it make for good feeling? Would it be an expression of the compassion he felt?

"Though we might with propriety," he said after a moment, "call ourselves the Grassy Lick Church because of our larger numbers, yet we should as Christians go from each other in peace. We leave you, therefore, this house, the grounds, the books. I propose we go over near Somerset and raise a new meetinghouse." He bowed his head and brought the meeting to a close with a fervent prayer for God's guidance upon them all.

He and Nancy made their way without comment to their buggy, and rode for a time in silence broken only by John's occasional absent-minded sighs. The reins hung limp in his hands; the horse sauntered, stopping to munch grass along the roadside, to snap at flies. Nancy twisted in her seat beside him, and finally reached over and took the reins from his hands and urged the horse into a trot.

"You're working yourself into a state, John," she said as they bounced along the rutted road. "You got yourself thinking it's more important to hold on to the Baptist church than to hold on to God."

CHAPTER XXVII

WITHIN a week John left for Frankfort.

He had been in that part of the state only a few times, and he rode leisurely, savoring the countryside. He went through Lexington and paused for a few minutes to watch the workmen already starting to rebuild the main building and law library of Transylvania University, burned to the ground a few months before, and then rode out the Leestown Road, widened now and covered with crushed limestone. He paused at Hickman Hill, viewing with a wry smile the cabin built and occupied for years by the great pioneer Baptist preacher, William Hickman. The old man had died there only two years before, a rugged, unrelenting Calvinist to the last. John hastened his horse; he would stop at nearby Old Stone Inn for the night.

Philip Fall was preaching in Nashville, but John had written him of his plan to visit Frankfort, and Philip had said he would be there and make arrangements for his speaking.

As John entered the town which was the state's capital, he rode slowly, marveling at its beauty. The Kentucky River cut a sparkling path through the main section; two-story structures with imposing columns lined both banks; churches were everywhere—Baptist, Presbyterian, Methodist, Episcopal—jealously staring at each other. He rode down Montgomery Street, following the river's course until it crossed Ann Street, named for the beautiful young wife of the city's founder, General James Wilkerson, and stopped at Weisiger House, a popular tavern for the legislators when in session. But he could not obtain lodging; the Legislature was meeting, and the inn was filled. He went another block to St. Clair Street and secured a room without difficulty at the Mansion House.

It was early Saturday afternoon; he had planned to preach that night if Philip Fall could make arrangements. They would meet in front of the capitol building, Philip had written him. He refreshed himself and walked toward the classic two-story structure in the center of a great open greensward. It was the third capitol building erected by the state, and was still in process of construction. The first two buildings had burned, but this one was built of brick and stone, its six fluted columns shielding a portico on which a dozen men now mingled and bartered, some of them wearing deerskin jackets, others, probably Tidewater people, dressed in broadcloth and silk top hats. John remembered that many Virginians from the Tidewater section had settled in Frankfort, and they gave the place an air of settled gentility. Kentucky could well be proud of her capital, John thought, looking about. It was a meeting place of the old and the new. The town was on the edge of the wilderness, but it represented the same penetrating thrust of civilization he had been conscious of in Lexington, with its handsome buildings and brick sidewalks and a water system constructed of a pipeline of hollowed cedar logs which brought enough water from Cove Springs to supply all the town's needs.

A sharp breeze had sprung up, but the afternoon sun was still warm. He was making his way toward the steps of the capitol to sit in its warmth when his attention was caught by a sign swinging from a post supporting a bear-oil lamp by the brick sidewalk. He read in amazement:

> Raccoon John Smith of Montgomery County will preach Sunday evening at 7 o'clock in the Franklin County Courthouse—by order of Judge Owsley.

John read the words over several times, puzzled, proud, yet disappointed. He had hoped Philip could arrange for him to preach in Silas Noel's church. The courthouse would be cold and uninviting; few people would attend. Yet it would be a distinction to speak in the courthouse of the state's capital; such public rooms were not being opened as freely as they once were for preaching services.

He was still staring at the sign when he felt an arm slip about his shoulders and turned to see Philip Fall's wide blue eyes looking into his, a grin on his lean face. They embraced in unabashed affection.

"You're curious about that sign, aren't you?" Philip said after the greetings were over. He wagged his head. "I tried to get Silas Noel to open his church, but he wouldn't hear of it. I tried every church in town, in fact, but not one would have you," he told John in candor. "Even the Presbyterians and the Methodists are afraid of you. I feel it's Dr. Noel's influence; he's warned them against you."

John laughed. "They didn't need his warning. They'd probably heard of my inroads on their sacred bailiwicks. Guarding their own starving sheep is more important to them than allowing an outsider to feed them," he said. "Closing churches to me is no new experience. I've preached in homes and on the streets. It's not too cold to hold a service here on the lawn."

Philip shook his head. "I'm glad that won't be necessary. I knew you'd baptized some of Judge Owsley's family back in Montgomery County, and when I told him the churches were closed to you, he insisted you preach in his courtroom. The announcement is creating quite a bit of interest; we should have a crowd."

"From the number of handsome churches I see, each prettied up like it was trying to outdo the others, I'd say Dr. Noel's sectarian spirit must have been contagious in this town," John said. "I'm not sure people will come out to hear me."

They had turned toward the street, John leading the way back to his tavern, when a carriage pulled to a stop at the edge of the curb in front of them. A woman of about thirty, her wide, intelligent brown eyes smiling, was leaning from the tonneau as the liveried Negro driver in the high box reined in the team of high-stepping bay mares. Her dress was of the finery of the Tidewater people, and the plumes on her hat nodded as she bent forward.

"Brother Fall!" she exclaimed. "I didn't know you had returned from Tennessee."

Philip Fall doffed his weather-beaten hat as he went to the carriage and extended his hand. "I'm back only on a visit," he said, "as I see you are. I came mainly to put plans in motion for opening a school for girls here next year if it seems feasible. In the meantime, I've been arranging a preaching service for my friend for tomorrow night." He motioned John forward. "Mrs. Tubman, may I present Brother John Smith," he said.

"Not Raccoon John Smith?" Mrs. Tubman's eyes twinkled as she extended her hand. John shook it awkwardly. He had heard of Mrs. Richard Tubman. Emily Thomas she had been, a ward of Henry Clay, reared in Frankfort but married now to a wealthy Georgia planter. "I've seen notices posted about town, and I've also been hearing stories about your unorthodox views," she went on, smiling. "Why aren't you preaching in Dr. Noel's church?"

John glanced at Philip and shifted his feet.

"Dr. Noel wouldn't allow it, Mrs. Tubman," Philip answered for him. "Brother Smith is a good Baptist, but he feels as I do about the need to change some of our Baptist doctrine. And Dr. Noel is opposed to such innovation. He's . . ."

"I know, I know," Mrs. Tubman interrupted him, nodding, a shadow crossing her face. "I love Dr. Noel dearly, but I've had the impression he is rigid in his thinking."

"You are a member of his church?" John asked.

She laughed. "Yes and no," she said. "My husband is a vestryman in the Episcopal church, but I was never interested in joining any church until I became a student of the Bible and discovered that immersion is essential. Dr. Noel as a Baptist believes that, too, so he baptized me only this month right here in the Kentucky River, although I told him at the time I wasn't sure I wanted to be baptized into the Baptist church." She turned to John, laughing. "Do I scandalize you?"

"Not at all," John said, his face thoughtful. "I know what you mean."

"Well, I scandalized him," she said. "Especially when I told him I was reading *The Christian Baptist*. Have you gentlemen seen that paper?"

Philip and John glanced at each other, and broke into laughter. "It's next to the Bible on my list," John said. "And on Mr. Fall's, too."

Mrs. Tubman wagged a finger at him. "Then I'm coming to hear you preach tomorrow night," she said. Her face grew serious. "The editor of that paper, Mr. Alexander Campbell, seems opposed to all this dogma and machinery that is bogging down the church, and I agree with him. I've seen so much of it in the Episcopal church, and now I'm discovering it is not confined to that group, that other churches are dogmatic, too. I want to feel the breath of God when I attend a worship service."

John smiled. "I may not be speaking with the breath of God tomorrow night," he said, "but I'll try to pry open the fancy windows of the church so you can get a whiff of it."

Her eyes studied him a moment. "I believe you can do it," she said. She tapped the shoulder of the Negro driver, motioning for him to drive on. "I'll be there," she called back as the carriage started to roll.

Every space was filled in the big courtroom when John arose to speak the following night—the lobby, the jury box, the window ledges; and people pressed against the narrow platform which served as the judge's bench, sitting on camp stools and upturned logs. He saw Mrs. Tubman near the front by an aisle. Every member of the Legislature, Philip had whispered to him, was present except four. Seven preachers of the town were in the audience, and Silas Noel, John saw, had slipped into a rear seat and was pressed now against a corner window.

John's hand shook as he turned the pages of his Bible. He had never addressed such an audience, and the effrontery of his coming for a moment swept over him. Who was he, Raccoon John Smith, to speak before the chosen representatives of the people of Kentucky? Who was he to attack the Baptist creedal position in the presence of one of its most vocal and capable advocates, Dr. Silas Noel? Who was he to boast that he would open church windows and let in the breath of the Almighty?

"You don't have to be a great man, John, to be used of God," he could almost hear Nancy whispering. "You just have to be willing."

"And when John came to Frankfort," he read solemnly from the Bible in his hand, "his spirit was stirred within him when he saw the city wholly given to sectarianism." He paused and adjusted his new spectacles, looking over the crowd. "I have not read the scripture exactly as it is in the Book," he said. "The city spoken of was wholly given over to idolatry; but the difference between sectarianism and idolatry is so slight that the error is hardly worth correcting. For I do aver, my friends, that sectarianism has done the cause of Christianity more harm than all the idolatry in the world."

He spoke for almost two hours, the great audience giving earnest attention as he pleaded not only for the Baptist sect but for all churches to renounce sectarianism. Dramatically he checked off on his long, bony fingers the steps by which fellowship could be reestablished: reject the creeds that divide us and accept the Bible alone; receive any repentant sinner on his simple confession of faith; recognize that lay people have equal access to God with the clergy;

restore to local congregations the right to govern themselves relieved of the authority of a hierarchy.

"Folks, something is wrong," he said as he concluded. "All of us are praying for what God can never grant; that is, that everybody will leave his own church and join us. The Presbyterian is praying for Christian union, but is he willing to cast aside the *Westminster Confession?* You know he isn't. We Baptists pray that we'll all be united in faith, peace, and love. Fine words, but ask our Calvinist Baptist brethren if they are willing to put away their *Philadelphia Confession of Faith* and take the word of God alone. The same is true of the Methodists with their *Articles of Religion*, the Lutherans with their *Augsburg Confession*, the Episcopalians with their Thirty-nine Articles, the Catholics with their Nicene Creed." He came to the edge of the platform and leaned forward, dropping his voice to almost a conversational tone that carried in the stillness to the furthest corner of the room. "Isn't it time to transcend our opinions with our faith? Isn't it time to unite on the Bible alone?"

He was wet with perspiration and his voice was hoarse when he finished and the crowd rose to its feet, breaking the tradition of a religious service with a thunderous applause. John stood, a sudden trembling again upon him as if a return of his old palsy. Philip noticed it, and took his arm and led him through a rear door.

"I was hoping to speak to Dr. Noel," John said, wiping his face.

Philip held out the short woolsey jacket Nancy had insisted he take, and John slipped it on. "He's probably more anxious to speak to you," Philip said. "I saw him squirming, and that's a sure sign he's gunning for you."

They went out a side door, avoiding the stream of people emerging at the front, and made their way to their horses tethered at the long hitching rail at the rear. Philip's horse stomped impatiently at the sound of their voices. Next to it, John's horse had been hitched, but now only the bridle was attached to the rail. The horse was gone.

"Now who would steal my old mare?" John said, peering about.

The figure of a man leading an animal approached them in the darkness. "Here she is, Smith," the man called, and John was startled to see it was Silas Noel. "I found her wandering on the grounds near the front."

"I thank you, Brother Noel," John said. "She must have slipped her bridle."

"You can't blame your horse; her master has already done the same thing himself."

John felt an anger filling him. The patronizing air of the man, the absence of the customary courtesy in offering his pulpit, the unveiled sarcasm. And then his good humor asserted itself, and he laughed and held out his hand. "We'll shake on that, Brother Noel," he said, grasping Dr. Noel's half-extended hand and wringing it. "Those of us in the Restoration Movement will wear no man's bridle nor yoke of human creed; only the yoke of Christ himself."

"And I intend to take on only the yoke of the Master," a cool voice spoke from the shadows, and the men turned to see Mrs. Tubman, a dim figure in the half-darkness. She was making her way toward her carriage, but she stopped before John and extended her hand. "I'm returning to my home in Georgia next week," she said, "returning as a baptized Christian." She inclined her head toward Dr. Noel, her brown eyes full of tenderness. "Although it may grieve you, Dr. Noel, I shall not unite down there with the Baptist Church. Surely," she looked again at John and Philip Fall, "surely there is a church for people like us; people who do not claim to be the only Christians but do insist on being Christians only."

CHAPTER XXVIII

"YOU so-called Reformers!" James French shouted. The words rang out in the crowded meetinghouse at Unity. It was the closing session of the North District Association, assembled in annual meeting in the brutal heat of the following July. "You're actually revolutionists. You're bent on upsetting the whole Baptist church. I say, Out with you and your doctrine! Get out and leave us alone!"

An undercurrent of unrest had marked the meeting, held in check until the last by the pious counsel of Jeremiah Vardeman. "Nothing is to be gained, brethren," he had protested in his golden voice when points of dissension had arisen, "from heat where there should be light."

Time and again John had challenged him. "Let them name the

charges," he had cried out. "Let them give us Reformers a chance to defend ourselves."

It was Silas Noel who had fanned into flames the smoldering fire, taking his revenge, John felt sure, for John's assault on his sacred citadel. As a messenger from the Franklin Association he had sat stiffly erect on a back bench during the meeting, his arms folded across his chest. But as the final session was drawing to a close, he had waved for recognition from David Chenault, the moderator, and had stalked to the platform amid cheers and some jeers.

"By our forbearance and their partial success among the Baptists, the Reformers have become vain and impudent," he cried when the crowd had stilled. "They have, as they think, waged a war of extermination against our altars, our church institutions, and our faith. The reckless spirits of the day have opened wide the floodgates of detraction and abuse; they insult the pious spirits of the dead." He had stood, glaring out over the assembly. "Make no compromise with this error! Do as the Franklin Association has done! Esteem it your duty to drop correspondence with any and every church where this heresy is tolerated!"

John, sitting beside Buckner Payne, saw a look almost of anguish cloud the discerning, tolerant eyes of the merchant. He glanced to the other side of the room and caught the eye of Barton Stone, who had come to the meeting as an observer and was sitting between John Rogers and John T. Johnson. Stone smiled, a wistful, melancholy smile, and shook his head, and John answered with a nod, a gesture, he suddenly realized, that somehow acknowledged how interwoven their thinking had become. Billy Vaughn was near the window, his face averted, his gaze directed to the fenced pasture beyond the clearing on which the meetinghouse stood. He had returned from Ohio opposed to the Reformers more vehemently than ever, John had learned, but he had avoided public argument. Jonathan was sitting toward the front of the room, his elbows on his knees, his head in his hands. He would not publicly condemn his brother, John knew, but neither would he uphold him.

The outburst of Silas Noel had precipitated a sudden, almost an impulsive, summation from David Chenault as moderator. He had begun quietly, almost dispassionately, listing the doctrinal points of difference: the distinction between the old and the new covenant; the design of baptism; the operation of the Holy Spirit in conversion.

But when he came to the practices of the Reformers, he grew livid with rage.

"They reject all creeds, covenants, and constitutions," he cried. "They receive members on confession alone without the requirement of an experience. Baptism and the Lord's Supper they claim can be administered by any believer. They require no special call to the ministry, no special rights or functions reserved to the clergy. They deny the authority of such an association as this over local congregations." He paused and looked over the crowd. "There is then only one course left to us," he said, banging on the pulpit stand with his gavel. "That is to withdraw ourselves from them."

A stunned silence followed, and it was then Judge French had cried out.

Someone called for a vote, but Jeremiah Vardeman arose hurriedly and began intoning a benediction, and the meeting stood adjourned. The people filed out, bewildered. What had happened? No one was sure.

"That does it, Jacob," John said quietly as he encountered young Jacob Creath in the aisle, and the two men moved through the crowd to make their way out a side door. "When North District meets next year at Spencer, we'll be a divided church. I don't know how things will be handled; there's no precedent for anything like this."

"Well, they won't bring it to a vote," Jacob said. "Both Judge French and David Chenault were speaking out of turn; Silas Noel is master-minding things, and I can see his strategy. He didn't risk being outvoted in his Franklin Association but had his group instead withdraw voluntarily, and he'll get David to handle it that way in North District. I overheard him back there as I left my seat, asking some of the Calvinists to meet in special session at Goshen."

John had no feeling for visiting; something felt dead inside him. He made his way toward his horse, tethered at the far side of the grove. A Negro man, one of David Chenault's slaves, was sitting in the Chenault buggy, waiting to drive the moderator home. He jumped to the ground and untied John's horse, grinning. John thanked him and climbed into the saddle. Slavery was a monstrous evil, a blot on the country's life, a crime against humanity, he thought as he looked at the man. Yet the church did not express even a prick of conscience about it. He tugged at his cravat. The church had forgotten what it started out to do. He turned to see Jeremiah Vardeman untying his horse and swung toward him, a sudden surge of anger, a pent-up frustration exploding within him.

"I'm sorry the charges against us Reformers weren't put to a vote, Brother Vardeman," he said, his voice hoarse. "Did you have good reason to see that they weren't?"

"Why would you want such a vote, my friend?" Vardeman said, easing his big frame into the saddle.

"Well, at least we'd know where everybody stood," John said.

Vardeman spoke quietly, his face blank. "You expect me to support you, I suppose?"

John shook his head, his anger spent. "No, I know better than that."

Vardeman twisted, shifting his weight in the saddle. "It would only lead to more controversy; let us have peace." He sighed and pulled on the reins, and the horse backed up a few steps and then started forward.

John stuck out his hand and took hold of the bridle. In the glow of the afternoon sun he could see how lined the man's face had become. "Peace at the price of truth, Brother Vardeman?" he inquired. "What passage in the Bible says we're wrong? You say you love the truth and that you love me. How, then, can you bear to see me in the wrong and not enlighten me?"

Vardeman pulled out his watch and studied it. "I must go, Brother Raccoon John," he said wearily. "All this controversy calls for divine wisdom." He nudged the horse with his knees, and the animal started forward. Then he wheeled about as if on impulse and faced John. "Why do you think you're ordained to strip us of our doctrinal creeds, or the clergy of their authority? Why do you talk as if we were all hypocrites?"

John shook his head, a sudden twinkling in his eyes. "I don't think you're given to hypocrisy, Brother Vardeman. I give you credit for actually believing in Calvinism, more's the pity. You high-back preachers are good men gone wrong, not wrong men pretending to be good. But you're blind; you can't see that since Alexander Campbell started the Restoration Movement, there's been a big change." He sat high in his saddle and threw back his head, a slow smile on his face. "Remember that old rhyme?

"Old Grimes is dead; that good old man,
We ne'er shall see him more;
He used to wear a long-tailed coat,
All buttoned down before.
And as those coat-tails disappear
Over the horizon's brim,
I own it with a furtive tear
That I was fond of him!"

Vardeman's face flushed. "There's no use arguing with you, Raccoon John. You do things with words the Lord never intended." He slapped the horse with the ends of the reins and started forward but at the edge of the grove stopped and looked back. "You know, I suppose," he called to John sitting motionless on his horse, "that Alexander Campbell is actually advocating an unpaid ministry. If he has his way, we'll all be paupers."

Like a dying creature gasping for breath, North District struggled through its meeting the next year at Spencer. Again no vote was taken. Similar confusion existed in every district association in the state, John found as he toured the countryside all during the winter and into the spring, torn by mixed emotions. The winter snow was light, but the rain came in torrents. Oblivious of it he rode the narrow lanes and walked the streets of the towns, preaching, explaining, trying to end the confusion. In the Elkhorn Association the Creaths were, as Jacob had hinted, the focal point of the wrath of the Calvinists, and during the tumult of its meeting they were denounced as heretics, denied a hearing, and the Reformed Baptist churches in the district ordered dropped from membership.

And then it happened. In 1830, meeting in a grove at Spencer's Creek, North District Association was split asunder. The gathering had opened in an atmosphere of suspicion and distrust, with the credentials of messengers challenged; allegations of heresy coupled with charges of disorder; church after church ordered dropped from membership. But the Reformers persisted in their demand for a vote until it could not be denied.

One by one the churches responded as their names were called. John listened with bowed head, glancing up to see David Chenault's stern features quiver with emotion as his beloved Cane Springs

Church took its stand openly with the Reformers. A pain gripped his heart. The morning had been cloudy, but as the afternoon session started the sun broke through, and now it cast dancing shadows through the sycamore trees on the men and women sitting on the backless benches.

When the result of the vote was announced, it was learned of the twenty-six churches represented twenty had gone over completely to the Reformers. The dissolution of the old North District Association was complete.

Someone called for Raccoon John Smith. Like a rising whorl of leaves in the wind, the call grew in volume.

"What have we done, John?" James Mason called from the rear.

John waited until David Chenault stalked down the narrow aisle, a procession of one, and made his way toward his buggy, his thin lips tight, his eyes staring straight ahead, unseeing. As if his departure were a signal, he was followed by Judge French, betraying no sign of emotion, the minute books and records of the Association clutched in his hands, followed by others who had held fast to their Baptist position. The group sat in silence until they had departed, and then John went to the front.

"We rejoice in the promises of God," he said simply, standing alone on the narrow planked stand, staring over the hushed assembly. "We have set at naught all Babylonish terms and phrases not found in the Word of God, and all traditions and all commandments and doctrines of men. And now we urge all to disregard everything as matters of faith or practice, not found in the Word of God. We, therefore, now profess to be followers of our Lord Jesus Christ, and of no mortal man. Our enemies, by way of opprobrium, who will call us followers of Alexander Campbell, while we are following only in the footsteps of Christ, do insult the King of Kings by robbing God of his own glory and giving it to man."

It was late afternoon in May, but the heat of the day was unbroken; summer was coming on fast. Shimmery dry waves covered the land, heralding a heat that would crack the ground, already sucked dry by a thirsty sun. John had been preaching in Madison County, south of the Kentucky River, within sight of the foothills of the great Cumberland range. A road of crushed limestone led to the buffalo trace he had followed when he had first moved to the bluegrass region from Wayne County, now almost fifteen years ago. On impulse he followed the trace for a distance, reliving the trip, and then, impelled by a sudden decision, as if drawn to a sanctuary, he hastened his horse. He would follow the trace back to Wayne.

He rode until midnight and then hobbled his horse and slept in a rock house, a shelter formed by an overhanging stone ledge. He refreshed himself at daybreak in a nearby creek and ate some wild strawberries, and resumed his ride. He stopped at a farmhouse for a noon meal; the family were unbelievers but allowed him to pray with them. He left with them a copy of the New Testament and went on his way. Early the next afternoon he rode up the winding trail that led to Monticello.

The countryside was little changed, but the town of Monticello had grown. Joe Beard's store boasted a new wing, and a two-story structure of planed lumber now stood next to the courthouse on the other side. Several sturdy new cabins faced the street. Micah Taul, John learned from Joe Beard, was living in Winchester, Tennessee, still a staunch and hearty man, unbroken in body or spirit despite his rumored heavy drinking and gambling, and the troubles his son, Thomas Paine Taul, had brought upon him. The Academy had been enlarged, and a new schoolmaster held classes now the year around. Rodes Garth practiced law in the town when he was not in Frankfort as a legislator from the district.

He rode out the familiar trail leading to William's place and reined in his horse at sight of the new house William had erected. His call brought William and Maggie to the lane, and the greetings were warm and joyful. William's two boys, Joel and Jake, were sturdy lads in their twenties, excellent farmers and already sparking the girls. William sent them to summon the neighbors for a gathering at the house that night. Yes, they had heard rumors of his heresy, but the news did not disturb them.

But the news had disturbed the others, John found, when he had greeted them and they sat about the yard in the cool of the mountain evening. Sam Hinds and John Parmley questioned him closely, and Philip's face plainly revealed his distress.

"We hear you even deny the work of the Holy Spirit in conversion," Philip said finally, as if pronouncing final verdict.

John corrected him. "I don't deny it; I just say a man can't depend entirely on the Holy Spirit to do his thinking for him. Do you believe the Holy Spirit always speaks the truth?" The question was directed at all of them and was met with a vigorous assent of nodding heads. "Then how come the Holy Spirit told you, and you," he pointed at each of them in turn, "that each of you were the greatest of sinners at the time of your revealing experience? How could each of you have been the greatest?"

Sam Hinds got to his feet. "I can see you haven't ever known what true religion is, John. You seem to be utterly in the dark."

The liberal-minded blacksmith, Elisha Franklin, had been taken with the Ohio fever and moved north, but John Woods and Alexander Hayes were receptive to his views, and he preached in both their cabins, heartened by the response of a young medical student, Isaac Reneau, who sought him out after both services and questioned him closely on points of the new Restoration Movement. Isaac Reneau had been seeking just such an interpretation of the gospel for eleven years, he said, and intended now to identify himself with it. Watching his earnest, sensitive face, listening to his easy manner of speaking, John knew he would make an able advocate of it.

He lingered in Wayne County four days and then went on toward Stockton's Valley. A settlement had grown up at the junction of the trace that crossed the road leading west into the Cumberland region, and he drew in his horse to get his bearings from old landmarks, and sat for a moment remembering. George and Beulah had moved back to Christian County, and the others were scattered; he decided to make no effort to contact them. But he must see Ma, and then Brother Isaac Denton. He felt a compulsion to preach his new-found truth in the old Clear Fork Church where he had so often proclaimed the old doctrine.

Ma was living just across the state line in Overton County, Tennessee, with Betsy and her husband, Ezra Matlock, and he turned his horse south. The next day he located the Matlock place, and the meeting with his mother served for a time to dispel the sense of alienation with the past with which the trip had filled him.

"They tell me, John, that you've deserted us," she said after the greetings were over. "They say you tell poor sinners that water alone can wash away their sins." She was badly stooped, but she tottered about with much of her old alacrity, and her tongue was still quick and her eyes sharp.

"I've never taught that, Ma." He spoke gently, wondering how much to try to explain to her. "But I preach other things that aren't in line with Baptist doctrine. Do you want me to keep still about them? Do you want I should not be true to my convictions?" He picked up her worn hand and pressed it, his voice taking on a teasing tone. "I'll tell you what I'll do, Ma," he said. "I'll turn back and preach Calvinism if you'll agree to answer for me on the Day of Judgment for not preaching the truth as I see it. Will you do that?"

She threw back her head in a familiar gesture, and her hearty laugh bridged the years as nothing else had done.

The next day he retraced his steps north. As he neared Stockton's Valley he cut across an old trail he had known in his youth, now almost obscured, a short cut to the Clear Fork Church. The trail ended at the creek, and he pulled in his horse as the animal lowered his head to drink. The banks were covered with the same riot of trailing vines he had remembered, but the meetinghouse across from it seemed smaller than he had remembered and somehow lonely and unkept. He was on the point of hobbling his horse and going over to look in through the shuttered windows when he heard the galloping thud of an approaching horse, and around the curve in the lane that ran back of the church appeared Brother Isaac.

The old man dismounted at sight of him and threw his arms about him in undisguised affection, and it was not until the greetings were over that a troubled look crossed his face. John saw it and guided him to a log, and together they sat, silence for a moment upon them.

"You've heard, Brother Isaac?" John said finally.

The old man nodded. "I've heard, John," he said. "And I'm grieved. Satan never tempted me to doubt that you were a Christian, even when I knew you were in error. But now . . ." He paused and picked up a twig and slowly broke it into small pieces. "Now I hear you are gone, John, gone completely over to the Campbell heresy. I've set Alexander Campbell down as the most erroneous and corrupt man in the world."

John sighed. Discussion was useless. He waved toward the church. "I want to preach in the old church while I'm here," he said. "Could we have a meeting tonight?"

Brother Isaac got to his feet. "You can never have my consent to preach in that pulpit again," he said firmly. Suddenly his face contorted with emotion, and he turned to mount his horse.

But John held him by the arm. "Brother Isaac," he said gently, "if I have gone into error, won't you help me to see it? Won't you hear me out? I'll confess all my departures from the Baptist doctrine and give my reasons for every change. When I'm done, I'll take it as the part of a father if you'll tell me wherein I have made any departure from the Word of God."

The old man shook his head. "You well know, John, that you can out-talk me." His voice trembled, and tears filled his eyes.

John watched him ride away, tears blinding his own eyes. Isaac Denton loved him as a son, he knew, but he loved the truth as he saw it even more, and he would never relinquish it. Men of conviction, even when their convictions differed from his own, were of a breed the country needed.

CHAPTER XXIX

IT was in early November that the unrest in John's spirit and the sense of impending change in his bones were given release by a letter from John T. Johnson. All summer he had tried to shake off the foreboding that had enveloped him since his trip to Wayne. What had he done?

In many places the Reformers were being called Disciples, and were congealing into separate bodies; in other places they were nameless, anchorless groups. "What shall we do?" was the question John met time and again as he counseled with the bewildered men and women.

"Meet every Lord's Day," he invariably replied, groping himself for an ultimate answer. "If others occupy the meetinghouse, meet in your own homes and gather around your own firesides. If you cannot exhort one another, pray together; if you cannot do that, then read the Book and sing."

But for what purpose had he created a scattering of nameless, drifting churches? How long would it be before they would be seeking refuge in their old group, having no anchor with other groups of kindred mind? Could such isolated, bewildered people be expected to battle the world, combat evil, change lives? For what had he struggled?

And then John T. Johnson's letter had come. "Come over to Great Crossings and preach for a week," he wrote. "Give us direction; point out our path. Where do we go? To what body do we belong?"

John sat now on the horsehair sofa in the big sitting room of the Johnson home and slowly uncrossed his long legs. He felt a little frightened and yet strangely calm. He had acted long enough on his own wisdom; now he must await word from God. He picked up a copy of Barton Stone's paper, *The Christian Messenger*, from the table by the sofa. Under it, he noticed, was a copy of the new magazine Alexander Campbell had started, *The Millennial Harbinger*.

"Strange," he mused aloud, "that just at this time of crisis with us here in Kentucky, Mr. Campbell should discontinue *The Christian Baptist*."

The tall man standing by the marble mantel poked the fire with his foot. "He sensed that it had served its purpose in arousing us from our apathy, and so it has. The debt I owe that man of God, Alexander Campbell, no language can tell." He motioned toward the copy of the new paper. "In *The Millennial Harbinger* he seems now to be telling us we should start building up the new order."

"The name indicates that," John said. "It's the harbinger of a new day, the triumph of the Kingdom of God on earth."

Johnson laughed shortly. "If he means that, he's too optimistic," he said. He put his elbow on the mantel and leaned his head against his hand, staring into the fire. "The church will have to be much more purified and unified before the Kingdom is established."

John smiled. "I agree," he said, and added slowly, "I was coming to that." He paused and then went on, feeling his way toward an expression of something he could not himself define. "We've been doing some purifying, ridding it as much as we can of man-made opinions as tests of faith. Now, my friend, we need to unify." He got up and went toward the fire and held out his hands, warming them. "You asked me to come over and preach to the little group of Reformers meeting here in your home. Shall I preach to them that the Bible is the only creed, and Christian is the only name? Does that describe us?"

Johnson looked at him, puzzled. "Of course it does, absolutely."

John grinned and picked up again the copy of Barton Stone's paper, thumbing through it for a moment. "Stone says here," he said with pointed emphasis, underlining a passage with his bony finger, "that it describes his group."

He raised his eyes to meet those of Johnson, and the two men looked at each other in the gathering darkness of the November afternoon. The implication was inescapable. The crackling of the fire was the only sound to be heard, and then Johnson cleared his throat.

"He's right," the tall lawyer said slowly. "There is no distinguishing doctrine between us. I have been conscious of it for some time. What's to be done?"

John walked to the window and looked out before he spoke. "Shall we ask Barton Stone to come over and worship with us in this meeting?" he said.

For a week the men were together, preaching by turns each night, at first to only a handful of people and then to growing numbers; their sermons devoid of any trace of sectarian doctrine, centering on God's love and care. One by one people began to signify a desire to identify themselves with such a brand of Christianity; then whole families came; well-known sinners joined, accepting Christ as Lord, changing their lives. By the end of the week the group had swelled to fifty-seven men and women.

"We are beginning at Jerusalem to demonstrate what God can do," Barton Stone said as the week neared its close, "when men work with Him and with each other."

John Rogers from Carlisle had joined them. He had dropped by Georgetown to see Barton Stone, and had come out to Great Crossings, expecting to stay only the night, but as the significance of the meeting deepened, he had stayed on, wide-eyed in wonder at the direction the Spirit was leading.

"Not as unconcerned spectators have Mr. Stone and I looked on at the mighty war you Reformers have been conducting," he said wryly at the conclusion of the fourth evening's service. "We've discussed many times how your views accord with our own. This experience brings us squarely to the question: Should we undertake together the job of uniting the scattered flock of Christ?"

At the close of the last meeting they lingered all night, discussing, analyzing, clarifying the possibilities of such a step. Their points of agreement were profound and basic; their differences by comparison almost trivial. But each knew there must be no compromise with truth; they must move cautiously. Above all, they stressed time and again, they must avoid establishing by their union another sect, proclaiming it was right and all others were wrong; it must be only a fellowship, a communion, a brotherhood. Gray daybreak found them on their knees, praying for guidance, and when they parted it was agreed they would meet again in a month, this time at Barton Stone's meetinghouse in Georgetown.

The thin sunlight of the winter morning slanted through the bare tree branches as John rode home, his body weary beyond caring, his mind burdened with an awesome sense of responsibility. At this moment in time, here and now, what he said could alter the course of church history. He realized now that he had tried to conceal from himself what he had known all along—that a union with Barton Stone's Christians could be in God's plan. Would Alexander Campbell see it too?

The December issue of *The Millennial Harbinger* had arrived in his absence. He thumbed through it as he sat the next night before the hearth with Nancy, recounting to her the strange turn of events at Great Crossings. Suddenly he jerked erect.

"Nancy, God's hand is indeed in this!" he said. "Alexander Campbell had no more idea than I had, or anybody else, what would come out of my visit to Great Crossings. Yet listen to what he has written:

> "In Kentucky many of the congregations called 'Christians' are just as sound in the faith of Jesus as any congregation with which I am acquainted. With all such, I, as an individual, am united. We plead for union, communion and cooperation of all such; and wherever there are in any vicinity a remnant of those who keep the commandments of Jesus, whatever may have been their former designation, they ought to rally under Jesus and the Apostles and bury all dissensions."

The next day John wrote Mr. Campbell of the meeting at Great Crossings, of the trend of the discussions, of the point to which the four men had been led. "We'll meet again the latter part of December, Brother Campbell," he said in his exuberance. "We hope to explore the possibilities of actually uniting. Will you send us your blessing?"

They would meet, it had been decided, on Friday, December 23, spending the Christmas weekend in a dedicated searching of mind and heart. Nancy at first demurred when she learned the plan; he would not be with the family on Christmas Day. But she agreed the significance of the day would give impetus to their thinking. "Christmas comes this year on a Sunday," she said, adding with her rare insight, "your minds should have a clear channel on that day to the Lord."

"At least," John said, "it should dispel the fog of our uncertainty."

In two weeks John received a reply from Mr. Campbell. The note was brief. "I rejoice to hear that the utmost harmony and Christian love prevails," he wrote hurriedly, "not only within the group of Disciples composing the congregation at Great Crossings but between that group and those Disciples meeting under the name 'Christian' in connection with Brother Barton Stone."

John took the letter with him to the meeting in Georgetown, and the men read it carefully as they sat about a small table in the meetinghouse of the Christians.

Barton Stone's face clouded. "It isn't so much what he says as what he doesn't say," he said. "But it's obvious the name 'Disciples' is Mr. Campbell's preference over the name 'Christian.' Surely, however, he would not allow that difference to mar our union!"

"I detect a note of gentle remonstrance," Johnson said. "He may think the union a bit premature, yet our two groups in various parts of the state have been meeting occasionally together. At Millersburg they are doing it, and at Cooper's Run."

"Perhaps Mr. Campbell just has some honest doubts," John Rogers spoke up. "And so have we, for that matter. For instance, the view you Reformers take..."

John held up his hand, grinning. "Call us Disciples, please."

Rogers laughed. "For the time being only I shall," he said. "We're all Christians, and the choice of a name will take care of itself." He looked at Stone nodding in agreement, and then went on. "Regarding the view you Disciples take of baptism for the remission of sins, for example. This doctrine has not generally obtained among us, although some of our brethren have received it. What then? Shall those who embrace it condemn those who do not? God forbid! We shall never have union if we insist on agreement on all such points!"

"You're right," Johnson said. "We do not see eye to eye on all aspects of the atonement either, or on the matter of inviting the unimmersed to the Lord's Table. But I allow to you what I claim for myself—the right of private judgment in such matters."

"Of course, we don't deny the atonement," Barton Stone said quietly. "We only deny the explanation which some give to it. And we neither invite nor exclude the unimmersed from the Lord's Table. We spread the Table, that is all." He rubbed his hand across his eyes and then stood up. "Brethren, why argue over such things? Even if we should be in perfect agreement on all such points, that would still not unite us. How vain are all human attempts to unite a bundle of twigs together so as to make them grow and bear fruit! They must first be united with the living stock and receive its sap and spirit before they can be united ever with each other." He leaned over and rested his hands on the table, looking at the men earnestly, his eyes moving from face to face. "What else can we do but unite? As two separate groups, we have both found our way back to the Bible as our only foundation. Should we Christians leave it to you Disciples and go off and find another? Should we remain as two separate groups and fight over possession of it?" He laughed shortly. "No, we have a living relationship; we ignore it at the peril of our very souls."

John Rogers got up and stood beside him, placing his arm about Stone's shoulder. "And you have led us to that relationship, Brother Stone. You are our leader."

Stone shook his head. "I appreciate such a tribute, but Alexander Campbell is the real leader. He has clarified much that I have seen only dimly; he has thought his way through where I have only felt my way. He is still in his early forties and can give leadership to this movement for years, while I at sixty am already feeling the weight of age."

"Campbell is a man of tremendous intellect," Rogers agreed, "but there are those who say he is all intellect and has little heart religion; that he is too severe in his strictures. He arouses controversy."

"And so did Christ," Stone said quietly. "And so, thank God, do we! I will not say there are no faults in Brother Campbell, but there are fewer, perhaps, in him than any man I know on earth, and over those few my love would throw a veil and hide them from view forever. I am constrained, and willingly constrained, to acknowledge him the greatest promoter of this reformation of any man living. The Lord reward him!"

At the Sunday worship service the next morning in the Christian meetinghouse, Barton Stone preached in an atmosphere tense with expectancy. The word had been rumored that John and John T. Johnson were in conference with Stone and John Rogers over matters vital to the church, and John sensed a mixture of curiosity and concern in the faces of the members as they shook his hand.

All afternoon and far into the night the four men sat, their differences receding in importance as their points of agreement were brought into sharp focus. Both groups accepted as their primary task the establishment of the unity of all Christian believers. Both repudiated any creedal system that denied a man access to God and fellowship with Christians. Both agreed that Christ was the Messiah, the Son of God, and that he died for all; both emphasized that salvation came by an act of the mind and heart in accepting rational evidence of the truth. Both accepted immersion as the Scriptural form of baptism; both opposed the use of unscriptural names.

"Our chief obstacle," John said, "will be the willful blindness of the clergy to the advantages of union; they have a vested interest and a pride of position. The people themselves will hear us gladly. They are sick of the sight of a hundred heads attached to one body, and that is what exists in the religious world—the innumerable religious sects each with its own separate church affixed to the body of Christ."

"I'm not so sure it will be an easy task, however, even with the people," Johnson said. "I have been astonished not only in private life but in the army, in Congress, and even on the judge's bench at the obstinacy of men in clinging to chains that bind them into slavery. Even during the Revolution, there were thousands of good citizens who openly preferred their fetters to independence."

Barton Stone smiled. "Many people will not know what to make of us," he said. "Many will actually be astonished that Christians of different theological opinions can meet on the public highway, recognize one another as soldiers of the cross, embrace each other as heirs of the same kingdom, and, as Paul said, press forward together toward the mark of the prize of the high calling of God in Christ Jesus."

Midnight struck, and John arose from his chair, stretching his lanky frame. "There is a difference between talkers and doers," he said, his voice weary, "and the Lord knows it. Talking about unity is no substitute for practicing it. Why not just declare ourselves as brethren united into one church, we Disciples and you Christians, and be done with it?"

Barton Stone shook his head. "It isn't as simple as that, John. We have about eight thousand avowed Christians in Kentucky; you have about ten thousand Disciples of Christ. Can we commit them?" He looked at Johnson for his judgment.

"We cannot commit them legally," Johnson said. "This is a movement only; not an organization. Perhaps we should unite at first by simply worshiping and working together."

"Then let's get started," John insisted. "Let's get word to the people we are doing it. How shall we go about it?"

Barton Stone studied the planked flooring for a long minute and then looked up at John T. Johnson. "How much time are you prepared to give to this movement, Lawyer Johnson?"

Johnson hesitated and then wadded into a tight ball a scrap of paper he had been toying with. "I'm prepared to give it my full time," he said simply. "Compared with the significance of this Restoration Movement, the practice of law or politics dissolves into nothingness. I dedicate my life, gentlemen, my time, my talents, my resources, to this work." He got to his feet and stood for a moment before them and then, one by one, they sank to their knees.

Thirty minutes later they again sat about the table, outlining the practical steps by which their purpose could be made known.

"I propose that John T. Johnson join me in editing my paper, *The Christian Messenger*," Stone said, "thereby symbolizing our union for its readers. John, you and John Rogers could ride and preach together, you representing the Disciples and Rogers as my Timothy, presenting a united message, going wherever you judge most profitable to our cause, encouraging our two groups in every locality to work together as one body."

John got up and paced the floor for a moment, and then came to the table and struck it with his fist. "All that is fine for the future," he said, "but the Lord had some reason for bringing us together just at this time. The Lord is nudging us, gentlemen. The new year is upon us. Why not usher it in with a great experiment in Christian unity in some central locality, perhaps in Lexington, for all the world to see? We can let that meeting decide our course!"

Barton Stone nodded, his face glowing with approval. "In its purpose and ultimate result," he said, "such a gathering, if successful, could be the most portentous meeting since the disciples were first called Christians at Antioch. The Lord give it guidance!"

The Kentucky Reporter for December 28 carried the notice: "We are requested to state that a four days' meeting will be held in the Christian Church on Hill Street commencing on Friday, the 30th. Messrs. J. Smith of Montgomery and J. T. Johnson are expected on the occasion."

"It sounds like just another meeting," Nancy said, looking up from the coarse oversock she was knitting as John read it to her. "You think anybody much will come? The weather's pretty bad."

"We've sent word as far as we're able; there hasn't been much time, and there may not be many there," John said, adding with a tone of cheerfulness he did not feel, "It's in the hands of the Lord. God's way is the sea; his path is the great water; and his footsteps are not known."

The rain came in torrents as they climbed into the buggy on Friday morning for the trip to Lexington. John had arisen before dawn, an excitement in him he had not known for years, straining to realize that he had pledged to risk the destiny of his group by an alliance with those of Barton W. Stone. It was a bold step; it could reverberate for years; it could change religious history. He found Nancy was already in the kitchen, an unaccustomed apprehension about her as she shook the stove, sending out waves of heat to drive the winter cold from the room. The children were still asleep.

Despite the rain Nancy wore her new velvet bonnet and broadcloth cape over her brown woolsey dress and stomacher, covering her finery with a deerskin rug as she snuggled beside John in the jogging buggy. She insisted John wear a linen shirt she had made him with a double pleated cambric frill, and a white cravat.

"In this weather," John said, his spirits dropping as they neared Lexington and no slackening was apparent in the rain, "there won't be a handful. Want I should drop you at the Postlethwaite's Tavern and go on to the meeting first? You could dry out and get some rest."

"I want to go straight to the meetinghouse," Nancy said. "A little wet won't kill me. Maybe I can help with the singing; you'll probably need somebody to fill the seats."

The rain had swollen the town fork of the Elkhorn River, turning it into a seething torrent which covered the wooden bridge at Water Street and came up to the buggy steps. Two small boys were fishing with bent pins for crawfish and minnows as they crossed and drove on toward Hill Street. Nancy studied the meetinghouse as it came into view, and they drove to the hitching rail and John tethered the horse beside that of Kenez Farrow of Mount Sterling. It was a two-story structure dedicated only the year before. The planed lumber siding was still in need of paint, and the doors were sagging. A few wagons and buggies were bogged in the mud of the dirt yard, and several horses were tied to the hitching rail. A scattering of people milled about the entrance.

Across the street the rain made little pools of water in an open field, dripping in monotonous rhythm from clusters of white birch trees and sycamores and elms, their bare branches stark against the brick wall of a hemp factory on the far side, spewing and sputtering in the crisp December air.

John helped Nancy out of the buggy and walked behind her as she gingerly picked her way along a walk of narrow planks laid across the mud to the center doorway. They were nearing the entrance when John heard his name called and looked around to see young Jacob Creath coming along the plank walk, holding a black cotton umbrella over a woman in front of him, shielding her dark cape and feathered blue bonnet from the slackening rain. He had not seen Jacob since the momentous final meeting of the North District Association, now almost two years ago. Jacob had been preaching, he had heard, for the First Baptist Church in Lexington, chosen by the church in spite of his liberal leanings in preference to Jeremiah Vardeman, who had denounced him as a Campbellite and had left the state in anger. John waited with Nancy for him at the church doorway, and their greeting was happy.

"I hear the heretics plan to make history by practicing some Christian unity in this meeting," Jacob said with a grin.

John looked in polite curiosity at the woman. She had placed her hand in the crook of Jacob's arm, and he was patting it affectionately. "But I've beat them all to it. I've become united in marriage last September to the former Mrs. Susan Bedford, widowed by Sidney Bedford of Bourbon County."

The woman flushed and smiled, her face dimpled, as John stared in delighted amazement and clapped Jacob on the shoulder.

"It's high time," he said, and bowed to the woman as Nancy leaned forward and kissed her on both cheeks.

They entered the church together, chatting happily, and then the women made their way to join a scattering of other females on the far side while the men stood talking with others who pressed forward.

John looked about. A gallery ran across the back of the room, extending over the rows of high-backed benches divided by a single center aisle. A wide platform at the front supported a boxlike pulpit and four pulpit chairs. The room would seat, he estimated roughly, at least two hundred people.

People were streaming in now; the place was filling. It was evident word of the impending move had spread. Who were these people? Well-wishers or critics? Sympathizers or scoffers? He saw William Poindexter, James Schooley, William Vanpelt, and the well-to-do farmer, Tom Rogers, seated together near the front. They were all loyal members of the group that had followed Dr. James Fishback out of the Baptist fold, renouncing all creeds, constituting themselves a Church of Christ. But now Dr. Fishback had swung back to the Baptists, temporizing his convictions with expediency, half-heartedly embracing the new doctrine but loath to leave the old one entirely, and the group he had forged into an unsectarian Church of Christ was left bereft. John looked toward Nancy and saw her introducing the new Mrs. Creath to Mrs. Joseph Ficklen and Mrs. Thad Bell, both of them also from the little Church of Christ. The group was probably all here, he suddenly realized, seeking the sheltering warmth of like-minded groups.

Near the platform he saw Barton Stone and John Rogers, talking with David Cassell and his brother Ben, and Philip Coffman. These were the men who had made this Christian meetinghouse possible, underwriting its cost, dedicating themselves to its dream. John T. Johnson joined them, and John caught Stone's eye. An understanding smile passed between them, and he started toward them, pushing past others he knew: Purnell Bishop, Alex Graham, Elwood Chinn, John Hewitt, Buckner Payne, James Mason, Alex Gibney. The benches were filled, and the aisle was becoming crowded. A sense of chagrin came over him. Where had been his faith? People were here from every part of the state; every district association of Baptist churches was represented. He recognized others from Barton Stone's groups, and here and there he saw Methodist and Presbyterian friends finding seats. It was the hand of God.

He stopped as Jacob Creath grabbed his arm. "Here's someone who wants to shake your hand," Jacob said, and John turned to see Philip Fall, his luminous blue eyes sparkling with excitement.

"I thought you were in Nashville, Philip," John said, clasping his hand.

Philip shook his head. "I came back to Frankfort to start the young ladies' seminary on Poplar Hill as I had planned," he said. "When I heard what was afoot here, I couldn't resist coming over." He pressed John's hand between both of his. "God's power and blessing on you, John," he said.

It was past time for the meeting to begin. There had been no set schedule prepared for this day's sessions, the four men agreeing to follow God's guidance, allowing all present to give utterance to their views as the spirit led them. By tomorrow the drift would be determined and, if God willed and the meeting was successful, they would sit down together at the Lord's Table on Sunday morning, brethren of one church, united in body and in heart.

"It would be premature to attempt a formal, organic union," John T. Johnson said in one of the opening talks after a prayer and brief statement by Barton Stone. "That will come in time. If we determine to keep together we should grow together gradually. Rome was not built in a day. All we have to do today is open our hearts and minds, and be receptive to God's leading."

And God's guiding hand was felt as the day progressed. The brooding spirit of the Almighty seemed to almost visibly hover over the deliberations as man after man spoke, freely airing honest doubts, holding with stubborn adherence to principle, voicing frank apprehension for any compromise with truth. John's hopes alternately rose and fell until it became apparent that the two groups had come by God's grace more in penitence, confessing their own shortcomings, than in pride in the rightness of their positions. Their very frankness revealed a burning, passionate longing for understanding, for tolerance of their views, a tolerance they would in turn give to those of differing opinions. It was the basis for unity of which Barton Stone had spoken. With such a spirit, they could be joined, not as a bundle of sticks tied together but as branches of a vine with common roots.

By Saturday afternoon it had been decided that Barton Stone and John Smith should give the culminating talks.

"You speak first, John," Stone whispered, conferring with him hastily as the session was about to open. "I will then say whatever needs to be said for my group."

John reached down to pick up his Bible and found his hand shaking, as if a return of his palsy. The magnitude, the responsibility of the task gave him the feeling he was on a pinnacle; how had he got there? It was as if he were alone, closed off by a depthless, foggy void from human contact. "What shall I say, Brother Stone?" he asked, his voice strained, trying to down his agonies of self-doubt. But he knew Barton Stone could not tell him. Nobody could tell him but God.

He advanced slowly to the platform and laid his Bible on the stand, realizing he had never faced squarely up to the possibilities of this moment. Were they standing on the threshold of a united church? Was he competent to say the word that would lead this host of men into such an unexplored land? He opened his Bible, and a hush fell over the crowd; murmurings died away; rustling ceased; a stillness filled the room as if God himself were waiting, breathless.

"God has but one people on earth," he began, and stopped. He caught the eye of Philip Fall. All the persecution that such men had suffered for this hour rested on him; they had committed to him their dream. A gleam of understanding flashed between them. "He has given to them but one Book, and therein exhorts and commands them to be of one family." His voice rose. "But an amalgamation of sects is not such a union as Christ prayed for. To agree to unite upon any system of human invention would be contrary to his will. The only union practical or desirable must be based on the Word of God as the only rule of faith and practice."

He paused and looked toward several earnest Reformers who had questioned the beliefs of the Christians during yesterday's discussions. "There are certain speculative matters, such as the mode of Divine Existence, the Trinity, the nature of the atonement, that have for centuries been themes of discussion. These questions are as far from being settled now as they were in the beginning; by needless discussion of them much feeling has been provoked and divisions have been produced. But the gospel is a statement of facts, and no deductions or inference from them, however logical and true, forms any part of the gospel. No heaven is promised to those who hold them, and no hell is threatened to those who deny them."

He saw Jacob Creath standing under the overhanging gallery, cupping his ear to hear better, and he raised his voice. "There is but one faith, yet there may be ten thousand opinions. Hence, if Christians are ever to be one, they must be one in faith and action, and not in opinion." He leaned forward as if speaking to each person individually. "When certain subjects arise, even in conversation or social discussion, about which there is contrary opinion, speak of them in the words of the Scripture, and no offense will be given, and no pride of doctrine encouraged. We may then come in the end by thus speaking the same things, to think the same things, and to be of one mind and body in Christ." He held up his Bible. "This is the foundation on which Christians once stood, and on it they can and must stand again. While for the sake of peace I have long since waived the public utterance of any speculations I may hold, yet not one single gospel fact, commandment or promise will I surrender for the world. One faith, one God, one baptism, one book, one name, one brotherhood! By this shall all men know that we are His disciples, that we have love one to the other."

Jacob Creath, Sr., his bushy hair now white, his erect form bending with age, was sitting near the center aisle, and John saw tears streaming down his face. And then the old man raised his cane and thumped it on the floor as he gave release to his emotion. "Amen! Amen!"

Others echoed the shout until John raised his hand for silence. "Let us then, my brethren," he said quietly as the room settled into stillness, "be no longer Campbellites or Stoneites, New Lights or Old Lights, or any other kind of lights. But let us come to the Bible and to the Bible alone, as the only book in creation which can give us all the Light we need! Let us stand together united in the Church of Christ as his disciples and as Christians only!"

For a moment there was silence, and then as one man the audience stood. Shouts of "Hallelujah!" "Amen! Amen!" mingled with cries and utterances of emotion too deep for words.

Barton Stone was beside him, pressing his arm. As the crowd stilled, he motioned it to remain standing.

"I have not one objection to the grounds laid down by John Smith as the true scriptural basis of union among the people of God," he said. "I am willing to give him now and here my hand."

John's eyes were misty as he felt his hand grasped. For a moment they stood, then unannounced and unexpected, men all over the room began shaking hands with their neighbors, triumphant and joyful. A song arose, faint at first but swelling in volume as the refrain was taken up until it seemed to burst the walls of the church and rebound against the gates of heaven itself:

"All hail the power of Jesus' name
Let angels prostrate fall;
Bring forth the royal diadem
And crown him Lord of all!"

"A pure instrument of God, rid of bigotry and dogma, releasing the redemptive power of the Almighty." John spoke the words almost to himself as he untied his boot laces and slipped off his shoes in his room at Postlethwaite's Tavern that night, his mind still whirling, unable to grasp the full significance of the day's happenings. Here at last was that unity for which Christ had prayed, the first voluntary union of two entirely separate religious communions in the history of the world as known to man.

"It's the end of the struggle, Nancy," he called exultantly. "The perfect church! January 1, 1832, will be a great day in history. Nothing can stop the sweep of victory."

Nancy finished braiding her hair by the washstand before she spoke. "At least, it's a beginning," she admitted. "But perfection's mighty hard to come by. Somehow we never quite make it."

John looked at her a moment, and then he sobered. Nancy was right. The complete victory was a long way off. It was the beginning of beginning again.

AN AFTERWORD

BOTH Raccoon John Smith and Barton W. Stone considered the union of their separate church parties as the climactic achievement of their lives. For the next three years Raccoon John Smith and John Rogers traveled Kentucky as Paul and Barnabas, going to the separate congregations of Disciples and Christians, uniting them as one body in Christ. Barton Stone and John T. Johnson jointly edited *The Christian Messenger* until Stone removed to Illinois in 1834, and Johnson began his triumphant evangelistic tours which were to continue until his death twenty-four years later. The union symbolized on that memorable New Year's Day in 1832 continued and grew in power and influence until today the resulting church bodies encompass the globe and number their adherents in the millions.

It was given to Raccoon John Smith to outlive all his contemporaries, preaching wherever opportunity presented itself for thirty-six more years. And wherever he went, multitudes of the people flocked to hear him. His dedication, his knowledge of the Scriptures, his sometimes searing but never unkindly wit, his logical, incisive approach to all problems endeared him to thousands, feared by some, hated by a few, and respected by all who knew his name. As old age advanced, a palsy settled upon his hands, but his step remained firm, his eye undimmed, his white mop of hair a prophetic, triumphant plume, his power of the preaching word never lacking. Nancy died in 1861, but he continued his travels and his preaching until he ventured for the last time to brave the wintry elements on Sunday, February 9, 1868, and preached at Mexico, Missouri. Pneumonia, followed by a steady fever, came upon him, and nineteen days later he died there at the home of a daughter, secure in the knowledge that he had fought the good fight and had kept the faith, and was buried beside his faithful Nancy at Lexington. On his simple tombstone shaft are inscribed these words:

In Memory of

JOHN SMITH

born

October 15, 1784

died

February 28, 1868

True, genial and pious, the good loved and all respected him. Strong through affliction and wise by the study of the Word, he gave up the Creed of his fathers for the sake of that Word. By its power he turned many from error; in its light he walked, and in its consolations he triumphantly died.

ACKNOWLEDGMENTS

If I were as Calvinistic as my early forebears, and as Raccoon John Smith was in his youth and early manhood, I would be convinced that it had been foreordained before the foundations of the world were laid that I would some day write this story of the now almost legendary pioneer Kentucky preacher who shook the bastions of hell itself, and converted thousands to the vision of the union of God's people. Due probably to the influence of Christian parents who reveled in the stories of his mighty feats and witticisms, the name of the great pioneer was as familiar to me as the names of my own playmates. My maternal grandfather George Washington Archer had been converted as an idealistic youth during one of Alexander Campbell's preaching tours through the South during the 1850's, and became and remained the rest of his days a "preacher of the Reformation." All the members of my numerous family on both sides of the house were loyal and vocal advocates of "the peculiar plea" for Christian unity with the sole exception of my grandfather Andrew Jackson Cochran who, true to his namesake, kept his own mind, and although he stood alone in the family circle, stubbornly insisted on remaining an unreconstructed Methodist all his life. Peter Cartwright would have loved my Methodist grandfather, and would have called upon him often for prayer at revival meetings, for 'tis said he had the gift, and Raccoon John Smith would have argued with him from sunrise to sunset in the effort to lead him onto that straightened pathway to the heavenly throne, since he had so little way to go.

The writing of the story of Raccoon John Smith may thus truthfully be said to be the ultimate result of a lifetime of unconscious preparation. It was a labor of affectionate tribute and respect, long delayed, to the great untutored, God-gifted pioneer evangelist who feared no man, nor the devil, only God.

The field research for the actual writing consumed most of the year of 1960. Five drafts were made of this book, three of them complete drafts and, although it broke my heart, whole chapters of the pioneer days, when the youthful John was still struggling under the bondage of Calvinism in the mountains of Kentucky, were eliminated for reasons of space, or sternly briefed. In assessing the individuals and the institutions to whom I am indebted for original source material, or for helpful suggestions and encouragement, I am overwhelmed by the sheer weight of numbers. I cannot name them all. But to those of immediate assistance during the last arduous, hopeful, frustrating months of effort, I bow in humble acknowledgment and appreciation. They helped more than they knew.

Especial thanks, therefore, to the Disciples of Christ Historical Society at Nashville, that unique repository of religious, historical, and church-related information, and to its patient and erudite staff. Particularly, my gratitude to those scholarly gentlemen, Dr. Claude E. Spencer, Curator; Dr. Willis R. Jones, President, and Dr. W. W. Wasson, Archivist, not only for their co-operation in the furnishing of original data but for their understanding and many courtesies far beyond the realm of duty during weeks of research there by me and my wife.

Most rewarding, also, was our extensive research at the one-hundred-year-old graduate theological seminary, The College of the Bible, in the heart of the Barton W. Stone and Raccoon John Smith country at Lexington, Kentucky. Because of the co-operation of the dedicated librarian, Mr. Roscoe M. Pierson, we were permitted access to many contemporary periodicals and documents, personal journals, and manuscripts, not available elsewhere. While in Lexington, contemporary documents and other original source materials were also examined in the libraries of Transylvania College, the oldest institution of learning west of the Alleghenies, thanks to Miss Roemel Henry, librarian, and at the University of Kentucky, due to the co-operation of that scholarly enthusiast, Lawrence S. Thompson, Director of Libraries, as well as in the Lexington public library, where we pored over old files of the justly famous *Kentucky Gazette* and the *Kentucky Reporter.*

Rewarding research was also conducted at the Christian Theological Seminary, with especial reference to information furnished by Librarian Henry K. Shaw relative to the diaries of Raccoon John

Smith, and at Butler University, both at Indianapolis; and the Midway Junior College, Midway, Kentucky. The David Lipscomb College, Vanderbilt University, Peabody College, the City Public Library, and the Tennessee State Department of Archives and History, all at Nashville, were generous in their supply of original information relative to pioneer folkways, customs, religions, routes of travel and other historical data. Dr. Dean E. Walker, president of Milligan College in the once "Free State of Franklin" in East Tennessee, furnished particular information relative to the birthplace of Raccoon John Smith, and due to the enthusiasm and personal assistance of another life-long admirer of the great pioneer, Frank Hannah, Jr., of Kingsport, valuable information was secured in regard to the boyhood of John Smith and the property holdings of the Smith family in Holston Valley from the records in the Sullivan County Courthouse in Blountville, and in the public library at Kingsport.

Other college and public libraries to which profitable access was had with particular reference to the early years of the Restoration Movement were the George Pepperdine College in Los Angeles; Texas Christian University, Fort Worth; Bethany College, West Virginia; Georgetown College, Georgetown, Kentucky; the Southern Baptist Theological Seminary, Louisville, Kentucky; the public libraries of Santa Monica and Los Angeles, California; the Methodist Publishing House, Nashville, Tennessee; the Filson Club, Louisville, Kentucky; the Library of Congress, Washington, D.C.; the Kentucky Historical Society, Frankfort, Kentucky; the Shaker Museum, Shakertown (South Union), Kentucky; and the Philip Fall Memorial Library of the First Christian Church at Frankfort, founded and guided with loving care by Mrs. Robert Gum, Librarian. Many other church libraries graciously furnished their own measure of original data, of which particular acknowledgment should be made of the Christian churches at Lexington, Mount Sterling, Versailles, and Cane Ridge, Kentucky.

In addition to the court records of Sullivan County in Tennessee, official Kentucky court documents and records were examined in the courthouses of Logan County at Russellville, Wayne County at Monticello, Cumberland County at Burkesville, Clinton County at Albany, Caldwell County at Princeton, Fayette County at Lexington, Franklin County at Frankfort, Green County at Greensburg,

Montgomery County at Mount Sterling, Scott County at Georgetown, and Woodford County at Versailles.

Contemporary periodicals, newspapers, original manuscripts, old sermons, and almost vanished records of the early years were cheerfully made available for study on personal visits to the great publishing houses of the Gospel Advocate Publishing Company, Dr. B. C. Goodpasture, Publisher and Editor, Nashville; the Christian Board of Publication, Dr. Wilbur H. Cramblet, President, St. Louis; and by the Standard Publishing Company, Dr. Burris Butler, Executive Editor, Cincinnati. Other religious publishing houses which furnished needed source material and pertinent data were the Methodist Publishing House, Nashville; the Association of Methodist Historical Societies, Lake Junaluska, North Carolina; Dr. Harry R. Short, Historian, Louisville Conference, Methodist Episcopal Church, Louisville; the Firm Foundation Publishing House, Mr. Reuel Lemmons, Editor, Austin, Texas; and the Old Paths Publishing Company, the late John Allen Hudson, Publisher and Editor, Rosemead, California.

The basic document in any study of the life and times of Raccoon John Smith is *The Life of Elder John Smith with Some Account of the Rise and Progress of the Current Reformation*, written by John Augustus Williams and first published in Cincinnati in 1870. Other especially rewarding material consulted were the *Philadelphia Confession of Faith* (*Baptist*); the *Westminster Confession of Faith* (*Presbyterian*); the *Memoirs of Micah Taul;* the *Autobiography of Barton W. Stone* (completed by John Rogers); the *Biography of John T. Johnson*, by John Rogers; *Memoirs of William Vaughn*, by his son, Thomas Vaughn; *A Century of Wayne County, Kentucky*, by Augusta Phillips Johnson; and for an excellent portrait of the early pioneer life of Kentucky, *Benjamin Logan, Kentucky Frontiersman*, by Charles Gano Talbert, published by the University of Kentucky Press.

Among other informative contemporary periodicals and documents consulted were bound volumes of *The Christian Baptist* and *The Millennial Harbinger*, both edited by Alexander Campbell; *The Christian Messenger*, edited by Barton W. Stone, and later with John T. Johnson as associate; and such fascinating journals as *The Christian Pioneer, The Evangelist, The Christian Preacher*, the *Christian Sentinel, The Gospel Proclamation, The Bible Advocate, The Primi-*

tive Christian and Investigator, *The Christian Magazine*, the *Christian Mirror*, *The Heretic Detector*, and the *Ecclesiastical Reformer*.

Grateful acknowledgment is made to Harriette Simpson Arnow, Ann Arbor, Michigan, author and nationally recognized authority on pioneer Kentucky history, who, in addition to other valuable data, supplied original snapshots of the Raccoon John Smith log house in Horse Hollow, Kentucky; Reverend Edward Coffman of Russellville, historian of Logan County, Kentucky, who is an authority on such divergent subjects as the Harpe brothers, the Shakers (the United Society of Believers in Christ's Second Appearance), and Methodist Circuit Rider Peter Cartwright; to former County Judge Joseph William Wells of Burkesville, historian of Cumberland County, Kentucky, and to Helen Hardie Grant, New York City, who furnished valuable personal information as the result of her years of research into the life of Peter Cartwright.

Others who supplied pertinent data and encouragement at needed times were Dr. Charles M. Watson, Santa Monica, who at eighty-eight is a walking encyclopedia of historical data pertaining to the Christian church; Dr. Jesse Randolph Kellems, Los Angeles, scholar, writer, and preacher of the Restoration Movement; Dr. Paul Jordan Smith, Los Angeles, literary critic and author, and Dr. James E. Davis, Muncie, Indiana. And there are Professor Olan L. Hicks of Freed-Hardeman College, Henderson, Tennessee, who supplied one of the few original authenticated anecdotes of Raccoon John Smith; Reverend George C. Frey, Owingsville, Kentucky, who through his own research supplied original information of the pioneer days; Reverend John C. Chenault, pastor of the First Christian Church, Frankfort, Kentucky, great-great-great-grandson of Elder David Chenault, mentioned in this book—who was always the friend and ever the theological opponent of Raccoon John Smith—who furnished a valuable original history of his doughty Calvinist ancestor; Isaac O. Reneau of Albany, Kentucky, direct descendant of Isaac T. Reneau, noted "Timothy" of Raccoon John Smith, and himself an authority on the early days; Dr. Charles C. Ware, Curator, Carolina Discipliana Society, Wilson, North Carolina, who furnished data on the Separate Baptists and on Barton W. Stone, on both of which he is a recognized authority; and Dr. W. E. Garrison, Houston, Texas, great scholar and church historian, whose suggestions, encouragement, and information, supplied through his own histories, are gratefully acknowledged.

Other persons to whom I am indebted for pertinent data through personal consultation or correspondence are: Dr. Jesse M. Bader, General Secretary, World Convention of Churches of Christ (Disciples), New York City; Dr. Hampton Adams, Park Avenue Christian Church, New York City; Dr. Perry Gresham, Bethany College, West Virginia; Forrest F. Reed, Nashville, Tennessee; W. C. Campbell, Russellville, Kentucky; Dr. Wesley LeRoy Baker, Princeton, Kentucky; J. Edward Moseley, Indianapolis, Indiana; Reverend Fred E. Gardner, Middleport, Ohio; Reverend Lanis E. Kineman, Carlisle, Kentucky; Edward R. Prewitt, Mount Sterling, Kentucky; Dr. Howard E. Short, Editor, *The Christian*, St. Louis, Missouri; Dr. Edwin V. Hayden, Editor, *The Christian Standard*, and Jay Sheffield, Editor, *The Lookout*, both of Cincinnati; Dr. B. C. Goodpasture, Editor, *The Gospel Advocate*, and Elders Jay Smith and Jim Bill McInteer, of the *Twentieth Century Christian*, all of Nashville, Tennessee.

A unique and important contribution was made by three direct descendants of the Raccoon John Smith family, who supplied necessary, and otherwise possibly unavailable, information about the family tree of their illustrious kinsman, without which this book might have been inadequate and incomplete: Miss Gussie Smith of Marion, Ohio, and Mrs. Maggie Reneau Miller of Ivanhoe, California, both of them granddaughters of Zerelda, the surviving infant daughter of Raccoon John and Anna Townsend Smith at the time of the tragic fire in Hickory Flats in the Mississippi Territory, and Bertrand Smith of Long Beach, California, a great-grandson of Philip Smith, John's brother and the first of George and Rebecca Smith's thirteen offspring.

To all these, and to any other sources who may have contributed to the completeness of this book but who may have been omitted here through inadvertence and human frailty, I make acknowledgment. Whatever else this book might have been without their aid, it would certainly not have been as it is, and to them all I offer my deep appreciation, and my lasting gratitude.